Reflections from the Past

D0951729

About the Author

Audrey Howard was born in Liverpool in 1929. Before she began to write she had a variety of jobs, among them hairdresser, model, shop assistant, cleaner, and civil servant. In 1981, living in Australia, she wrote her first bestselling novel: there are now thirty. She lives in St Annes's on Sea, her childhood home.

AUDREY HOWARD

Reflections from
the Past

coronet

CORONET BOOKS

Hodder & Stoughton

First published in Great Britain in 2003 by Hodder and Stoughton
A division of Hodder Headline
This paperback edition first published in 2004
by Hodder & Stoughton
A Coronet Paperback

1 3 5 7 9 10 8 6 4 2

A CIP catalogue record for this title
is available from the British Library

ISBN 0 340 82402 6

Typeset in Plantin Light by Palimpsest Book Production Limited,
Polmont, Stirlingshire
Printed and bound in Great Britain by
Mackays of Chatham Ltd, Chatham, Kent

Hodder and Stoughton
A division of Hodder Headline
338 Euston Road
London NW1 3BH

1

The strange sound began just as they turned the corner from Bamford Street into Edge Bottom Row: a rumbling sound reminiscent of thunder. In fact they both glanced up at the sky, the grey, snow-laden sky which had crept up on them unnoticed during the day and which lurked threateningly above the rooftops, but thunder didn't roll in January, at least not in their part of the world.

"What were that?" Roddy questioned anxiously, moving a little closer to her, looking about him for an explanation, his lean face uneasy, his slanting, pale grey eyes, which Abby thought were like those of Mrs Hodges' pampered striped tabby which spent its time curled up in front of the kitchen fire, alert with speculation, for there was nothing that did not attract the notice of the inquisitive mind of Roddy Baxter. "It seemed ter come from glass works."

He began to hurry her, taking her elbow in his eager young man's grip so that she winced, for though he might be thin he was strong and wiry. He was not yet fully grown but when he reached maturity he would be a big man, his shoulders already giving promise of width and strength.

They were just approaching the wide, wrought-iron gates to Edge Bottom Glass Works, which stood open, when the first scream rang out. It was followed by another and another, overlapping, tearing the icy air to ribbons, hurting the ear as some unimaginable horror surely must be hurting the flesh from which the sound came. There were shouts, cries of great confusion, chaos even, but still the screaming went on, many voices joining the clamour, and from the open doorway of one of the two great warehouses a massive cloud of dust began to billow. The noise and the dust rose to the rooftops of the many buildings that were clustered round the enormous yard, disturbing a flock of sparrows perched on the tiles of the sawmill. The sparrows took flight, winging away to the trees just outside the walls surrounding the works, settling there with a great twittering and ruffling of feathers. Horses pulling wagons that would take the finished glass in their wooden frames to their destination shied and laid back their ears, jinking sideways in an attempt to escape the terrible noise and blinding dust. The men who were loading the crates clutched at one another in order to avoid being thrown off the wagons.

"Bloody 'ell!" the youth whispered, but despite the din that had taken over the works, the girl heard him. Her hand slipped into his as though for comfort and his gripped hers tightly for the same reason.

"What is it, Roddy?"

"Nay, don't ask me," Roddy gasped fearfully. "Summat bad . . ."

They took a hesitant step inside the gate. A good-looking boy and a pretty girl, probably about fifteen; it was hard to tell ages in this town of hardship and poverty with starvation very often staring you in the face, a lack of nourishment that stripped the flesh from young bones, but these two were better fed than most. By this time there were men coming from every direction, spilling out from every doorway, men with white, pallid faces, for surely something dreadful had happened. They came from the mixing rooms, the cutting rooms, the offices, from the laboratory where Mr Noah worked, from the smithy and the joiner's shop and from the double rows of tiny cottages towards which the young man at least had been heading.

The doors to the cottages were thrown open and women stood in the doorways, women in aprons and shabby skirts and bodices, shawls thrown hastily about their heads, women with youngsters huddled against them. One held a frying pan from which fat was dripping, to the delight of a mangy cat curling round her feet, another wielded a broom and a third still clutched a bucket and a scrubbing brush. They all had men employed by Edge Bottom Glass Works to which the cottages belonged.

"What's ter do?" they were all begging one another, taking hesitant steps into the yard and when the first man stumbled from the warehouse, his face a mask of blood, it stopped them, men, women and children, bringing the whole running crowd to a paralysed standstill.

"Dear Mother," a woman faltered, one of the women from the cottages, the wife of Stan Jolly who was a 'teaser', a man who fed the coals on to the fire in the furnace. "Poor man . . . who is it? Yer can't tell wi' all that blood on 'im. See, Annie" – turning to her next-door neighbour – "gimmee a hand with 'im, fetch 'im inter my place. Oh, Blessed Mother, there's another," as a second man blundered from the warehouse, then a third, each one dripping blood and calling out hoarsely for help.

The yard was by this time full of men from the joiner's shop, the mason's shop, indeed every department at the glass works, all, that is, except the glasshouse. The men who worked there in the glasshouse cone which housed the furnace, the 'blowers', the 'gatherers', the 'flashers', the 'flatteners' and 'pilers', indeed all the men who were involved in the actual making of glass at the furnace, could not just run out into the yard willy-nilly whenever they had a fancy to. The aristocracy of the glass-making sphere, the skilled blower was involved in work that could not be put down and left while the man had a smoke or a glass of ale or popped his head out of the door to see what all the commotion was about. With eight or nine pounds of molten glass on the end of his blowpipe, ready to be rolled to and fro on a smooth iron plate, needing great skill and strength, the blower had to make sure the malleable glass did not come into contact with any other surface. Once started, the process continued until it was ready for the annealing chamber where the glass was very gradually cooled, an operation that could take from six to sixty hours depending on its weight.

The two young people, still hand-in-hand, watched the scene with mounting horror. A man crawled out from the warehouse doorway, his forearm held defensively against him, and when some woman went to him, hushing his piteous cries with sounds that soothed her children in the night, he was found to have misplaced his hand. Blood gushed from the mangled stump and the woman, not knowing what else to do for the poor bugger, wrapped it in her pinny. It was none too clean, for she had been blackleading her stove when the drama started but it was all she had. Another seemed to have had his ear sliced neatly away and many, hit by what must have been broken glass, had deep cuts about their faces, their brawny arms, only their sturdy flannel shirts saving them from worse injuries.

"Yer'd best get 'ome ter yer mam, Abby," the boy said absently, his mind already intent on what he might do to be of help, turning to the girl who still clung to him. His was a protective manner, for surely a young lass as she was should not see such dreadful sights. It was turning his own stomach a bit and he was hard put not to vomit, but the girl remained where she was and when they brought Master Richard out, his slack figure carried on a frame, though his face was unmarked some sort of wrapping had been placed across his chest from beneath which blood seeped, he felt her sway. He was ready to sway himself, for he'd never seen so much blood in his life. Not just on the young master but on the other men who staggered from the warehouse. The crowd seemed to sigh collectively, for this was the son of Bradley Goodwin, the owner of Edge Bottom Glass Works, the son who held first place in his father's heart. The *only* place, come to that, for he was an only child. This was the young man who would, with no effort on his part, inherit Edge Bottom. He was thirty-one years of age and due to be married in the spring to the daughter of a wealthy colliery owner, a grand lass by all accounts and a grand match for them both, but by the look of him, to those of a pessimistic, or should it be called *realistic* turn of mind, was unlikely to make it up the aisle then, or ever.

"It were the frames," they heard one chap moan, not so badly injured as others but still in a state of shock. "Glass were stacked in't frames, nigh on a dozen of 'em but some bloody thing set first one off and the whole lot went. Like a bloody row o' dominoes. Oh, Jesus . . . lads between was crushed . . . glass crackin' everywhere."

"Never you mind, lad, let's get yer . . ."

"We couldn't see fer't dust an't noise were so loud . . ."

"We 'eard 'em go, lad, but never you mind. Yer can tell us later; it's a doctor yer need."

"I were near't last one an' managed ter jump clear but Master Richard got whole bloody lot on him."

"Leave it, lad. He's bein' tekken care of."

"We dragged 'im clear but 'is chest were caved in like an eggshell. Blessed Mother, 'e were squashed ter pulp."

It was Mr Noah who pulled it all together, sending men who could ride a horse, one of them the mare Richard Goodwin had cantered into the yard this very morning, men with sweated faces and hair all awry, galloping off for the doctor, in fact more than one doctor if they could be found, for there were many men with injuries. The women had begun to run from their cottages, flinging off clutching, wailing children, running towards the warehouse with their hands to their mouths, their eyes wide and frightened, for several of them had men working in the building where the accident had happened. Noah Goodwin, engineer at Edge Bottom, was calm, decisive, pushing through the crowd, which stood in a silent, appalled group, speaking quietly, steadily, directing who was to go where, himself covered in the dense pall of dust which the fall of the heavy glass in their wooden frames had disturbed. It floated about the yard, obliterating the buildings so that those who were doing their best to get the injured from the warehouse and laid as gently as they could where the doctor might attend them, were forced to feel their way almost as though they had been blindfolded.

Abby found herself pressed against the wall of the second warehouse. Roddy, with a muttered word which she had not quite caught, had disappeared into the pall but some woman with a pile of sheets in her arms shouted at her as she ran by.

"Don't just stand there, lass, gimme a hand wi' these men. I need someone ter tear me sheets up though only the blessed Mother knows what I'll put on me beds when all this is over. 'Appen the old master'll put his hand in his pocket though this'll knock stuffin' out of him. Poor Master Richard . . ."

Abby followed the woman obediently, doing her best not to lose her in the dust-laden yard though by now the cloud was beginning to settle. "Is . . . he dead then?" she faltered.

"As good as, I heard. They've tekken him inter th'office, may the Holy Mother watch over him," she said, crossing herself hastily. "But there's others need bindin' up an' the doctors can't be everywhere at once."

Abby spent the next couple of hours running here and there at any woman's bidding, fetching water and hastily contrived bandages, even kneeling at Martha Jolly's command to hold some poor boy, no more than twelve or so, an apprentice who happened to be in the warehouse, not his usual place of work, when the tragedy happened. He was terribly cut about his face, a great gash above his eye which, in Mrs Jolly's opinion, should be stitched and so, the doctors happening to be occupied elsewhere, she proceeded to do so, making a very neat job of it, for wasn't she used to mending tears in her family's clothing.

She found Roddy leaning against the office wall, himself streaked in blood, other men's blood, for he had been helping to carry men to the tiny cottages where many of the workmen lived. Thirty of them had been erected on the extreme edge of the glass works, one of them the home of Roddy Baxter. He had been giving their wives a hand in getting them to bed, those who had not needed the services of the doctors. His young face was white and strained, as was hers, and smeared with blood where he had wiped the sweat from it. Abby brooded on the way the day, which had started out with so much secret excitement, could have changed in the space of half an hour into such horror.

They had been skating, she and Roddy, slipping away, he from his mam's cottage in Edge Bottom Row, she from the labourer's cottage in Sandy Lane, one of a row belonging to Mr Hodges of Updale Farm where her pa was a hedger and ditcher. Pa's own family had come from Ireland when he was a boy during one of the never-ending famines back in the late twenties, the famines that were the scourge of the country. Many of the Irish, the Connors, the Doyles, the Murphys, the Gallaghans, had settled in St Helens, since it was no more than a twelve-mile tramp from Liverpool. They had travelled as deck cargo on the cattle steamers which had established a regular service across the Irish Sea, congregating in Greenbank, Smithy Brow-Parr and Gerard's Bridge, shunned by the rest of the population, and were willing to take any man's money for the lowliest job available. They brawled with one another and with the male population of St Helens; they drank and kept their pigs and it was said in the town that the Irishman loved his pig as the Arab his horse, eating with it, sleeping with it, his children playing with it and if food was short, which it frequently was, it was the pig who got it.

Her pa had been different. He did not fight nor drink and after what he had known as a lad in Connaught the cottage he and his family occupied was like a palace to him. There were ten of them, counting Mam and Pa, shoved higgledy-piggledy into the two rooms which would have been cramped with half the number. You stepped through the low front door into the kitchen, the only room on the ground floor, and up the steep, ladder-like stairs to a single bedroom. It was damp and to Betty Murphy, though she did her best to keep it, and them all, clean, it was an uphill fight. The walls were greyish green with mould and the floor was of plain earth. It was ill maintained, the accumulation of effluvia of old clothes and unwashed bodies, of smoky fires kept going by any fuel that came to hand, and of the potatoes that were the Murphy family's staple diet. And yet compared to some it was a clean cottage. Her ma was a good worker, trudging up to the Bird in Hand Inn every day to stand at Mrs Thatcher's dolly tub, washing and mangling, taking Dicky, the youngest at two years old, with her, while Pa laboured for ten bob a week in all weathers, clearing Mr Hodges' ditches and mending Mr Hodges' hedges. Abby herself worked in Mrs Hodges' dairy and had done since she was ten years old and as a great favour to her mam, for whom Mrs Hodges had great admiration, she had been allowed to live out. Of course then, five years ago, there had been three fewer of them! Next week though, at Mrs Hodges' insistence, she was to "live in". Mam was unhappy about it, for Abby was a grand lass about the crowded cottage, caring for the little ones while Mam had a bit of a rest. Mam was thirty years old but looked more like fifty, her body so distorted by continuous pregnancies, six of which had ended in a miscarriage, it was difficult to tell with certainty whether she was carrying a child or not. Still, she was always unfailingly cheerful, optimistic and, as Mrs Hodges said to Mr Hodges a dozen times a week, the best worker she'd ever had and her lass was shaping to be the same!

Because of the coming change in her circumstances she had played truant from the dairy, claiming terrible cramps in her belly. Roddy had had no need for deception since he was on the last shift in the glasshouse cone. As a live-in dairymaid Abby was aware that she would be unable to get out as often to meet Roddy though he had promised, when the nights became lighter with the coming of spring, to walk across the fields to Sandy Lane and Updale Farm where it might be possible for her to slip out and meet him briefly.

This morning they had met at the corner of Sandy Lane, then, hand-in-hand, sauntered in the lovely, rose-pink dawn light of winter through the stretch of frost-rimed wood that led up to Little Dam. The sun hovered at the back of the stark trees, the bare, frost-coated branches like white lace against the rose and duck-egg blue of the sky, the ferns and bracken frozen into stiff spears which were brilliant as the rising sun caught them. The trees flung deep shadows across the frosted ground and a faint mist hung, still and mysterious, about their legs. A fox had made his way along the track, leaving his paw marks in the thick white frost, and here and there pools of water had thin slicks of ice on them, some broken where the fox had drunk. It crunched beneath the iron soles of their sturdy clogs and their breath misted and mingled about their heads which were close together as they talked.

Roddy had made their "skates" from thin wedges of the

hardest wood he could find in the sawmill, helped by old Jos Knowles, the head joiner, who knew a bit about wood, he told Roddy laconically. Jos, interested and not a little sceptical about this new pastime which was becoming increasingly popular in the hard winters known in these parts, had helped him to shape and fit the wooden skates on the bottom of their clogs. He was clever with his hands, was Roddy, though Jos, being a northcountry man, wouldn't have said so for the world, and the contrivance was remarkably effective.

The frozen dam had stretched like a sheet of gold as the sun rose above the trees, the sun itself forming a pathway from one side to the other. The dam was surrounded by oak, birch and rowan, the berries on the latter glowing a deep orange-red in the sunlight. Holly bushes, again bright with the red of berries, and yew grew side by side, all clothed in the beauty of the winter, but the couple had eyes for no beauty but what they saw in each other. They were dressed warmly, for they were among the lucky ones who had decent jobs. Mrs Hodges could not bear to see her dairymaids suffering in the ice-cold conditions of the winter dairy and Mr Hodges had been known to grumble that had his wife had her own way she'd have put a fire in the dairy! But the dairymaids were supplied with warm flannel petticoats, good woollen gowns, plain, of course, shawls to wrap about themselves and *mittens, of all things*.

Roddy gave his mam ten shillings out of his fifteen shillings wages, buying his own clothing from the market in town. He was careful to purchase good hardwearing trousers, flannel shirts, a waistcoat that once might have belonged to the gentry in a bright canary yellow, over which he wore a jacket and a scarf, knitted by Abby, in a yellow to match his waistcoat. He looked very dashing against Abby's rather sombre attire, but her young beauty, the brightness of her vivid hair, the brilliance of her blue-green eyes more than made up for any lack in her dress.

They had been the only ones on the frozen stretch of water for the first few hours, since this was a working day and those who ventured later to skate on the dam were among the lucky few who came from the wealthy and well placed of St Helens. The day was well under way before *they* left their warm beds.

Neither of them could skate and for the first hour they had spent most of their time on their bums, hauling one another to their feet, pulling and pushing, hanging on to one another and laughing hysterically, their eyes like diamonds in their rosy faces, two youngsters giving no thought to the responsibilities which were theirs. Roddy's mam was a widow and would be hard pressed if her eldest son lost his job, for those who came after him could do little but rook-scaring and stone-picking in the fields about the town, as she did. They were a good deal younger than Roddy, for like most women in their world she had lost several in between to the prevalent fevers.

Abby at least had a mam *and* a pa, with Tommy and Bobby for the past three years working in Mr Hodges' cowsheds, the others doing any menial job within their grasp, but she would still be in a great deal of trouble if Mrs Hodges, who was a kindly, maternal sort of a woman with no children of her own and a good mistress – which was why Abby had chanced this day – took it into her head to be harsh.

Abby Murphy loved Roddy Baxter and he loved her and one day they would marry, they both knew that, but until he had finished his seven-year apprenticeship at Edge Bottom and became one of the élite of the glass-blowing world they would wait and save, and not until he was able to support her and the children they would have would they marry. Neither could read nor write but they were hardworking, intelligent, practical, far-sighted beyond their years with great plans for their future and though it was hard at times to overcome the call of their young, healthy bodies, which clamoured to move on from chaste kisses and modest embraces, they were determined to do so. Their lives would not be as their parents' were: a child every year, scraping together a few pennies for a *new* second-hand pair of clogs for a growing child, living on scraps, terrified of losing a job, making do on next to nothing, clutter and crowding in a clod cottage, sleeping four or more to a bed in the only solace known to the poor, which was sleep.

They became quite adept after an hour or two, skating hand-in-hand round and round the edge of the dam, moving in dizzying whirls as Roddy, as lads will, began to show off, *twizzing* her at the end of his two clasped hands so that her hair flew out like a banner. And what were a few bumps to him who worked in danger every day, danger from burns and falls and the extreme heat which drained the moisture out of you.

Reluctantly they had made their slow way back to Sandy Lane, laughing still.

"I reckon I'll have more bruises than Jack Whistler after he come from the prize fightin'," Roddy had remarked ruefully, rubbing his thigh. Then, turning to Abby, he smoothed his big-knuckled hand across her rosy cheek. "An' I wouldn't like ter have ter explain that there bruise yer got on yer cheek. By Gow, yer didn't half come a cropper. It's tekken a bit o' skin off. What'll yer say ter yer mam?"

"Never mind me mam. It's Mrs Hodges that I'm bothered about. She'll think someone's landed me a fourpenny one. Anyroad, she's not goin' ter tekk up against me fer a bruise on me cheek when I've bin missin' all day. That's what she'll be more bothered about. Poor old Agnes an' Nancy'll have had to do my work as well as their own."

"Serve 'em right, lazy beggars. You do it all every other day."

"Oh, they're not so bad. An' Mrs Hodges is a good mistress. I could do worse."

"It'll not be fer long, sweetheart. Three years ter go then I'll be outer me apprenticeship an' we'll be wed. But Jesus wept, it's hard ter . . . yer so lovely."

He had begun to tremble as his hand moved into her hair which was the exact shade of the fox that had meandered through the wood earlier in the day. It hung to her waist, for her mam had refused ever to cut it, a tangle of thick curls which Mam seemed to love, rinsing it with chamomile which brought out its streaks of pale gold. She brushed it for her every night, smoothing it back from her wide, delicate brow, her eyes gazing at something it seemed only she could see. It had started the day falling in a plait from the crown of her head, thicker than Roddy's wrist and so heavy it tipped her head back in a way that was almost queenly, but now it hung about her neck and shoulders like a living mantle. She walked like a queen, too, holding herself erect, not stiffly, but with the grace of a young deer Roddy had once seen on Lord Thornley's estate.

He placed his flat lips against hers which were full, soft and moist, straining her to him, for he was a young man with a young man's passionate needs and when she responded his hands began their journey to cup her face, his thumbs beneath her small chin, the nape of her neck where her hair snapped and curled about his fingers. Their kiss became deeper, caressing and folding, and they groaned together for it was hard, as hard as his erect manhood, to break apart. Delight ran through them, a dizzying delight that was as old as the human race, this meeting of male and female, this tenderness, this wild feeling that was becoming dangerously difficult to control. They were both breathing heavily when he reached up and dragged her hands from about his neck.

"Don't, darlin' . . . Jesus, I want yer an' I know yer want me but we mun remember what we planned." He began to smooth her hair back from her face, patting the shawl that had been tied round her shoulders as they skated and which had begun to slip away. He kissed her chastely on the brow, keeping his body well away from hers, for, like a young animal looking for comfort, she would keep trying to snuggle up to him.

"Roddy, I love yer . . ."

"I know, my lass, but we mun wait. When I've finished me apprenticeship we'll be wed. I'll be a glass-maker. I mean ter work hard an' become a blower an' bringin' in forty shillings a week. Best paid workers in't country, yer know that." Which was true, for her own pa was paid a mere ten shillings a week though he did have a cottage as one of Mr Hodges' labourers.

She sighed and leaned against him, but without that hot flame of desire that had flared through them and he held her gently, the flat plane of his lean cheek against the tangle of sweet-smelling curls on the top of her head. After a moment or two they parted and, clasping hands, began the walk back to their present life, leaving behind the dreams of their future.

And so it was they were there when the accident at Edge Bottom Glass Works occurred. The chaos that had reigned was easing. Those men who had needed sewing up had been hastily stitched. Men with broken limbs had been splinted and all about the place could be seen women offering themselves as crutches, small broken-down handcarts trundling those who lived off the premises to Greenbank or Gerard's Bridge, for there were many Irishmen employed at Edge Bottom. The dust had settled and though there was a lot of activity about the warehouse where the accident had occurred, it had become relatively quiet. It was a Friday, a traditional day for pot-filling. The raw materials had been weighed, mixed and partly fused in an oven to liberate any gases and burn off impurities. Cullet was added and the batch was shovelled into the pots, allowing one load to melt down before the next was tipped. It was over the weekend that the furnace was tended by the teaser and by Monday morning the melting process would be complete and the glass fit to work. The men would begin work at six a.m. on Monday morning, working a ten-hour shift, the second shift would start at four p.m. on Tuesday, the third at two a.m. on Thursday and the fourth at noon on Friday, finishing work late on Friday. This left them with Saturday and Sunday completely free. It was not for nothing that the glass-makers were called the aristocracy of craftsmen.

Roddy stirred. Despite his youth and strength he was weary after the hectic activities of the day. First the skating, which had been no hardship, but then the frantic haste of helping men and their women to pull themselves round, the carrying of the injured, the careful handling of the chaos in the warehouse that had to be cleared up before any man could think of his bed.

It had begun to snow, soft, white flakes coming to rest on Abby's tangled hair.

"Master Richard died," he said simply. "They say all his ribs were crushed. Poor sod. I know he weren't a young man" – for to Roddy Baxter thirty-one was ancient – "but it's sad, in't it. The old man'll go mad."

"Did anyone else . . . die?"

"No. Some bad injuries though. Andy Richards lost his hand."

"How awful, an' with all them children."

"Aye, but yer'd best get home, my lass," he murmured into her hair, "before this lot gets goin'." He looked up into the leaden sky. "I'll walk wi' yer."

"No, yer'll not. I'll cut across fields an' be home in ten minutes." She put up a tender hand to his tired face, then placed a kiss on the corner of his mouth.

"Now then you two," someone shouted and they sprang

apart, for they were still young enough to be embarrassed by a show of feelings in public.

"Right then, chuck. I wish yer'd let me walk . . ."

"No, I'll see yer . . ."

"Termorrer?"

She managed a tired smile as she turned away. "That's if Mrs Hodges is in a good mood."

2

When Abby entered the cottage Mam was bending over the kitchen fire stirring something in the big saucepan which was used for almost every cooking purpose, pans being expensive and therefore hard to come by. This time it was stew, made from the remains of the joint of beef eaten by the Hodges the previous Sunday. She was generous with leftovers was Mrs Hodges and there had been a few scraps of meat still clinging to the bone. To the stew were added the vegetables that Pa grew in the tiny square of garden at the rear of the cottage, those not eaten in the summer stored carefully for winter use. Potatoes, carrots, onions, leeks, cabbage, all carefully planted in every available inch of earth, row upon neat row, not one bit of space wasted, the soil fed by the muck which Declan Murphy brought by the bucket from the farm. As an Irishman his love of the land was born in him. He was mild-mannered, with the easy-going nature of his race but without the feisty inclination for arguments that was the trait of many of his countrymen. He was sitting in a broken-down rocking-chair, again a cast-off of Mrs Hodges, his boots and socks off, his bare feet to the glowing fire, for he had been out in the frosty fields since early morning and he was frozen to the marrow. That bloody Buttercup of Mr Hodges would keep breaking through the hedge, nobody knew why, and Declan was forever mending the damage she caused.

Ma turned in surprise, the spoon with which she was stirring the stew dripping juices on to the scrap of a rag rug before the fire.

"Yer 'ome early, chuck. Mrs 'Odges let yer go afore yer time?" She smiled at her daughter, a sweet smile and it was obvious that Abigail Murphy was exactly what her mother had been at the same age apart from the colour of her hair. Betty's was grey now and scanty, just a trace of the honey brown it once had been, but she still had the high cheekbones, the long, firm mouth, the same delicate eyebrows and wide forehead, though it was scored with lines. She had lost most of her teeth and her cheeks had fallen in. But despite her ruined face and figure her eyes were quite beautiful. The same soft blue-green as Abby's with a fan of long, dark brown lashes, and despite the constant anxiety of her life she had a kind, maternal look about her.

"There's bin an accident," Abby blurted out, closing the door behind her hastily, for they could not afford to lose the heat. Five children were already sitting up to the kitchen table, their wooden spoons in their hands, an expectant look on their young faces. Tommy and Bobby were not yet home but there was Albert who was nine and about to start in the cowsheds at Chadwick's Farm just beyond the Bird in Hand, Cissie, seven, Sara-Ann, five, Freddy, four, and two-year-old Dicky. None of them was working yet apart from Cissie and Sara-Ann who were handy about Uplands Farm, rook-scaring, stone-picking, potato-gathering at the right season, keeping an eye on their Freddy, bringing in a few welcome pence for the family coffers.

They all turned to stare with interest at their sister. Pa sat up, leaving the rubbing of his frost-nipped toes though he was careful to keep them on the bit of rug.

Ma put her hand to her mouth. "Not Tommy . . . Bobby . . . ?" she quavered, for though she was overburdened with children she loved them all and would be devastated if anything happened to any one of them.

"No, at glass works." Abby advanced further into the room and sat down suddenly on the bench that was set to one side of the table. She, like her father, was chilled to the bone and the shock of what she had seen that day had begun to set in. It had started out so lovely and finished in a nightmare of blood and screams, of agony and death. She began to shiver uncontrollably and at once her mother threw the spoon back into the saucepan and clutched her daughter to her.

"What is it, love, tell us. What 'appened? Not . . . not Roddy?" For they all knew of Abby's partiality for the lad. They'd been close since they were nippers, had Abby and Roddy and made no secret of the fact that when they were old enough they'd be wed. "Let it out, lass, yer'll feel better." As long as it wasn't one of hers Betty Murphy could stand anything her lass had to tell her but she did hope it wasn't Roddy.

Abby sank into the comfort of her mam's arms, pressing her face into the sagging bosom, her arms wrapped tight about her and clasped at her back. Mam smelled of fresh baked bread and the lavender that grew along the edges of Pa's vegetable garden and which Betty collected and dried. She also smelled of woodsmoke, sweat, onions, clothing not laundered often enough, but then none of them got a decent bath from one month's end to the other, except her, Abby, who was privileged to bathe once a week in Mrs Hodges' tin bath in the dairy where hot water was in abundance. Dairymaids and the tools of their trade must be spotlessly clean or they could spoil the milk, sour the cream, turn the butter, and Mrs Hodges insisted that she, Agnes and Nancy must have an all-over wash and their working clothes went with hers and Jack's into the wash which Abby's mother laboured over.

"I don't know exactly what 'appened," Abby stuttered,

for her teeth had begun to chatter. "Summat ter do wi'
warehouse. Big sheets o' glass fell onter't men, a lot of 'em . . .
Oh, Mam, it were awful." They were all so engrossed none
of them thought to question why she was at the glass works
and not in the dairy at Updale Farm.

"Blood . . . I never seen such blood. One chap's 'and were
chopped off."

"Holy Mother save 'im." Declan crossed himself, for
though he no longer practised the faith in which he had
been brought up the habits were ingrained in him.

"What a sight fer a lass ter see," her mother murmured,
holding her girl more closely to her.

"I 'elped ter bandage some of 'em an' Mrs Jolly sewed
up one lad, just a bit of a lad who kept cryin' fer his
mam."

"Poor bairn . . ."

"There were doctors there from all over, it were awful,
Mam. And poor Master Richard were killed, crushed under
the weight."

She felt her mother sway and the arms that were holding
her so comfortingly fell away. Betty staggered back as though
some unseen hand had pushed her and slowly, so slowly, she
slid to the floor. Her face had lost every vestige of what colour
she still had and her eyelids fluttered. At once they were all on
their feet and Declan Murphy, in some corner of his mind that
was always concerned with where the next penny was coming
from, hoped the Blessed Mother was not to burden them with
another child.

"Mam . . . Mam," they were all crying, from the youngest
to the eldest. Abby herself lifted Mam's head from the dirt
floor, patted her hands, smoothed her hair from her face,
none of them knowing what to do, for their mam was the
backbone of this family; she was the one to direct it and how
could she when she lay senseless on the floor.

"See, our Albert, mekk a pot o' tea. A *real* one," by which Abby meant not one of those that used the precious tea leaves again and again. "Can yer lift her, Pa, put her in your chair." For nobody but the head of the house sat in the rocking-chair. It did not matter that Betty Murphy worked as hard as he did, or that the children did their share, the rocking-chair was reserved for the man of the house. Mostly the others crowded round the table on the benches that surrounded it on four sides.

Mam was beginning to come round, making strange sounds in the back of her throat and Dicky began to cry. It was perhaps this that brought Betty Murphy from her strange faint, for her instinct was to nurture. She pulled the toddler on to her lap and buried his tearful face in her vast bosom. She did her best to smile though it was a ghastly parody of her usual cheerful, loving beam. She cuddled him to her, smoothing back the riot of tangled brown curls that swirled round his baby head, kissing him, holding out her hands to the others.

"Nay, I don't know what come over me, I really don't. 'Appen it were the terrible news." Which was strange, for many a terrible thing had happened in Betty Murphy's hard life and none of them had made her faint. She couldn't even blame it on the *change*, which came to all women, for she was still only thirty. She only wished she could, then she would be sure that there would be no more babies in this house.

She drank the tea gratefully. Tea was a real heartener to women like her. She meant the tea that their Abby had poured out for her, hot, strong, with milk and sugar, not the weak dregs they usually drank, and though she was still pale she began to look better.

"Now then, let's get our supper an' then it's time we was in our beds. Mrs Hodges wants me ter scrub out pantry an' kitchen flags termorrer so we'd best get our rest or we'll be

fit fer nowt. See, our Cissie, hutch up an' let our Abby
put 'er bum down. Ah, 'ere's the lads," as Tommy and
Bobby came noisily into the kitchen, their thin faces red and
chapped, their hands tucked into their armpits. Like Abby,
they suffered from chilblains but Mrs Hodges, good soul that
she was, provided them with goose grease to prevent them
from cracking and bleeding. As Betty Murphy settled down
in the biggest bed with Dicky between her and Declan, she
gave silent thanks to the good God who had led the Murphy
family to Updale Farm and the benevolence of Jack and Aggie
Hodges. The rest of them, boys on one palliasse on the floor,
girls on another, sighed and shifted as they settled to sleep and
it was only as she drifted off herself that it occurred to her
to wonder what the dickens their Abby was doing at Edge
Bottom Glass Works when she should have been hard at work
in the dairy of Aggie Hodges.

The glass works was closed on the day of the funeral. Richard
Goodwin was buried in the family plot in the corner of
the graveyard of St Thomas' Church. Next to him were
his grandfather, Tobias, and his great-grandfather for whom
he had been named. There were others, Eleanor, Francis,
William, George, Anne, Simeon, Margaret, Mary, Albert, all
wives or children of past Goodwins, the names repeated as an
infant died and the next to be born was given the deceased's
name. All had ornate headstones of gold-lettered marble, as
the Goodwins had been wealthy for many generations, and
above them a great hawthorn tree reared its leafless crown, its
branches stripped bare by the winter wind and frost, but which
in summer was smothered in clusters of pale pink flowers and
in autumn with berries known as haws. Its trunk was gnarled,
twisted and furrowed, like the angry old man who stood at
his son's graveside and cursed the world, his rage terrifyingly
awesome, and those about the graveyard, and there was a

great multitude, wondered what he would do with his glass works and his money now that he had no one to step into his shoes.

It was noticed, as he climbed from his carriage, that he glared about him, his sharp eyes assessing every face, making a note of who was there and who was not, who had come to pay their last respects to his son and who had had the temerity to ignore his importance. The road to the church was lined on both sides with black-draped carriages and from them stepped top-hatted, black-gloved gentlemen, their wives in black crepe and mourning veils, for none of the businessmen of St Helens dared offend Bradley Goodwin. He had an iron in every fire in the town, so to speak, and there were not a few who would find it *all up brew from here on*, as they said in these parts, if he withdrew his support. Every man who worked for him, and many who didn't but hoped to, crowded the churchyard, so many that they could not fit into the church. Among them were Abby Murphy and her mother, for, surprisingly, Mam had stated a wish to see Master Richard laid to rest.

"What the divil for?" Pa had questioned. "Sure an' what was 'e ter' the likes of us?" But Mam had her way. They stood on the edge of the huge crowd, their heads bowed and wrapped in their shawls, their clogged feet deep in the wet grass. Mam seemed to cling to her as the coffin was lowered into the deep black hole, but the old man never wavered though it was noticed that Noah Goodwin, who was related in some way, offered his arm which was waved roughly away. He planted his feet foursquare on the ground, his mouth twisting into a grimace of what might have been hatred at the gods who had taken his lad, an old, desolate man, unutterably bitter, alone. For a moment Abby felt sorry for him, then it was over and the mourners began to thread their way through the gravestones towards the lych gate.

It had begun to rain and Mam urged her through the crowd, eager to get back to her warm kitchen.

"Come on, chuck, we'll be soggin wet threw if we don't get a move on. Why does it always rain at funerals?"

The town of St Helens was once described as a village *and* a town but that was before ugly urbanisation came to lay siege to it. It was set on a piece of level ground surrounded by a few gentle hills, like a set of tumbled bricks set in a shallow bowl, and on a weekday was seldom without its overhanging acrid cloud of smoke. There were irregular rows of brick houses, churches with square towers, tall chimneys vomiting smoke and conical glasshouses giving out occasional bright flashes of flame, for St Helens was a glass-making town. The smells from the chemical works were obnoxious and the clang of hammers ringing against iron hurt the ear. The streets had been laid out with what seemed to be no particular plan, some built up on one side only, leaving vacant spaces of ground where ragged, barefoot children and mangy dogs played in the pools of stagnant, disease-ridden water that collected there.

And yet take a step away from this and at once the surrounding areas became pleasantly rural, a short walk bringing those with the desire for fresh air and exercise to the gentle hills, to pleasing country walks along lanes whose hedges were heavily laden in summer with may blossom and submerged by a rising tide of growth. Sweet Cecily, fragrant with the scent of aniseed, stood waist high, almost blocking the cottages and sunken lanes, along with hedge parsley, which Betty Murphy made up into a potion to alleviate the painful monthly cramps suffered by her daughter. There was dock and nettle, meadow cranesbill for the relief of sore throats and mouth ulcers, ragwort, foxglove and willowherb, colours and fragrances that made the senses swoon. Honeysuckle and wild guelder roses could still be found, with elderberry and wild angelica in blossom. Climb a small incline and the rambling panorama of hedged fields was spread out like a colourful handkerchief, fields red with poppies, yellow with corn and barley, green with the neat lines of potatoes and beet, for this was farming country.

It began over a hundred years ago. Richard Goodwin the first and his forefathers had lived as small but prosperous farmers in the foothills of the Pennines, laying claim to more and more land and becoming even more wealthy. Looking round for some suitable investment Richard found himself in St Helens. And so he was one of the first to begin what was to overtake farming in his life in the middle of the eighteenth century, with a small bottle-making factory on the very site where Edge Bottom Glass Works now stood. Being an astute businessman, for even in farming a man needed a good head on his shoulders to get anywhere, he had looked about him and sensed that here was the beginning of what would one day be a thriving industry. Everything that was needed for the making and selling of glass, of any sort, was to hand, though the early glass-makers were not very particular about the quality of their product with a virtual monopoly in the area they supplied. There were canal communications with London, vast quantities of sand, which was admirably suited for glass-making, and coal. With the building of mills and factories, warehouses, shops, came the cottages to house the thousands who flocked there in search of work; with their numbers increasing the need for glass, the industry grew with its market and with it the change from bottle-making to the production of window glass was introduced at Edge Bottom Glass Works.

Richard's son Tobias took over from his father in the late eighteenth century and it was he who largely replaced what had always been produced by his father: domestic glazing by glass made in a completely different way. This was known as crown glass. Instead of the glass being blown into a cylinder it was formed into the shape of a small pear until it produced a sphere which was then flattened, opened out – or flashed – into a flat circular plate which could extend up to sixty inches in diameter. This was known as a table of crown glass. It was of a superior quality to the cylinder glass and the business begun by Richard Goodwin expanded, and Tobias Goodwin learned to call himself one of the wealthiest men in St Helens. Not only wealthy but influential, powerful in the town with an iron in many a fire, a respected man of business. It seemed that each generation was stronger than its predecessor. More vigorous, more ambitious, more far-sighted, more astute, so that the business grew with the years. They were alike in many ways: big men in youth, turned heavy in middle age, full-blooded, hearty of appetite. Bradley, son of Tobias, was taller than any of them, convinced, presumably because of those who had gone before him, that he was invincible, perhaps even immortal.

But in one respect, at least in the eyes of other men, and perhaps secretly in their own though they would not admit it, they were somewhat of a failure. Each master through the decades to Bradley had bred only one child, thankfully a son. Enough to carry on, certainly, to inherit, but in these days of sudden infant death, it was considered wise to have one or two to spare, so to speak. It was with this in mind that the future wife for young Master Richard had been chosen. A well-bred young lady from a wealthy and, more importantly, a large family of brothers and sisters. One of *eleven* which surely boded well for the continuation of the Goodwin line.

At the beginning of the century Tobias had married, not a lady in the genteel sense but somewhat above him in station. She had taste and discernment and Tobias had built Edge Bottom House where he brought his bride. She had helped to plan it, from its construction to its décor. It was large enough to shelter the great brood of sons and daughters she and Tobias meant to have. It was a gracious, stone-built house with, naturally, many fine windows and graceful chimneys, set in five acres of garden where, on a fine summer's evening, Tobias could sit and smoke a cigar and gaze across the intervening fields with great satisfaction at his cone chimneys, his warehouses, the discreetly placed rows of cottages which housed many of his employees. But like his father before him he sired only one son!

And now that son, Bradley Goodwin, sat in his lovely house, alone but for the handsome housekeeper, Mrs Harriet Pearson, he had employed when his wife died some years ago. She was thirty years younger than he was and had he been anyone else but Bradley Goodwin there would have been talk, but, despite her attractions which had led to the services she performed for her master, she was a superb housekeeper. The servants, the cook, the kitchen- and parlour-maids were firmly under her command, for she was, to all intents and purposes, and for the moment, mistress of Edge Bottom House. She had held it all together when Richard had been killed and was the only one who could control Bradley Goodwin when, shouting with gigantic fury and grief since he had lost his only son, he rampaged through the house. He had terrified the servants, threatening them with dismissal should one of them happen to meet him on the stairs. Only Mrs Pearson seemed unafraid, coaxing him to his room and doing there whatever was needed to console him, the kitchen-maids shuddering as they imagined what that might be!

But now it was April and Bradley walked across the fields each day to oversee the running of his glass works, for the bloody thing wouldn't run itself, he was heard to snarl at his young engineer. With Richard gone he had been forced to come out of the semi-retirement he had begun to enjoy, but on this fine day he had ordered up his carriage for the first time since January.

"Wheer's he off?" Olly, one of the grooms asked in amazement when Ruby ran across the stable yard to inform him that the carriage was needed at ten o'clock.

"Nay, don't ask me. 'Appen church. It *is* Sunday."

"Church! He never goes ter church."

"Well, he don't tekk me into 'is confidence, Olly Preston. Why don't yer ask him when he comes out." Ruby tossed her pretty head haughtily and Olly watched in admiration, for he was sweet on Ruby and longed only for her to feel the same about him.

"I might at that," he answered, and they laughed, both of them knowing he would do no such thing.

The lane from the gate of Edge Bottom House led westwards through the burgeoning spring growth that lined it. It was a beautiful morning, the hawthorns coming into full blow, ox-eye daisies beginning to open in hayfields, cuckoos calling to one another and cattle lowing as they moved slowly about the grassy fields, a plaintive sound, though what they had to be sad about Olly, who was a country man, couldn't imagine. Fed on the lush greenery of well-tended meadows, nothing to do but eat and laze about and he wished he might do the same. Not that Mr Goodwin was a tyrant, as far as the grooms were concerned, for now that Master Richard had gone, so had the saddle horses and Olly and Clem had little to do except pretend to be working should the master take it into his head to stroll out and look at them. This was a real surprise, this jaunt out this morning and even yet he was not sure where they were going.

Sandy Lane, into which he had been ordered to turn, was narrow and deep-rutted. It, like all the country lanes beyond the town, was overhung with the blooming spring greenery. Olly, for lack of any further instructions, continued past a closed gateway set in the hedge and across a little stream, if it could be called that, for it was almost dry with no more than a trickle of water still shining over the rounded pebbles in the middle of the dry, cracked-mud bed. There were cows, their tails lazily twitching, peering over the hedge as though word had got out that an important personage was to pass along this way and they were afraid they might miss it.

They came to a row of dilapidated cottages in front of which several children played a vigorous game of some sort. There was a line of washing hanging to the side of the last one and as the carriage drew near, to the stunned amazement of the children who all froze at the sight of it, a young girl came out and stood on the doorstep. She had bare feet and wore an apron of sorts over a clean but much mended cotton dress.

"Mam ses yer've ter come in at once, our Cissie. You too, Sara-Ann. Dinner's on't table an' yer've not ter let it get cold . . ." Her flow of words came to a faltering stop as she too caught sight of the carriage.

Olly waited for some sort of command from his employer, for surely this was not his destination but with a sharp word Bradley Goodwin brought him to a halt.

"This will do, Oliver," he barked, sitting for several moments while the groom drew the horses to a halt, climbed down from his seat and opened the carriage door. The old man stepped out of his grand carriage, the likes of which had never been seen by the inhabitants of Sandy Lane cottages, here or indeed anywhere, and stood looking about him.

The girl in the doorway gaped and behind her a voice stressed that she was to "shut bloody door" but she was so astonished she merely stood with her hand on the latch and stared at the old gentleman who stared back.

The voice that had spoken at the back of the girl suddenly transformed itself into a woman, a seemingly old woman with greying hair and a shapeless figure. She stood beside the girl, her hand to her eyebrows, shading her eyes from the low sun's glare and what she saw so evidently alarmed her, every vestige of colour in her face, which was not a lot to begin with, drained away so that it resembled a suet pudding. She made some sound, a sort of moan, and though she did not exactly crumble she was seen to lean heavily against the rotting door frame. The old gentleman watched and at his back Olly moved to protect his master's carriage and his master's fine carriage horses from the attentions of the now unfrozen and inquisitive children.

"Get away from there," he bellowed, as one lad laid a hand on the shining rump of Hercules who twitched nervously away. "Get off, yer cheeky little beggars. Them's valuable hanimals an' don't like handling by them they don't know."

The old gentleman and the old woman stared at one another and when he began to move towards her front door she put out a hand as though to ward off a blow. The girl beside her watched her with total bewilderment, then turned her attention to the old gentleman who looked strangely familiar to her though she could not at that moment have said from where.

Abby reached out and took her mam's hand; again she could not have explained why except that Mam seemed to be mazed, her mind to be meandering between terror and horror. She appeared to be shrinking in front of her daughter's very eyes. She looked as though she might faint again.

"What the divil's goin' on?" her pa's voice asked behind her. "By all that's holy yer'd think we'd coals ter chuck away, so yer would, wi't door open wide an'—" At the sight of the old gentleman he stopped in mid-sentence, his childhood memories of fear, fear of the landlord or his agent, carrying him back in time, for surely this was one or the other.

"What . . . ?" Betty began bravely, her voice wobbling, what teeth she had left doing their best not to chatter, so great was her fear and her hand gripped her daughter's so fiercely Abby winced.

"I've come for what's mine," the old man said harshly, amazing Declan Murphy, Abby Murphy, the fascinated children and most of the occupants of the cottages who had come out to watch. What could the Murphy family possibly have that this old man should want? They were all as poor as church mice, just about managing to subsist above starvation level and he was clothed in the best, driving in a carriage drawn by magnificent horses and obviously had never been hungry in his life. They did not know who he was, for most of them had barely been beyond the end of Sandy Lane in their lives. Not even to one of the three fairs that took place in St Helens every year.

"Please . . . oh, please, Mr Goodwin," Betty quavered, "please . . . no . . ."

"Don't waste your breath, madam. I've come for my granddaughter so kindly get her ready."

3

Noah Goodwin studied himself critically in the long cheval mirror that stood in the corner of his bedroom. The room was small and sparsely furnished and the mirror looked out of place, for it was a handsome piece of furniture come from Yorkshire as part of his mother's dowry. It was all that was left, the rest having been sold to feed his father's addiction for gambling, to keep an expensive mistress in a villa on the edge of Liverpool and to live grandly, which he could not afford to do. The room, as bare as that of a housemaid's, contained, besides the mirror, a pine chest of drawers on which stood a ewer and basin, plain and functional, a towel stand holding two white towels, a small wardrobe and a chair. On the floor was a rag rug. It was evident that a great deal of scouring and dusting and polishing had taken place, for it was achingly clean. On the single iron bedstead lay a lumpy flock mattress covered by an exquisite, hand-sewn quilt with a pattern of birds, lover's knots and flowers, stitched by Joanna Goodwin before she gave up hope of a husband!

Noah adjusted his snowy cravat, which his sister had laundered and ironed to perfection, pretending to her friends and callers that the job had been performed by the maid of all work, the only servant they could afford. Just as she pretended that the cakes and biscuits she served to them had been baked by the same half-witted girl, a pretence that fooled no one! Joanna had a strict code of conduct, a great deal of pride and a very small income on which to support it, the income derived by her brother from his work at the Edge Bottom Glass Works where he was employed as an engineer by Bradley Goodwin.

Noah frowned as he tweaked again at his cravat and studied intently his plum-coloured jacket, his dove-grey trousers and his tucked and pleated shirt which was as snowy a white as his cravat. His boots were highly polished and his hands were scrupulously manicured. He was undeniably handsome with the Goodwin build but leaner, finer than Bradley or Richard. His eyes were dark, almost black, and his hair was the rich colour of the polished mahogany table that had once stood in his mother's dining-room. He was shrewd, cunning, ambitious, which was why he had accepted Bradley Goodwin's offer of a position as engineer at the Edge Bottom Glass Works. It was not exactly clear to his employees what his relationship to the old man was. His grandfather and Richard Goodwin's grandfather had been brothers; Bradley had been cousin to Noah's father Jonathan, who could have lived comfortably on the profits of his small but prosperous colliery but who had gambled it all away.

Noah did not mean to do the same. He had returned to St Helens in his early twenties, his apprenticeship to a Liverpool engineering firm completed, interesting himself in processing glass. He spent hours after his day's work in the laboratory at Edge Bottom, working far into the night to improve apparatus for grinding, smoothing and polishing plate glass, crown glass and sheet glass, taking out a patent which Bradley Goodwin chose to ignore, calling it a damn fool idea. He was not employed to *experiment*, Bradley thundered, but to put in a fair day's work for a fair day's pay and it was of no interest to him that the young idiot spent most of his evenings perfecting his invention and therefore could not be said to be wasting Bradley's time and money. And no, he did not care to be bored with details of Noah's ideas for the design of a new flattening kiln, he told him peevishly. A flattening kiln did what its name described, flattened the sheet of glass; had his son lived and come to him with Noah's suggestions they would have been greeted with cries of joy and amazement at the cleverness of the lad, but this was not the case with Noah. The old man was soured, jealous of Noah's ingeniousness, his health, his looks, and in the months following Richard's death he was seen to brood for hours on end, no doubt on the future of his glass works, for who was to inherit it now, those about him asked one another.

No one had a keener interest than Noah Goodwin. He had been summoned to Edge Bottom House, not to dine, but to discuss something of great importance and he could feel the excitement seething through his veins, pumping with his own hot blood. Was this what he had been waiting for ever since the day of the accident? A chance perhaps to . . . what? He dared not put into words what was in his heart, but it was certainly not to be at the beck and call of the old man for the rest of his days. He had known right from the beginning when he had accepted the old man's invitation to work at Edge Bottom that it would not be for ever. With Richard standing in his way there was nothing for him here, but it had been a chance to work in a decent laboratory on his own inventions and one day, perhaps when the old man had gone and Richard, a young, go-ahead man, was in charge, he would have a chance to put his ideas into production. But was this now the moment? Was the old man, who had told everyone who came to sympathise with him on his loss to leave him alone, about to make some decision that would affect himself? The old man had been heard to mutter, talking to himself as the old do, that he was not down yet, that he was not broken yet and surely that could only mean one thing. That Noah Goodwin was to take the place of the dead Richard?

Giving himself another critical look, he turned away from

the mirror and ran down the narrow staircase to the even narrower hallway. Joanna waited there for him, his well-brushed top hat in her hands. She helped him on with his greatcoat, her hands lingering for a moment on his shoulders.

"Good luck," she said, for she of all people as his sister knew of his hopes. She made no attempt to kiss him, for they were not a demonstrative couple but he knew she was, as she had always been, firmly behind him. They had stood together ever since their mother had died, of a broken heart, Edge Bottom said, all that was left of the half a dozen babies Amelia Goodwin had borne and seen die. Noah had been her last and, her husband having very little interest in anything beyond the turn of a card or the running of a horse, had left the naming of his son to his mother. Noah was derived, she had read, from the Hebrew meaning "to comfort" and that was what he had been to her until she went to her grave.

He walked up from Mill Brook Cottage where he and Joanna had spent their days since old Jonathan had died, the property belonging to Bradley Goodwin and meant for an overseer but grudgingly rented to his distant relative. It was but a short step along an overgrown lane already becoming deep in convolvulus to Edge Bottom House and on to the Edge Bottom Glass Works. This evening, instead of continuing on to the works, he turned in at the tall wooden gate that was let into an archway, covered at this time of the year by an explosion of yellow forsythia. The bush had been carefully trained by the Goodwin gardener to creep over the archway set in a high stone wall which surrounded Bradley Goodwin's home. It was almost dark and the garden was but a vast shadowy square where deeper shadows loomed, trees and shrubs, two wrought-iron garden seats, flowerbeds and a great oak tree which was said to have been ancient when George I was on the throne.

Noah crossed the lawn to reach the paved pathway that led

to the arched front door of the house. Yellow lights showed in most of the windows, warm and mysterious against the twilight sky. Bradley Goodwin was not a miser where his own comfort was concerned and Noah knew that there would also be fires in most of the rooms. Smoke drifted from chimneys, trailing in the almost windless night against the darkening sky, which was pricked by a few early stars. He knocked, using the heavy brass head of a thistle with which it had pleased the dead Mrs Bradley Goodwin to decorate her door.

A smart housemaid opened the door to him, immaculate in her black dress and white apron. On her head was a frilled, rather attractive white mob-cap. She bobbed an automatic curtsey.

"Good evening, sir," she said, reaching out to take his hat and coat.

"Good evening, Kitty," he answered and was rewarded with a pleased smile. There were not many gentlemen callers, especially young ones, who remembered the names of Mr Goodwin's maids, unless they were pretty, of course, which Kitty was not. She had been with the Goodwin family since the old gentleman had married, coming as a ten-year-old scullery-maid. She had been in the kitchens on the night the young master was born, and all the other babies who had come and as quickly gone, but this one, a relative in a roundabout way, was a charmer when he wanted to be. He seemed to be in high spirits and what would he say when he saw what awaited him in the drawing-room?

"This way, sir. Mr Goodwin . . . and . . . er . . . is in the drawing-room." She opened the door for him, ushering him over the threshold, longing to hang about and see what was to happen; after all she was almost one of the family but she knew Mrs Pearson would have something to say if she did not immediately return to the kitchen.

He did not at first notice the still figure crouched in the

chair opposite the old man, or if he did his whole being was so concentrated on the old man himself, trying to read by his expression what was in his mind, he overlooked her. The fleeting glance he did manage showed that she was young, a child really and he could see she was very frightened.

"Come in, come in," the old man said irritably, before he had time to wonder. "Don't just stand there with your mouth open." He waved his hand towards the sofa which faced the fire. "Sit down, for God's sake. I want to talk to you."

Hiding his astonishment, not at the idea that the old man wanted to talk to him, though that had come as a surprise, but at the sight of the child in the chair, he sat where he was told.

"Sir?" he questioned.

The girl cowered even further in her chair. She was dressed, as far as he could see, in a plain grey cotton dress, rather short, which revealed her bare ankles – and clogs! The shawl, which she huddled about herself, was also drab but as she moved her head, looking fearfully from him to the old man, the light caught her hair and for a moment he was mesmerised. It was the most beautiful colour. There was copper in it, like that of a fox but there were also streaks of gold and cinnamon and amber. It was long; he could see the curling ends of it protruding from below her buttocks against the cushions of the chair, thick and springing. Her face was in shadow but there was something in it he thought he recognised.

The old man laughed. "You see it too," he remarked genially. "And well you might, for this is my granddaughter. Aye, Richard's lass and about to become a member of—"

The girl sprang up and Noah saw at once that she was not as young as he had thought. Fear had made her vulnerable, as a child might be in an unfamiliar situation, but this was no child. Her figure was that of a woman, high-breasted with a narrow waist and slender hips. But she was still young and very, very mad!

"I am not yer granddaughter, yer daft old man," she shouted. "Me name's Abigail Murphy. Me mam's Betty Murphy an' me pa's Declan Murphy. An' I'll not bide 'ere another—"

"Spirited too, which is all to the good, don't you think, Noah Goodwin? What I have in mind requires a woman with a bit of life in her, for she'll need it if she's to overcome—"

"What the devil are yer talkin' about? Yer nobbut a crazy old fool, fetchin' me from me family an' why I let yer's a mystery ter me." She pulled her shawl about her with a grand gesture and swung towards the door, her magnificent hair swinging with her, but the old man merely chuckled as though she had pleased him inordinately.

"I had hair that colour once," he remarked confidentially, "though Richard's was more . . . well, ginger, I suppose you'd call it." The girl had begun to stride across the thick carpet with the evident intention of leaving but suddenly the old man stood up, his huge bulk barring her way, his seamed face menacing and she stopped abruptly.

"Sit down, girl," Bradley Goodwin snarled, "and do as you're told." But instead of returning to her chair as many a lesser female might have done she faced up to him and Noah knew at once that this girl was indeed what the old man said she was.

He spoke for the first time, his voice mild though his heart was pounding, for he knew that this was going to be of importance to him in some way. Why had he been invited here otherwise? "May I ask what is happening here, Mr Goodwin, and more to the point why I am included?"

"Aye, you may ask and happen I'll tell you when this lass does as she's told. Sit down, I say."

"No, I will not. I want ter go 'ome an' if yer don't get out of me way I'll scream the bloody place down. I don't know why I let yer bring me 'ere in the first place." When she thought back she could only assume that she had been so stunned she would have gone anywhere with anyone. But now she had come to her senses and was having none of this daftness!

Her mind returned her to that moment in the cluttered kitchen of her home with Mam on her knees, well, almost on her knees, begging the old man for something. Tears were streaming down her face and she held out her clasped hands in a plea so pitiful Dicky began to cry in sympathy. They were all there, crowding into the cottage, mouths agape, the splendour of the horse and carriage quite forgotten at the sight of the gentleman entering their humble home.

"What the divil's goin' on 'ere?" Pa was blustering but he was of the class that did not question the gentry and his attempt to do so was half-hearted. The old gentleman ignored him. He was looking at *her*, his eyes running over her in a way that in a younger man might have been offensive and it was then that the great terror struck her and took away her senses.

"Madam," the old man was saying in that particularly sarcastic way the gentry have with those they believe are beneath them, "you know and I know that this girl does not belong to you. She is a Goodwin—"

"No, please," Mam screamed and poor Dicky cowered back against Cissie who happened to be the nearer. His mam was not his mam at the moment. "She's bin wi' me for nearly sixteen years. She knows nowt else."

"She'll learn."

"Sir, please . . . don't tekk 'er away from 'er family."

"*I* am her family and mean her to—"

"Yer can't. She doesn't know, yer see, an' the shock'll turn 'er 'ead."

"Don't be so ridiculous. She is my son's daughter. I

mean to adopt her. What better life could she have than the granddaughter to the wealthiest man in Edge Bottom? She'll have the best of everything, education, mix with decent company, dress as she should, all the things she would never have if she remains with you."

"She's our lass. We love 'er."

The old man sneered. "Love, like you have here, you mean," looking round the untidy cottage. "A life of drudgery with a labouring man. A child every year, living on the edge of poverty."

"Now then," Declan Murphy began, "an' what's wrong wi' bein' a labourin' man? 'Tis 'onest work, so it is, an'—"

"I'm not here to argue with you. The girl is my blood, the daughter of my son and I mean to adopt her, bring her up—"

"*Bring 'er up*," Betty Murphy shrieked. "We brung 'er up. She's nearly sixteen not a babby. I'm not goin' ter let yer tekk 'er. She's ours not yourn."

"I think you may have trouble proving that, madam. I have conferred with a lawyer on this. The authorities are more likely to believe my story than yours, whatever that might be. What possible reason would I have for taking a girl from the family into which she had been born if she was not connected to me in some way? You only have to look at her to see she is different to the rest of you. Her hair, for instance, is the same colour as mine when I was younger—"

"We don't know that."

"And she is finer than these others." Which was true, for the Murphys were all tow-headed, pale-eyed, somewhat scrawny like their father.

Bradley Goodwin turned to his granddaughter. "Do you believe me when I say you are not related to these . . . these persons. My son – he was only sixteen himself – got a child on a woman, a girl, and you are the result. We – my wife was alive at the time – decided that . . . well, it was not unusual for a lad to sow his wild oats, but we could not acknowledge that child . . . the scandal; but believe me when I tell you, you do not belong here and so I propose to . . . to tell the world who you are and train you . . . have you trained to become a true Goodwin. You will have . . . Do you understand, girl?"

His old face was as hard as flint and as immovable. He would have his own way, it said, and these people who were nothing to him would be swept away like so much discarded chaff if they made a fuss. She nodded. She was almost senseless with shock and the great dark confusion that had come upon her. Her mam was still screaming, the children crying, Pa babbling on about nothing at all, but she allowed herself to be led, just as she was, into the old man's carriage. She trembled violently; her face was as white as alabaster, her eyes enormous blue-green caverns, tears which she had not known she was shedding slipping from them. The old man had not spoken again and now here she was in this room, with a strange, younger man regarding her and the man who said he was her grandfather barring her escape.

"Get out o' me way," she told him, "or I'll—"

"Scream the place down! Yes, you told me, but won't you sit down first and listen to me?" The old man's face had softened imperceptibly and she found herself returning to the chair from which she had risen. She would not stay, of course. Mam would be worried sick, and though it was dark now she meant to hurry home and reassure her that the old gentleman was talking nonsense. She was Abigail Murphy, dairymaid to Mrs Hodges at Updale Farm where she would be ready to milk the cows first thing in the morning. The old man must be off his head, but as she looked about her, having calmed herself down with these thoughts, a picture above the fireplace caught her eye, a picture of a young boy in a fancy suit made from some material she had never before seen. He was a handsome boy, smiling just a little and about his head rioted a mop of short red curls. The face was familiar to her, for did she not see it every day in Mam's bit of broken mirror in which she checked that she was tidy before she set off for Updale. The picture fascinated her though, and as the old man talked and she glanced curiously about her at the rest of the room, her eyes kept returning to it.

"That was your father," the old man said, evidently noticing where she was looking. "He was only a child, six or seven, but you must surely see the resemblance."

The second man suddenly sprang to his feet and Abby and the old man turned abruptly to look at him.

"Am I to believe, sir, that you are claiming that this . . . this girl is your . . . your granddaughter?" His face was like bleached bone and his eyes, which were such a deep brown as to be almost black, seemed to have sunk into the sockets of his strong face. The scorching heat of his apparent anger surprised them both, for what had *he* to be angry about? He began to stride about the room, almost blundering into several small occasional tables. Bradley Goodwin held a glass of brandy in his hand but he had not offered one to Noah; now, without being invited, he moved to the table by the fireside and poured himself a glass, drinking it straight down then pouring himself another. Bradley watched him with amusement. Noah had been in this room more than once and without so much as a by your leave he strode to the fireplace, took a cigar from the massive gold and onyx cigar box, lit it with a taper, inhaled deeply and blew smoke towards the ceiling. He seemed suddenly to be in command of himself again and Bradley smiled.

"Have you finished?" he asked lazily.

"For the moment," Noah answered.

Bradley's smile deepened. "Don't worry, my boy, you are not to be . . . deposed, is that the word? I have plans for you, as well as the girl, but that is for later. It's getting late and I'm sure the girl . . ." He turned to Abby who blinked. "By the way, what did you say your name was? Did your . . . did the woman at Sandy Lane say?"

"D'yer mean me mam?"

He winced. "Yes, I suppose I do."

"Abby. Abigail, but everyone calls me Abby."

"I shall call you Abigail. We all will." He reached out and pulled something that hung beside his chair and within seconds the door opened and an attractive woman entered.

"Yes, sir?" she enquired. She was dressed entirely in black. She was thirty years younger than her employer and far too good-looking for her own good but she was evidently a servant. Around her slender waist was a wide belt from which hung her badge of office, known as a châtelaine. Hanging from it were keys, a tiny pair of silver scissors, a thimble, a notebook and pencil, also silver, and, an indication of her nature, a tiny scent bottle.

"My granddaughter is tired, Mrs Pearson. Show her to the room that has been prepared for her and make sure she has everything she requires."

If Mrs Pearson was surprised she did not show it. Without altering a muscle of her smooth face she said, "Come this way, miss," turned towards the door, and, surprisingly, Abby went with her. The two men watched her go, then, when the door had closed behind her, the old man leaned forward and tapped Noah on the knee.

"Now then, lad, here's what I intend."

The room to which the woman in black showed her was so lovely Abby felt a moment's regret at what she must do. Downstairs, being in such a state of shock, she had noticed nothing beyond shapes, rich panelling, glowing fires, lamps, deep carpets, mirrors. She had sat in a wide chair of the utmost comfort but it had all seemed shadowy, muted, just images on the periphery of her vision. But here, in this room where the woman took her, were light, pale colours, warmth, with creamy lace and a pale duck-egg blue carpet on which she hardly dared place her clogs, the ones that stepped through the muck of Mr Hodges' cow yard. There were curtains at the window, soft and fine, the same colour as the carpet, tied back with pale blue ribbons, and on the wall, which was papered in cream printed with tiny bluebirds, hung pictures. Pictures of flowers and birds and one with a great expanse of water with boats on it. Delicate and misted, and reflected in the glass which fronted them, were the flames of the fire dancing a warm and merry jig in the white fireplace. There were several bowls of flowers, roses, *roses* in April, and others which she did not recognise, unaware that they had come from Bradley Goodwin's conservatory.

"Would you like to bathe?" the woman asked politely, her eyes straying to Abby's bare ankles.

"Bathe?" Abby's mouth fell open.

"Yes. Take a bath. I can arrange for the maids to bring up hot water. The bath is behind the screen."

Abby turned to stare at the screen, painted with vivid birds and flowers, to which the woman had pointed.

"No." For this would entail removing her clothes and she'd no time for that.

"Very well. Perhaps . . . something to eat?"

"No, thanks."

"Then I'll leave you to sleep. Ring the bell should you need something." The woman's voice was completely toneless, her face expressionless.

"The bell?"

"Yes, it's just there hanging by the fireplace and there is another by the bed." So that was what the old man had pulled to summon this frozen-faced woman!

"Goodnight, then."

"Goodnight."

The woman turned, glided to the door, opened it and left the room, closing the door so quietly Abby wasn't sure she had gone. To make sure she tiptoed across the beautiful carpet, tempted to take off her clogs, opened it and peeped out. The candlelit hallway was empty. She closed the door again and moved at once to the window, opening it wide. She smiled triumphantly when she saw the branches of the oak tree no more than a foot from the window. With the expertise which many years of climbing trees had taught her she climbed from the window, lowered herself swiftly from branch to branch and, without looking back when she reached the ground, ran silently across the lawn, through the gate and into the lane that led to Edge Bottom.

4

When she arrived at the row of cottages, which were so dilapidated they seemed to lean against one another for support, it was long past bedtime. Beating on the door with her clog brought no answer so she flung several handfuls of grit and small stones at the tiny upper window before it was opened and a timid voice which she recognised as Mam's asked who was there and what they wanted.

"It's Abby, Mam. Let me in."

"Abby!" Betty Murphy said in a stunned voice just as though she never expected to see her daughter again, in this world or the next, then at once it became joyful and though it was dark Abby was certain she could see the wide grin on Mam's face.

There was a short pause and then the bolt on the door screeched and the door opened.

"Lass . . . lass . . ." Then she was dragged into Mam's crushing embrace. "I thought yer was gone. I thought I'd never see yer again. Blessed Mother in heaven," voicing one of Declan's oft-repeated sayings. After all she was a mother and the One above must surely have heard her pleadings tonight. "Come in, come in, chuck, an' tell us what 'appened. That wicked old man . . . we was all cryin', even Declan who's no blood ter yer but he's bin a good pa—"

She stopped speaking abruptly then very gently she led Abby to Pa's chair and sat her down in it, for she could see the girl was overwrought. The fire was nearly out but, fiddling with a few bits of kindling, Betty got it going and brought the kettle, which always stood on it, to the boil. She reached down the tea caddy and, seeing that this had been such a bad, bad day, heaped two spoonfuls of precious tea into it and poured on the hot water. In a minute she pushed a mug of tea into Abby's hand and, with one for herself, lowered herself heavily on to the old stool on which Pa rested his feet and squatted in front of Abby. They sipped their tea in silence, then, putting her mug on the fender and doing the same with Abby's, she took her daughter's hands in hers, looking down at them sadly, sighing deeply. She stroked them and Abby watched her, waiting for her to speak, for speak she must. In the space of an hour or two their whole life had been turned upside down and Mam owed her an explanation.

Mam was still her mam, of that she was sure, but it seemed Pa was not really her pa and the story of what had happened in Mam's early years must be told. The rest of the family was asleep; only she and Mam were here in the room that had been the centre of Abby's life ever since she could remember. The room where they had lived and loved and squabbled, she and her brothers and sisters, where they had, despite the hardship of their lives, known laughter and tears, not much in the way of joy, but steady day-to-day living, familiar, well-known, and now she realised it had all been a sham. She had refused to believe it, shocked beyond measure, unable to comprehend what was happening but in her heart of hearts she knew that what the old man said was true. The picture of the small boy above the magnificent fireplace had told her that, that and her mam's manner, her sadness, her terrible grief.

"'E told the truth, lass," her mam said at last. "'E's yer grandfather all right, bad old bugger that 'e is. Me an' Richard, we were only bairns, sixteen mebbe, but for the whole of that summer he loved me an' I loved 'im. You know what love is, you an' Roddy, so yer'll know what I mean. It tekks all sense from yer. All yer want is ter be wi' 'im, ter see 'is face light up when yer meet, ter feel the smile in yer own 'eart . . . yer don't think, or look ter the future. We used ter meet, laugh – he were allus jokin'. It were the loveliest thing what ever 'appened ter me an' it's still 'ere in me 'eart." She placed her work-worn hand, the one that had been kissed and fondled by the master's son, on her sagging bosom, the bosom that had once delighted the handsome young man who had been the love of her life, and her head bowed in remembered joy and grief. "When I 'eard he were dead it brought it all back an' though yer pa has allus been a good, kind husband it never was the same. He married me when you were on the way. He knew you weren't 'is but he treated yer as though you were an' there was great . . . fondness atween us. 'E didn't know who yer real pa was and I never told 'im, or anybody. It were summat precious ter me. A treasure inside me I couldn't share wi' anyone. It broke my heart," she said simply, "when we had ter part, which o' course we did. Well, the son o't master of Edge Bottom Glass Works couldn't wed the daughter of a farm 'and, could 'e? The old man give me five guineas and me an' Declan – 'e worked on't same farm as me pa – was wed. It set us up wi'a few bits o' things and then when you were born . . . it were like having Richard back. You're the spit of 'im, lass. I loved 'im. I love you but you're a Goodwin."

Abby snatched her hands away, almost pushing her mother over in her distaste and horror. *A Goodwin!* Never. She was the daughter of Declan and Betty Murphy. A dairymaid with her life all set out before her with Roddy, the man she loved. The old man who had come to them with this fantastical story was off his head and she didn't care what Mam said; even if it was true about . . . about her and Richard Goodwin, it didn't alter things. She looked round the kitchen, at all the familiar, beloved . . . yes, *beloved* things in it, which, although they might be old and tattered and dented and cracked, were her life and her heart was racked with pain. This was her place. This *was* Abby Murphy. She could smell the rabbit stew they had all eaten for their midday meal, the last she had shared with them before her life fell in rubble about her ears. Rabbit stew was a luxury to them all, the rabbit shot by Pa with the old gun Mr Hodges had passed on to him. Only a small rabbit, but they had all had a bit of tasty flesh from the pot, full to the brim with onions and carrots and potatoes to make it go further among the ten of them. How they had enjoyed it, chewing on the bones and scraping up every drop of juice with the bread Mam had baked that morning, the aroma of which still tantalised her nostrils. How they had laughed at Pa's old joke about the pattern on the plates, which he swore they would take off with their enthusiasm!

"Lass." Her mother's voice came at her softly and she rose heavily to her feet. Betty had cause to believe she was again with child and her heart dragged at the thought of how they were all to manage, especially if this good girl of hers was to be taken from her, which she was, of course. How could anyone, anyone in their station of life, stand against a man like Bradley Goodwin? If he said Abigail Murphy was his son's daughter, *his* granddaughter, who were they to argue with him? True, she, Betty, was Abby's mam but it would make no difference. Abby was intended for great things, that was for certain, else why would the old man take her into his home? She would learn to be a lady. With his son dead she would be a great heiress – was that the right word? – and could she, Betty Murphy, the wife of a hedger and ditcher, stand in her way, or even argue with it? But the girl must be made to see it, to recognise it, to accept it and not keep running home every time she felt like it. She would be Abigail Goodwin, a member of the wealthiest family in the district. She would be educated to that station of life and though it broke her heart Betty Murphy must persuade her to it.

Abby turned to look at her and in her eyes was a terrible clouded fear. Her face was like stone, even her lips colourless.

"Don't, Mam," she whispered. "Don't make me."

"I must, my lamb. I've no choice an' neither 'ave you."

"What about Roddy?" Even as she spoke his name the colour slowly returned to Abby's face and she straightened her back and squared her shoulders. Roddy wouldn't let this happen to her, would he? She and Roddy were to be married when he had finished his apprenticeship and nothing nor nobody was going to interfere with that. She wouldn't allow it and neither would Roddy. She wasn't awfully sure what the old man would have to say about it but with the resilience and confidence of youth – and love – she knew they would overcome that difficulty when it arrived. She and Roddy had loved one another since they were children. No, if it meant losing Roddy the old man could whistle. She'd rather live in abject poverty with Roddy than in that grand house with the old man and if it came to . . .

"You could give your Roddy a hand up if you was Miss Abigail Goodwin of Edge Bottom 'Ouse. Have yer thought o' that, child, not ter mention yer family." Though the very idea of taking anything from that old man, even through her own daughter, was ashes in Betty's mouth. But the important thing was to get Abby to accept her new life of her own volition. It would do no good to take her kicking and screaming up to that grand place. She *would* go, that was a certainty, for the old man would have his way. Hadn't he done so when she had confided to Richard she was to have his child? He was powerful, rich and vindictive and her lass must be protected from him in any way she, Betty, could contrive. He was a man who believed in the continuation of his line. With his son gone the only way he could live for ever was through his descendants, his *direct* descendants, a line of Goodwins just like himself. There was the glass works. With Abby he would have, not a son, but children who would have his blood in them. Not exactly what he would have dreamed of but his own flesh and blood nevertheless.

"So what must I do, Mam?"

Her mam sighed and straightened her own shoulders. "Yer must decide fer yerself, lass, but if the old man has set his heart on it yer'll not have the strength ter say him nay. Not him."

"Then I must do it."

Her mother's eyes, so like her own, were moist with tears and one escaped, sliding down her cheek to drip on to the old garment which did her for a nightgown. Upstairs someone coughed and she saw Abby turn her gaze up to the ceiling. It would be their Sara-Ann who had a weak chest and was always plagued with it through the winter and even now into the spring. It was perhaps this that decided Abby, for even as her mother watched her she could see by the expression on her face, the expression that said Abby's mind was turning to thoughts of doctors, cough medicine, the best of care for her little sister, for all of them, when she was Miss Abigail Goodwin of Edge Bottom House. Warm clothes, good food, perhaps an education for her brothers and sisters, decent jobs for the lads, all the things she would be able to provide, and if the old man didn't like it, then he could go hang himself. And then there was Roddy. What might she be able to do for him when she was the granddaughter of Bradley Goodwin, the owner of the glass works? To what heights might Roddy rise with her to help him? They might be able to marry even earlier than they had hoped!

"Sleep on it, my lass," Betty said gently, breaking into her thoughts. "If yer won't 'ave it I'll fight tooth an' nail ter keep yer, yer know that."

"I know, Mam." Abby put her arms round her mother and they stood in a loving embrace for a long time, both of them knowing in their hearts that they were saying good-bye.

The scullery-maid was astonished when she answered the knock on the back door to find a pale-faced but pretty young girl on the doorstep. She was clutching a bundle. Wrapped about her head was a slipping shawl which revealed the glorious russet red of her hair and on her bare feet were iron-soled clogs.

"Yes?" said Nessie the scullery-maid, lifting her head superciliously, for it was not often that she had the opportunity to feel superior to another human being. She was the only one up, though Kitty, Ruby, May and Cook would be down soon. It was Nessie's job to rake out last night's fire and get another going, to put on the kettle, make tea and begin the preparations for the servants' breakfast. Mrs Pearson, the housekeeper, was, naturally, down last and was the only one who could have told Nessie who the young woman on the back doorstep was.

"I'm Abby," the girl said, just as though Nessie should know exactly who Abby was.

"Oh, yes, and who might that be?"

"Abby Murphy. I'm here ter see Mr Goodwin."

"Yer what?" Nessie was taken aback, then she smiled, ready to shut the door in this mad girl's face but something *in* the mad girl's face stopped her and she dithered, not knowing what her next move should be. She had heard whispers that a girl had been brought to the house last night by the master, but for what reason she did not know and anyway they were not about to confide in her, a lowly scullery-maid, were they? So was this her? And if so what was she doing banging at the back door at six o'clock in the morning?

The girl stepped over the threshold and moved past Nessie into the huge kitchen, looking round her as though she might be thinking of buying it if the price was right, and Nessie was so astounded she let her. She stood holding the latch of the still open door and watched as the little madam walked slowly to the table and placed her bundle on its snow-white surface which Nessie had scrubbed last night before she dragged herself to her bed. She watched, her mouth open, as the girl's gaze wandered round the room. She was not to know that the room was a marvel to the intruder. Abby had been too stunned to notice fully the drawing-room to which she had been taken last night, and apart from the picture of the boy had scarcely noticed anything in it. But this room, this shining kitchen was something she recognised. Not that even Mrs Hodges' kitchen was as amazing as this one but the dazzling white walls, the dozens of gleaming copper pans hanging thereon, the racks of crockery, the shelves crammed with objects, shining and lovely, whose purpose she couldn't imagine, the big clock ticking on the wall, the high ceilings, the tiled areas at the back of immaculate sinks, the joints of red marbled meat hanging from the ceiling, the nets of onions and mushrooms, birds in neat rows, trussed and ready to go into the ovens, she supposed, and the ovens themselves, great blackleaded creatures that took up half of one wall were a wonder to a girl brought up in a sod cottage. The tables, four of them, were of scrubbed pine and alongside two of them were benches, all neatly placed. The whole spoke of order, discipline, cleanliness, harmony, a punctilious eye for small details and yet it was warm, homely and infinitely more comforting than the room to which she was taken last night.

She turned and tried a small smile on the young girl who had let her in.

"Is he about?" she enquired politely.

"What?" Nessie stammered, then, remembering who she was, closed the door.

"The master. Is he about?"

Nessie glanced in consternation at the clock as though to

confirm that it was not she who was mad. "At this time? 'E don't come down till eight. Then he'll be off ter't glass works."

"Very well, I'll wait."

Nessie cast about her like a horse tormented by a persistent fly, her young face a picture of bewilderment. Her indecision was plain. What the dickens was she to do with this haughty – yes, she had decided the girl was haughty, despite her working-class dress – young woman who seemed to be perfectly at ease with the situation even though it was only six o'clock in the morning? She even appeared to be somewhat startled that the master was still in his bed at this hour! Should she allow her to stand by the table or send – who should she send? – for one of the others to tell her what to do? Kitty would be down soon, or May, but in the meanwhile was she to offer the visitor a cup of tea? The kettle was just on the boil.

Her problem was solved, bringing her great relief, as two neatly dressed maids entered the kitchen, both yawning behind their hands and stretching their necks. For a second or two they did not see Abby standing by the table and when they did their mouths dropped open, especially the older one, for it was she who had shown Mr Noah into the drawing-room where this very girl had drooped in the chair opposite the master. She didn't know what the dickens had been going on, or what had happened after she had left to return to the kitchen. She only knew that Mrs Pearson had told her that on pain of death, so to speak, she had not to breathe a word of it to the other servants. Now here was the lass standing in the Goodwin kitchen and how had she got there? And who the devil was she? Kitty Spencer asked herself, though something in the way the girl stood, the shape of her mouth, the set of her chin and the vivid colour of her hair reminded her of . . . of someone, of something, but for the moment she was so taken aback she could not get her shocked brain into a functioning mode.

"What's going on?" she managed to ask and Nessie passed the burden thankfully on to her.

"Nay, don't ask me. She just knocked at door an' said she wanted ter see t'master. Abby . . . somethin' or other."

"Abby . . . Abigail Murphy," Abby offered.

They all three continued to stare at her curiously. Perhaps she was a new servant, though none of them had been told of one. Mrs Pearson was the one who employed new staff but as far as they knew none was needed. Perhaps they had better fetch her, May, who was second parlour-maid, proffered, and at once they began to shuffle about awkwardly, for it was not something they relished, summoning the housekeeper who might not even be in her own room. She was a woman of great stature, dignified, handsome, of proud, easy carriage, shrewd and unapproachable. She was fair with those who worked as she demanded and though it was well-known that the master and she were . . . well, close, not one of them would dare to criticise her for it. To her face or behind her back! She was a good mistress, if she could be called by that name, in the real sense of the word and not the other, but the idea that one of them should go and knock on her door at just gone six in the morning quite literally terrified them.

The third housemaid, Ruby, clattered into the kitchen, still tying the ribbons of her apron, her maid's cap awry on her head, for Ruby was a bit of a scatterbrain, always the last up, full of laughing excuses, thankful that she had reached the kitchen before Cook who would have given her what for, but the sight of her three fellow servants gawping at the strange girl by the table brought her to a skidding halt.

"Who's this then?" she asked, her hands still at her apron, then going to her cap, and as she spoke the fifth member of the kitchen staff entered the room with the dignified majesty of their little queen up in London whom she greatly resembled.

"Well, and who might this be?" she demanded, crossing her arms under her capacious bosom and heaving it up towards her chin, and if she had not been so frozen with fear Abby might have laughed. One after the other they had come to a full stop and asked virtually the same question but she couldn't tell them, could she? Not until she had spoken to the old man who, she supposed, thought her to be still tucked up snugly in that pretty bedroom where she had been put last night.

"Well," the plump little woman demanded ominously as though she had caught her staff entertaining a friend behind her back.

"Me name's Abigail Murphy as I've already told this—"

"Don't you sauce me, young lady," Cook began, advancing threateningly on Abby.

"I'm not saucin' yer. You asked who I was an' I'm tellin' yer. Now if one of yer would be good enough ter go an' tell the old man Abby Murphy's here I'd be obliged."

"*The old man!* Who d'yer think yer talking to, yer little madam. This is my kitchen and I'll have a bit of respect in it, not just for me but for the master of the house. I don't know who you are or what you think yer doing here but I suggest you tekk yerself off quick smart before—"

"Oh, fer goodness sake, go an' fetch Mr Goodwin or that woman I saw last night. I'm not standin' here arguin' with you." For by this time Abby's hard-won courage was rapidly draining away. She longed to be back in her mam's familiar cluttered kitchen, or in the dairy where everyone knew her and where she was accepted for who she was. And that was another thing. Somehow she must get word to Mrs Hodges – or would Mam do it and if so what would she say? What would *everyone* say when they heard the news? And of course, before the day was out she must somehow get to speak to Roddy. She didn't know how, for what the devil was she to do in this great house all day long? How was she to be occupied? How did the granddaughter of a wealthy man spend her time? Whatever it turned out to be she was determined to slip over to the glass works and see Roddy. Explain to him what had happened to her, tell him it would make no difference to them, that though she might have a different name and be . . . be *someone* else . . . Dear God, would he ever believe her? But she must make him understand and . . . well, if only these gawking women would get a move on she could see which way the land lay and make her plans accordingly.

"I think yer'd best get the old man," she managed faintly, "an' I wouldn't mind a cup o' tea if there's one going." There was always a cup of tea going in Mrs Hodges' kitchen!

"Yer cheeky young madam," the plump little woman spluttered and there might have been mayhem in the kitchen of Edge Bottom House if, as though some instinct had warned her that there was trouble in her domain, Harriet Pearson, still in the rich brocade housegown she wore whenever she slipped from her room to *his*, had not opened the door and entered the room.

"Ah, there you are," she said to Abby, ignoring the others. "Come into my sitting-room and, Cook" – turning to the turkey-faced little woman – "we'll have tea and toast at once. Hot buttered toast, if you please, the tea good and strong." Just as though Jane Grimshaw, who had been cook in this house for over fifteen years and had prepared positive *banquets* for Mr Goodwin's dinner guests, had no idea how to prepare tea and toast!

Abby watched apprehensively as the little dumpling of a woman opened her mouth to say something in outrage but she evidently thought better of it, so, submissive as a little mouse, Abby picked up her bundle and followed the tall, imposing woman through a door set in the far wall and into another room. To Abby the room was as splendid as the others she had seen in the house, for she was not to know that this was merely the housekeeper's private room and though comfortable was quite plainly furnished. There was a fire laid in the hearth, small scraps of kindling, paper and wood and, kneeling gracefully, her brocade skirts falling about her, the woman put a match to it.

The room, which was central to the smooth running of Bradley Goodwin's home, served by turns as office, sitting-room and dining-room. It housed a number of Harriet Pearson's personal belongings, ornaments and pictures, but the array of cupboards and shelves that lined the walls, painted in a pale shade of grey, proclaimed that this was very much a place of work. It was kept immaculately tidy by Ruby or May, for it was here that the housekeeper discussed accounts with tradesmen, entered her accounts in enormous ledgers, gave orders to the housemaids or laundry-maids and interviewed applicants for a job. There were two high wing chairs, a large table covered with a fringed, chenille cloth around which were placed four dining chairs. Heavy velvet curtains hung at the two windows which looked out on the stable yard. There was a small tripod tea-table on which Ruby, her face rosy with excitement, placed a tea tray bearing a plate of hot buttered toast, a silver teapot, milk jug and sugar bowl and two dainty china teacups and saucers.

Abby stood quietly until the lady in the brocade gown indicated that she was to sit in one of the wing chairs before the fire which was beginning to crackle cheerfully. The lady poured tea, fragrant and steaming, into a teacup and handed it to Abby.

"Drink," she commanded, "and help yourself to toast." Then she sat back with her own cup of tea and watched as Abby, who had never, ever touched, let alone drunk out of a cup so beautiful and so delicate, sipped the tea appreciatively.

It was hot, strong and Harriet Pearson had stirred in two teaspoons of sugar and Abby thought she had never tasted anything quite so delicious.

"Have you eaten?" the lady asked her and when Abby shook her head, for how could she eat for the last time in the kitchen with her mam crying quietly and the children staring at her in wonder, the lady passed her the plate of toast. The toast was dripping with *best* butter and she should know, for hadn't she made pounds and pounds of it in Mrs Hodges' dairy. She was young and her appetite was healthy and she found herself tucking in, drinking her tea, a second cup forthcoming as the first was drained and eating every scrap of toast. She was not to know that Harriet Pearson watched her intently, noting with approval that the girl who was Bradley Goodwin's natural granddaughter ate daintily, delicately, careful with her cup and saucer and the empty plate which she placed on the small table beside her when she had finished. She licked her lips of the last scrap of butter then, obviously feeling better, sat up straight and turned her gaze to Harriet who still sipped her tea.

"Well," the girl said with a brave lift of her head, "where do I start?"

5

Roddy Baxter was just sitting down to his dinner after coming off his ten-hour shift in the crown furnace as the glasshouse was often called. It was half past five but not yet dark, or even dusk on this April early evening and he ate quickly, for if he could manage it he meant to walk over to Sandy Lane and spend half an hour with Abby. Perhaps take her hand and walk her down the lane until they were out of sight of the cottages and exchange a kiss or two. It was three days since he had seen her as his shifts had been awkward during the past week but today, starting at seven and finishing at five meant that he could get over there and if she was not yet home, set off to meet her at the dairy. Stroll with her along the blossoming country lane between the farm and her home, smell the refreshing fragrance of windflowers and violets and primroses, walk beside the little spinney where the great round-leaved willow tree bushed, covered all over with great golden catkins. Listen to the bees humming and the cows lowing to be milked. It was all they asked, he and Abby, just to be together in their dreaming world which would one day soon be spent for ever in one another's company.

He stoked himself up with the good, hearty, shin beef casserole his mam had left in the oven for him, along with a great panful of mashed potatoes. Willy and Eddy had already eaten theirs and he could hear their shouts as they scuffled with other lads outside the row of cottages. The meal was tasty, filling, but he was in a hurry and he ate it with the sole purpose of fuelling the engine that was his virile body. The heavy and exacting work he did had little effect on his young man's vigour, for he was strong, his mam's nourishing food, his own youthful ability to sleep the moment his head touched his pillow for as long as he was allowed, his love of sporting activities in which he was a keen participator and at which he excelled, hardened his young body to the peak of fitness. He was lucky, he knew, in his wellbeing, thanks to his mam who worked her fingers to the bone to provide decent food for her family, and it was perhaps the death at a young age of his father, and his many brothers and sisters, leaving only himself, Willy and Eddy to clothe and feed, that was the reason for it. Willy and Eddy, six and five years old, earned a few pennies in the fields about the town but it was himself and his mam who brought in what to the other families in the row was considered good money. His mam was unusual, he knew that, in her steady guiding of his and his brothers' lives, allowing nothing to stand in his way to the life he had worked out for himself, and would do the same for her two younger sons. She was careful, treading delicately through this world of theirs which was a tough one for most families. She was polite to the other women in the row but formed no particular friendships, for her whole existence was concentrated on the betterment of life for her lads. They were all she had and though she was not a demonstrative woman they all three knew they were the centre of her world. She was a wise and careful shopper, going from shop to shop, market stall to market stall to find the best she could for the money she had and with his wage as an apprentice at Edge Bottom Glass Works and hers which she earned scrubbing, cleaning, washing, ironing, doing a stint at the Glassmakers Arms as a barmaid several times a week, anything that would bring in a few extra pennies, they were well fed, decently clothed and housed.

And Roddy was happy which added to his sense of well-being! His world was just as he wanted it to be. He was in love and was loved by the most beautiful girl in the village of Edge Bottom and when he had finished his apprenticeship in the work he found so satisfying they would be married, he and his love. They would have their own cottage, children, not too many to drag Abby down though he was not sure how that might be managed, and live out their lives in the peace and contentment which they had been planning ever since they had discovered that not only did they like one another, they were in love as a man and woman can be in love.

When he had finished his meal he fetched a bucket of water from the tap at the back of the row, bringing it into his mother's immaculate kitchen and pouring some of it into a bowl. He added hot water from the kettle which simmered on the fire and put his and his brothers' plates into it to steep. He knew Mam wouldn't mind if he left them, for she was aware of, and approved of his eagerness to get over to Abby's. He had already had a good wash before he sat down to his meal, another of his mother's rules. He slipped his jacket over his yellow waistcoat, opened the door, checked that his brothers were where they should be and was just about to stride out down the row and into Bamford Street when he was surprised to see his mam hurrying as though the devil himself was at her heels from the opposite direction. He knew she was to do a couple of hours at the Glassmakers Arms this evening and had only been there for half an hour so what the hell was she doing positively *running* along Bamford Street? Her shawl had slipped to the back of her greying head and her clogs rang on the cobbles, striking sparks as she ran. When she saw him she stopped so suddenly she might have run into a brick wall.

He began to hurry towards her, his hand already going out to her, for surely she had some terrible news to impart by the look on her face.

"Mam . . ." he began but without a word she grasped his hand and began to pull him along the pavement towards their own cottage.

"Mam . . ." he protested but she continued to hurry him along until they reached their own front door. It was not locked. She thrust it open with such force it hit the wall behind it and as soon as they were inside she closed it firmly, standing with her back to it as though to keep out the screaming hordes of China.

"Mam, fer God's sake, what's up with yer?" He pushed his hand through his thick thatch of hair in which brown and gold was equally mixed, his usually good-tempered face pulled into an expression of irritation. Mam knew he hadn't much time to see Abby, for her pa would be at her to come in the minute it started to get dark but his mother continued to stand and stare at him, her chest heaving, her face, which had been red with her exertions, suddenly looking pale and strained.

"What is it, Mam?" he said more quietly. "Tell me."

"I've just heard. It's all over the Glassmakers Arms."

"What is?" As he spoke he knew it was something bad, something to do with him, or his mother wouldn't look so terrible. Something to do with him and . . .

"It's Abby," his mother croaked.

"For Christ's sake, Mam." His young voice was suddenly savage. "Tell me . . ."

"She's at Edge Bottom House."

He was so relieved to hear that Abby was not dead or injured or . . . or . . . He began to smile, his shoulders slumping in relief.

"Mam, yer scared the bloody life out of me."

His mother's voice was harsh. "Son, it seems Abby Murphy is Bradley Goodwin's granddaughter and she's gone ter live wi' 'im at Edge Bottom."

"Don't talk so daft."

"It's true, son. It's all over t'village. Master Richard an' Betty Murphy were . . . years ago and Abby is—"

"I never heard anythin' so bloody daft in me life. Someone's coddin' yer." Roddy's voice was flat, harsh, and his own face was as white as paper. He turned in a circle, then strode to the window, staring out at the hectic activity of the yard, at the children, most barefoot, screaming in play, at the women gossiping on their doorsteps, at the horses and wagons that were being loaded or unloaded. He didn't know how to respond to this *ridiculous* revelation of his mother's. His brain seemed to have frozen and yet at the same time was whirling about like a flock of starlings. He couldn't *think*, for the whole idea was so bloody crazy. Abby and that old man! Edge Bottom House! If only he could think of a plausible explanation but there was none and the only thing he could think of was to get over to Sandy Lane and demand one from Abby's mam. Perhaps it was all a mistake. Perhaps he would find Abby calmly eating her evening meal with the rest of her family. Oh, dear God, let him find her eating her evening meal with . . .

"Oh, lad, I wish they were," his mother said in answer to his last remark, "but the old man's carriage was in Sandy Lane yesterday an' 'e took 'er back wi' 'im. Go to see 'er mam an' pa if yer don't believe me. Charlie Potter, him what does odd jobs up at the house, ses 'e saw 'er this mornin' settin' off in the old man's carriage wi' that woman who . . . the housekeeper, settin' off fer town. 'E were full of it in't bar, everyone buyin' him a drink, tellin' 'is tale over an' over again."

"She wouldn't do such a thing. Not wi'out tellin' me."

"'Appen she didn't know. It'd be such a shock to 'er."

"Even if it's true she'd no need ter go with him."

"No, I suppose not but there's only one way ter find out, son, an' that's ter speak to 'er."

"I bloody well will." His young voice trembled, becoming

high as it had been in adolescence and his face was like that of the boy he had been then. Vulnerable, unsure, fearful, and it was all Dorcas Baxter could do not to drag him into the comfort of her arms. But he was a man. A big man, taller than her and already he was turning violently away, ready to dash off somewhere to find out the truth of this unbelievable story. The door banged to behind him as he left her and even as he began to race towards Bamford Street, his mother, who watched him go from the window, was conscious of the fascinated stares of all those in the yard.

Abby was not at the cottage in Sandy Lane. The moment the door was opened to his frantic knocking Betty Murphy began to weep. They were all about the table, Declan and the children spooning into their mouths whatever Betty had managed to put in front of them, which was mostly the last of the vegetables Declan had planted at back end and stored in the bit of a dilapidated shed at the rear of the cottage. Into the pan had gone a bacon bone on which little meat remained, given to her grudgingly by a mortified Mrs Hodges who could not get over the fact that her dairymaid had upped and left her without a word of warning. Oh, yes, she'd heard the rumours which she could scarcely believe and could you blame her when you looked at fat, slovenly Betty Murphy as she was now. An affair years ago with Richard Goodwin and the result of it, Abby Murphy, gone off to live up at the big house with the old man. What was she to do with a dairymaid short and a big order just come in from the wife of one of the colliery owners, Mrs Arbuthnot, for trussed chickens, butter, pints of cream, cheese and only two girls to see to it all?

Betty had stood with her head hanging and her tears dripping under the tirade, but at last Mrs Hodges, on the whole a fair and kindly woman, had relented and shoved the bacon bone in her hand. Without Abby's wage the family would be hard pressed to survive. They were only just this side of poverty as it was with so many of them and if she was not mistaken, though it was difficult to tell, it looked as though there'd be another mouth to feed before long.

"Is it true?" Roddy's mouth could hardly form the words, for from his position on the doorstep he could see Abby wasn't there.

"Oh, Roddy, I'm that sorry," Betty blubbered. "It 'appened so long ago . . ."

"Where is she?" He'd no time for Betty Murphy's troubles. He'd his own to manage.

"Yesterday he come . . . the old man . . ."

"Edge Bottom House?"

"Aye."

"Why'd yer let her go?"

"She's 'is granddaughter."

"That don't mean she belongs to 'im."

"Oh, but it do, Roddy. She's a Goodwin."

"*No . . . no*, she's mine . . . we're ter be wed."

But Betty merely looked at him pityingly, for there was nothing more certain in this life than the fact that there was no way Bradley Goodwin would allow any granddaughter of his to marry an apprentice in his own workshop.

Nessie Hardacre was astonished for the second time that day when, just as the lamps were lit in the house, she opened the back kitchen door to a thunderous knocking and found a wild-eyed, tousle-haired young man on the doorstep.

She stepped back in alarm but held on to the doorlatch as she cried out. The others, just about to serve dinner to the old man and the whey-faced young girl who sat in the drawing-room with him, crowded behind her, Kitty brandishing the carving knife, Cook the big spoon with which she had been basting the succulent shoulder of pork in the oven. The smells in the kitchen were mouth-watering, the roasting pork, the delicate aroma of chantilly soup, made to her own special recipe, and the dessert, which tonight was Swiss cream made with macaroons, sherry, a pint of rich cream, sugar and the rind of a lemon, the whole garnished with strips of angelica.

"Where is she?" the young man shrieked, and across the yard in the stable where they were settling the carriage horses for the night, Olly and Clem lifted their heads and looked at one another in consternation. For a moment they were paralysed, then as one they made a dash for the stable door, jostling to get through it at the same time, racing across the yard, closing in on the lad at the kitchen door though he didn't seem to notice they were there. It was to do with the girl, of course, the one Olly had driven to town with Mrs Pearson this morning, the one who had looked like a pretty working lass on the way in, and an elegant young lady on the way back.

"Excuse me, young man," Cook said with great dignity, "I'll not have me kitchen door battered on at this time o' night and—"

"Where is she?" Roddy said more calmly. "I'm not 'ere ter cause trouble, I just want ter speak to 'er. Tell 'er its Roddy. I'm not 'ere ter make trouble but I must speak to—"

Olly laid his hand on Roddy's shoulder, not roughly, just a hand to let him know that he and Clem'd stand no nonsense, but at once Roddy, poised on the brink of a tension he could not control, turned and struck out at him. Among his sporting pursuits he had done some prize fighting though it was illegal, and had won a purse or two, and his fist caught Olly on the point of his chin, lifting him from his feet. He fell in a heap to the cobbles, spitting blood, and for a moment Clem backed off, staring down in amazement at his fallen workmate.

But the commotion had brought another person on the scene, one who had the authority and icy command none of

the others possessed. Harriet Pearson had known a colourful
life in the vast seething underworld of Liverpool until she had
caught the eye of Bradley Goodwin. She had known a life of
luxury as the mistress of wealthy men, passed from one to the
next, sliding lower and lower in the social strata of prostitution
as her youth faded away and she had been brought so low she
had been on the brink of jumping into the River Mersey. They
had been precarious times but she had survived and by sheer
willpower, bred in her by her hard life, she had come to rest in
the home – and bed – of the wealthiest, most powerful man in
St Helens. She had known many men but had loved only one,
the first, the young squireen who had taken her innocence then
deserted her to a turbulent life on the streets and in the beds of
any man who could pay for her talents. Somehow along the
way she had learned the art of running a home and it was this
which – along with her fading charms – had brought her to
Edge Bottom House. Her life was still an unstable one, for
Bradley Goodwin could cast her off whenever he felt like it
and when he died she would inherit none of his money. She
had wondered many times if she might have done far better
had she listened to the gardener's lad who would have married
her when she was a kitchen-maid instead of falling in love with
the son of the house, but in that direction madness lay. But
her housekeeping was superb, her manners impeccable and
her authority absolute so that as she glided majestically into
the kitchen they all fell silent, even Olly who had climbed
unsteadily to his feet.

"What is going on here?" she asked quietly. "Who is this
young man?"

They all spoke at once.

"I only want a word wi' Abby . . ."

"I thought he were goin' ter attack . . ."

"Just burst in like a . . ."

"Landed a right one on Olly . . ."

"I'll not have such goings on in my . . ."

"Stop, stop at once, all of you. I can make no sense of it if you all speak at the same time. Now, boy, who are you and what are you doing?"

"Clutterin' up my kitchen, he is an' . . ."

"Thank you, Cook. Let us just hear what the young man has to say and then . . ." Cook subsided unwillingly, still muttering beneath her breath.

"I want a word wi' Abby," Roddy asserted arrogantly, sure of his right. "I were told she'd come 'ere an' I want ter know why. Anyroad, she'd best come home wi' me. Her mam's skrikin' an—"

"May we know who you are?" Harriet interrupted him smoothly. "Your name, if you please."

"Roddy Baxter. Me an' Abby are ter be wed an' I'll not 'ave 'er . . ."

The servants watched with fascinated interest. They knew something strange was going on and had been agog with it since the girl, who it was said was the daughter of Richard Goodwin, had entered their domain early this morning. She had been taken to see the master and then, wonder of wonders, had gone off in the carriage with Mrs Pearson. None of them had seen her since she had been taken in to the master, not even Kitty who had served his lunch.

The pork, which had been ready to come out of the oven ten minutes ago, was beginning to burn and if the soup wasn't taken off the hob soon it would boil over. Nessie had moved away from the door and the young man who hovered just outside it, for who knew what he might do in his fury, despite the presence of Olly and Clem, and the others had begun to exchange glances, for what the dickens was to happen next? And this chap who said he was to wed her, what were they to make of that? Their dull lives had been enriched by the events of this day and the excitement was intense. At the back of Olly and Clem had gathered Frankie and Jacko, along with Mr Renfrew the head gardener, but the lad just stood there, white-faced and trembling.

"If you'll wait there for a moment I'll see if . . . if . . ." Harriet hesitated, for was she to call the girl she had been told was Bradley Goodwin's granddaughter by what she presumed was her correct surname? She compromised. "If the young lady is at home."

"She's 'ere all right," Roddy blustered. "Her mam said she'd bin taken away—"

"No, she came of her own accord," Harriet interrupted smoothly.

"What . . . what?" Roddy's mouth hung open and he made as though to take a step inside the kitchen. At once several pairs of hands took hold of him. His face was chalky white and he clamped his lips shut. His Abby? Come willingly to this house? No, never! Even if she proved to be the old man's granddaughter she'd not leave him, Roddy, to stand out here under the curious gaze of all these men and women just as though he were some intruder, someone who meant harm which wasn't so. All he wanted was to speak to Abby. Ask her what the bloody hell was going on. What the devil she was doing here, and, if he could, persuade her to come away with him. He thought it might be tricky if the old man had . . . well, kidnapped her in some way, but if she was here willingly . . . oh, Jesus, what was he to make of that?

All the women began to feel sorry for the lad. He looked absolutely desolate. Like a small boy who has been unfairly punished but he was *not* a small boy he was a man and he lifted his square chin and took the blow full on it.

"I don't believe yer an' until Abby tells me it's so I'm stoppin' right here."

"Very well, but I must close the door. The servants are preparing dinner for Mr Goodwin and his granddaughter."

The women all gasped but stood like stones that have been petrified by some disaster. So it was true! Their minds could not quite grasp the true import of Mrs Pearson's words and each one mulled it over excitedly. "They are expecting a guest," she went on. Even as she spoke the front doorbell rang and Kitty, whose job it was to answer it, nearly jumped out of her skin.

"Answer the door, Kitty," Mrs Pearson directed and Kitty scuttled off, praying that nothing would happen while she was away. And perhaps she'd get a glimpse of . . . *had Mrs Pearson said granddaughter*?

The door was shut in Roddy Baxter's face but he continued to stand with his nose almost touching it, surrounded by the male servants who were as stunned by the meaning of Mrs Pearson's words as the women in the kitchen. This lad had struck one of them and might he not prove awkward if he was not allowed to see . . . to see whoever it was he was asking for? Best keep a sharp eye on him, they decided. It was April and though spring was here there was still a sharpness in the evening air. Their wives and hot dinners would be waiting for them but nothing on this earth would move them until this drama was over.

It was almost half an hour later when the door opened and in that time Roddy had not moved an inch though the men about him shuffled and muttered.

Harriet Pearson, though she had known nothing but adverse circumstances that had hardened her heart ever since the young squireen had cast his lustful eyes on her pert prettiness, felt a pang of sadness for the young man. He didn't stand a chance against the wicked old man to whom she had just spoken. Power, wealth, a self-willed old man with his eyes fastened on what *he* wanted. He and his forebears had built a small empire and he was not about to see it all wither away to dust for want of a name, *an heir* to carry it on for him. This lad was nothing. A shadow without substance who could be made to disappear like mist blown by the wind. He would not be cheated of his dream by a lad who worked in his crown furnace, or so he had been told and he was to be got rid of at once. The man who was to marry his granddaughter and provide the heir, a *Goodwin* heir, was sitting in the drawing-room, a brandy in his hand, doing his best to draw out the tongue-tied girl who was perched like a frightened animal on the settee by the fire. It was all arranged between them: him and Noah Goodwin. Give the girl a bit of polish, dress her up as Harriet had dressed her up for this evening, a woman to teach her the minimum a young lady needed for her education, and within three months a wedding and within a twelvemonth *his* grandson. His own flesh and blood to mould, as he had moulded Richard.

"Get the men to throw him out," he told Harriet in the privacy of his study, turning away, expecting to be obeyed.

"I don't think it will be that easy. He's a determined young man. He wants to talk to her and if you stop him now he'll find a way."

"Is that so? Then *I'll* find a way. She's not for him and he must be made to see that."

"Very good. What shall I tell him then? That she doesn't want to see him." Harriet was perfectly calm.

"Yes. Say she is . . . with guests."

"He won't be satisfied."

"Really." The old man was savage in his outrage. "Then we'll have to deal with him in another way. Send one of the men to fetch Paddy O'Connell – no, not now but tell him I want him . . . No, I'll meet him in the wood at the back of the house first thing tomorrow morning. It wouldn't do to have that Irish lout come to the house. This young whippersnapper must be made to learn I will not be harassed in my own house. See to it, Harriet, and tell them in the kitchen that we'll have dinner in fifteen minutes."

"Very good, sir." Even though she might share his bed later Harriet Pearson never called Bradley Goodwin anything but "sir".

It took a great deal of persuading to convince Roddy Baxter that Abby could not be disturbed at the moment.

"Surely she can just come ter't door an' let me see how she is. Tell her I won't try ter do owt, just talk to her."

"They are about to dine."

"Bugger that. I'll not go till I've seen her."

"Mr Goodwin has given me instruction that if you won't go he has no alternative but to call the constables."

Roddy was desperate. "Does Abby know I'm 'ere?" he pleaded.

"Yes, she has been told," Harriet lied, "and begs to be excused." A remark which totally confused Roddy Baxter, for his Abby would never talk like that.

"What the 'ell does that mean?" he snarled savagely and the men about him moved in closer. Harriet knew she must make this young man leave of his own accord or the men would handle him roughly and, what was worse, he would keep coming back and coming back until he saw the pale, pretty girl who huddled in her new finery in the drawing-room.

"Why don't you come back tomorrow?" By which time Paddy O'Connell would have done what Bradley Goodwin needed of him. She felt shame and a quiet hatred for the man who was her protector but she was approaching her middle years and if she defied him and helped these two young lovers he would throw her to the wolves. She was a superb housekeeper and tended to his every whim and fancy in his deep bed but that would make no difference. Women like her were not hard to replace.

"I'll be 'ere at first light."

"Just as you like, lad, but I'd go now if I were you."

Roddy stood for a moment, irresolute, as though he were

not at all sure he was doing the right thing, but what choice had he with the old man's stable lads and gardeners at his back.

"Right, first thing," he said warningly, then strode off into the gathering gloom towards the stable yard gate.

6

Noah Goodwin looked appreciatively about the high-ceilinged dining-room of Edge Bottom House, its carved wooden walls glowing the colour of honey. The dining table was long, highly polished, the sideboards along two walls were carved with cupids and grapes and acanthus leaves and set with shelves and niches holding crystal lamps, silver and porcelain figures backed by shining mirrors to reflect each costly object. The windows were shrouded with deep blue velvet, French windows that he knew led out on to a wide terrace with steps directly into the garden. The room was luminous with candlelit crystal and silver, fragrant with blooms from Bradley Goodwin's hothouses and the tantalising odours of fine wines and foods designed to please not only the palate but the eye.

Harriet Pearson certainly knew how to do things well, he thought, watching her as she supervised the two immaculate housemaids in the serving of rich soup, salmon and game, French pâtés and intricate savoury moulds which melted on the tongue. There were ices, whipped cream stuffed with nuts and cherries, an epergne overflowing with fruit and ferns, and opposite him sat the girl, wary and wide-eyed, giving the impression she was about to make a bolt for it. Again he had to admire Harriet Pearson's taste, for it was evident it was she who had dressed her. The girl's hair had been fastened on the crown of her head with a velvet ribbon the colour of aquamarine, but not in a stiff or formal style. Curls had been allowed to fall about her neck and over her ears, a careless tumble which, though contrived, he was sure, looked entirely natural. And what hair! It was the red of a fox's pelt and yet contained shades of gold that caught the light, glinting as she moved her head. Her gown was the same colour as her hair ribbon, silk, he knew, for Noah Goodwin was well versed in the fashions of ladies, of whom he had known a great many. The gown was simple, modest, low enough to reveal the marvellous cream of her shoulders but not the tops of her breasts. Now she had shed the plain working clothes in which he had last seen her she was lovely, her eyes, those wide, wary eyes that stared about her watchfully, the same colour as her gown, a vivid blue-green, set in a fringe of dark brown lashes. Her skin was fine, her eyebrows delicately arched, her mouth a soft coral pink, wide and generous, and her teeth, which he caught a glimpse of, white and even. Often those of the lower classes had bad teeth, the result of a poor diet, he presumed, but this one must have eaten better than most.

She had not as yet spoken a word and could you blame her? She had until two days ago lived in a tumbledown cottage with a family of God knows how many and was used only to the ways of the working classes, the *poor* working classes, and here she was transported to wealth and luxury which must have been beyond her wildest imaginings. She had managed the meal and the accompanying cutlery with quiet dignity, obviously primed by Mrs Pearson who must have told her to watch himself and Bradley Goodwin and follow their lead, and he felt compelled to admire not only her delicate loveliness but her composure. But then she was a Goodwin who were known for their steely strength. She was granddaughter to the old man who sat at the head of the table, eating little, gazing with a certain satisfaction at the slender, graceful figure of the sloe-eyed woman who later would share his bed, and at the two young people who sat one on either side of him.

"We'll drink to the future," he said, his glance flickering from the young girl to the man. "Yes, the future," lifting his glass first to Noah then to Abby, the latter having not the faintest notion of what that might be. Noah Goodwin had, of course, as he worked out in his clever, jubilant brain exactly what he would do with the works when it was all his.

"The future," he echoed. He looked extremely handsome in his plum-coloured coat which he had worn for more years than he cared to remember but which Joanna had cleaned and brushed and pressed to such perfection it looked almost new. His trousers were dove grey and his cravat was a snowfall against his artfully pleated and tucked shirt. His hair was as dark as midnight and his eyes almost black in the candlelight as he smiled through it at the girl, but he was aware that she scarcely noticed. His mouth lifted at the corners with wry amusement, not at her expense but at the machinations of the old man who would have his way in all things and was to do the same with his granddaughter.

"And what do you do to occupy your days, Miss Goodwin?" he asked equably, then could have kicked himself, for it was the sort of question that was asked of a gently reared girl at the dinner table. And Abigail Goodwin was not that!

The old man snorted and at the sideboard Harriet paused and held her breath.

"What?" Abby asked hesitantly, raising her incredible eyes to his, her mouth falling open in surprise.

"I'm sorry, perhaps that was a rude question," he went on smoothly. "I only wondered what you were . . ."

"I were a dairymaid," Abby answered loudly, as though glad to raise her voice about an area that was familiar to her. She had been brooding on the matter of how she could get over to Roddy's without attracting the attention of all these men and women who seemed to work at the old man's place. So far she had never been left alone, trailing to St Helens this morning with the woman at the sideboard. She had been stripped . . . aye, stripped to her skin and then shoved into the most peculiar garments whose names she didn't know. Underwear, she was told, pretty, white, frilly in soft material which was like mist on her skin. Drawers into which she stepped and petticoats that swayed about her like the bell in the church tower. Over these in quick succession several dresses, already made up, for which the woman apologised, had been draped one by one about her. She had been pushed and prodded and pinned until two, which the woman and the housekeeper – was that what she was called?– had decided were suitable, had been purchased, one of which she wore tonight.

She had barely glanced at herself in the long mirror in the room where she was to sleep before she had been brought down here to what they called the drawing-room. A sweet drink had been put in her hand and she and the old man had stared at one another from opposite sides of the fire. Then the other chap had come, taking her hand and bowing over it, and telling her she looked very smart. After some conversation between him and the old man, none of which she understood, or even listened to, he had taken her hand again, surprising her, for she had been quite enjoying the syrupy drink, lifting her to her feet and leading her into this room, the dining-room, and seating her at the table. Her appetite, which was normally healthy, had failed her and she had picked at whatever was put before her, wondering desperately how she was to get through this, not just this meal or this evening, but the whole damn charade. Well, she couldn't, could she? She missed her mam and her home so much her heart hurt her and as for Roddy she didn't think she could manage another hour without seeing him.

"A dairymaid," the handsome young man said politely. "That must have been hard work." The old man frowned, not liking the way the conversation was going, but Noah knew that this girl could talk of nothing except what she knew and though it was not exactly dining-room conversation perhaps it would take that look of a trapped animal from her eyes.

"Aye, it were. Up at five, cows milked by six and then into't dairy. Mrs Hodges were very particular about bein' clean so't floors had ter be scrubbed, shelves, pots an' pans . . ."

The two housemaids listened in amazement, so intrigued they had to be prodded back into service by the house-keeper.

"Yes, yes," the old man said irritably, "I'm sure we all know what the work of a dairymaid is—"

"I don't, sir," Noah interrupted smoothly. "I don't believe I have ever been in a dairy." Made love to a few dairymaids, of course, which this girl's father had apparently done, but what they did when they were not pleasing him had not concerned him.

Abby shot the man a grateful look. What had they said his name was? Noah? She wondered who he was and why he had been chosen to eat with them on this particular night, but his teeth gleamed whitely in his dark face and his eyes were soft and strangely gentle as they sent her some message through the candlelight.

"There's no good going over what's past," Bradley Goodwin fumed, waving away the maid who offered him a plate of cheese and grapes. The maid was Kitty and she couldn't wait to get back to the kitchen where she knew they all waited for her to give them a description of their master's granddaughter and perhaps shed some light on where she had come from and, more to the point, what she was to do in this house.

"No, sir, then perhaps we – Miss Goodwin and I – or may I call you Abigail?"

"Abby."

"Pardon?"

"I like ter be called Abby."

"Very well then, Abby it—"

"Her name is Abigail and so she shall be called. Abigail Goodwin. I have seen the lawyer and she is now legally my granddaughter."

"So soon?"

"Aye, there was no point in dragging our feet," leaving Abby to wonder what he meant by that remark. Noah's attempt to talk to her had opened a slit through which began to flow a minute trickle of curiosity. One of the servants took away her plate and the other offered her something but she shook her head, the first decision she had made of her own accord. Previously food had been put before her and, when not eaten, taken away again but this time she actively refused. She glanced up into the girl's face. It was Ruby, a girl of nineteen who had been in the service of Bradley Goodwin and his son for nine years. A bonny lass who had caught the eye of Olly Preston, he who had been given a clout by Roddy. She was a good-hearted girl who felt sorry for this young lass chucked down in the midst of all this unfamiliar luxury and the old sod who was her grandfather. She smiled at Abby encouragingly.

"That'll do," Bradley grunted, indicating to Harriet that she and her minions could leave the room. "We'll have coffee in the drawing-room. Take Noah's arm, lass, and lead the way."

"I'd like ter get ter me bed," Abby answered, standing up abruptly and pushing back her chair so violently the housemaids jumped in alarm. Harriet drew in her breath and waited for the old man to remonstrate. "I'm tired an'—"

"We've things to talk about, girl, so I'd be obliged if you'd do as you're told."

The two serving girls, who were about to gather up the detritus of the meal and escape to the kitchen, stood perfectly still against the sideboard and Harriet held the breath she had drawn in. Was this the first clash between Bradley Goodwin and his granddaughter? Though the lass had barely spoken Harriet had a feeling that Abigail Goodwin – she supposed she'd best get used to calling her that – would prove to be as strong-willed as her grandfather.

"Sir, perhaps tomorrow would be soon enough—" Noah Goodwin began, but the old man turned on him, ready to snarl, the old lion showing his teeth to the young, to the interloper, to the one who was only too keen to take his place.

"The girl is to be trained, educated, shown how to be the granddaughter of Bradley Goodwin and it must be talked about. She must be told what is expected of her." His mottled, irate head nodded and shook in agreement with his own words and his thin lips twisted into a grimace, a challenge. "She'll have them all sniffing round her, Noah Goodwin, when it gets about," he continued. "She's somebody now, an heiress and they'll be on the scent before the week's out. There'll be Alfred Hardwick's lad, Tom Lucas's, and a score of others wanting to court her, so don't think you've a monopoly no matter what's been said between us. She'll have her pick but she'll wed—"

"I'm ter wed Roddy." The words were flung into the dialogue like a firecracker and with the same effect. Abby lifted her head with great pride and the three women held their breath in horror. *Roddy!* He must be the lad who had caused such a commotion at the back door and who had sworn he would be back in the morning. Dear God, what was to happen next? The master was not a man to be thwarted.

The old man, who had just risen to his feet, turned slowly and shot a look of such venom at her Noah made a small movement as though he would go to her side, but she needed no one's protection as she spoke of her love.

"Me an' Roddy" – innocently unaware that, had it not already happened, she was tolling the death knell for herself and Roddy Baxter – "are ter be married as soon as he's finished his apprenticeship. I meant ter mention it to yer. I know things 'ave changed but . . ."

The old man lifted his head, tenacious and eternal as the ancient tree in his garden. Harriet wanted to run to the lass and tell her to be quiet. Did she not see how impossible it was to disobey him? No one ever had, not even Richard Goodwin who had been the apple of his eye, but the girl stood straight and proud and unafraid. Her love for this Roddy shone from her gleaming eyes and the old man recognised it and, for the moment, let it go. There was plenty of time to solve this little problem. When the lad was no longer in the picture the girl would be more malleable, the certainty of it was in his seamed old face.

"Get to your bed then. The lad and I have things to discuss. Harriet," turning to snap his fingers at his housekeeper. "See her to her room and then come back here. I've a thing or two to say."

Harriet crossed the room to take Abby's arm, watched by the open-mouthed maids, but she was shaken off. She moved with great dignity for one so young, opening the door herself but making no demur when Harriet followed her. They moved up the stairs, and only when she had gained the warm and peaceful sanctuary of the bedroom that was to be hers did she allow her shoulders to slump. Harriet watched her. She could be sharp when she wanted to but something in this defiant young girl reminded her of herself at the same age and she felt a great sympathy for her. There were things to be said but this was not the time or place to say them. She would learn soon enough.

"Shall I help you with your dress? Your nightgown is laid out on the bed—"

"I've been dressin' an' undressin' meself since I were a bairn," Abby said coolly.

"Of course, but I just thought . . ."

"I can manage. I'd like ter be by meself now. I'm tired."

"Yes, but if—"

"Oh, fer God's sake, let me be."

"Of course, but let me warn you that your grandfather will not be crossed. He will have his own way and you'd best accept it."

"Please . . ." Abby sank down on to the low satin-covered chair by the fire and gazed desolately into it, the flames tinting her cheeks to a rosy hue. There were suddenly deep circles beneath her eyes.

"Very well, I'll leave you. Sleep well." Harriet quietly left the room and for the first time that day Abby was left on her own.

Roddy sat opposite his mother at the kitchen table, the cup of tea she had pushed into his hand as yet untasted. He looked distraught, his usually merry face hollow and drawn as though he were just recovering from a long illness. The two young boys, silent and afraid of this brooding man who was their fun-loving brother, had gone willingly to their beds, and his mam watched him anxiously. She knew his feelings for Abby Murphy, or should she call her Abby Goodwin now, ran strong and deep and she also knew in her own mother's heart that the chances of him marrying her now were absolutely at rock bottom. Bradley Goodwin had lost his own son at the beginning of the year and it had been thought that he would go under. That his glass works would be auctioned off to one of his keen-eyed competitors, sold for a profit and he himself would wither away and the line of which he was so proud die with him. Now he had a granddaughter, which, naturally, was not as good as a son but he surely had plans for the lass and they would certainly not include her son. He had been to Edge Bottom House, he had told her, and been turned away but he wouldn't give up. Tomorrow he meant to go again and this time he meant to speak to Abby, make plans. No, he didn't know of what sort but she, his mother, was to be sure he would not give her up. He loved her and, young as she was, she loved him and in due time they would be wed.

"Go ter yer bed, son," she pleaded with him. "Get some sleep and then tomorrer, when yer more rested yer'll know what's ter be done."

"Mam, I know what's ter be done. I'll . . . she an' me, we'll have ter get away. I know that old man's a tyrant, they all say that in't works an' he'll do his best ter keep 'er, turn 'er into the kind o' lass that their sort value. A lady fit ter live up at Edge Bottom House but Abby an' me have bin in love fer years and I'll not give her up."

"Lad, they say she went willingly up ter the big 'ouse."

"No," Roddy said violently. "Never! She were – what's the word? – reluctant. She'd not go with that old bugger unless she were forced."

"They say in Sandy Lane she got in 'is carriage wi'out a word."

"She's bin promised summat, 'appen for 'er family. I dunno." Roddy shook his head, tormented beyond measuring by the thought of his love being hounded by that old man to do his bidding. *She'd not have gone of her own accord.* That was the one thought that kept him sane: that she'd been forced and that he must rescue her, take her away where the old man couldn't reach them. They were both young, healthy, hardworking and would find jobs, Abby as a dairymaid and he in a glass works in another part of the country. It would be hard, especially for him since it would mean breaking the contract of his apprenticeship and he would have to start over again, but they would manage. They would be wed and live the life they had planned somewhere else. To leave his mam, who would miss his wage, to leave this life of theirs which was all they knew would be almost impossible, but it was the only way.

"Go ter yer bed, son," his mother said gently, laying a hand on his clenched fist. "First thing termorrer get over there and ask politely ter see her. They can't say no, can they?"

Nessie absolutely refused to be the one to open the kitchen door to his frantic knocking and so it was left to Harriet, whose own face was paper white, to do so.

"Where is she? I said I'd be back ter see her. Ask 'er ter come out. I promise I'll not mekk a scene or owt but I must talk to 'er."

"She's not here," Harriet faltered, for this was a dreadful thing she was about to do but what alternative was open to her? She had nowhere else to go and Bradley Goodwin had made it quite plain that if she disobeyed him she could pack her bags and leave before the end of the day. Without a reference! She was called Mrs Pearson but she had never had a husband. Her family were dead or scattered. This was her home and had been ever since Mrs Goodwin had died and Bradley had taken a fancy to her and brought her here. What could she do if she was turned off? Go back to her old profession, but she was older now, not as pretty and the life would kill her. Besides, the life the old man had planned for his granddaughter was not a bad one and who was she to stand in the way? The lad would be taken care of, given some money and sent on his way, Mr Goodwin had promised her and that would be that. The way wide open for the future he had mapped out for himself, for his granddaughter and for the man he meant her to marry, and for continued growth of his business. This boy, this white-faced youth who was bravely doing his best to stand up to him had not the faintest notion of what he was doing. He would keep on knocking on this very door and if he didn't get in to see her he would hang about and waylay her. They couldn't keep her a prisoner. She must be allowed out to live the life Mr Goodwin had in mind for his granddaughter and this lad stood in the way. He must be made, one way or the other, to stand aside. *One way or the other.*

"Not 'ere?" Roddy spluttered, clearly not believing her.

"She . . . she left a message." Harriet felt her heart, which had been turned to stone years ago, ache for this unhappy pair of young lovers but she had to put herself first, hadn't she? They were young and would get over it but she was approaching middle age and could not start again.

"A message." In his eagerness Roddy put out a hand to her and God forgive her she nearly took it. The rest of the servants were pretending to be doing something in the kitchen, the door to which she had shut behind her. They were agog with curiosity, wondering what the devil she was telling this poor, desperate lad, but her master had impressed upon her the need to let no one, certainly none of the servants, hear what she was saying. It must all be kept a secret, for he had no wish to have his granddaughter pining over some lad from the glass works and certainly no desire for speculation on their part. He must be got rid of, paid off, he told her, and made to leave. She was to see to it.

"Yes, she's gone over to the woods at the back of the house. D'you see that path beyond the gate . . ."

He turned eagerly, following her pointing finger.

"Well, go along there and into the woods at the end of the path. She'll be there."

Olly and Clem were engaged in blacking the hooves of the carriage horses, their heads bent to their tasks and though they had seen the lad knock at the kitchen door they did not see him run off in the direction of the wood.

Harriet Pearson turned back into the kitchen, her face set like stone. They watched her, the others, exchanging glances, those glances asking what she had said to get the boy to run off so willingly. They had expected a great set-to, which was why they had all refused to answer the door but Mrs Pearson was not about to tell them, it seemed, for she went directly into her own sitting-room, speaking to no one, looking at no one, closing the door behind her.

She sank into the wing-backed chair in front of the fire, her eyes unfocused as she stared into the glowing fire and was surprised to find that her cheeks were wet with tears.

7

Abby picked up her clogs and pulled her old shawl more closely about her head. It was still dark beyond her window and totally silent so she was pretty certain that the servants were not yet up. She was undecided whether to climb down the tree as she had done the first night she was brought here or to chance going down the stairs and through the kitchen, but perhaps it might be better to save the tree for an emergency. She wasn't quite sure what she meant by that, but as long as no one knew about the tree and its escape route it might be best to keep it so.

She opened the door quietly, peeping into the corridor to make sure the coast was clear. It was well lit by a branch of candles set on a table at the far end where stairs went up to the servants' quarters. Satisfied that there was no one about, she slipped through the open doorway, closed it silently behind her and glided across the velvet carpet towards the head of the stairs. The carpet felt lovely on the soles of her bare feet and for about the hundredth time she marvelled at the wonders she had seen in this house. It was like a fairy tale. Not that she knew much about fairy tales, nor the books in which she presumed they were written, never having seen one, but Mrs Hodges, who could read and write, had sometimes talked of them, of fairy princesses and wondrous things like that, remembering them from when she was a child. Thinking of that life and the one she had now, had it not been for the heartache she suffered at being parted from her family and

Roddy, she thought she might have taken more interest in the
things about her. But still, what a tale she would have to tell
them all when she managed to get over to Sandy Lane which,
if she'd anything to do with it, would not be long. She'd walk
across the fields, skirting the glass works, and give them all a
surprise. Perhaps she could manage to take them something
from the kitchens. Not steal, of course, but get to know the
girls there and ask them to save anything that was left over.

There was a lovely smell in the kitchen, a reminder of the
meal she had eaten with the old man and – what's his name?
– Noah, last night. She'd eaten very little, not knowing what
the dickens most of it was, but there had been so much of
it there must surely have been some left over. She tiptoed
across the kitchen, careful not to bump into anything, and
was considerably startled when something curled itself round
her leg. Her heart jumped then she smiled, for it was only
a cat. It purred loudly and for a moment she was afraid it
might wake somebody, then her smile deepened, for she was
sure they were all sleeping the sleep of the dead as she had
done when she was a dairymaid. Hard work made for sound
sleepers!

The door was bolted and she prayed it would not make
a noise but Charlie Potter, who was a handyman and joiner
about the place, the one who repaired anything that was
broken, whether it was a gate or a clock, kept all the bolts well
oiled. Bradley Goodwin was a man who liked everything in his
house, or his glass works, to be in perfect working order. It
opened noiselessly and she slipped through, closing it behind
her, making sure the cat was inside. The maids would wonder
how the door came to be unbolted, but by then she would
have seen Roddy and be back here in her bedroom. In fact
if she got back before they were up she would need to gain
entrance, wouldn't she?

The sky in the east was showing a pale wing of grey against

the dark and as she put on her clogs at the stable gate, which again opened noiselessly, the grey turned to a pale tawny pink, then to apricot as the sun rose towards the horizon. She had no idea of the time but she knew if Roddy wasn't still in his bed he would be in the glass house on his shift. She was surprised that he had not been over to Edge Bottom House to see her, for by now he would have heard the news about her, then she realised that all this incredible thing had only begun the day before yesterday! The day before yesterday at this time she had been Abby Murphy, dairymaid to Mrs Hodges at Updale Farm and now she was *Abigail Goodwin* of Edge Bottom House, granddaughter to one of the most important men in St Helens. But it made no difference, she told herself as she hurried across the field to the south of the works, turning into Bamford Street, making for Edge Bottom Row and the cottages where the Baxter family lived.

On the north side of the glass works Roddy Baxter struck out across the fields towards Edge Bottom House, running in his eagerness to get to his love. He had debated whether to take the alternative route to the south then decided it was as broad as it was long and besides, this was the way he had come yesterday and was more familiar to him. He had never, until yesterday, had occasion to call at the Goodwin home. The woman at the big house, who was obviously a person of some authority, had promised him he would see Abby today and though it was barely light, a soft spring morning with the chill of winter almost gone as the sun rose behind the woods at the back and to the east of Edge Bottom House, he couldn't wait another minute.

It is of such small things that lives are changed!

Abby knocked on the door of the Baxter cottage, smiling shyly at the woman who answered. It was Roddy's mother, she knew that, though as yet they had never spoken. Roddy had told her about Abby, he said, and when the time was right

Abby herself would be invited to Sunday dinner, which was the traditional way for a courting couple to advertise their intentions. Nothing would be said, not until the actual plans for the wedding were discussed, but it would be known and accepted that Abby Murphy and Roddy Baxter were walking out and would eventually be married.

Mrs Baxter looked flushed and harassed and Abby was not to know that she had just been arguing with her son. He was to go to the big house again, he had told her, where he would be allowed to see Abby. This would not stop them from being married, he had said confidently, but naturally they needed to make plans, arrange where they were to meet until they were wed. He must speak to the old man to let him know of Roddy's honourable intentions and Dorcas had been horrified by the naïvety, the innocence of her son, who firmly believed that the love he and Abby bore one another would win the day. That though she was Miss Abigail Goodwin she was still, in her heart, Abby Murphy, the girl he would marry. He would make some excuse when he returned to the glasshouse for being late on his shift, he added, but he was well thought of in the crown furnace where he was apprenticed and his record was good.

"Don't worry, Mam," he had told her. "Now I must be off ter see Abby and get back ter work. It wouldn't do ter lose me job. Not wi' me a man about ter get wed." The Lord bless him and him only sixteen!

"I'm Abby, Mrs Baxter," the bonny girl on the doorstep told her. "Has Roddy gone ter work? I just wanted a word ter let 'im know—"

"Lass, yer've just missed 'im. He's gone up ter the big 'ouse ter talk ter yer. Not ten minutes since. It's a wonder yer didn't bump into 'im." Dorcas grimaced, then turned to look at the two small boys who had just clattered down the carpetless stairs behind her. "I'll not be but a minnit, lads. There's a

pan o' porridge on't stove. Sit yer down." She turned back
to Abby who was all ready to run like a deer back the way she
had come but was too polite to leave without speaking once
more to the worried mother of the man she loved.

"Right, lass, off yer go then an' tell our Roddy ter get
straight ter work after yer've seen 'im. His job's important."

"I will, Mrs Baxter, an' thank you."

They were all in the kitchen when she burst through the door,
her face scarlet with her exertions, her heart pumping, for
like his mam she didn't want to keep Roddy away from his
good job. Just a quick word to let him know that nothing had
changed between them and then she'd let him go and get on
with whatever Mr Goodwin had in store for her.

They all turned to stare. Cook was at the stove turning
bacon in a frying pan, a neat pile of uncooked mushrooms
on a plate beside her waiting their turn. There were sausages
and sliced tomatoes all ready to be placed under their heavy
silver covers and be taken into the breakfast-room where the
master would eat his usual hearty breakfast. Kitty carried a
tray which she was about to take into the breakfast-room
bearing cutlery, napkins, crockery, all the paraphernalia for
the master's breakfast and the tail end of what Cook was
saying to her about "a lazy man's load" was being ignored
by the parlour-maid. Ruby and May were missing, for the
downstairs rooms had to be cleaned before the master came
down and Nessie was scrubbing the scullery floor.

They gasped when they saw her, for they had thought her
to be still in her bed. May had got the rounds of the kitchen
for leaving the back door unbolted, though she swore she
had bolted it last thing. She smirked, looking about her
triumphantly as though to say, 'There you are, I *did* bolt
it," but they were all staring at the girl, the girl they didn't
even know how to deal with let alone address.

"Well, miss," Cook began, but at that moment Mrs Pearson walked into the room, halting abruptly when she saw Abby. She had been up to Abby's room, knocking gently on the door and on finding her not there had hurried downstairs, hoping to God the stupid girl had not come across the equally stupid lad, for she really had had enough of this charade, this need for secrecy and deception.

"Has he been?" Abby gasped and the servants looked at one another, frozen and silent, for what was to happen next in this house gone mad? Mind you, it made a change from the tedium of their lives!

"He's been and gone, my dear—" Harriet began but was interrupted fiercely.

"Where? Did he say? Has he gone to the works?" Abby balanced on the doorstep, ready to run in whichever direction the woman instructed her but the woman – was it Mrs Pearson? there were so many of them it was difficult to remember their names – merely shrugged and moved towards the table where a loaf of bread was waiting to be sliced for toast. "I'm afraid I don't know. He didn't say. Just ran off."

"Why did he run off? Why didn't you come and fetch me?"

"I did but you weren't in your room." Which could have been true. It wasn't, of course, but who was there to argue with her?

"Right, he'll 've gone ter the glass works." And without another word Abby sprinted off in the direction from which she had just come.

No, they hadn't seen him this morning, the fully trained glass worker to whom Roddy was apprenticed at the furnace told her angrily. The heat in the glasshouse was intense and though Abby went no further than the door she was soon slicked with sweat. The room was a hive of activity, assistants wiping blowpipes before the molten glass was gathered from the pots, some carrying the cooled cylinders from the splitters to the flatteners. Some of them, Roddy among them, had graduated to punty-sticking, the process of sealing the piece to the pontil or punty on which the piece of glass was twirled into a circle. They would all, in time, become skilled blowers, flashers of crown glass, or flatteners of sheet. There were five hundred men employed at Edge Bottom Glass Works but of those only four were blowers and four gatherers to each of the three glasshouses though altogether there were fifty fully skilled glass-makers. The rest were employed in the cutting rooms and warehouses, sorting, cutting, packing, and loading the finished product, in the polishing rooms, the joiner's shop and in the pot rooms.

"I were told he'd come ter work," Abby said hesitantly, though this was not strictly true. The woman had said he'd run off and Abby had just presumed he'd come to the glass works.

"Well, 'e'd best get 'ere sharp," the glass-maker said testily, "or 'e'll find 'e's no work ter come to."

"But 'is mam said—"

"Lass, it's nowt ter do wi' me what 'is mam said. If that lad's not 'ere within the 'our 'e'll be out of a job."

"But where can 'e be?"

"Nay, don't ask me, lass. Now I've work ter do so yer'd best 'op it."

For the second time that morning Dorcas Baxter opened the door to Betty Murphy's lass and this time they were both of them grey as the ash in Dorcas's uncleared grate. They stood and looked at one another, neither wanting to be the first to speak, for in their hearts they were deadly afraid. Of what they couldn't have told you but there was something wrong, that was evident. Roddy Baxter seemed to have disappeared. He was not at his home, nor at the glass works, the two places where he spent his days and nights unless he was with Abby.

His mam had seen him dash off eagerly to talk to Abby at Edge Bottom House and the housekeeper there had confirmed to Abby that he had been but where had he gone?

"Will yer come in, lass?" Dorcas asked her. "'Appen he'll turn up." Her face showed her indecision as though for the moment she, who was never uncertain, was in a dither on what she should do next. She had been due at Mrs Arbuthnot's half an hour since to deal with the family's laundry and should for the next six hours be bent over boilers, dolly tubs, wringers, scrubbing and pounding, hanging the many garments out to dry since it was a fine day, then ironing and folding and placing each one up on the airing rack. She had her reputation to think of and Mrs Arbuthnot was very particular. She could not afford to lose this job in the delicately balanced life of hard work and financial reward which were necessary to keep her family fed and clothed and housed. When she had finished at Mrs Arbuthnot's she would run across the village to Mrs Hardwick's, the colliery owner's wife and do several hours' scrubbing and when that was finished to Mrs Hardwick's satisfaction she would make her way to the Glassmakers Arms and work behind the bar until closing time. Sixteen hours of hard, back-breaking work but she had not minded, for it all showed in the fine, straight limbs of her lads, in the decent clothes they wore, the best the market could offer, in the shining cleanliness and relative comfort of her home. Because Roddy worked at the glass works he was allowed one of the cottages in Edge Bottom Row, but if he did not report for work within the next hour he would lose his job, this cottage. Oh, dear sweet Jesus, where the devil had the boy gone? It was not like him to be so irresponsible and, though she tried not to, she blamed this lass who hovered on the doorstep.

"I can't, Mrs Baxter. I'll not settle till I've found Roddy. We must've missed each other again. Now I'll set off for the big house this way," indicating the way that led round the south side of the works, "then come back the other way. If he comes tell 'im ter wait here."

"I should be at work, my lass," Dorcas said worriedly.

"I know, I'm that sorry but I can't settle until we find 'im."

"Yer right." She turned briskly to the two boys who were at the table tucking in to the bacon butties she had made them. "Will, get dressed an' run ter Mrs Arbuthnot's. Tell 'er yer mam's took poorly and can't come terday but I'll be there first thing termorrer." For surely by then their Roddy would be found safe and sound and this nightmare would be over.

"Oh, Mam," Willy whined but his mother clasped him by the arm and dragged him from the table. "Do as yer told unless yer want a clout round lug'ole," hoping to God Mrs Arbuthnot would accept her absence without turning her off. Laundry-maids, *any* sort of servants, were ten a penny and Mrs Arbuthnot was a bit of a tartar.

Noah Goodwin was again at table that evening, dressed as he had been the night before and Abby wondered wearily if he came to eat dinner with the old man every night. She knew vaguely that he was related in some way so she supposed that was the reason. It didn't really matter to her, for she was trapped in such a world of misery, such worry, she would not have noticed if the queen and the Prince of Wales had sat down with them.

The meal was as superb as ever, the service quiet and efficient. She was unaware of the guarded looks Kitty and Ruby cast in her direction for they had heard – as who had not – the old man's anger when he had been told that his granddaughter was not in the house and nobody knew where she was. The one who bore the brunt of it had been Mrs Pearson, thank God, who was in charge of her, so the old man thundered, and what the devil was he supposed to do with the woman who had come to teach his granddaughter how to be a lady? The woman, a Miss Holden, had sat all morning in what was still called the nursery, for it was where all the Goodwin children had started off their short lives. Master Richard had had his first lessons there before he went to the grammar school and Miss Abigail – as they had been told to call her – was to do the same.

They had seen neither hide nor hair of her all day and it was said that she had been seen scouring the woods and the fields, shouting the name of the lad who had come twice to the house looking for her. As dark fell she had returned and had made no objection to being hustled upstairs, put in her pretty dress, had her hair brushed and tied with a ribbon and hurried down again to her grandfather, who had given her what for, only stopping when Mr Noah had arrived. She had sat impassively under the barrage and Kitty, who had served brandy to the gentlemen and a glass of sherbet to the young miss, told them in the kitchen, which was agog with speculation, that she seemed to be in a trance.

Noah, even in the laboratory at the glass works, had heard what had happened during the day: the girl accosting the glass-blower in the glasshouse, tales of her running round like someone not right in the head, and not only that but the mother of the lad who was missing doing the same. He himself thought it strange that this young man had vanished and, being a man of the world and knowing him as he did, wondered if Bradley Goodwin had had a hand in it.

He did his best to engage the silent child, for that was how she seemed to him, in some sort of conversation. It was impossible really, for he knew barely anything about her and how could he talk to her, as was polite, and *kind* perhaps, in the circumstances, when she was clearly not really at the table.

"Have you nothing to say to our guest, girl?" the old man

bellowed at one point and, startled, Abby had looked up from whatever was on her plate and stared from one man to the other.

"What?" she stammered.

"What . . . what! Which proves my point that there is no time to be lost in the start of your education, wouldn't you agree, Noah."

"Surely it's early days yet, sir. Abby has only been here—"

"*Abigail!* How many more times must you be told that my granddaughter's name is Abigail?"

"Give her time."

"Time is not something I have a lot of, boy. There is much to be done."

"Certainly, sir and if there is anything I can do to further Abigail's . . . education you have only to ask." His dark eyes fastened on Abby's downcast face and bore an expression the old man couldn't read. "She will need more than lessons. Perhaps she might care to take a walk with me one day, or perhaps a ride in the carriage." Anything to get her away from this old man and from the sombre atmosphere of the house. She was young and pretty and he wanted to make her laugh, or perhaps just a smile, but it was hardly possible here with Bradley Goodwin looking on suspiciously.

Abby looked up and her eyes met those of Noah and in the depth of her wretchedness she felt a small spasm of warmth. She did not know this man or even why he seemed to be favoured by the old man, but he was offering her something. He might even be able to help her find Roddy. Oh, please, dear God, let me find him, let him not be . . . be . . . what? She didn't even know what it was that frightened her so much. She meant to slip out tomorrow morning and with the help of her family and all the inhabitants of Sandy Lane who had today promised to search with her, she would find Roddy wherever he was. He might be lying hurt somewhere . . .

*   *   *

Pedestrians hastily stepped to one side as the two men stumbled along the pavement. They were big men, tall, but the older one in contrast to the younger was overweight with what looked like muscle gone to fat. He it was who appeared to be supporting the younger.

"Pick yer feet up, laddie. We don't want yer ter be falling down in front of all these grand folk, now do we." He grinned round at the busy throng, most of them women heading towards St John's Market which was to the rear of St George's Hall on Lime Street. The main railway station in Liverpool lay just across the street and even when a train whistle pierced the air the young man, whose arm was draped about the shoulders of the older man, did not lift his head. His chin rested on his chest and his feet seemed to slide across the flagged pavement, one following the other in slow alternation.

"Now then, boyo, it's too much drink yer've taken but 'tis not far now." Again he grinned round at the women as though in apology for his companion's awkwardness. When they came to a doorway over which the sign *Lancashire Fusiliers, Recruiting Office* was written, the two men stumbled inside. An officer, accompanied by a sergeant major, sat behind a desk. They both glanced up as the two men staggered towards them.

"Now then," the sergeant major rumbled, but the bigger of the two men bowed as though to the aristocracy, almost allowing the younger man to slip to the floor.

"Begorra, yer lordship, but this young chap's a wish ter join up. Drunk as a fiddler's bitch, begging yer pardon, so 'e is, but before he . . . ahhm, succumbed in the Old Swan, he told us, me an' me mates, 'e were on his way ter the recruitin' office. So 'ere 'e is, all ready ter sign up if yer'll show 'im where."

The officer looked the younger man up and down and

though he had the supercilious demeanour of his class, his eyes were sharp. This man was well set up, tall, strong, healthy by the look of him and just the sort of man they could do with in the army. The ranks were on the whole made up of the rag, tag and bobtail of the human male race, misfits, the helpless and homeless, those who had nowhere else to go except the gutter. The Lancashire Fusiliers was a good regiment and had fought bravely in the Punjab, South Africa and India and needed good men to replace those who had died. This chap looked promising material.

"What's his name?" he asked the Irishman, picking up his pen and addressing a sheet of paper before him.

"Now, sur, I couldn't be tellin' yer. But a nice lad."

"Yes, yes," the officer said irritably. "Can he sign his name?"

"Again I couldn't say, sur, an' if yer'll excuse me I'd best get back ter me mates. Will I put 'im in this chair?" He grinned ingratiatingly and with the sergeant major's help deposited the flopping form of Roddy Baxter into the nearest chair, then escaped hurriedly.

"We'd best get his cross, Sarn't, but he'll have to have a name to put it under."

"'Ow about . . . Patrick O'Reilly? It were me mother's father's name an' he's probably Irish. I'll sign 'is cross fer 'im."

"Very well, Sarn't, then get some of the lads to take him to the barracks."

8

She scarcely remembered the next few weeks. She was calm, doing her best in the appalling weariness of her spirit to fight her way back to reality, the reality of the loss of her home and family at Sandy Lane, and Roddy, both of which no longer existed in her world. She moved through days of hopeless misery and only when she escaped from Edge Bottom House did her heart lift a little with fresh hope.

At first she just walked boldly out through the kitchen door, ignoring the apprehensive looks of the servants who knew she was not supposed to go. The bodice and skirt she had worn when she first came to her grandfather's house had been washed, cut up and thrown in the rag bag to be used as dusters but, knowing she could not go to Sandy Lane, nor search the fields and woods in either of the two elegant gowns Mrs Pearson had provided her with, she had calmly walked to the market in St Helens and, to the astonishment of the stall-holder, exchanged the silk gown she had on for a dark grey bodice and skirt of wool, a shawl and a pair of clogs. She felt no guilt. In fact she barely felt anything except the need to be with Roddy, wherever he was, with her family in Sandy Lane or at Edge Bottom Row where she and Dorcas Baxter did their best to lift up their spirits by telling each other that Roddy would soon be found. They wept a little when Dorcas took down the glass *frigger* from the wall, the one Roddy had made as an example of his work, his in the shape of a walking-stick. It was a task all apprentices were expected to do to show their skill, or otherwise, in the art of glass-making. She spent days with the residents of Sandy Lane and anyone else she could persuade to help her, moving in ever widening circles, searching for him.

The old man was incensed, snarling at her that if she did not give up this madness he would have her confined to her room. No granddaughter of his would be allowed to make such a showing of herself, he stormed, and she was to give over this nonsensical roaming about the countryside looking for a man who surely was long gone. And as for the get-up she wore, referring to her plain, countrywoman's outfit and clogs, Mrs Pearson was to burn them at once. Abigail was to get up to the nursery where Miss Holden was still patiently waiting for her and start the process of becoming the lady he meant her to be. Did she understand?

"Mr Goodwin, if you burn me frock I'll tekk summat from that bedroom I sleep in and sell it on the market and buy meself another one. Yer'd best get used ter the fact that I'll not rest until I find out what 'appened ter Roddy. If yer lock me in I'll get meself out—"

"You impudent young . . ." Bradley Goodwin could not find a word bad enough to call this defiant young woman who was his flesh and blood. He was enraged by her attitude yet at the same time he could not help but admire her courage. He had hoped to get her and Noah to the altar within three months of seeing her for the first time but here it was June and the matter had not even been raised with her. Not in her present state of mind. She lived in his house, ate at his table and on a couple of days a week decked herself out in one of the half a dozen new dresses Harriet had had made up for her and went up to the nursery. Miss Holden was teaching her first to read and write and had reported to him that she was bright and quick and could already stumble her way through the child's primer. But she would not give up this obsession she had with finding the lad who, Paddy O'Connell had confided to him, was now a soldier in the Lancashire Fusiliers. A whisper in the right ear with an accompanying bribe had ensured that the soldier, though nowhere near properly trained, had already been despatched with his regiment to some spot on the globe where Her Majesty's soldiers were at war, probably to Burma where the "natives" as they were contemptuously called by the British fighting man, were ill-treating British subjects.

She stood before him, her back straight, her head high, her shoulders rebelliously squared. Her hair hung to her waist in a curtain of flame and her eyes, which were the only thing she had not inherited from his side of the family, flashed a desperate blue-green. He was often intrigued by her eyes, for sometimes they were as now, glowing with the fervour of her belief that one day this boy would be found, and at others they were quiet, introspective, unfocused, sad. Still, it mattered not to him. All he required of her was that she marry Noah Goodwin and pass on his own bloodline to the children they would have. He would sleep easy in his bed when his first grandson was in his arms and Noah Goodwin the protector of the Goodwin undertakings. Noah was a good businessman, probably better than Richard would have been though he would never admit it to anyone. Abigail could not run the works but she would bear children who could. After he had gone it would all be in safe hands, but the obsession she had with finding this apprentice from his own works was standing in the way.

And it had done no good locking her in her bedroom, for she had merely climbed out along the branch of the oak tree and dropped to the ground, showing a great deal of her long, bare legs. Mr Renfrew, Frankie and Jacko had seen her do it and though the two lads had been filled with glee, Mr Renfrew had been shocked and had wasted no time in telling Mrs Pearson.

Abby was increasingly and hopelessly aware that the chances of finding Roddy were becoming slim. Every inch of ground from here almost to Liverpool, east to Newton in Makerfield, north to Up Holland and south to Farnworth had been searched and no trace had been found of him. But she had come to realise that she must accept her new life here at Edge Bottom House, with or without Roddy, taking advantage of all being a Goodwin offered her, and not just her but her family. And Roddy's! Mrs Baxter could no longer afford to take time off in the search for her son. Privately she had come to believe that he would never be found and that she, Willy and Eddy had best get on with their lives before they went under. As yet they had not been turned out of the glass works cottage, for even Bradley Goodwin knew what ill-feeling an eviction of the widow would stir up. And the lass, meaning Abby, must also get on with hers!

The lass meant to, but not without first gaining something for those she loved, and for herself. One day, when Roddy came back from wherever he was, or until his . . . his body – please not that, dear God – was found, she meant to make something for herself and only this old man could help her.

"I want an allowance," she said firmly, even briskly, as though there was no use in arguing. "I need ter help me family and 't family of Roddy Baxter. His mother's destitute wi'out his wage and—"

The old man rose in his chair, gasping, an expression of outrage on his face, his colour choleric, then, considering, it was replaced with one of cunning and a certain vindictiveness. No one had stood up to him for many years; in fact he couldn't remember when anyone had, not even Richard. But this lass, seeing something to her advantage and having a bargain with which to negotiate, was using it and he could not but admire her for it.

"That is nothing to me," he said sourly.

"It is ter me. I can't be running ter you or that woman every time I need some money."

"Buy what you like and have the bill sent to that woman, as you call her."

"That won't do. I mean ter help Mrs Baxter an' her children, and that's another thing—"

"Now you listen to me, young woman—"

"No, you listen to me, old man. Mrs Baxter is terrified, now that . . . that 'er son is missin' that she'll be turned out of 'er cottage. It belong ter't glass works but she's nowhere else ter go. I'll not see 'er turned out."

"Will you not?" His tone was silky.

"No."

"I see. And what will you do for me in return? If I grant all these favours you demand, what will you do for me?"

"Anythin' that's in me power."

"Really, well I shall remember that, lass."

"So will yer do as I ask?"

"I might."

"Yer might."

Abby watched the old man, not trusting him an inch, afraid of him, for he was powerful and could make or break her and those she held dear. But it seemed to her that he might be prepared to allow her certain benefits if she did not obstruct him in his plans. He wanted her to be a lady. She was his granddaughter and she must be trained to act as a member of his family should. It had not been talked of yet, but she supposed he meant her to mix with his own class of people, entertain and be entertained, wear the lovely gowns Mrs Pearson had brought back from the dressmaker and milliner in St Helens, the gowns chosen not by herself but by the housekeeper. The woman, Miss Beckett of Market Street, a cobbled square in the centre of town where the best shops lay, had taken her measurements on that first day and at Mrs Pearson's request had made up half a dozen gowns – a morning dress, two afternoon dresses, a walking outfit and two evening gowns – her assistants stitching far into the night on the crepe de chines, the gauzes, the taffetas and the brocades that would make Miss Goodwin into a fit granddaughter for Bradley Goodwin. There were cashmere shawls and others of silk crepe. An evening cloak of midnight-blue velvet, bonnets with ribbons and lace, gloves and stockings and a froth of lace and lawn which turned out to be further undergarments. She donned them on certain days and on others turned to her plain grey wool and her clogs, her frayed woollen shawl, ready to tramp the countryside looking for Roddy.

She had been surprised one day when Kitty came up to the nursery to tell her that Mr Noah was downstairs asking for her.

She put down *Lessons made Easy* which was teaching her her numbers, floundering through *one two, buckle my shoe, three four, knock at the door* and had just reached *fifteen, sixteen, maids in the kitchen*, when Kitty knocked at the door. Miss Holden tutted irritably, for it was difficult enough to get this awkward girl to the nursery or, as she preferred to call it, the schoolroom, and the servants had been instructed not to interrupt lessons.

Miss Holden found it quite a challenge to teach this girl who, though she had been brought up in a working-class environment, was, astonishingly, the granddaughter of one of the most wealthy and powerful men in St Helens. Miss Holden was thirty-two and had for the past twelve years, ever since her parents had died, been a governess to several good families. She was, of course, a lady, a soul of propriety with a vast knowledge of English, French, arithmetic, history, geography and even Latin learned from her father who had been a parson. For twenty pounds per annum she passed on this knowledge to the child or children of those who employed her. She had the best references and yet she had in her time acted as nursery-maid, mending stockings, for she was also a good needlewoman. She could play the piano and could paint prettily in watercolours and was the ideal person to teach Abigail Goodwin all she needed to know to move in the society, the *good* society of her grandfather's world. She knew the girl's history and her crazy search for some young man to whom she had been attached. And she was astute enough to realise what plans her employer had for his granddaughter. She was clever, her quick mind seeing far beyond what the other servants saw and if the girl had been in her right mind, which she apparently was not, she would have seen it too.

And this was a good place that she didn't want to lose. If she could teach this girl to the old man's satisfaction and a marriage took place between her and Noah Goodwin, would it not follow that a governess would be needed for any children they might have. She had never known such a comfortable place. This schoolroom was large and spacious, an enormous fire in the grate, an endless supply of coals brought up by the maids. There were toys on shelves, puppets, rag dolls, a doll's house, spinning tops, toy soldiers and many, many books. Her own room on the first floor of the house was comfortable and though she did not mix with the servants, having her meals brought to her in the schoolroom, she was not lonely. She was accustomed to her own company, her books, her diary which she wrote in each day. She meant to hang on to this job for as long as she could.

"You'd best go, child," she said, for if Noah Goodwin was asking for her it was with the permission of her grandfather.

He rose as she entered the drawing-room and for a split second she was surprised at how handsome he looked. Bradley Goodwin, in anticipation of things to come, had given him a raise and Noah had ordered several new suits to replace the outfits that, though well pressed and cleaned by his devoted sister, were very shabby. Today he was in a swallow-tail morning coat in a rich blue and his trousers were a dove grey. His waistcoat was the same shade as his trousers and his shirt and cravat a sparkling white. His dark hair curled vigorously and his brown eyes snapped with some inner excitement. His teeth were white against the amber of his skin and he smiled in what she thought might be mischief.

"I've come to take you for a walk," he told her without preamble. "It's time you got away from your lessons and from the rather, dare I say, *tedious* life you lead at the moment. Later, with your grandfather's permission, I intend taking you to . . . well, I'd best wait until . . . Now then, get your wrap and—"

"Mr Goodwin, what the dickens are yer . . . you talking about? I never said I'd come fer a walk wi' . . . with you. The old man'd have a fit if . . . he don't . . . doesn't like me going about looking for Roddy an' I'm sure if he found out I was off walking wi' you he'd—"

"No, no, I have his permission, Abby. You see, despite what he says I have decided to call you Abby and that being so will you not call me Noah. After all, we are related."

She blinked. "We are?"

"Oh yes, very distantly, I must admit, but I believe we share a great-grandfather."

She looked bewildered but before she could question him he said, "Now get your shawl." He looked down at her light slippers which were the same shade as her gown, apple green and very pretty but totally unsuitable for outdoors. "And you'd best put on a pair of stout shoes. I suggest boots. This rain has turned the ground to mud."

"What ground?" Her voice was suspicious. This man had dined with them on many occasions since she had come to Edge Bottom Hall but she still linked him with her grandfather whom she did not trust, so what the dickens was he up to now?

She knew nothing of the conversation he had just had with Bradley Goodwin.

"Sir, will you not allow me to have my way in this? You cannot force your granddaughter to marry me. We can hardly drag her to the altar screaming that she loves another man."

"Love—" the old man began contemptuously.

"She thinks she loves him, sir, and that is enough to make her dig her heels in. She must marry me of her own free will and it's no good you shouting at her to do this or that."

"She is my granddaughter and will do as I tell her." The old man glared round his study, the bright shimmering flames of the fire turning his already florid face to scarlet. He reached for the bell and when May scuttled in ordered her to pour himself and Mr Noah a glass of port. May had been cleaning the silver in the scullery and was most put out to be disturbed when the damn port was at the old man's elbow and could be reached by either gentleman, but her irritation did not show on her impassive face.

"They're up ter summat," she told the inquisitive servants when she returned to the kitchen. "You mark my words."

"What?" squeaked Nessie but May didn't know the answer to that one.

"Never you mind," she answered knowingly, going back to her silver.

In the study the two men continued their argument. "No, sir, she won't. If I may point out, she is a Goodwin and is as stubborn as . . . well, as yourself."

"You young beggar."

"I don't mean any disrespect, sir." He could scarcely afford to when his whole future depended on this bad-tempered old man and the young girl in the nursery. "I believe she should be left alone for a while. Let her get used to the disappearance of the boy *and* to my presence in her life. If I may be allowed to take her about, perhaps she may learn to enjoy it. Let her do things that a young lady in her position would do. We could start with a simple walk not far from the house. It would be a start for her on her new life. She will, eventually, get used to the loss of the lad, wherever he may be, and, with time, be persuaded, if she knows and trusts me, to accept me as her husband. It is what we both want, you and I, but we must go slowly."

"You young devil . . ." But there was approval in Bradley Goodwin's eyes and Noah was aware that he had won the first round in his courtship of Abigail Goodwin.

Now he smiled at Abby, for she really was the most suspicious young creature he had ever come across. But then could you blame her?

"The ground between here and there," he said in answer to her question.

"Where, for God's sake?"

"It's a secret. Look, the sun is shining after the rain and a walk will do us both good. I've just come from the works and the smell of chemicals is in my head. I'd like to clear it. So, run and get your wrap and boots and let's go."

"You're very free with your orders, Mr Goodwin."

"Noah." He smiled engagingly and Abby could not help smiling in return. He was so good-natured with a curl to his mouth which seemed to say he might have a sense of fun and she'd had none of that for a long time.

They walked side by side along what he had known would be a muddy lane. It was rutted with cart tracks which led off to some farm but the sun was warm and was already drying up the rainwater that had gathered during the night. Edge Bottom village was set in the same shallow bowl as St Helens. It was June, high summer, and the sky behind them as they climbed was yellow with smoke through which the sun could not penetrate. It was streaked with the grey of the many filthy industries of St Helens. Once there had been oat fields, barley fields, cattle and fruit gardens, peat mosses and wild heaths, mixed farming which had for the most part vanished in what was being called the industrial age when coal was found. Coal which heralded all the industries it fed. A great deal of building went on, which destroyed much of the countryside. Alkali-making was begun, which erupted such gases it caused men's teeth to decay and clouds of filthy smoke to lie across the roofs of the town. There were cone-houses vomiting smoke and flames, mill chimneys and factory chimneys spewing out their filth to cover the town and the people within it, but it did not take long to get away from the urban sprawl.

They turned their backs on the town, striding quickly away from it to a point where the tufted upland grass was sharp-scented and even the sky shredded, first to a cleaner grey and then to blue. There was the nearby music of moorland water, the tangy feeling of space and solitude, and Abby felt a gentle peace settle about her.

As they topped a low rise a sprawl of buildings came into view and a man dressed in the garb of a countryman, a pipe in his mouth, his face as brown as the peat he was stacking, rose from behind a dry-stone wall. He nodded his head in greeting but that was all before continuing with his task.

The wind struck her a blow, whipping her bonnet from her head so that it hung down her back from its ribbons. Her hair, which Mrs Pearson had taught her to dress in a fat chignon at the crown of her head, became loose and flew out like a banner. Roses bloomed in her cheeks and her eyes sparkled with pleasure and for the first time in weeks she felt a lifting to her heart. She stopped and turned, her back to the pale blue sky, her face to the smoke, then turned again to look at the spectacular scenery. There was a tumble of rocks and without speaking they moved towards them and sat down, facing not the town below but the wide stretch of moorland.

Tussocks of cotton sedge moved in the wind, a cotton-grass moor, it was called and was a feature of the southern Pennines, wild and desolate, their only moment of unforgettable colour when the white cotton sedge heads were ripe in May and June, their edges splashed with the bright yellow-green of young bilberry leaves.

"Have you been up here before, Abby?" Noah asked her casually.

"Only when I were lookin' fer Roddy." Her voice was clipped and cool.

"Ah yes, Roddy."

"What does that mean?" She turned to look at him, her hand going to her cheek to push back a bright strand of hair that whipped across it.

"Has it ever occurred to you that – now please don't take offence – but that Roddy left the area because of you?"

"What!" She was scandalised, her poppy mouth falling open in astonishment.

"I'm sure his feelings for you had not changed but *your* circumstances had. Perhaps he could not picture himself, an apprentice in the glasshouse at Edge Bottom, as the husband of the glass works owner. It must have been very daunting."

"Daunting? What d'you mean by that?"

"You are the granddaughter of Bradley Goodwin. He is the son of . . . a woman who scrubs for the local gentry and works in a public house. The step he would have to take would be enormous."

"I've never 'eard anything so daft in all me life," she said flatly, standing up and striding away from him, refusing even to turn and look at him and he knew the remarks had struck home.

"I'm sorry to distress you but it is a possibility. He must have been a very proud young man and the thought of taking what he would see as charity from his wife might not have

Reflections from the Past 113

been something he could stomach." He did not add that Roddy Baxter, being an intelligent lad, would have realised that there was not the slightest hope that Bradley Goodwin would let him marry his granddaughter.

"He would have left a note."

"Could he write?"

"No."

"And at the time could you read?"

"No."

"Then there would have been no point. Abby, look at me." She turned reluctantly. He had stood up and moved towards her so that his dark eyes, which she noticed for the first time had golden glints in them, or was it a trick of the moorland light, were looking down into her face.

"I'm not saying this is what happened, for, like you, I don't know but it's worth thinking about. It's the end of June, nearly three months since he disappeared." He watched, strangely affected by the spasm that crossed her face. He did not love this child, this lovely young girl. He had never been in love in all of his twenty-eight years but he was eager to marry her for what she would bring to him. And she *was* lovely. It would be no hardship to be her husband. As his wife he would protect her. She would be all right with him. He knew she could have just about anybody, the way things had turned out, but he could look after her affairs better than the lot of them.

"You're very pretty, you know," he added gently, putting a tentative finger on her chin, but she jerked away and began to stride in the direction from which they had come. He sighed, but he knew he had taken an important step today in the healing of Abby Goodwin.

9

It was September and in the port of Rangoon on the eastern shore of the Bay of Bengal a young man shivered, though the heat and humidity was intense. He crouched behind an enormous tottering edifice made up of bales, though what they contained, the young man neither knew nor cared. As long as they protected him from curious eyes. He had bartered his blue drill trousers, his scarlet coatee with its white lace and high collar, his tall cap called a shako and heavy boots for the skimpy cotton trousers and shirt he had on, but he knew if he was found he would be shot as a deserter.

The sailing ship berthed at the dock was called the *Rainbow* bound for Liverpool and was the most beautiful craft he had ever seen. It was what was known as a clipper, the fastest ship to sail the oceans, elegant and graceful. Men swarmed all over her, polishing brasswork, patching sails and touching up paintwork while coolies, dressed as scantily as himself, loaded the cargo of rice and timber on to her deck.

The dock was heaving with activity, skinny little men running frantically here and there as they helped with the loading of the ship. Dogs foraged among the noisome heaps of rubbish and rats stirred at his back. A rickshaw deposited a well-dressed couple before the gangway of the ship, the woman holding a scrap of handkerchief to her nostrils and with the other hand doing her best to keep the hem of her silk gown from dragging on the filthy, juice-spattered ground. They were hurried up the gangway, disappearing into a cabin.

For a moment activity had slowed and, taking the opportunity the interruption had caused, the youth clapped a coolie hat on his head, hefted a bale of what appeared to be rice on to his shoulder and joined the shuffling line of men waiting to carry their burdens on to the ship. Keeping his head down and bending his back, for he was at least a foot taller than the other men, he crept up the gangway, following the man in front to an open hold where a seaman was supervising the lowering of the bales into its interior. The youth dropped his where the seaman pointed, then, swift as a mouse seeking safety down a hole, he slipped over the lip of the hold, dropping on to the bales already stacked. He slid across them on his belly making for the far corner where he burrowed down in a nest against the ship's bulkhead and curled into a tight ball. He waited for the cry, the shout of alarm, but astonishingly there was none. The bales were lowered and the men stowing them continued swiftly, for the ship was to sail on the next tide. He was afraid that he might be smothered by the growing bulk of the cargo but mercifully he found he could shift his hidden position and breathe though the air was stifling and filled with dust. He settled to wait, as he had waited for the past six months!

Though she still dreamed of Roddy she was settling herself without knowing it into the daily rhythm of her new life. She had blossomed into a lovely young woman, becoming refined and even elegant. She had grown up, matured, no longer the ignorant lass whose only thought had been to marry as her mother had done and have babies in a home of her own. She had developed into an adult, leaving behind for good the naïve child she had been. She began to take a vital interest in what Miss Holden had to teach her and the sound of her practising her scales on the piano in the drawing-room, though it drove her grandfather mad, gave him a great deal of satisfaction, for it seemed she was moving in the direction he had mapped out for her. She could read quite fluently and write in the good clear copperplate Miss Holden had taught her. Her manners at table were flawless and she had perfected the art of dinner conversation, practising with Miss Holden in the schoolroom, so that though Miss Holden only knew the genteel way in which young, well-bred girls should speak, and that when spoken to, it was a good beginning, the basis for the day when she would enter good society.

She and Noah had many a lively discussion at the dinner table, in which the old man took very little part, about every subject under the sun that interested her. About faraway places which she read of in her geography books and of which Noah knew a little. He had been to Choisy-le-Roi, near Paris, to investigate the way Charles Singre, a sheet glass-blower held in high esteem, worked with glass. The supply of sheet glass-blowers and flatteners was so strictly limited in England that Bradley Goodwin had during the past six months sent him to the Continent in search of additional hands. He had travelled extensively across France and he kept her entranced with his tales of the country. He could talk about books, advising her on what to read, though Miss Holden didn't always approve of his choice. He was country born and bred and though his tastes were sophisticated he knew about birds and animals and on their walks, which became more frequent, could talk knowledgeably about their habits.

But Noah Goodwin was a man who had been until recently much addicted to cards, to gambling, to pigeon flying, prize fighting and laying bets on the foot races that were so popular in the vicinity; to fancy wines and spirits, to expensive women, the theatre, the music hall which had recently opened in St Helens. He was a fiercely ambitious man, prepared to play his part in this undertaking that was the brainchild of the old man. Abby was a lovely girl, though his taste did not run to innocent virgins, but the only way he was to get his hands on the Edge Bottom Glass Works was through her. She was bright, and, as time passed and nothing was heard of the lad she purported to love, she no longer spoke of him and had, under his own tutelage, he liked to think, become an amusing companion. The old man was increasingly impatient and roared at him in the privacy of his study that he'd best get a move on. Noah might have time to spare but *he* certainly hadn't, but Noah, afraid of moving too quickly, and as there seemed to be no rivals for her hand as yet on the horizon, begged the old man to be patient.

Though the memory of Roddy was still strong in Abby's loyal heart, she had begun to accept that he had gone and was not coming back. She didn't know where or why he had gone but the words that Noah had said to her on their first walk had taken root in her mind. They made sense. Roddy had been proud, proud of his success at the glass works, proud of the way in which he looked after his mam and the boys, proud of her and the way he meant to give her what so many other women of their class lacked. He had been a young man who would go far, he had told her that, and, given the chance, would have done so.

It was in September when she realised with appalled horror that she was beginning to think of him in the *past tense*. She had learned about grammar, and about tenses with Miss Holden. Past tense, future tense and it seemed that Roddy did not fit into the latter. She had no idea what she was to do with *her* future so she threw herself into her learning. She drew great comfort from seeing the growing improvement in her family's circumstances and not only her family but that of the Baxters. Every Sunday afternoon after church, which her grandfather insisted upon, for it was here he introduced her gradually to his own class, she donned her sensible grey dress, pushed her stockinged feet into her clogs, threw her shawl about her shoulders and strode across the fields to Sandy Lane.

At first her brothers and sisters had been shy with her, Tommy and Bobby and Albert racing off to some boyish pastime of their own, embarrassed by this girl who, it had been whispered, had been got on their mother before she was married. They were country lads, lads who worked on the farm and they knew all about breeding. Not only had they been embarrassed, they had been shocked. Not so the little ones, Cissie, Sara-Ann, Freddy, Dicky and the new baby, another boy, two months old now and named George, or Georgie. He thrived rapidly as those before him had not, for every week Abby slipped five shillings into her mother's thankful hand and not only that brought a basket of food that she begged from the kitchen. The servants had all become used to what they had first called her "scrounging". She was polite and smiling, had learned all their names and, feeling at home in the warm bustle of the kitchen, had sat down at the big, scrubbed table and, when Harriet Pearson was not about, drunk tea with them, to their astonishment. She praised Cook's biscuits to such an extent, Cook was encouraged to make up a big batch for the children at the Sandy Lane cottage.

Everything that was left over from Saturday's meals, and even stuff that had not been offered to Bradley Goodwin, found its way into what became known as the "Sandy Lane" basket. Best butter, home-made jams, fruit jellies, a lump of cheese, half a chicken, pork pies, the remains of a boiled Yorkshire ham, enough food to feed the family for a week and the effect on the Murphy children was immediate. They began to put on a bit of spare flesh, to have more energy, and more bloody cheek, their mam said indulgently. She herself had plenty of milk for the new arrival and though she missed her she thanked God for the day her lovely lass had fallen so propitiously on her feet. Not that she used the word propitiously, for it was not in her limited vocabulary, but she was grateful for the extra money and food none the less. She had more time now that she need no longer work so hard, but Abby noticed that she did not spend it in keeping the place clean, or even tidy.

Had it always been like this? Abby wondered as she watched her brothers and sisters stuff their faces with fruit cake. Did I live in this clutter for fifteen years of my life and take no heed of it? She had become used to the immaculacy of her new home, her pretty bedroom with not a thing out of place, the bathroom with its white enamelled bath and brass taps, its black and white tiles, the mirrors, the lavatory set in its wooden frame and the ceramic handle on the end of its chain that flushed the contents of the lavatory away. The fragrant soap, the bath salts and toilet water that she had begun to take so much for granted. *Hot* water that gushed from the taps through some miraculous technique which joined them to the boiler in the basement. And the shining kitchen where she often whiled away a pleasant hour talking to the maidservants as they worked. She had only to step out of her drawers or petticoats and they were whisked away to be washed and yet here in her family's home there was still a smell of unwashed bodies, of the boiled potatoes they had eaten for last night's meal, and the underlying odour that was the heritage of the poor.

But perhaps the best thing of all was the miracle that Albert, Cissie and Sara-Ann were learning their letters and numbers at the Church of England School at Moorflat in College Lane. The Cowley School, it was called, the funds to run it left from the estate of Sarah Cowley for the bringing up of the town's poor children. The two older boys, Tommy and Bobby who, having worked for their living for three years, had flatly refused to go. Abby had sighed sadly but at least part of her family was bettering itself.

It was the same at the home of Dorcas Baxter. Though she said nothing to Abby, Dorcas had given up hoping to see her boy again. If he had not been taken or done away with, he had gone voluntarily and she thought the same way as Noah Goodwin, deciding he could not live as the son-in-law of Bradley Goodwin, had he been given the chance. He could not, of course, write but she was surprised he had not sent her some word. Perhaps he still would! Abby had used her new influence to ensure that Roddy's family did not starve, nor were turned out of their snug cottage. Dorcas worked long hours as she had always done but she was not too proud to take the few shillings a week Abbey offered her. And then there were her boys! Already able to write their names and add a simple column of figures, sitting next to Abby's own sisters and brother at the school in St Helens. Though she ached for her son who was lost to her she had a lot to be thankful for.

Abby often sat with Harriet, as she now called her, in the housekeeper's sitting-room. Harriet had thought it a good idea if she learned the intricacies of the accounts that, as the mistress of this house as one day she would be, she would need to know.

"Why can't you continue to run the house, Harriet?" she had asked anxiously. "I'd be no good at it." They were drinking tea, not the dark, sweet brew from earthenware mugs she drank with the servants but the expensive China tea that Harriet kept locked in an ornate tea caddy. Ruby or May would bring in the tea tray and place it on the occasional table and then carry in the hot water which could be reheated over the fire as required. Dainty bone china cups and saucers, a silver teapot, sugar bowl and milk jug, all very different from what was used in the kitchen.

"Because I might not be here, my dear. When your grandfather . . . goes you will be mistress and will need to know the way of things."

"Why should you go when Grandfather dies, Harriet?"

"Well, a housekeeper will no longer be needed, not with a mistress to supervise the running of the house."

"*I* will still need you." Abby's voice quavered. "I couldn't manage on my own."

"Eventually you will have a husband and children and . . ."

"All the more reason for you to stay on. Anyway, when I'm mistress I shall do as I like and that means I shall be able to choose whether to be married or not."

She was staring blindly into the fire and did not see the quick glance Harriet cast in her direction.

She lay in bed that night, her head turned to the window where a bright full moon lit the branches of the tree. It was like black lace against the silver-blue sky, the remains of autumn leaves still clinging on and giving it a beauty that made her heart ache. She had lost so much and yet at the same time she had gained so much. Now that she had settled in, become accustomed to the luxury, the warmth, the comfort, the lessons that she enjoyed, even the old man's taciturnity, she found herself delighting in so many things she had not even known existed. This pretty bedroom, the colours in it, delicate and muted, the pictures, the constant vases of flowers that were everywhere, the garden during the summer when the flowerbeds had been filled with a glorious rainbow of shades from the palest cream to the deepest scarlet; the formal herb garden, a knot garden Mr Renfrew called it with its interflow and knotting effect of the shapes and fragrance. She spent as much time as she could in the magnificent conservatory, as it was known, though Mr Renfrew preferred to call it a winter garden, the delicate tracery of its roof edged with fretwork, its tiled floor in lustrous shades of rose, vermilion and pale cream, the wickerwork chairs and tables where she sprawled to do what Miss Holden called her "homework" and the forest of plants, camellias, gardenias, lilies, azaleas, vines, ferns, creepers trailing, all of which Mr Renfrew had named but were too numerous to remember, and canaries in cages singing their hearts out. She loved the elegant gowns that she wore, the fabrics, the colours and the never-ending appearance of new ones in her wardrobe; the shoes and boots of the softest leather, all made to measure her foot so that she walked in total comfort. She had discovered that she could find no fault with her new life apart from the tearing wrench of her separation from Roddy and missing her mam, for though she had become friendly with Harriet it was not the same as your own mam, was it?

An owl called from the woods at the back of the house and she heard soft footsteps moving along the hallway outside her room. That would be Harriet returning to her own bed, and though it had shocked her at first she had become used to the fact that Harriet's duties consisted of more than running the house. The window was slightly open, for the cold depths of winter were not yet upon them and a slight breeze lifted the net curtains. It grew stronger and seemed to blow across the room, a breath full of the odours that country folk unconsciously learn to associate with the approach of autumn. Not unwholesome. Not the scent of decay, for it carries a hint of slowing down gently as the great pulse of nature eases from the beating of spring and summer, ready for the onslaught of winter.

She turned on her side, sighing, wondering sadly where Roddy was then her eyes closed and she slept.

"Mrs Pearson wants ter see yer, Miss Abigail." May poked her head round the schoolroom door, ignoring Miss Holden's sigh of annoyance.

"Does Mrs Pearson not realise that this is lesson time, May?" she exclaimed.

"Don't ask me, miss. I were told ter fetch Miss Abigail an'

that's what I'm doin'. She don't confide in me." May smirked at Abby, for she was proud of the word "confide" which Abby had told her the meaning of.

"There is no need for impertinence, May."

"No, miss."

"Very well, Abigail, you'd best go and see what Mrs Pearson wants." Jane Holden knew that Harriet Pearson would not send for the old man's granddaughter unless the old man himself had instigated it. Not during lesson time.

Harriet was sitting in the fireside chair in her sitting-room. It had comfortable knitted cushions which Abby had noticed before, wondering idly who had made them. The housekeeper leaned against them as though weary.

Harriet had decided that she must be sharp, quick to make her point, for what she had to say would be a shock to the girl and the sooner it was said the better.

"Listen carefully, Abby," calling her by the name which the old man had forbidden her to use. Somehow it seemed more personal, less formal, and to tell the truth she had grown quite fond of the child, for that was how she thought of her.

Abby blinked solemnly. "Yes?"

"Someone has asked for you."

"Asked for me?"

"Yes, someone has asked to marry you."

"Someone?" Abby actually smiled, for it seemed so silly . . . daft . . . improbable, which was a word she had learned quite recently.

"Abby, are you listening to me?"

"Yes, I'm listening." If she was surprised or alarmed she did not show it, for it made no sense and Harriet watched her closely because it seemed as though Abby did not fully understand.

"Well then," she said, "since you are listening I suppose you realise that your grandfather has long had this in mind for you. To marry sensibly, not for your sake but for his. I know you once loved a young man but he is gone and is, after all this time, unlikely to return. There is no one else?"

"No."

"Good, I thought not. Does it surprise you that the man your grandfather has chosen is Noah Goodwin? A good choice, for it means there will be someone capable of looking after the business, and you, when he is gone. Your grandfather, I mean. And then there is the blood."

"Blood?"

"You have your grandfather's blood in your veins, and so has Noah, though not *through* your grandfather. Bradley Goodwin intends to live for ever through his descendants, to be constantly reborn in a line of young Goodwin men exactly like himself. Surely you understood this when he took you from your mother? You are all he has left. You cannot run the glass works but Noah can. Your grandfather will make sure that Noah has no power while *he* lives but he is a Goodwin and so, as far as your grandfather is concerned, this is an excellent arrangement. You could refuse, of course, but when Bradley Goodwin has set his mind on something anyone who stands in his way does so at their own peril. He would make your life a misery. Are you listening? Do you understand?"

Abby felt an enormous desire to yawn, to settle down in the fireside chair and doze just as though this were nothing to do with her. As though she and Harriet were discussing the future of another girl and quite frankly she didn't care.

"Noah is a very handsome young man, Abby, and will make you a good husband. After all, there is no one else, is there?"

For a fleeting moment an image of a young man, tall, lean, with laughing eyes and a thatch of brown hair which fell into them flashed across her vision. His white teeth gleamed in his brown face and his kisses had been sweet on her mouth. Strong he had been and good, good-natured, good-tempered and he had loved her as she had loved him. Where was he, that first love of hers? And then she was shocked, for again she had put the memory of Roddy Baxter into the past, calling him *her first love* just as though there would be a second, or even a third.

Harriet's voice cut into her brooding. "Unless Noah Goodwin is positively hateful to you and I can think of no reason why he should be then I think you should take him. There have been other approaches. Alfred Hardwick, who is almost as wealthy as your grandfather, has put forward his son, Charlie. Frank Lucas and Philip Arbuthnot are two more who are eager to ally themselves with the Goodwins, but Noah would work hard, not just for you as your husband but because he wants the business. He is good at it. He knows it, and your grandfather is aware of this."

There was a lengthy silence. Harriet poured herself another cup of tea, offering one to Abby who stared blindly into the fire and wondered why she should feel so little interest. When Abby ignored her Harriet sipped the tea and watched her.

"They won't let me refuse, will they?" Abby said at last.

"I'm afraid not."

"I loved Roddy, you know."

"Yes, but I think we both know that he is not coming back. So it would be wiser . . ."

"To take Noah?"

"Yes, my dear."

The tall lad, thin as a post, so thin that every bone of his spinal column stood out, pressed his forehead against the mast, his hidden face wrenching in agony. He was spread-eagled, his sinewy arms raised and tied, the ropes that held him cutting into his wrists, which ran with blood, as did his back. His body was the colour of mahogany, brown from the tropical suns under which he had sailed.

". . . twenty-eight . . . twenty-nine," a voice intoned and at each utterance the sound of the lash cutting into the lad's back made a kind of a squelching noise. On and on it went, the punishment, and the crew of the *Rainbow* watched stoically, for it was common practice on a sailing ship, or indeed on any ship, for a man to take forty lashes for some misdemeanour. Fighting, the lad had been, over what none of them knew, or cared. Something one of them had said that the lad didn't like, but then they were used to that, and to him. A stowaway, he was, working his passage back to Liverpool. A real hellion who, though he was half-starved and hardworked, could be provoked into a fight over nothing at all.

". . . thirty-nine, forty," the man wielding the lash pronounced and at once the bosun stepped forward and threw a bucket of salt water over the boy's back. He arched and when they cut him down staggered against the rigging where he had been tied. He lifted his head and though his mouth was bloody and bitten through, he grinned.

10

The wedding took place in December on a day so cold and
crisp it brought tears to the eyes of the spectators and put
poppies in the cheeks of the bride, giving the illusion that she
was radiant with happiness. The sun shone from a cloudless
sky the colour of pale duck-egg blue and was reflected in a
million diamond drops of ice that clung to every blade of grass,
every bush and bare branch. Hoar frost crunched under the
feet of the bride and groom as they stepped from beneath the
porch of the church, and at their back Bradley Goodwin's face
twisted into a satisfied smile. It seemed he was well pleased
with this union he himself had engineered and it was in the
minds of those who knew him that he would be expecting
to get himself a great-grandson within the twelvemonth. It
was not far from the thoughts of the gentlemen who watched
that it would be no hardship on Noah Goodwin's part to
achieve this, for the bride was quite enchanting. So young,
just sixteen, it was said, slender and virginal as a bride should
be and tonight Goodwin could surely be relied on to get her
with child. The old man obviously hoped so.

Abby had never heard the wedding service before and had
not given much thought to its meaning. She must obey Noah,
it told her, honour him as well, but as for love some part of
her cringed, for her heart was still grieving the loss of Roddy
Baxter who surely must be dead. She had made her vows,
repeating what the minister told her she must repeat, but none
of it meant anything to her and passed her by in a drifting blur

which she scarcely noticed. It had been the same ever since she had agreed to marry him.

She had spent her days since walking the moorland paths, heedless of Joanna Goodwin's warning that now Abigail was the betrothed of a gentleman it was improper for her to walk alone. Joanna, who would be her sister-in-law, had reluctantly been invited by Bradley to dine at Edge Bottom House and had taken the invitation as a sign that she was now part of the future household of the would-be Mrs Noah Goodwin, calling frequently to dispense her advice to the girl who surely needed it. She was on calling terms with most of the *good* families of Edge Bottom and St Helens and the old man had come to the conclusion that if his granddaughter was to be accepted by them Noah Goodwin's sister would be of immeasurable help. She was a woman much involved in the church and in the good works with which she occupied herself, in the Sunday school movement, in the movement for the abolition of the slave trade in the colonies and many other worthy causes. She could not say she approved of her brother's choice of a wife but had accepted it, since it benefited financially both him and herself. She loved her brother and his advancement in the glass trade was of great satisfaction to her.

When it rained, which it did during the month of November, Abby sat on Harriet's hearth-rug, dreaming into the glowing coals, watching Harriet, Miss Holden and one of Miss Beckett's young seamstresses sew on batiste, muslin, cambric, intricately pleating and frilling, for it seemed that the dozens of nightgowns and petticoats already in her wardrobe, though they might suffice Miss Abigail Goodwin, would certainly not suit the wife of Noah Goodwin.

Her wedding gown of creamy velvet was, naturally, created by Miss Beckett herself, as were the multitude of gowns of taffeta, silk, satin, mousseline-de-laine and others whose names Abby could not remember. She must have morning gowns, afternoon gowns and evening gowns, for Noah told her that when they were married he meant to entertain many of the businessmen of St Helens, and their wives, of course, and as their hostess she must outshine them all. Harriet would show her the way, he told her casually, and, naturally, Joanna would be only too glad to put her expertise in such matters at Abby's disposal. There was a three-quarter-length mantle lined with silky fur, a pelisse for warmer days and half a dozen diaphanous shawls. There was a riding outfit of rich blue gabardine, since he meant to buy her a quiet mare and teach her to ride, he informed her. With it she would wear a black beaver hat and veil and under the habit trousers of chamois leather with black feet. He himself had a fancy to join the local hunt since he was an excellent horseman but had not until now been able to afford a decent hunter. By God he could now!

It appeared to her in those lazily unwinding days before the wedding that getting married was more concerned with fashion, fabrics and colour than with the man she was to marry. There were trips in the carriage to Miss Beckett's smart little shop in Market Street where she was fitted and pinned at great length and where earnest discussions between Harriet and Miss Beckett took place and in which she seemed to have no part; to be fitted for shoes and boots and dancing slippers and, when all was concluded, lessons in etiquette from Miss Holden. Discourses on her duties as the mistress of the house, how to be a prudent wife and a careful matron for so would she make her husband happy. On forming friendships and how they should be conducted; on charity and benevolence to those less fortunate than herself; the courtesies of receiving and making morning calls, the characters of servants and their supervision and the correct procedure for seating those at her dining table.

She listened dutifully, still in that state of suspension that had begun on the day her grandfather had come to claim her. She breathed and moved, spoke and even laughed, to all outward appearances recovered from her loss, but deep within her lay that part of Abby Murphy who had loved and been loved by Roddy Baxter. She was not even conscious of it. She enjoyed the trappings of wealth and if she was honest she even admitted that she liked Noah Goodwin. He was a good companion, enormously fascinating to a girl of just sixteen. He made no attempt to touch her, to kiss her, treating her as perhaps a brother might treat a favourite sister. She saw little of him, for he was closeted for hours with her grandfather.

On the day of the wedding Harriet had surprisingly kissed her, holding her for a moment before she was taken downstairs to be delivered to her grandfather. She held her away for a moment, searching her face with anxious eyes.

"Is there anything you want to ask me, Abby?" she asked quietly.

"About what?" the lovely, lifeless reflection of Abby Murphy asked.

"Have you ever . . . do you know . . . ?"

"Of course," knowing Harriet's meaning but unwilling to admit to it.

"There's nothing you have to do, my dear. Noah will know what he's about and all you have to do is follow his lead." Harriet frowned, sighed, then let go of her, perhaps remembering her own first time.

Her wedding gown had a bell-shaped skirt held out with a dozen of the petticoats that had been sewn on over the past eight weeks. The bodice was simple, fitting smoothly to her breast, the neck cut low enough to show the skin of her neck, which was no less creamy than the velvet. Tiny seed pearls, thousands of them, had been sewn on the skirt and bodice and clever Miss Beckett had designed a small coronet with the same pearls gleaming in her hair which had been brushed into a curly knot on the top of her head. She wore a string of beautifully matched creamy-coloured pearls that had once belonged to her grandmother and carried a simple posy of cream roses.

She looked quite glorious as she was led up the aisle on the old man's arm towards Noah who was as handsome as she was lovely. A dove-grey jacket, a white brocade waistcoat, a froth of white for a cravat and a single cream rosebud in his lapel. His dark hair curled vigorously and he took her hand with the eagerness, not of a bridegroom, but of a man who is, at the last moment, afraid the prize he has coveted might still be lost to him. His hand was warm, firm, smooth and his smile was deep and enigmatic. But he was excited, the congregation was inclined to think and who could blame him. This beautiful young girl was to be his, but more to the point, so was her fortune, her glass works and all the other business concerns that Bradley Goodwin had built up in his lifetime.

Since the glass works had a prior claim on his time, and besides, Bradley Goodwin had made it clear he had no affinity with such foolishness, there was to be no wedding journey. There was no question that Abby, as the wife of Noah Goodwin, should move into her husband's home and so after a polite smattering of good wishes and some snide teasing which made her stomach churn, Abby was left alone in the bedroom she had slept in for the past nine months and which she was now to share with Noah Goodwin.

He was patient, gentle, stroking her arms and shoulders, doing his best to prise her loose from the frozen rigidity into which his alien presence in her bed had spun her. She did not struggle, knowing what was expected of her, for how could a child who had grown up with the sound of her parents coupling in the same room where she and her siblings slept be ignorant? She submitted, making no sound. He took her nightgown from her, one of those sewn on so diligently by Harriet and Miss Holden, then removed his own, the candleglow washing their young, beautiful bodies to a golden bronze. She kept her eyes tightly closed and, becoming impatient with her lack of response since he was doing his utmost to please her, Noah penetrated her quickly, thinking it best to get it over and done with, then fell gasping on to her supine body.

"Don't worry," he murmured when it was all over, turning away from her, "the first time can be . . . awkward. It will get better, my pet, believe me. Now sleep, it's been a long day and you must be tired."

"No, not at all," she replied stoutly to this stranger whom she was now to call husband.

He turned back, balanced himself on one elbow and looked down into her face. "I'll say this for you, Abby Goodwin. You're a brave lass. You hardly know me, at least not in this way but we'll get along. You're mine now and I take good care of what's mine. No one will hurt you. Not even your grandfather."

He turned his back to her once more and though she knew nothing of men, of their needs or desires, she was aware that his body had not been totally satisfied by what he had just done to her.

The first months of marriage were awkward, dominated as they were by the old man who watched her like some ancient and tenacious goblin, waiting, she knew, for the news that she was pregnant and becoming grimmer with each month that passed when it did not come. It was not for want of trying, for Noah took her each winter night in the fire-glowed comfort of their bed. He seemed pleased with her, for at Christmas she and Harriet had planned a dinner party, her husband providing her with the names of the businessmen and their wives, those who could do him the most good in his building up of Bradley Goodwin's glass works. Influential men like Alfred Hardwick who owned a printworks, Tom Lucas who was a master builder and Jack Arbuthnot, a colliery owner, all of them worth cultivating. For once the old man agreed with him. He was well aware that his granddaughter, even now, was considered beneath them but they dared not refuse, and with Harriet's help and Miss Holden's guidance the party was a mild success. They had taught her well, these two women, so different in their backgrounds but both with something to offer. Miss Holden made her practise again and again the art of conversation between ladies and what was suitable for discussion with a gentleman. Every aspect of entertaining was learned from the setting of the table, the glassware, the cutlery, the flowers, the seating, to the niceties of polite society to which her guests were accustomed.

The table looked superb. Harriet was pleased with her, for she had remembered all she had been taught. The dining-room was bathed in a subdued light from the candles, for, as Harriet said, it was considered kinder to the ladies. A separate table had been set at the end of the room for serving dessert and Kitty and Ruby had put out the silver compôtes and tazzas piled high with fruit of every kind, most grown by Mr Renfrew. Nectarines, peaches, figs and the green and black grapes of which he was justifiably proud, for it was difficult to cultivate such exotic fruits in this cold climate, even in a hothouse.

The main table was set with the Goodwin porcelain dinner service manufactured by Josiah Spode and so translucent light could be seen through it. The silver cutlery gleamed from the hours of polishing by May and Nessie, and the fragrance from the bowls of roses arranged by Miss Holden filled the warm air. There were even finger bowls, which quite astonished Abby, containing scented water and the napkins had been folded and arranged in wings before each setting. It quite took her breath away. Miss Holden told her that in the households of the gentry there would be a butler who would be expected to know exactly where each guest was to be seated but in the absence of one at Edge Bottom House, name cards had been placed above the array of cutlery, alternating lady and gentleman as was the custom.

"Where have I to sit?" she asked apprehensively, the prospect of conversing with a complete stranger who would probably look down on Betty Murphy's daughter frightening her to death.

"At the head of the table, my dear. You *are* the hostess. Now it is proper for each gentleman to help the lady on his left with her fan and her napkin then, when the plates are changed he will turn to the lady on his right and converse with her."

"And what about me? I can manage my own napkin, Holdy," which was the affectionate nickname she had given the woman who had until recently been her governess and was now her mentor in so many things.

"I know that, and so does every lady at the table but it is the custom."

"Dear Lord, I shall never manage, I know I won't."

"Nonsense, dear. You are a clever and lovely young woman and with your husband to help you, to guide you, you will be a successful hostess."

She looked radiant, as she had on her wedding day, dressed this time in a gown of silver gauze, a lustrous, shimmering thing with a wide skirt and a fitted bodice that was cut so low it revealed the tops of her breasts. Noah had fastened a thick rope of gold, elaborately twisted and set with diamonds, about her throat, not, she was certain, for her pleasure but for his own. It was a declaration to the gentlemen with whom he did business and who were to dine at his table tonight that he was able to buy his wife expensive jewellery. She stood beside him and, taking Holdy's advice, said very little.

She smiled and answered when spoken to and it seemed the gentlemen thought she was charming and the ladies told one another that she knew when to hold her tongue. The meal was splendid, thanks to Harriet and Cook, the service impeccable, again thanks to Harriet, and the two gentlemen who had been placed on either side of her were inclined to be enchanted with her smiling modesty, her interest in every word they spoke and her gentle laugh at every small joke they made. Her grandfather, unwilling to give way to Noah, sat at the foot of the table and watched her, pleased with his investment in the future, *his* future and that of the glass works. She had only to become pregnant and his plan would be complete.

Noah was down at the glass works before dawn the next morning, as he was every morning, watching the shifts come and go, irked, she knew, by her grandfather's demands that each day he explain every action he took. He brought the accounts books and old ledgers home, secretly poring over them in the privacy of their bedroom.

"You'll say nothing of this to the old man, Abby," he warned her. There were explosive arguments when Noah altered even the smallest thing in the warehouses, the crown furnace, the glasshouse, Bradley Goodwin unable or unwilling to see that an improvement in this or that could only be good for the business.

"It was good enough for my father and for me," he growled, "and no slip of a lad is going to change it."

"But, sir, it is for the best."

"I'll say what is best."

Abby existed between them, barely noticed in the glare of their mutual hostility and it was not until April, when for the fourth time since her marriage she was made aware that she was not pregnant, that her grandfather took her to task. He and Noah had just had a snarling match over the breakfast table which it seemed Noah was winning when the old man turned on her.

"And where the hell's that grandson I was promised?" he thundered. "Wed three months and not yet with child. I can't think it's this lad's fault since it's well known that his bastards are littered all over the county. So . . ."

Noah stood up so violently his chair crashed backwards and tipped to the floor. Both Kitty and Ruby squeaked and huddled together against the sideboard. They were used to the master and Mr Noah's violent arguments and took no notice, indeed scarcely heard them, but what their master had just said to Miss Abigail was dreadful. The poor lass . . . to be accused of . . .

But as Noah leaped to his feet so did his wife. Abby had sat through so many of these incidents and had said nothing since she knew nothing about the glass works but this attack on her was beyond reason. Her face was scarlet with rage and Noah retrieved his chair and sat down slowly, watching her admiringly. She was so quiet, so amenable, he had begun to think the spirit she had once shown had been destroyed. She had done well at the dinner party they had given and had been acknowledged a great success at a ball given in the Assembly Rooms in St Helens last week to celebrate the birth of Her Majesty's eighth child, a son. Gentlemen had flocked about her, begging to be allowed to put their names in her dance card and even more gratifying, at least to those who watched, the young son of Lord Thornley of Thornley Green, whose party had deigned to put in an appearance at this – in his opinion – clod-hopping affair, had monopolised her for several dances! Not that any man, father or husband, would be pleased about that, for the handsome young man was known for a womaniser and a rake.

"Who the hell d'you think you are to tell me when I must produce a child?" Abby shouted now. "Surely it's the privilege of a husband and wife to decide that?" She knew as she spoke that this was not true. Women had no way of preventing childbirth but why she had not conceived she could not say. Not that she cared precisely.

"Don't you dare address me in such a manner, girl. Sit down and hold your tongue. You know why you were brought to live in my house and it was simply that, as my grand-daughter, you could give me an heir. Do you imagine I would have taken a snivelling by-blow of that Murphy woman, even if the father was my own son, for any other reason? I've had you turned into a lady so that you would make a suitable mother for my grandson and married you to this upstart so that not only would Goodwin blood run in his veins but the glass works would be kept in readiness for the lad when I've gone. So I'll take no more of your . . ."

He was surprised, as was Noah, into speechlessness when his granddaughter simply turned on her heel and strode from the room. Kitty and Ruby watched her go with open mouths, then, as the door banged to behind her, turned to see what the master would do now.

"Bloody girl," he muttered, banging his knife and fork irritably to his plate, scattering fried tomatoes all over the snow-white cloth.

"It is hardly her fault, sir," Noah said coldly. "It takes two to make a child and she has not been . . . unwilling."

"Don't tell me what you get up to in the night, Noah Goodwin. I can only say that whatever it is it isn't enough."

"That is our business, sir, mine and my wife's and now, if you will excuse me, I must . . . I have things to do."

"Really! Perhaps if you stayed away from a certain house in Tontine Street you might be more successful. You're a tomcat, Noah Goodwin. Oh yes, I make it my business to know what is going on, and not just in Tontine Street. I don't pay you a handsome wage to spend your time with—"

"You're a foul-mouthed old man—"

"Who holds the purse strings so go after your wife and earn the wage I pay you. Go on, take her to bed and get her with child. And you two" – turning savagely on the two dithering housemaids – "bugger off back to the kitchen and fetch me something decent to eat."

She climbed the slope behind the house, bending her head against the thin, sleety rain which seemed to come at her horizontally. It was cold and grey but the weather could not match the coldness and greyness in her heart. She had known neither joy nor affection, except that given her by servants since she had left her mother's cottage in Sandy Lane. She thought Noah might be fond of her in an odd sort of way but the realisation that he had made other women pregnant, that there were bastards hereabouts with his dark eyes and hair, though not distressing her in any particular way, was not pleasant.

She wandered up along the track, her boots sinking into the growing tufts of rough grass which were soggy with the rain, not bothering to drape her warm shawl, the one that always hung behind the kitchen door, about her head. Her hair tumbled to her waist, thick, springing, becoming curlier as the rain spangled it, but it did not concern her. She wondered what did? There was a drift of wild daffodils on the edge of a small bluff, clustered round a sprawl of rocks and she moved across the springing turf, plucking one idly and lifting it to her nose though she knew it had no strong fragrance. It smelled of rain and the coming of spring and its bright and cheerful yellow was like the sun which today hid behind a cloud. She crouched down against a rock and stared across the rooftops of the town below her.

Sulphurous smoke poured from a score of chimneys, coating every surface of the town in which so many industries thrived side by side. Brass foundries, copper smelting works, chemical manufacturers, glass-makers and the collieries which provided the power to serve them all. There was a flourishing alkali trade supplying the local manufacturers of soap. The era of canals had begun here when the first to be built in the country was constructed by deepening Sankey Brook from St Helens to the River Mersey, linking the town to the sea and to the rest of the trading world. A great yellow pall hung over them all, drifting with the prevailing wind across the blackened buildings. It was a town of machinery and chimneys, black canals and steam engines, overflowing privies and open ash-pits. A town of sharp contrasts in which appalling poverty lived in close proximity to new and immense wealth such as that belonging to her own grandfather.

She sat quietly, her heart dragging in pain. Her shawl was soaked, her hair hung down her back and drifted in wet tendrils across her wet cheeks and it was several minutes before she realised that it was not rain that dampened them but her own bitter tears.

Approximately forty miles away a young sailor, barefoot, his thin body shivering inside his ragged gansey and patched trousers, swayed in the rigging of a tall-masted clipper, his eyes not on her graceful bows, her slim hull nor the figurehead at her prow but at what was ahead of him. There were other men beside him, reefing some of the twenty or so sails in readiness for their entrance into the wide outer estuary of the River Mersey. The Mersey was as broad as a channel of the sea and on that channel were dozens of sailing ships such as the one the young sailor was aboard but none was as elegant. There were schooners carrying stone from North Wales; packet ships making for Philadelphia and New York; Mersey lighters, ferry boats, two masted brigantines and steam ships, noisy, dirty, smelly, but fast and reliable and ready to take the place of the beautiful ships in which he had sailed for the past six months. More than half a dozen of them, for their captains did not care for stowaways and had put him off at the first available port. It had taken much ingenuity and patience to slip unseen on to other ships at these ports, sailing ever westwards. Since last October he had been making his way back to her and from the lofty rigging he gazed with tear-dewed eyes at the skyline of Liverpool and the land where he would find her.

11

The month of April is the most changeable in the calendar. No other month shows so many variations of mood. It can be brilliant sunshine with the most breathtakingly blue sky and white islands of snowy clouds yet within an hour it will have changed to blistering, blustering winds, scudding clouds, horizons so dark that the seagulls riding the winds above the waters look even whiter against the leaden skies.

It was such a day when Roddy Baxter slid down the rope that was attached to the berth in the Princes Dock Basin. He had rubbed his hands raw on the thick hempen rope and wrenched his ankle as he landed in the muddle and hubbub of the dockside but the tumult was welcome for it hid his escape. He felt as though a skewer had pierced his ankle but he ignored the pain, darting among the heaped cargoes that were ready to be loaded on to the dozens of ships that would sail, probably on the same route he had just travelled, to the far corners of the world. He leaped nimbly across a pile of timber, cursed by a brawny docker in whose path he had almost fallen, then raced along Princes Dock Parade, past enormous warehouses, an edifice that proclaimed itself as the Public Baths and for a moment he felt a great longing to plunge into hot water and get rid of the stink that had accumulated about him over the months at sea. His eyes darted everywhere, looking for a way out of the dock area, and his bare feet slapped painfully on the cobbled roadway. He was conscious of the agony of his ankle but he did not stop. The dock area was lively, vigorous, energetic but he did not linger, longing for the quiet and peace of his own home. Men cursed and whistled and shouted incomprehensible orders to one another. Shire horses pulling loaded wagons neighed, dogs barked and women with baskets on their head shouted their wares. He wondered what they were selling but again he had little interest, for he had been part of scenes like this in every port between here and Rangoon.

Before the great warehouses of Albert Dock he spied a wrought-iron gate standing open to allow the passage of even more wagons and horses and he could see a road along which a multitude of vehicles passed. Moving through the gates he stood indecisively, unsure which road to take of the many that led away from the docks. His journey, his long, long journey was almost over and he could not wait to get to the end of it. He paused at the kerbside, shivering in the threadbare garments that covered his thin frame. His flesh was bronzed to the colour of mahogany but there was an overlying greyness to it that spoke of semi-starvation, hard work beyond even his strength, once considerable, and a general poorness of health. His hair, which had been streaked with brown and blond, was now bleached to a pale dusty gold, for Roddy Baxter had sailed under skies where the merciless sun struck down like the fires of hell. He had grown used to it and to the blinding sunlight his eyes had squinted against, forming lines about them which looked out of place on so young a man. He was seventeen but looked a great deal older. His long dark lashes framed the slanted grey of his wary, narrowed eyes, and he had formed a habit of glancing over his shoulder at almost every step, watching his back as he had learned to do in the past twelve months.

The road was filled from kerb to kerb with horse-drawn carriages, cabs, wagons fully loaded going to and coming from the docks. There were small carts and dozens of barefoot, filthy urchins darting about between the legs of the animals. A policeman's whistle shrilled and he froze for a moment, then, careless of the traffic, diving as the urchins did, crossed to the other side of the road. He was bone weary, hungry, cold, disorientated, since his life for the past twelve months had been directed by others, but nevertheless he chose a street at random, Water Street, and moved as inconspicuously as possible along the pavement, hugging the walls of the buildings that reared up on either side. He moved eastwards, for he knew that that was the direction where St Helens lay. He had learned the points of the compass the hard way on the ships he sailed in and could have said in a windowless, unlighted room which was north, south, east or west.

Nobody took the slightest interest in him, or he them, but at last he reached the edge of the city and the open countryside. The road became a rutted track, bordered on either side by verges thick with the white of stitchwort and big-faced white daisies and lush with the late spring and early summer greenness of grass. In the hedges honeysuckle twined round the bursting growth of hawthorn and may. Beyond the hedges in the lush pastures of the Lancashire farmland fat cows grazed. He stopped, held in thrall by such beauty which he had once taken for granted. He had been in places so hot and arid nothing grew and now he was looking at his own homeland, his place and, bending his head, he began to weep. The cows in the meadow raised their heads curiously and began to wander towards him, but crouching down in the ditch lined with lady's-smock he allowed, through his tears, the terror, the horror, the longing, the despair to run out of him, drenching his face and thin shirt, for he was going home.

Dorcas was sleeping the sleep of the overworked, the sleep she fell into every night after working for sixteen hours which she did every day, even Sunday. Abby Murphy, as she still called her, had tried a dozen times to slip some money into her hand but after the first shock of Roddy's disappearance, when she had been out of her mind with worry, had become more bearable, she had refused. She was glad to accept lessons for her two lads, for she had the illiterate woman's reverence for schooling, but as for wages, she would earn her own. Which she did, any honest labour that would bring her in a few pence. Her lads had a roof over their heads, nourishing food in their bellies, sturdy clogs on their feet and though she herself might look shabbier and shabbier with each passing day she was at least clean and tidy. And she had her pride which was of great value to her.

The noise that woke her up was no more than a scratching at her door and for several minutes she told herself it was her imagination. Who would come to her door in the middle of the night? And if anyone did they would knock firmly. Was it a rat in the woodwork or perhaps next door's cat at the wrong door? The boys slept soundly on the palliasse beside her own but then they were young, safe, protected, with nothing to fear with her to guard them which was their right as children.

But the slight noise persisted. She reached for her shawl and got out of bed, creeping to the window with as much stealth as if she were the intruder, peering from the small bedroom window. There was something on her step, a bundle of some sort, piled against her front door and even as she watched the bundle moved and the scratching came again. Her heart rose in her throat, for though she could not be said to be thinking coherently, her mother's heart knew who it was. With a small cry she turned and flew down the narrow stairs, across the kitchen where a small fire still glowed, flung open the door and crouched down, lifting her boy into her arms. She rocked him in a frenzy of love and thankfulness, her senses in such a state of shock she was mindless, unable to think clearly.

"Roddy! Roddy! Oh, son! My son! What's been done to yer? Lad, oh lad . . ."

"Mam . . ." Roddy Baxter had walked barefoot from Liverpool, living on scraps left out for pigs and on the kindness of farmers' wives who had felt sorry for the emaciated lad and had the spring weather not been unseasonably mild he would have perished. He was too weak to say more, or even to lift himself those last few yards across the threshold of his mother's cottage.

Leaving him for a moment even though it hurt her physically to do so, she flew up the stairs and shook her two surprised younger sons out of their sleep. Ignoring their bewildered questions and even their delight at seeing their Roddy again, even in such a poor state, she instructed them how to help her to lift the skin and bone and hank of hair which was her son across the threshold and lay him on the rug before the fire. He looked like a dead man except for his eyes which were as flat as beaten pewter in his hollow face.

"Mam . . ." he whispered again, incapable of saying more, nor even of moving.

"See, our Willy, run up the dancers an' drag down me palliasse. Eddy, fetch the blankets. 'Urry, lads, 'urry . . . an' then stir up fire an' put that broth on ter warm." They clattered off in great excitement and she turned back to her boy who had been lost but was returned to her. "Come on, my son, let's 'ave these . . . these . . . off yer." For not by any stretch of the imagination could she call the rags that hung on him *clothes*.

He made no resistance as she gently removed what he wore, nor when she gathered him into her arms and wept at the sight of his abused body. The soles of his feet were raw, blistered and bloody, looking as though he had walked on glass. The long, thin lines of him, his fine chest, his broad back, his strong arms and shapely legs, which had once been covered by sleek, healthy flesh and strong muscles, now looked as though the bones were ready to break through. The scars on his back, white lines criss-crossing his skin where he had apparently been flogged again and again and others, more recent, were turning bad. He was filthy, crawling with vermin which jumped merrily about him and on to her but she was his mother and did not flinch.

She and her young sons sponged him gently and put him in a clean shirt, one that had been his but which he had grown out of. She hadn't thrown it out, of course, for it would do for Willy but now it was too big for Roddy. Tomorrow when he was stronger she would get out the tin tub and fill it with warm water and he could have a proper bath, she told herself. She fed him a few spoonfuls of broth which was all he could manage and held his hand as he fell asleep, sending the boys to their beds and watching over him, for no man was going to take her lad away again. She crouched next to him, her thoughts busy, brooding on where he had been. He would tell her his story when he was stronger, but until that day came she had the strangest feeling that she must let no one know of his return. Someone had done this to him, whatever it was, and until the lad's strength was restored and he could protect himself she must keep his return secret. Their Willy and Eddy must have it impressed upon them that they were to tell not a soul that he was home. It would be hard for them, they were so young, only seven and six and just at the age when boys long to boast, but if she had to keep them fastened in the house, this must not get out.

As she sat through the night, watching the slight rise and fall of her boy's chest, a girl's anguished face swam into her vision and her heart was sore but not even *she* must learn of it, not yet. After all, she was married to Noah Goodwin now and was nothing to do with Roddy Baxter.

*   *   *

It was almost the end of May and she was in the meadow at the back of the house when Willy Baxter sidled up to the gate. Noah had kept to his promise and purchased a small chestnut mare which she had christened Poppy, to the great amusement of Olly who was teaching her to ride. Her grandfather had flown into a rage when the mare was introduced into the stable, swearing that Abigail and Noah were determined to deprive him of a grandson, for it was well known that women who rode, even side-saddle, did not conceive.

"If I want to buy my wife a mare then I believe that is my business, sir," Noah had replied distantly. "She is a good girl and deserves—"

"You young puppy! Just because you married my grand-daughter does not mean you are in charge, of the glass works or in this house. I still own everything, including the clothes on your back and you will do as you're told or learn the consequences. Those fancy wines you're so fond of, and the fancy women—"

"That's enough. I earn every bloody penny that is paid me in wages. From dawn to far into the night—"

"Oh aye, I've heard of the damned experiments you carry out in my shed . . ." And they were away in one of their interminable arguments. The old, decaying lion challenging the young who was out to steal what was his.

He would have been even more outraged if he knew his granddaughter rode astride. Her habit, which was very full, hid the breeches she wore and though Olly was shocked he had to admit his young mistress did much better when the cumbersome side-saddle was removed and a light ladies' saddle was placed on Poppy's back.

She was on what Olly called a lunge rein, walking Poppy round and round the meadow before allowing her into a trot and it was at this stage that the small boy appeared at the gate. Abby had not yet been out of the meadow on the mare and would not be allowed to do so until Olly decided she was ready. Then, with him beside her, she would take gentle rides up to the moorland tracks.

"Sit in't centre of saddle, Miss Abigail, an' follow movement of horse. Don't snatch at reins and keep them feet in proper position. Back straight . . . that's right, head up . . . Good lass."

She really did look well, he thought, in her smart riding habit, at the same time wondering what the old man would say if he knew she was riding astride. He'd be blamed, he supposed, but it was hard to say no to Miss Abigail who, though quiet and biddable, he had heard, had a streak in her that could be stubborn when she wanted. Her top hat was tipped over her forehead and the small veil was held under her chin. Her stock was snowy white and though they could not really be seen beneath the full skirt of her habit, he knew her boots would have a polish on them like a mirror. She wore pale grey kid gloves and carried a small riding crop. She knew, of course, that should she hit the mare with it he himself would take it to her and she'd not sit down for a week. Bradley Goodwin's granddaughter or not!

The boy watched for at least five minutes, afraid to interrupt what he saw as a lady, one of the gentry, on her grand horse. He knew who she was, naturally, for hadn't she been to his mam's cottage a time or two, but just the same he couldn't quite get up the nerve to try and attract her attention and it was not until the groom spotted him and shouted to him to "be off" that Mrs Goodwin turned to look at him.

She hesitated, her concentration gone. The reins slackened in her hands and the chestnut mare faltered to a stop, nodding her head up and down and blowing through her nostrils. She pricked her ears, swivelling them on her pretty head. She was young, only three years old and though well trained was not sure what the person on her back wished her to do.

"Trot on, Miss Abigail," Olly commanded, but Miss Abigail had gone a peculiar shade of white, staring across the meadow to the boy who was standing on the lower rung of the gate. She had begun to shake. Throwing her leg clumsily over the rump of the mare she slithered to the ground, almost falling in the flower-studded grass of the meadow.

"Miss Abigail?" Olly was flummoxed and not a little annoyed, for the mare was upset, but his young mistress was flying across the meadow, her skirts bunched up almost to her waist, her long legs in their tight breeches racing towards the gate. She stopped abruptly when she reached it.

"Willy?" Her voice was hesitant. "Or is it Eddy?"

"Willy, miss."

"What is it, Willy? Is your mam sick?" Despite her training at the hands of Miss Holden, when she spoke to one of her own class, as she still thought of them – apart from the servants in the house – she was inclined to use the words that were familiar to her own childhood.

"No, not me mam, miss. She ses yer must come."

She felt as though some large hand had been clenched into a fist and driven deep into her stomach. In fact she bent over with the shock of it and her face, which had lost its colour at the sight of the boy, turned to a sweated, dough-like hue. Inside her head, spinning like the top that still stood in the nursery cupboard, the thoughts went round and round, faster and faster and her hand quickly grasped the top rung of the gate or she would have fallen. So this is what a faint is like, she remembered thinking, then Olly was at her side, leading the mare who had been petted and calmed and stood quietly when Olly did.

"What's up, Miss Abigail? 'Oo's this lad, then?"

"Me name's Willy Baxter an' I've come ter fetch Abby," Willy answered fearlessly.

"Oh, yer 'ave, 'ave yer? Well, we'll see about that, yer little tyke. An' 'oo are you ter be callin' the mistress by 'er name? Be off wi' yer before I give yer a clip round't ear."

"Me mam ses—"

"I don't care what yer mam ses." But his young mistress, though she was still very pale, seemed to have pulled herself round. She put her hand on his arm. Her eyes had fallen back quite alarmingly into their sockets, grey in the paleness of her face, and her lips trembled.

"It's all right, Olly. Mrs Baxter is a . . . a friend of mine. I'd best go. Open the gate, will you?"

"Yer what!" Olly was aghast, for the young mistress was in his charge. Did she mean to climb on to the mare's back and go off with this young lad? Jesus tonight, the old man would skin him alive, not to mention the young master, as the servants were beginning to call him since it was becoming increasingly obvious who was in charge. Of the glass works, of this house and of this girl.

"Miss Abigail," he spluttered, but before he could stop her she had thrown off her awkward skirt and, clad only in her breeches, clambered clumsily on to the horse's back and gone through the gate which the lad had obligingly opened for her. "Miss Abigail, fer God's sake!" he bellowed and began to run after her, the lad beside him but, given her head, the mare streaked across the field in the direction of the glass works.

Women scrubbing their steps, washing their windows, shaking out rugs and sweeping the bit of pavement in front of their own cottages, stood paralysed and gape-jawed as the horse and rider swung into Edge Bottom Row, the rider pulling on the reins in front of Dorcas Baxter's house. Men in the yard stopped whatever they were doing, every last one of them, their faces as astonished as those of the women, watching as the lad, or, dear God, was it a lass flung herself from the animal's back and hammered on Dorcas's door. It was opened at once and the rider slipped inside.

She kneeled beside the palliasse and looked down at the flushed, twitching face of Roddy Baxter. His skin was dry, stretched like parchment across his cheekbones, and the parched, fiery heat coming off him was strong and rancid. He mumbled continually and in that mumble the only clear word was her own name. She laid her gloved palms on either side of his face and bent to kiss his lips as the tears poured from her eyes and across her face, dripping on to the spotlessly clean sheet which was tucked about Roddy's chin, then she wiped them away resolutely, for this was Roddy, her love, and it did no good to sit and weep over him.

"How long has he been back?" she whispered and then felt irritated with herself, for what did that matter when he was obviously so desperately ill. She removed her gloves and placed a gentle hand on his forehead and for a miraculous moment he became still and his eyes opened. He did not see her, for his eyes were glazed with fever but his cracked lips formed a whisper on which her name echoed.

"Two weeks," Dorcas murmured softly, though it was obvious the St Helens brass band would not have brought him back to a conscious state, "but I were afraid ter let anyone know, even you, lass. Someone took 'im, Abby, an' if that person found out 'e were back they might—"

"Over my dead body, Dorcas. They'll never hurt him again, I promise you, but we must get help. He needs a doctor."

"I done me best but 'is back. Sweet Jesus, 'is back."

"What?" She turned for a moment from her concentrated inspection of Roddy's face, looking up at Dorcas who hovered behind her, her face as white and strained and *old* as a woman twice her age.

"I'm feared ter move 'im but . . . look at this. Help me to turn him."

Abby gasped and put her hand to her mouth. Roddy's back was a horrific sight. Barely a hand's breadth separated the welts, some old and some more recent and it was these that were suppurating, the flesh proud about them. "'E's bin flogged, Abby. Flogged until 'is backbone showed. It's gone bad, festered as yer can see. I've done all I could – infusions an' such, bathin' 'im, but I don't know what else ter do. 'E'll not eat. If yer could see 'im naked . . ."

"Let me look."

"Eeh, Abby, 'tis not right fer a young woman ter—"

"Don't be daft, Dorcas. I'm a married woman and—"

"I reckon that's why 'e won't mend." Dorcas bowed her head, appearing to be unaware of her youngest lad who sat quietly in the corner; of their Willy who had just slipped in through the front door; nor of the irate Olly who stopped on the threshold as if he had walked into a wall. To see his young mistress leaning over a lad, a bare-arsed lad who was badly by the look of him, was a terrible shock and how was he to explain the whole incident to his master? Which master did not seem to matter.

"'E were talkin' when 'e first come 'ome. First thing 'e asked was after you. 'I've come 'ome to 'er, Mam,' 'e said and when I told 'im you was wed 'e went off inter a sort o' faint. 'E's bin like this ever since," Olly heard the woman say, not knowing what the devil to do. There was Poppy wandering about outside the cottage untethered with hordes of children ready to climb on her back, and his groom's instinct was to get her safe home to her stable. Or should he run across the yard of the glass works and fetch Mr Noah, for he'd not like his young wife bending over this lad who surely was at death's door?

But the young mistress solved his dilemma by standing up briskly and turning to him, completely unsurprised by his presence. "Oh, Olly, good. Take Poppy and ride to the house and ask Mrs Pearson to come here at once. Tell her to use the gig, it will be faster. Explain that we have a very sick man and she is to bring every potion and unguent that she knows of. And to bring me some clothes, working clothes, my grey dress and apron."

"Miss Abigail, please, I can't do that. The master'd 'ave the 'ide off me if I was ter let yer stay 'ere," glancing round the small cottage as if it were a pigsty complete with pigs rooting about in the corners. But he might have leaned out of the window and spoken into the wind for all the notice she took of him.

"And ask Mrs Pearson if she knows of a good doctor . . . perhaps the one who came to the old man in January when he had that bad chest. He was young but he appeared to know what he was doing." She turned to Dorcas. "Have you plenty of sheets, blankets, that sort of thing?"

"Miss Abigail, please," the voice from the doorway pleaded.

"Olly, will you do as you're told." Her young voice had a ring of authority in it but still he hesitated. "And you'd best see to Poppy before those young ruffians ride off on her."

He bowed his head in defeat and left the cottage.

12

She knew he would come the moment word reached him. It took precisely ten minutes. Harriet had not yet arrived with the plain grey dress and all the other items she had asked for, and when he thundered on the door, bellowing her name, she was still bent over the restless body of the man on the palliasse, crouching on the low stool on which Dorcas propped her aching feet at the end of a long day. Her face was inches from his and her left hand smoothed the dry, tangled mass of his hair which had been uncut for months. Dorcas had shoved a cup of tea in her unoccupied hand and she sipped it absentmindedly while she watched over him. She barely recognised him. The skull-like face, the deep sockets of his plum-encircled eyes, the cracked lips which Dorcas had soothed with a damp cloth, the strange, yellow-white of his skin were not those of the young man she had loved. Even his slitted eyes, which had opened when she laid her hand on his cheek, were a blank, washed-out grey, the colour of gunmetal. Where was the laughing, attractive lad with his vigorous thatch of shining brown hair, thickly streaked with gold, who had kissed her so ardently over a year ago? What had become of the healthy amber of his smooth skin, the glowing golden mischief of his thickly lashed eyes? He was still tall but where once he had been muscled, not heavy but well proportioned, he was now thin and wasted.

Dorcas sighed and opened her door, letting the explosion of Noah Goodwin into her kitchen. The room, which had been calm, not empty nor even spacious but of a fair size, was suddenly crowded with his handsome, virile presence. His clothes were immaculate, for he was working in what used to be the old man's office but which was now his and today he had no need of the old clothes he always donned to work in the experimenting shed. He was freshly shaved and looked exactly as he did each morning before he set off for the glass works. But the unleashed, snarling anger of his temper was frightening.

"May I ask what my wife is doing here hanging over this . . . this slum-dweller?" The question was directed at Abby herself. His lips hardly moved and his eyes were dark slits in the gloom, narrowly glittering. Now that he was inside he was doing his best to keep his voice low. On the cobbles beyond the window a crowd had gathered, women from along Edge Bottom Row, tumbling out of their double row of cottages as word got round that there was excitement at Dorcas Baxter's place. Men from the yard and indeed from many of the buildings at the glass works, seeing their young maister stride from his office and almost run towards the cottages, were peering with great interest from doors and windows. Horses ready to draw heavily loaded wagons were momentarily left unattended as those whose job it was to see to them gathered outside the smithy to watch the fun.

"No, don't bother to answer," Noah went on. "Just stand up and come with me. I believe Olly has taken your mare back and will no doubt fetch the gig to bring you home. I will go with you though I have more than enough to do at—"

"Then return to it, Noah, please. I should hate to interrupt your work, for I know how important the glass works is to you. And to my grandfather who I'm sure will not be happy to hear you have left his precious business to run itself. I am staying here."

"No, you are not, madam. Get up and come with me at

once. This woman" – turning an icy stare on Dorcas – "can care for her own. He is her own, I suppose. The lad who disappeared last year . . ."

"Do you know anything about that, Noah?" Abby asked him almost idly as she continued to stroke Roddy Baxter's hair.

He did not deign to give her an answer. "Abby, I have had enough of this. You are my wife, the granddaughter of Bradley Goodwin, and this behaviour is reprehensible. I am aware that once you and . . . this lad were childhood sweethearts but your position in the community forbids you to—"

"I am staying here, Noah, and unless you want to drag me, screaming and fighting you every step of the way so that even those in St Helens hear me, this is where I shall remain. I have sent for Harriet, and Olly is to fetch the doctor. Until this . . . this man recovers . . . or dies," – she gulped and almost lost her composure – "I shall stay and help to nurse him. Mrs Baxter must rest. She has two other sons and cannot afford not to work."

"Lass . . . please, lass, do as yer 'usband tells yer." Dorcas was badly frightened by the barely controlled and vicious anger of Noah Goodwin which could be turned on her and her family. "Us'll manage, lass. Dear Lord, I wouldn't o' sent fer yer if I'd known but I were at me wits' end . . . 'im slippin' away, yer name on 'is lips. Oh please, Abby, Mrs Goodwin, go wi' yer 'usband before—"

Her words were cut short by a small commotion outside her door and they all turned towards it, even the two young boys who cowered in the corner as far from Mr Goodwin as possible. A polite knock on the door sent Dorcas to open it. The gig stood there, pulled by the small black and white cob, stocky, strongly built, but calm and steady and kept especially for the purpose. He could be driven by a child on a thread of cotton, the grooms boasted. The crowds that surrounded him did not appear to faze him but Harriet was clearly agitated, becoming even more so when she saw Noah Goodwin's savage face.

"Mr Goodwin, I did not think—"

"Apparently not, Mrs Pearson, and if you wish to remain in my employ you will get back in that gig and return home. My wife will accompany you."

"I've come on a . . . to bring help to a sick man, sir," she said bravely, but Harriet Pearson was no longer a young woman and should she be turned out of her job she would find it difficult to get another. She closed her mouth and waited.

"Very well, you may put what you have in the gig" – which was loaded with blankets and packages, baskets of mysterious bottles and jars – "inside the cottage and go back to Edge Bottom House. I appreciate that you are probably taking orders from my wife and so I will overlook this and say no more."

He moved to one side as Harriet sidled into the room and deposited her bundles on the table, then went back to the gig and brought in the rest which she put beside the others. She glanced apprehensively at Abby who continued her anxious contemplation of the desperately sick man on the palliasse.

Braving her master's wrath she spoke but once to her.

"The doctor's coming, Abby."

"Thank you, Harriet. You have been a great help, but perhaps you had better do what Mr Goodwin says. I will be home as soon as—"

Noah sprang forward and dragged her to her feet, his face contorted with rage. Dorcas, Harriet, Willy and Eddy seemed to fade into the walls in an effort not to be part of this contest between man and wife.

"Pull yourself together, girl and remember who you are. You do not belong here, do you hear me?"

"Yes, I hear you but unless you want me to tell you and all

the folk crowding outside this cottage what this man means to me then you will leave me in peace. I'm warning you . . ."

His face was like stone as he took a step or two backwards then slowly walked towards her, halting a bare inch away. He reached out and, holding her with one hand, he hit her twice across the face, viciously and accurately so that her neck muscles wrenched in agony and her head reeled.

Appalled by the terrible blankness in his eyes, they all gasped and the two boys began to cry, but Abby lifted her head and stared into his face. The blows he had struck her showed plainly across her fine skin but she was unafraid.

"Noah, I'm sorry to do this to you but I cannot stop myself. Because of me . . . oh, yes, I realise that now, this man has suffered more than any of us can know. None of us has been told his story, not yet, but I will not leave him, not while he is so ill and helpless. Let Harriet go home, for she is not to blame. The doctor will be here and when . . . when I am ready I will come home. I promise you. Don't force me. I suppose you can since I know in the eyes of the law I belong to you but I believe you to be a decent man."

He laughed harshly. "Do you indeed, and what of your grandfather? Do you honestly believe he will calmly sit at home and let his granddaughter, *my wife*, nurse her lover?"

"He is not my lover, Noah. You should know that. You—"

Dorcas had turned her face to the wall as the two protagonists faced one another but suddenly she turned back and forced herself between them. "That's enough, the pair o' yer. No more, I say. My lad's mebbe lyin' on 'is deathbed an' yer scrappin' like two dogs over a bone. This is my 'ouse an' I'm askin' yer ter leave, Mr Goodwin. She can do as she likes though it's 'er good 'eart what brought 'er 'ere an' I know it's that good 'eart what'll heal my lad. Think on that, Noah Goodwin. 'E can't tekk 'er from yer, not now. She's wed ter *you* an' that's the end of it so let's pull 'im through an' then . . . well, it's up to the pair o' yer what yer do."

Noah was beginning to back down. He was horrified at what he had done to Abby even though his rage still consumed him. He didn't know why, for Abby was really no more than a means to an end for him and he had already achieved it. He was fond of her. She was a lovely young woman and a good companion. Only in their bed did she disappoint him but that was remedied elsewhere. He wanted a son, not for Bradley Goodwin's sake but for his own. Though they had been married since December she had not conceived. He was honest enough to admit to himself that he did not believe that this wasted boy lying unconscious on the palliasse could be a threat to him so why did he not let her get on with it?

Because she belongs to you and you do not readily give up or share what is yours. That was why, but he could hardly drag her bodily home, not with half the glass works watching and sniggering. The old man would, that was certain, but then she might turn against them all and refuse to bear the child both he and the old man wanted so desperately. She had great power, had Abby Goodwin, though he did not believe she was aware of it.

There was a further ripple of excitement as a man riding a chestnut horse clattered round the corner from Bamford Street and into Edge Bottom Row. He looked about him as though not sure of his destination then, on seeing the crowd, "gidd-upped" to his animal and brought it to a halt at Dorcas's door.

"I presume this is the home of Mrs Goodwin?" he asked courteously, and the men and women who had never spoken to a doctor in their lives looked bewildered.

"I'm Doctor Bennett. I've been called out to a sick man. I wonder if one of you would be good enough to take care of my horse." He smiled round the huddle of people. John Bennett was that rare being, a clever young doctor who could have earned a pretty penny had he chosen to. But he cared little for the fees he could get from the wealthy although, should they ask, he would treat them. Not many did, for it was well known he went into the homes of the poorer classes and what might he bring back with him into *their* establishments?

Half a dozen men pushed forward for the privilege of seeing to the doctor's horse, though from the glass works irate overseers were beginning to descend on them. Mr Noah had deserted his office and it seemed half the workforce thought they could do the same. Only the men working in the crown furnace could not stop the delicate and expert work they were concerned with.

Doctor Bennett, reassured that his animal was taken care of, lifted a hand to knock on the door but it opened abruptly and a furiously angry man pushed past him and strode off in the direction of the glass works.

"The maister," a voice told him helpfully, but Doctor Bennett was concerned only with the sick man who had been reported to be at death's door by the groom who had hammered at his own door. Fortunately he had been at home, about to eat his midday meal and though his wife had protested half-heartedly, knowing it would do no good, he had leaped on to his already saddled animal and here he was.

He smiled reassuringly at the distraught woman who stood in the doorway. "Mrs Goodwin?"

"Nay, Dorcas Baxter's me name. My lad's badly so . . ." Dorcas, who, like the other inhabitants of Edge Bottom Row, had had no dealings with the medical profession, let her voice peter out uncertainly in its presence. The only time a doctor had been seen in these parts was when young Master Richard had been killed, and she was not sure how this one should be treated.

"I've been told there is a young man who needs medical attention. Have I the right house?"

"Aye, come in." Dorcas moved aside silently to allow the doctor to enter, then shut the door firmly in the faces of those who had come to watch. The men drifted back to their work but the women continued to stand, their heads together, in the roadway.

If Doctor Bennett was surprised when a tall, immaculately dressed and very pretty young woman rose from the bedside of the man he presumed was his patient he did not show it, nor his amazement at the sight of her long legs in skin-tight breeches.

He bowed politely. "Madam," he murmured, thinking her to be a lady.

"I'm Mrs Goodwin. I was the one who sent for you. Mrs Baxter's son is seriously ill." She turned with a distraught gesture towards the palliasse. "He's been away but returned like this . . . when was it, Dorcas?"

"Two weeks."

"Let me see." He crouched down on the stool which Abby had vacated and pulled back the covers that were tucked up about Roddy's neck. He was a doctor and had seen many a nasty sight in the poorer areas of St Helens but the suppurating pulp of Roddy Baxter's back drew an involuntary gasp from him. With Dorcas and Abby hovering at his side, he was aware that he must not show too much.

"He looks as though he has been flogged." It was as if he were talking to himself. "Poor lad, where can he have been to . . . ?" His sure hands moved about Roddy's thin frame, searching for further injuries, carefully lifting and turning with Abby's help. Roddy muttered and tossed and though he was not conscious seemed to object to the doctor's handling, gentle as it was.

"Well," the doctor said at last, "we have our work cut out

here, ladies, but with good nursing and attention we'll have this young man up and about in no time." He spoke with sure optimism which was assumed for their sake. "The wounds on his back have turned septic. There are germs in there which are poisoning his system."

"Germs? What are those, Doctor?" Abby asked hesitantly.

The theory of germs was something Doctor Bennett could talk about at great length but this was not the time nor the place. He had corresponded with Louis Pasteur, a French chemist whose work he admired, and had Abby and Dorcas chosen personally the man to heal Roddy Baxter they could not have made a better choice.

By the end of the day Roddy had been been treated with an antiseptic, a phenol spray which was directed on every area of his back after it had been thoroughly cleaned of all the pathetic unguents and ointments Dorcas had smeared him with over the past fortnight. She was devastated to learn that these had not only *not* cured him but had made matters worse. The two women were instructed on the cleansing and dressing of his wounds, dressings soaked in phenol, and the need for absolute cleanliness.

Dorcas was somewhat inclined to take offence, for was not her home immaculate, scrubbed and scoured and polished almost every day, no matter how tired she was, but the doctor patiently sat her down, held her hands and explained to her that it was not enough. No one, *no one* was to touch the patient without first washing their hands thoroughly. He was to be kept warm, covered by a clean sheet, which must be changed regularly, and kept as quiet as possible. If they could get him to drink it must be water that had been boiled and he was to be watched over at all times. He would be back this evening, he told them briskly, to check that . . . he had been about to say that his orders were being carried out but the two faces, one old and haggard, the other so pretty and drawn, held an expression that told him that the lad was in good hands.

It was later in the afternoon when the squall began again but this time it was the old man, Bradley Goodwin himself. Abby had changed into the plain dress and sturdy boots that Harriet had fetched from the house and after urging Dorcas to slip upstairs and have a rest on Willy and Eddy's palliasse, she was hanging over Roddy, her hands longing to touch him, to soothe his restless murmurings. She had washed her hands for the umpteenth time, topping up the water in the big pan and the kettle and bringing both to the boil again on the glowing fire. It was warm in the kitchen, stuffy, for the doctor's warning about germs had frightened both of them and they kept the windows and doors tightly shut to keep them out.

The closed door did not keep Bradley Goodwin out and the occupants of Edge Bottom Row were once again treated to the sight and sound of Abby Goodwin being roared at to get her things and get into the bloody carriage. There was even an attempt to manhandle her out of the cottage and into the vehicle. He had done it once before at her mam's cottage in Sandy Lane and had succeeded, but the girl who guarded Roddy Baxter was not the same one who had gone meekly with her grandfather a year ago.

Olly had hurriedly climbed down from his coachman's perch and was forced to stand at the horses' heads, for the sound of the old man shouting his rage was making them uneasy. There were children everywhere, which didn't help, and women who stood, arms wrapped in their shawls, telling one another they had never been so entertained in many a long year.

Abby's voice was calm though she did not feel it. "I told my husband early today that I would not return to Edge Bottom

House until Roddy Baxter has recovered and I'm saying the same thing to you so you might as well get in the carriage and go home. Mrs Baxter can't manage—"

"Bugger Mrs Baxter and bugger that lad in there. You're my granddaughter, the wife of Noah Goodwin and will do as you're told." His face was a mottled red and purple and Abby thought for a distracted moment that he meant to strike her, or fall in a heap at her feet. His colour was appalling, the red patches on his face leaking into his eyes. His lips were a thin line of pure venom and his hands were like claws, longing, she was sure, if not to strangle her then to force her into the carriage.

"You cannot force me," she told him quietly, wishing the doctor was here to lend her some support. Dorcas had crept down the stairs and was standing wide-eyed at the bottom, one of the blankets Harriet had brought draped about her shoulders, but she was no help, for she was of the class that was subservient to those above them and did not dare argue. Besides which she was seriously debilitated by the thought that her son was ill and might not recover. She had suffered the pangs of a loving mother these last months, not knowing where he might be, and the sight of the man who ruled them all in this part of the world weakened her even further.

"*Get into the carriage, madam, or I won't answer for the consequences,*" Bradley Goodwin hissed. "I will be obeyed and let me tell you that from now on you . . ."

It was strange really, Abby was to think later, that the young man who he had done his best to destroy, for she was certain that it had been Bradley Goodwin, should be the one to destroy *him*. The old man had moved menacingly over Dorcas's doorstep and was advancing into the kitchen, his intention to have his own way in this, as he did in everything, quite clear. The horses were proving a bit of a handful for Olly and when some chap, God knows who he was, offered a helping hand he left him to it. As he entered the kitchen, certain that murder was about to be done, he was in time to see the old man go down like a tree just felled, his head narrowly missing the corner of the table. Dorcas moaned, her hand to her mouth, but Abby made no sound nor movement. If she thought at all she thought of the man on the palliasse, for would this turbulence cause him further harm? That was all she cared about and the man at her feet was no more to her than an insect squashed by an uncaring foot.

Olly leaped over the bit of drugget which lay across Dorcas's kitchen and kneeled down at his master's side. "Mr Goodwin, sir?" he quavered, for it was obvious even to him that there was something seriously wrong with the old man. He put out a nervous hand and laid it, knowing of no other place, on the master's forehead, which told him nothing. "Mr Goodwin, are yer all right, sir?" he pleaded, which again evoked no response.

An excited male head peered in at the kitchen door, a crowd behind it, none of them wanting to miss a moment of this intoxicating event. They were none of them bad people, or unfeeling, but their lives were so hard and uneventful this was like watching a play. Or so they imagined, for not one of them had seen such a thing.

"Shall I go fer't maister, missis," he enquired, meaning, of course, the *young* master and it was this that brought Abby from her strange trance.

"Thank you, I'd be obliged," the wife of the young master said calmly. As he told his wife later you could have knocked him down with a feather, for they all knew where *she'd* come from and the way she had once spoken. Just like them, in fact!

Noah had no need to push them all aside, for they stood back respectfully as he skirted the carriage and entered the kitchen. The garbled message from the excited messenger had told him that the old master had fallen down, for the fellow knew no more and that the mistress "would be obliged" if the young master would step across to Dorcas Baxter's place.

He scarce gave his wife a glance. He dropped down swiftly on one knee and put his fingers on the old man's neck where his pulse should be and when he found none looked up at Abby, a flash of excitement in his face.

"He's dead." He turned to look at the groom who was still hovering at the bottom of the stairs. "Ride for the doctor, Olly. Take my horse from the yard and tell him that . . . that Bradley Goodwin has . . . that he is needed once more at Edge Bottom Row. And Abby, pack your things and get in the carriage. I believe your place is at home in the circumstances."

There was still an excited glitter in his eyes and as he stood up and moved towards her she heard him whisper so that Dorcas could not hear, "Thank God for that."

He was ready to take her arm, to help his bereaved wife to her rightful place beside him but she gently freed herself.

"I can't do that, Noah. I can't return to the house with you, not yet. I must help Dorcas to nurse Roddy. I'm sorry, but you have what you have always wanted, haven't you? The glass works are yours now and you really have no need of me."

13

She was dozing in the old armchair by the fire when the sound woke her. She had developed a knack of sleeping but at the same time of being aware of the man on the bed and his every movement, and when the sound was repeated, she leaped from the armchair and crouched down by the palliasse. He still lay on his stomach, his cheek pressed into the thin pillow, both arms pinioned at his side but by the light of the candles, those that Harriet had secreted to her with the rest of the stuff, she could see the gleam in the one eye that was visible.

"Roddy," she whispered. "It's me. Can you hear me? Oh, Roddy, my love, nod your head if you're able and let me know what . . ."

"Thirsty . . ." His lips were still cracked and peeling though she and Dorcas moistened them frequently. His voice was hoarse but she could see the light of sense in his eye. The doctor had left a ceramic cup with a spout, and with a glad heart she half filled it with boiled water and carefully guided the spout to his lips. He drank deeply and at once fell back into the unconscious state he had been in for days. He breathed so deeply, so harshly it was as if he snored. His mouth was partly open, the stink of his foetid breath in her nostrils, but as she hunched over him she could see what seemed to be a slick of sweat across the back of his neck and his cheek. Had his fever broken? Should she call Dorcas? Should she send for the doctor? Though he was washed as often and as gently as they dared, he smelled unsavoury. But she didn't care.

This was Roddy, *her* Roddy with whom she had loved and
laughed, shared sweet memories, shared her life with for as
long as she could remember. When they were no more than
bairns they had gone everywhere together, and her last truly
happy day had been spent with him when they went skating
on the dam. She could not bear to lose him again. She was
focused on nothing but restoring him to the endearing young
man he had once been and if it crossed her mind that she was
another man's wife, it did not trouble her. This was where
her life was, her heart, her future and without him she was
nothing. Noah Goodwin no longer existed, nor any of the
world she had known since her grandfather had brought her
to Edge Bottom House. Here was her world, her love and she
would fight to the bitter end to prevent him from slipping
away from her again.

She had barely shed a tear since she had been summoned
to Dorcas's cottage but she did so now, great fat droplets
that slid silently from her eyes and across her cheeks to fall
on the cheek and tangled hair of the man she loved. He
was not even recognisable as irrepressible Roddy Baxter,
this hollow-textured, bony, six-foot skeleton, this fretful,
mumbling stranger who had come back to them. Where had
that man gone? she agonised. What adversity, what nightmare
had he known? Where had he been? But until he was lucid,
and if she and Dorcas had anything to do with it, one day he
would be, they would never know. She could not bear to think
of it. For him to die would be unbearable, but the thought of
him slipping away without her knowing what had been done
to him and by whom was insupportable.

"Roddy," she sobbed soundlessly, "come back to me,
sweetheart. You see I can't live without you. I told you that
a year ago and it's still true." She dropped light kisses on the
cheek that was turned to her, across his closed eyelid and his
eyebrow. She put her own face on the pillow so that she was

face to face with him, the tips of their noses almost touching and when he murmured her name her heart lurched.

"Roddy . . . Roddy, love," she said, whispering through her tears and the thickness in her throat. She lifted herself carefully on to the palliasse, lying next to him. She slipped her arm under his neck and drew him gently closer. "Come, sweetheart, lay your head on my shoulder." She felt him tremble and knew he was conscious, if not fully to his surroundings, then of her. He sighed then relaxed and she knew he was sleeping, a natural, healing sleep.

Bradley Goodwin was laid to rest on a mild spring day a week later and in the churchyard the birdsong was at its glorious height. The dew lay heavily on the greening grass, wetting the footwear of the mourners, and sparkled in the bright sunshine on spider's webs, picked out with beads of moisture, every strand a silken maze like a necklace of diamonds.

For the length of time it took to put Bradley Goodwin in the ground, his granddaughter stood at her husband's side. She had left the cottage where, it was whispered, she had taken up residence and where her *lover* lay mortally wounded, wearing the decent black that the woman who called herself Goodwin's *housekeeper* was reported to have sent across for her on Noah Goodwin's instructions. She stood passively on view during the interment, showing no emotion, her mind elsewhere, those who watched were inclined to believe. No tears, though many of the ladies who scarcely knew Bradley Goodwin held a black-edged handkerchief to their eyes. Later, as the top-hatted gentlemen and black-veiled ladies were making their way back to their carriages the young newlyweds, such a handsome couple, could be seen arguing in the shadow of the porch and for a terrible moment those watching thought he lifted his hand with the intention of striking her. And that sister of Noah Goodwin's didn't help matters by refusing even to stand in the pew beside his wife, though one could hardly blame her, for in her and indeed everyone's opinion Mrs Noah Goodwin was behaving outrageously.

"When are you to come home, madam?" Mrs Agnes Holme heard her hiss at her sister-in-law in the church porch. "Your duty is with your husband and your husband's household and not with that . . . that low fellow you seem to think it necessary to nurse. I'm surprised my brother doesn't assert his rights and drag you home where you belong. I'd take a horsewhip to you if you were mine."

"Thank the good Lord I am not," Mrs Noah Goodwin answered icily, "and I'd be obliged if you would get out of my way."

There was to be the customary fruit cake and sherry back at the house, for some of the mourners had come a fair distance. All around the churchyard were men and women, workers from the glass works, which was closed for the day, rubbing shoulders with manufacturers and colliery owners, hundreds of them who owed respect to Bradley Goodwin and now knew that they must show the same feelings towards the man his granddaughter had married. It was all his now, for what a wife owned, earned or inherited went automatically to her husband.

The news of Bradley Goodwin's death and of how it had occurred had caused a scandal of such proportions in St Helens that wherever more than one person gathered it was the sole topic of conversation. On street corners and in public bars men speculated on what the lass thought she was up to, for there was nothing more sure than that Noah Goodwin, who was known for his temper, would not allow his wife to continue living under the same roof as that lad. In drawing-rooms over afternoon tea ladies gossiped, and when the rumour reached them that the young man she was purported to be nursing had worked in Bradley Goodwin's own glasshouse and that he and she had been . . . well, should they call them *friends* or *lovers* before she married poor Noah, the guesswork was intense. But then she had come from poor beginnings and really, you couldn't make a silk purse out of a sow's ear, one lady said to another behind her fan. Bradley Goodwin had tried, God knows, what with governesses and the like but see where it had got him. God had put folk on this earth where He intended them to be, everyone knew that, and there they should stay until He called them to Him. So said the ladies who had entertained her and been entertained in her grandfather's house but who had known really that beneath it all Noah Goodwin's wife was still of the lower classes. So it was repeated all over the town.

And not just among polite society! When the news reached Sandy Lane that Roddy Baxter had turned up a bit the worse for wear and that Betty Murphy's lass, who had once been sweet on him, had left her husband and moved in with the lad at his mam's place, they were as shocked as the rest of the community. Betty Murphy might be poor and hardworked, as they all were but, except for that one slip with Richard Goodwin, was a decent woman and it seemed the lass had shamed her and her family.

Abby was unconcerned with the gossip simply because she did not hear it. Noah Goodwin was a man whose pride and arrogance would not allow him to beg and after that first furious attempt to force her to come home he had not been near Dorcas's cottage. But on the day before her grandfather's funeral he rat-tatted sharply on the door with his riding crop, unable, it seemed, actually to touch the cottage door, and told her coldly that for the old man's sake she must attend since he was her grandfather. She had agreed absently. It was her turn to sit beside Roddy while Dorcas slept and she had been busy washing and boiling the bandages which were changed each time the doctor called. Doctor Bennett was pleased with his progress, telling them that his back, thanks to the phenol, was healing nicely and that as soon as his fever had broken he would make a good recovery.

She and Dorcas had been elated, hugging one another and ready to dance a jig round the kitchen.

"I'll mekk 'im a good pan o' broth. If yer'll watch 'im fer an hour I'll get down ter't market and buy some fresh vegetables an' a pound o' shin beef. There's nowt like shin fer nourishment. Eeh, lass, us'll 'ave 'im right by the end o't week, you wait an' see."

And now she was hurrying away from the graveyard of St Mary's Church, just off Church Street, where the funeral service and interment had taken place, eager to discover if, during the two hours she had been absent, there had been any improvement, even in such a short time. None of the mourners had spoken to her, or even acknowledged her presence and she had wondered at the absurdity of it all. Noah had insisted she stood beside him, probably thinking about the future when she was back at Edge Bottom House and entertaining would begin again, after a decent period of mourning, of course. His voice had hissed in her ear that she was to come back to the house for the refreshments but short of dragging her by the arm and thrusting her into his carriage in full view of everyone, there was nothing he could do. It was bad enough as it was but there was still the hope that he could make this look as though she was merely helping an old friend nurse her sick son.

Abby was astonished when, at the corner of St Mary Street and Foundry Street, a figure seemed to come from the very bricks of the wall that surrounded the abattoir which resounded with the noise of panicking animals. It was Harriet Pearson. Abby had seen her standing among the servants by the graveside and had smiled and bowed her head but now, looking agitated and very pale in her total black, she stood in her path, looking about her as though afraid to be seen.

A herd of cows were just being driven through the enomous wrought-iron gates of the abattoir, uneasy and inclined to be restless as though they sensed this was not a good place to be. The men driving them wielded cracking whips and shouted. The animals' hooves slipped and clattered on the cobbles and it was several minutes before Harriet could make herself heard.

"I've been ordered not to talk to you," she said breathlessly as though she had been running. "I daren't come to the cottage. Someone would report it back to him and I can't lose this job, Abby, you know that." Her voice was pleading. "But I had to speak to you. To warn you . . ."

Though she didn't know why, Abby took Harriet's arm and drew her close to the high wall behind which murder was being done, just as though they too were both in danger. Her drawn face became even paler and she was suddenly afraid. Again she didn't know why.

"To warn me? Against what?" Her voice rasped in her throat. She was tired, bone weary after so many hours crouched at Roddy's bedside and wanted nothing but to get back to Dorcas's cottage and roll into bed. Dorcas had promised she wouldn't go to her job behind the bar at the Glassmakers Arms but would chance the landlord giving her the sack so that Abby could have a decent sleep. They both needed it, for even when she was supposed to be resting as Dorcas took her turn, Abby found she couldn't relax and Dorcas was the same.

Harriet cleared her throat and took a deep breath. "He's . . . he's had a solicitor call on him."

Abby looked puzzled. "I don't understand."

Harriet took her by the arms and shook her so that the rather fetching black bonnet Miss Beckett had provided wobbled over her eyes. "The law, you fool. You're his wife. He's making sure of his rights should you ... not come back to him."

"His rights?"

"As your husband. Your grandfather left everything he owned to you, and consequently to Noah. If you continue to refuse to come back to him he has no choice but to ... ."

Abby's eyes narrowed. "What?"

"I'm not sure but you must know a husband has the law on his side. Are you to come back to him?" Harriet bent her head a little to peer under the brim of Abby's bonnet. Abby stared down at her own hands which were clasped placidly before her as though she were in church, denied by the churning and twisting of her insides, which were in turmoil. She had not thought beyond Roddy. Making him well. Bringing him back to the straight, tall, laughing young man she had once known. Healing him, returning him to the life he had led as a boy. Leaving behind the mumbling, restless wreck who had come back to them, but now Harriet's words hit her solidly in her chest and she could hardly breathe.

She was Noah Goodwin's wife. She had shared his bed since last December and had grown used to accommodating his need of physical pleasure, though she could not say she shared it. He was a powerful man, the owner, through her, of the largest glass works in St Helens, with enormous influence in the district, taking over from her grandfather. Could he force her to return to him? Would he want to after the scandal she had caused? Did she want to live as Mrs Noah Goodwin, taking part in all the trivial pursuits ladies of his class indulged in? His casual, tolerant affection had been pleasant enough, demanding nothing of her except a strict adherence to the rules and conventions of his society, and it would be expected that she would return to it when she had got over this mad desire to help nurse the son of Dorcas Baxter.

Abby was making for Market Street which led past Kidds Foundry, across a bridge and to the fields which were a short cut back to Edge Bottom. She had ridden beside Noah in the carriage which was now his to St Mary's Church, both of them turning their heads away from one another but though she would rather have made her own way, for his sake she kept up the pretence he demanded.

Market Street was a swirling throng of housewives, decent working-class women hurrying along the pavement from shop to shop, looking for a bargain. They would be on their way either to the newly opened covered market or to the open-air market stalls that stood before it and where anything from a packet of pins, bootlaces, fruit and fish, second-hand garments, rolls of material and boots might be purchased. They took little notice, it seemed, of the equally busy roadway they had to cross to get to it and which teemed with carriages, hansom-cabs, drays piled dangerously high with the dozens of products that St Helens and the area about it manufactured. Sacks of alkali, chemicals, coal, crates of glass, soap, barrels of beer, all making their way either to the canal boats which carried them to every part of Lancashire, or to the St Helens to Runcorn Gap Railway which finished up on the River Mersey. All over the world went the produce of St Helens and it seemed that most of it was on Market Street that day.

"I can't leave him, Harriet," Abby said desperately. "It's my fault he's in such a dreadful state."

"No, no, Abby. You weren't to blame. You were manipulated by two unscrupulous men for their own ends. Your grandfather was a man who would stop at nothing to achieve them. When his son died he turned to you, sweeping aside everything that stood in his way. Roddy Baxter stood in his way because you loved him."

"I still do." Abby's voice was passionate.

"Then what are you to do, my love?" Harriet asked gravely.

"I . . . I can't think. I must have time to think."

"You are his wife."

"I know. Dear God, d'you think I don't know?"

"I must go, Abby or they will miss me. They are going back to the house, most of them. Dear Lord, he will be in a foul temper. I think he imagined you were ready to come back."

"I don't know why he wants me," Abby said distractedly. "He's got the works and the house and I know he goes . . . goes somewhere to other women so why should it concern him what I'm doing, or where I'm doing it?"

"You don't know?" Harriet looked astonished. She was a woman of the world. There was no female who knew as much about men as she did and her face as she looked at Abby was quite comical in her amazement.

"Know what?" Abby was equally amazed. A bowler-hatted gentleman who was passing looked at them closely, his expression admiring, for though they were both deep in the black of mourning they were more than attractive, especially the younger one. Harriet, despite her age, was still a pretty woman and she suited black which gave an alabaster pallor to her unlined skin.

"Know what?" Abby repeated, but Harriet turned away and shook her head.

"I really must go but should you need anything, if I can I will do my best to help you. Clem is sympathetic," mentioning the older groom who worked with Olly. "He has a . . . a liking for me and will take a message. He drinks in the Glassmakers Arms."

Without another word or looking back she hurried away in the direction of a hansom-cab rank in Church Street.

Abby watched her go for a moment, a puzzled look on her face, then, shrugging her shoulders, she turned in the direction she must go. After crossing the bridge that spanned the canal she ran quickly along the track in the direction of the fields.

She climbed the stile and waded through the grass and wild flowers in the meadow, then another and a third, coming out on the lane known as Edge End. Edge End led directly to Edge Bottom Glass Works and the double row of cottages where the Baxter family lived.

It really was a glorious day, mild and sunny, the sky clear and unsullied in this part of the world with the glass works closed. She would love to have lingered in the fields, since it was a week since she had been out of doors. The usual pall lay over St Helens to the north but the small breeze was taking it northwards and she could see the rise of the moorlands which surrounded the bowl in which the town lay.

His carriage stood outside Dorcas's door, the hood down, and in full view of the occupants of the cottages, many of whom had been to the laying away of the old man, sat Noah Goodwin. She had turned the corner and though it was an unusual sight in this narrow street she was halfway along it before she realised its significence. Because of the day and respect necessary to their dead master, none of the usual clamour was about. Children had been kept indoors and the womenfolk refrained from gossiping, arms akimbo, in their own doorways.

She paused for a moment. His back was to her, for he had entered the street from the same direction as herself. Olly sat on the coachman's seat, his back straight, his eyes, she presumed, staring at nothing as he waited for his new master's command. But she must go forward. She felt she really couldn't manage another encounter, not in her debilitated condition, but she must. It had to be faced. *Again!* He had tried to force her into going home with him in the church porch, hissing that she was his wife and her duty lay at Edge Bottom House. She knew he hated himself for being in the position of having to beg and she knew he hated her for putting him in it. She had thought he would strike her but he had drawn back and turned away. Now he was here, leaving, she presumed, the astonished mourners to their own devices back at the house.

She lifted her chin. Squaring her shoulders she strode forward, coming to a stop beside the carriage. He still wore the total black of his mourning suit and his top hat was perched somewhat rakishly on his dark hair. It made her want to smile. He had always had that inclination to be different to the rest, to wear his clothes with a dash and style that made him stand out from other men. The tilt of his hat was an indication of this. He had a cigar clamped between his even white teeth and the smoke curled about his head.

He did not turn to her but continued to stare at Olly's back as she stood patiently, like a housemaid awaiting orders by the carriage door.

"Noah?" she said politely. An hour ago they had been arguing in the church porch but it served no purpose to alienate him further.

"Get in the carriage, Abigail. This nonsense is at an end. My forbearance is at an end so get in the carriage and let us go home."

"I cannot, Noah. Edge Bottom is not my home but that is not the reason I can't come with you."

"Then what is?"

"I think you know the answer to that. Roddy Baxter is still at death's door and until I'm convinced he is not to go through it I must stay by his side."

"You are my wife. In the eyes of God and the law—"

"Don't tell me you are concerned with God, Noah."

"In the eyes of the law then, you are my wife. We made a commitment to one another and we are bound to honour it. Your place is by my side not hanging over the sickbed of a man who is nothing to you. I appreciate that when you were both younger, you were sweethearts but when he went away . . ."

"Was *taken* away, for nothing but force would have parted us."

"When he went away you chose to marry me. You are my wife not only in name but in fact, as I'm sure you remember. You may be acting from a feeling of pity, or guilt, in nursing this man but I cannot condone it. I have kept my distance from you for a week but no man, even one in his state, will make a fool of me. They are already whispering about your behaviour and *mine* in allowing it and it must end, so get in the carriage. We will send for your things. I would really advise you to obey me, Abigail, for you know I can make things hard for . . . for the people in this cottage."

"She cannot manage without me. She has two young children and work to go to. She cannot leave Roddy in the condition he's in."

"I care naught for his condition, or hers. You are my wife so get in the carriage."

Her face worked and she could feel the tears gather at the back of her eyes but she must not weep, nor would she beg. She was this man's wife and the law was on his side, but it was not that so much as his veiled threat to hurt the family of the man she loved that frightened her.

"I will come back, Noah, but I need another week. That's all I ask, a week more. The doctor says—"

"Don't tell me what the doctor says, Abigail. It does not concern me."

There was a long silence, for they both knew there was nothing more to say. She had put her hands on the door of the carriage as she spoke, glad of the support, she supposed. She looked down at them then stepped away. Her face was bleached of all colour and the bones stood out but Noah Goodwin did not turn his head to look at her. He had not done so during the whole conversation.

"I will come home when he is recovered, Noah. Until then . . ."

Noah lifted his handsome head and spoke to Olly's back. "Edge Bottom House, Olly," he said, still not turning to her. She slumped against the door of the cottage and when Dorcas opened it she fell inside and into her arms.

14

"Yer goin' back to him, then?" The voice from the low bed in the corner of the kitchen was bitter, with a sadness in it that clutched at her heart.

She turned from the shirt she was ironing using the old sadiron, the name a corruption of the word "solid" and which was heated by standing it close to the coals of the fire. There were two, one being used while the other was heated. Care had to be taken when using them; the intense heat from the iron could scorch the fabric and there was an irritating tendency for the iron to become coated with soot from the flames. Dorcas, who was a stickler for cleanliness, tidiness and a general air of immaculacy in her family, had picked the irons up, she told Abby, from an ironmonger's stall on the market for a few pence and was inordinately proud of the resulting improvement in her family's appearance.

Now that her son's health was improving Dorcas had taken up full-time employment again, leaving Abby to tend to him during the day. Willy and Eddy were at school and the shirt Abby was ironing belonged to Eddy. It was much patched and darned, the patches come from old garments picked up for a penny a bundle from the same source as the irons, though a different stall.

It was four weeks since Roddy Baxter had come home and for two of them Abby had helped to care for him. Doctor Bennett had professed himself pleased with his healing back but until he was stronger he must not leave his bed. For hours Abby had sat beside him, staring into the thin, sleeping face on the pillow, the frail and defenceless face of the man who was in this state because of her. Because of their love for one another and the intrigues of the greedy self-willed old man who had been her grandfather, he had been sent across the world, from where, her grandfather must have thought, he would never return. The halting tale of his forced conscription into the army, the brutality of the men he had served with, the conditions under which he was made to live, his desertion, for which he could have been hanged, would have broken a lesser man. Better class men did not join the army, and the recruits with whom he served were drawn from the dregs of the working masses. Many officers believed that flogging was necessary to enforce discipline and Roddy, because of his defiance in the face of his circumstances which he would not accept, had been flogged more than many. Only his determination to get back to *her* had kept him from being broken. His determination and strong will and perhaps his endearing humour, his nimble mind, his obstinacy had brought him home. It had taken four weeks to get him back to himself and but for her and Dorcas's constant nursing and their good luck in having the medical attention of a man like John Bennett, he would have died. Many doctors today still believed in "blooding", which further weakened an already frail man, in leeches and old-fashioned remedies such as purging, and the constant washing of hands and instruments was looked on by many as laughable.

But John Bennett's modern outlook, his belief in what he called "hygiene", the antiseptics he used had steered Roddy back on to the road to health. He still had a long way to go but soon, Doctor Bennet said, with summer ahead of them, he would be allowed, with his young brothers to help him, to stroll in the fields and flowery lanes nearby. At the moment he looked like a bearded corpse ready for burial, but the doctor told them cheerfully that he was on the mend and they could only believe him. Nevertheless they agonised over where the carefree, easy-going young man who had not yet reached his twentieth birthday had gone.

She must answer his question, the flat statement he had made. How was she to tell him what she must do? She was terrified that the answer might send him spinning back down the long spiral of his illness. She could only be truthful, for what was the use of prevaricating? The week Noah had agreed to – well, if he had not actually agreed, he had not refused – was up today and though he was still weak, Roddy could be left alone. Jinny Hardacre who lived next door had promised to look in on him during the day when Dorcas was out, and though Dorcas was reluctant to leave her lad in any care but her own and Abby's she had accepted. Jinny was young, good-hearted, married to a flattener at Edge Bottom and had as yet only two children and for a few pence a week which Abby had promised to pay would gladly help out.

"Roddy, I must." She tried to keep her voice steady but she knew the words plunged a knife into his heart. She thumped the iron up and down the small shirt, not daring to turn and look at him. "He's my husband."

"Yer love me, yer know yer do. We were to be wed an' would be if that old bugger hadn't knocked me senseless an' sent me to the other side o't world. It's took me over a year ter get 'ome to yer."

"I know, I know, oh Roddy, I know, but I thought you were gone for good. I looked for you. I searched the woods and the fields, everybody did. I didn't know what to think but . . . but now . . ." She bowed her head over the small shirt and a tear dropped on to the fabric. "Now I know *he* did it. The old man. He wanted me to carry on the name so he married me to Noah and Noah was willing because of the glass works. You were simply in the way. He knew I wouldn't marry Noah if you had been still here. It took me a long time . . . December . . ."

"Yer call that a long time, April ter December?"

"You didn't know my grandfather."

"Yer even speak different."

"He made me as I am. He made me into Noah Goodwin's wife and that is why I must go back."

"He didn't get yer wi' child, so Mam tells me. Not man enough ter—"

"Don't, Roddy, please don't." She banged down the iron and moved across the room to kneel at his side. Her hand was on his brow, smoothing back his lank hair, her vivid blue-green eyes glowing into his with all the love she had felt for him ever since they were children. It flowed over him, ready to nurture and sustain him with every breath she drew, with her own steadfast heart which was breaking in her breast and her voice was hoarse with emotion as she spoke.

"I must go. He is my husband—"

"It's that bloody 'ouse, them dresses and carriages an'—"

"No, *no!* You know me better than that. I made vows in a church and I must try to keep to them. He could have me brought back in any case. In handcuffs if necessary. The law is on his side and he could lock me up, even beat me should I be disobedient. If I go back willingly I can help . . . your mam, mine, the children. Please, Roddy, I must. I have no choice."

"We could go away."

"He has enormous influence. He would hunt us and find us and . . . and he would destroy you. No man will ever take what is mine, he once told me, and that includes me."

"Jesus, I love you. Please, Abby, what am I ter do wi'out yer? Please . . . I just can't bear the thought o' yer in 'is bed. Say yer'll stay wi' me."

"I can't. I can't."

"Then go. Go now. Get yer things an' go."

"I can't leave you on your own."

"I've ter manage on me own fer the rest o' me life. I might as well start learnin' now."

She walked along the grassy track that led to the stable yard gate, her bundle clutched to her and had she not known the track and its surface so well would have stumbled and fallen, for her eyes were blind with tears. She could just make out Poppy browsing peacefully in the meadow, the two carriage horses beside her and, cavorting about like a butterfly on the wind was what surely must be a thoroughbred horse. It was as black as ebony. It was the most beautiful animal she had ever seen and the thought passed through her mind that it had not taken Noah long to begin spending the old man's money. Olly and Clem leaned on the fence, their faces wreathed in blissful smiles, like two women doting over a baby. Clem was in his forties, a widower with a grown-up daughter married and gone away, but he was a well-set-up man, still attractive and lean. He had a cottage in the row at the back of the vegetable garden, living alongside Olly and his family, Renfrew the gardener with Mrs Renfrew, and Charlie Potter with his missis and four children. Charlie's children were all out earning a living in a decent way, for the old man would not employ nor house servants who were not respectable.

The two men turned as one and almost fell off the first rung of the fence in their amazement. Clem removed his pipe and touched his forelock with it and Olly looked uncertain, for he had been the one who had overheard – how could he help it? – the last conversation between this lass and the master. He it was who had been the most involved in the dramatic scenes in Edge Bottom Row and had seen the wreck of the lad who had come back, it was rumoured, from China or some such place on the other side of the world. It had been the talk of the kitchen when Mrs Pearson had not been about. She would not have gossip about their young mistress, she told them coolly, so they were not even to begin to speculate. Young Mrs Goodwin was doing what many ladies in society did and that was to help nurse the sick and those less fortunate than themselves. The fact that the sick man had been her sweetheart before she married Mr Noah meant nothing. She was there with the permission of her husband and the rumours that were bandied about were to be discounted.

They held their tongues until she was out of earshot but the moment she left the house they gathered about the kitchen table with their cups of tea – for a house without supervision soon falls into slack ways – speculating on what was to happen, not only to them but to the master, the new master.

"D'yer reckon us'll be turned off, Cook?" Nessie asked tearfully, for her mam would be livid if she lost this good place.

"Don't be daft, girl," Kitty said scathingly. "Master has ter be served whether mistress is here or not. D'yer think he's goin' ter cook his own breakfast and make his own bed?"

They all tittered. "But will she come back?" This from Ruby who had always had a soft spot for young Mrs Goodwin. She was that friendly and not a bit stuck up as she had heard from her friend who was in service with the Hardwicks, *her* mistress was.

"She's his wife, isn't she? What else is she ter do?"

"Nay, don't ask me." And it was at this precise moment that the woman who was under discussion opened the back door and walked in. She was dressed in the plain grey dress she had worn at Edge Bottom Row, the bundle she carried containing her change of underclothes. Kitty herself had cleaned, pressed and hung up the riding outfit she had been wearing when she had galloped off to Dorcas Baxter's a fortnight ago and which Olly had returned to her.

"Is there a cup of tea in the pot?" she asked mildly, putting her bundle on the bench and sinking down beside it, then, remembering who she was and who she *must* be from now on, she stood up again. If she was to be the true wife of Noah Goodwin and the true mistress of this house she could not sit down and drink tea with her servants as she had done in the past. Then she had been no more than a careless child who knew no better. Now she was a woman. She had matured beyond reckoning under the weight of her sorrow during the past two weeks.

They were all gaping at her as though she had returned from the dead, their cups halfway to their mouths, every last one in a state of shock which gave her time to pull herself together. She felt as though a great cold, slate-grey wave had come up and engulfed her, she who had never even seen the sea. It had swept her down, battered her against sharp rocks and then thrown her back to the shore, dying, but not dead, limp, broken with pain and grief, not only for herself but for Roddy who had turned his face to the wall as she turned to say goodbye. The movement had pulled down the sheet and his upper back had been revealed in all its horror. It was covered with a criss-cross of faded white lines from an earlier flogging, with small lines of silvery scar tissue in some spots where the welts had crossed. In some places the skin and muscle had been gouged out and still seeped blood, and the sight of it, though she had bathed it a dozen times, had nearly broken her determination. This had been done to him because of her and yet here she was creeping back to the man whose fault, at least indirectly, it was. But she had no choice. None!

"Perhaps a tray could be brought to my room," she said, addressing her remark to Kitty, "and then hot water for a bath. Is my husband at home?"

"No, madam," Kitty quavered, setting her tea carefully on the table. Cook turned hurriedly and began to bang about with pans and a basting ladle while the others scuttled to their allotted tasks.

"I'll go up then. Is the fire lit in my room?"

"No, madam."

"Have it lit, will you and then, when I'm dressed, I'll be down to speak to you and to Mrs Pearson."

"She's out, madam."

"If she returns send her up to my room, will you, Kitty, but before that, the tea."

"Yes, madam." Kitty bobbed a curtsey but the dead eyes set in the dead face of Abby Goodwin did not see it.

She was sitting in the velvet fireside chair, staring blindly into the small, cheerful fire which Kitty had lit when, after knocking softly, Harriet came into the room. She stood for a moment, looking at the despairing figure of her young mistress, then hurried across the room and dropped to her knees beside her.

"Abby . . . ?"

"Oh, Harriet . . . Harriet, how am I to do this? I have broken him, coming back to Noah but . . ."

"You could do nothing else, my love. Your place is here with your husband. I am amazed he has been so patient. Not many men would. Think about it and try to think well of him. He is enormously attractive and not unattentive to you. He will, I'm sure, be generous with you."

"With my grandfather's money."

"You knew that when you married him. You could have a good life if you . . . you behave yourself."

"And Roddy?"

"Who can say, dearest? If you leave him alone he will get on with his life as you must get on with yours. He must make up his own mind what he is to do. He has a trade and if Noah won't employ him I'm sure someone will. There must be no pressure on him such as you could apply."

"I love him, Harriet."

"I know. I have been in love myself, Abby. When I was in service. Oh, yes, I was a parlour-maid, very pretty, young and pretty. I could have married the gardener's lad but I set my sights on the young master. I was a fool, reaching for the stars when the flowers in the hedgerows were just as lovely and far more accessible. I was asked to leave when the young master had done with me and so my feet were set on the road that led me here. I played whore for your grandfather and for other men but now, now I am to marry. Oh, yes, my love. A good man has asked me and I have accepted."

Abby sat up violently, almost knocking Harriet on to her back. Her face was terrified, as bleached as bone and her eyes were enormous. "No . . . oh, God, no. You can't leave me, Harriet. Not now just when I need you the most. You're my only friend."

Harriet laughed softly, cupping Abby's cheek then kissing it gently. "I'm not to leave you, my love. I am to marry Clem and live in his cottage alongside the other servants."

"You're not a servant, Harriet."

"Oh, but I am, as my future husband is, but I thought . . . if you please your husband he might allow me to be your maid. A lady's maid. What I believe is called a companion. I believe many ladies in society have them. I'm good with fashion and could help you with running the house until you can manage on your own."

"Harriet . . . Harriet . . ."

"Don't cry, please don't cry or it will undo us both." She put her arms about the weeping girl and held her firmly, stroking her hair and making little murmuring sounds over her as though she were a hurt child.

"Come, enough. Let us go through your wardrobe and pick

out your most elegant gown so that when your husband comes home you will look your best. He will be pleased and if he is pleased he will do his best to please you – and your family. They and the Baxters will need your help in the future, you know that."

Harriet brushed her hair, her bright red curls which snapped round the brush reaching her buttocks. When she had dressed it into an enormous coil she placed a pale cream rosebud in its centre, perfumed her shoulders and wrists and put her in a new cream gown of lace over silk. She dressed her as though she were a doll in whom a buyer might be interested. Over her bare shoulders she draped a cream silken shawl and led her down the stairs to the drawing-room where a good fire was burning.

"Drink this," she said abruptly, putting a glass of brandy in her hand, then stood back until she had drunk it and a flush of colour touched her cheeks. She looked quite glorious, her eyes burning feverishly, the brilliance put there by the tears she had shed but which were no longer in evidence and the brandy to which she was unaccustomed. Somehow, Abby wasn't really sure when or how, Harriet had ordered dinner and brought up a decent bottle of wine from the cellar. The table in the dining-room was set for two, candles and crystal and silver gleaming on the snowy damask cloth with a centrepiece of cream roses to complement her gown.

Noah, who had been warned by the grooms of her return, strode arrogantly into the drawing-room, frowning, ready to snarl and snap and tell her it was about time, too, but at the sight of her by the fireplace, a smile on her lips – for he really did look comical in his amazement – a glass of champagne in her hand, which Harriet had thought appropriate, he came to an abrupt stop and allowed his mouth to twitch into what would become a wide grin.

"Abby Goodwin, I must say that when you do something

you do it in style, and I like that." She did not tell him that the whole charade was Harriet's idea! He turned and looked across the hallway into the dining-room which gleamed and flickered with candles and then to the kitchen from where came the mouthwatering smell of one of Harriet Pearson's exquisite meals. "Well, it seems I can't sit down to eat dressed as I am. Give me ten minutes to bathe and change and . . . well, we will see. You look very beautiful, Abby."

It seems he could not have been more pleased and Abby was to learn that Noah Goodwin, so sure of himself and his hold on her, had not for a moment doubted she would return to him. She had been a virgin on her wedding night and it hardly seemed likely, at least to him who was well versed in such things, that she and that lad had made love in his mother's cottage. She was as she had been on the day she had left Edge Bottom House. He cared, naturally, about the gossip that had been whispered about the township and in the homes of his acquaintances, businessmen all of them, for Noah Goodwin could not be said to have personal friends. But she was here, back where she was supposed to be and the talk would die down and be forgotten. He would get her with child and that would be that. He had everything he had ever wanted except for the child and he knew how to remedy that this very night. It would be no hardship. She had made good progress in her training to be the wife of a gentleman and would continue to do so. The governess, whatever her name was, could be kept on to further her education and would be handily available when the children came. Harriet Pearson was on hand to help her with the house and with Bradley Goodwin's money jingling in his pocket what more could he ask?

He began the gentle, stroking exploration of her shoulders, the curve of her breasts and the outline of her waist and thigh as soon as Kitty left them in the drawing-room with their coffee. He had made an amusing companion during dinner, doing his best to set her at her ease, making her smile and smiling back at her through the candlelight.

"To you, my pet," he said to her, toasting her with the dry white wine Harriet had chosen, his eyes warm and approving, but something in the set of his chin telling her that though it seemed he had forgiven her she had best watch her step from now on. The past fortnight was not mentioned and never would be, she imagined.

"Come to bed now, my darling," he murmured, his mouth against her neck, his hands delicately probing the low neckline of her gown and when she stiffened, holding her firmly as he poured two more glasses of the champagne that Harriet – and he – believed to be an essential part of seduction, a second bottle of which he had instructed the flustered Kitty to bring in.

"Don't think about it, Abigail, just leave it all to me," he murmured as he lifted her to her feet, which she did, allowing him to lead her up the stairs and into their bedroom which was fragrant with flowers and candlelight and firelight.

She had set herself to endure it, expecting to feel revulsion but, helped enormously by the vast quantities of champagne he poured for her, she found herself floating somewhere near the ceiling, detached from what was happening to the woman on the bed. The woman allowed the man beside her to remove her nightgown. She watched as he explored the woman's body in a leisurely fashion from the tumble of her hair to the soles of her feet; in the most intimate and tender parts of her body, turning her this way and that for his own pleasure and when he came to a shuddering climax and the act was over she closed her eyes and slept as did the woman on the bed.

He woke her twice in the night and repeated the whole, lingering process and she made no objection. She didn't love this man. She was grieving desperately for Roddy and knew she must find some way to see him, if only to find out how he was, but this night with her husband was her commitment to the start of her life with him. She prayed that he had got her with child, the most binding affirmation a woman could make to a man, for though she fully intended to keep the vows she had made in church and the pledge she had whispered to herself as she left Dorcas's cottage, a child would tie her to Noah as nothing else could. Besides, she would like a child, perhaps a little girl on whom to lavish her love, or a son to please Noah. A family. A family of her own, for since she had come to Edge Bottom House she had none. Her mother, her father, her brothers and sisters, though she would still do everything in her power to help them, were lost to her. A child . . . Dear God, she prayed as Noah turned away from her, let there be a child in my womb.

15

She and Holdy were in the nursery, or the schoolroom as the governess preferred to call it, when Kitty knocked at the door and in a state of extreme excitement told her that there was a lady asking to see her. *A lady*, for Kitty knew a lady when she saw one! Abby and Miss Holden were beginning the rudiments of French, a language that would stand her in good stead should her husband require her to accompany him on one of the business trips he increasingly took, Holdy told her. *Merci! Merci beaucoup! Bonjour!* were as far as she'd got, for the novel idea that Noah might take her to France with him was highly amusing and not a bit conducive to learning.

"Is she in a carriage, Kitty?" Holdy asked loftily, for if the caller was as described by Kitty a real lady, then the equipage should be standing at the front steps with a coachman in attendance. Well, not exactly at the front steps, for there were none as such at Edge Bottom House. An old stone pathway bordered by a low lavender hedge led from a small side gate on the lane up to the front door dissecting the smooth lawns, and those who called were forced, whatever the weather, to leave their carriage in the lane. Abby had always thought that the heady fragrance of the lavender more than made up for the inconvenience.

"No, but she's a lady all right. She speaks lovely." Kitty beamed at Abby, evidently well pleased with the quality of the person who, at this moment, was perched on a chair in the hall. The custom of calling cards seemed to have been overlooked, probably because there had been no *proper* mistress at Edge Bottom House for many years. In fact since the old master's wife had died and Kitty had been no more than a kitchen-maid then.

"Did she—?" Holdy began to speak, for it was up to her to create in this lovely girl the proper wife for Noah Goodwin. She was progressing well but she still had this inclination to be impetuous, as now, interrupting her and leaping to her feet.

"Who is she, Kitty? Did she give her name?"

"Oh aye. Mrs John Bennett, wife of a Doctor Bennett. She ses yer know him."

Abby felt her heart miss a beat and then surge forward at twice its normal speed. Doctor Bennett's wife was here asking to see her and she shrank inside herself for what Mrs Bennett might be going to tell her. She had been back with Noah for six weeks now and through the servants' grapevine, to which Harriet secretly listened, she had heard that Roddy had been seen about the village which meant he was recovered. She didn't know to what extent, of course, or whether he had found employment, and the lack of knowledge was hard to bear. She longed to go to Edge Bottom Row and see for herself, and several times had donned her riding outfit with the sole purpose of going over there. She rode almost every day and had become what Olly called a nice little rider with a good seat but at the last moment she had backed down, for she knew that the polite accord that now existed between her and Noah would be badly damaged if she went against his will.

The young woman in the hall was perched on an intricately carved elm bench with a velvet seat and back and as Abby sped down the stairs with far more haste than Holdy would have liked, she stood up and smiled tentatively. Laura Bennett was a lady of good family and was well used to the ritual of calling cards. But Laura was as radical as her husband and despised the foolish conventions of what was called "good" society, and having heard of the unconventional Mrs Goodwin from her husband had decided to call on her. She was pretty sure that a woman who had come from good working-class stock would not take offence.

"Mrs Goodwin, how lovely to meet you at last. My husband has told me so much about you." She smiled widely, nodding at the card-tray holder that stood on a side table. "I'm afraid I don't possess a calling card. I don't believe in them." She held out her hand and, surprised, Abby took it.

Doctor Bennett's wife was one of the loveliest women Abby had ever seen, with a perfect oval face and a great deal of glossy brown hair which, when her bonnet was removed, proved to be piled high on her head in a huge coil. Her gaze was frank and open and her eyes, a startling violet-blue, long-lashed and set wide apart, were kind. She wore a gown of plain cream cotton sprigged with tiny yellow roses. About her small waist was a wide sash of plain cream silk and her straw bonnet had several freshly picked yellow roses pinned to the brim. She looked fresh and smelled of some fragrance which Abby thought might be lemon.

She couldn't help herself. The first words she ever spoke to the woman who was to become her closest friend were, "How is he? I've had no word. Is Doctor Bennett still attending him? Oh, please, please tell me . . ."

Laura Bennett's smile deepened and she put a comforting hand on Abby's arm. In the background Kitty watched with fascinated interest, for the two women had forgotten her presence and if she hung about long enough she might have something to tell those in the kitchen. If that there Mrs Pearson was not about. She had already learned something, for the young mistress's first words had been about that lad she had nursed. So what were they to make of that then? Kitty felt a certain resentment towards Mrs Pearson, for Kitty had been made up with her elevated position as Mrs Goodwin's maid, weeks ago now, but Mrs Pearson had taken over so not only was she housekeeper but the young mistress's personal maid and Kitty was not best pleased about that.

Laura Bennett was the first to notice her hanging about and, knowing that the young mistress of the house was in a state of agitation, said gently, "Perhaps your maid might bring us tea or, if you have it, hot chocolate. We could talk in your drawing-room, if you agree. John has told me a lot about you and I felt I must come and make your acquaintance. I hope I'm not interrupting . . ."

"No, oh no." Abby turned distractedly to Kitty and repeated what Mrs Bennett had said as though Kitty were deaf or something and the pair of them moved into the drawing-room where, the day being warm, no fire had as yet been lit. Instead Kitty and Ruby had begged a huge bunch of hydrangeas from Mr Renfrew and had made a charming floral arrangement to put in the hearth. As she brought in the silver tray with a silver pot of steaming hot chocolate and two dainty china cups and saucers, she heard Mrs Bennett admire it.

"Oh, don't give me the credit, Mrs Bennett. I believe Kitty here is the artist."

"She is to be commended on her talent." Mrs Bennett smiled at her, and though Kitty was not sure what *commended* might mean she instantly felt a glow of pleasure, running back to the kitchen to tell Ruby and the rest that the visitor seemed very pleasant. They were to learn that Laura Bennett had that knack, that talent of making people feel good about themselves.

"Have you . . . forgive me, Mrs Bennett, but have you news of Roddy?" Abby begged.

"Laura, please, and if I may I shall call you Abby." Laura Bennett was six or so years older than Abby and far more sophisticated so she took the lead. She could tell that Abby cared not a whit whether they were on first name terms or not, indeed had no realisation of how far they had already wandered from the path of convention.

"Has Doctor Bennett mentioned him?"

"Oh yes, indeed." She sipped her hot chocolate and smiled at the younger woman. "He was very . . . taken with Roddy. His fortitude in the face of such pain and suffering. His resolution to get on with his life despite the many setbacks."

"Yes, but *how* is he? Mrs Bennett, please."

"Laura, and very well, he has recovered physically if not emotionally."

"What the devil does that mean?" Abby leaned forward and seemed ready to take hold of Laura and shake her.

"He loves you, Abby, and he has lost you so how would you expect him to feel?"

"Oh, dear Lord, bless him. What am I to do? I'd give anything to help him but my husband is—"

"I know, my dear, and there is nothing you can do. But John has used what bit of influence he has and Roddy is to start work next week at Mulberry Glass Works near Denton. It is a small glass works newly opened and the owner is an old school friend of John's. Roddy is to start in a lowly position, an apprentice, but as he has already served several years as an apprentice glass-maker at Edge Bottom Glass Works he should soon get on. We have a house in Claughton Street off College Street—"

It was evident that, though she intended no rudeness, Abby's concern was not for Laura Bennett's place of residence but was only for Roddy.

"Is his back healed?" This time she clutched at Laura's arm, almost causing her to spill her chocolate down her gingham skirt but Laura only smiled and patted the hand that gripped her.

"It is, thanks to his youth and previous good health. He has been walking in the fresh air, for my husband is of the opinion that exercise is very beneficial. He even talks of foot racing which I believe is very popular in these parts but John says no, not yet. I don't come from round here so these pastimes are new to me. My family live in Buxton and it was not until John and I married that I came north. This is quite delicious chocolate. You must congratulate your cook."

"Does . . . does he speak of me, Mrs Bennett? Does he know that I have no choice but to stay with Noah?"

"Abby." Laura's expression was grave. "You must put this young man from your mind. Your life does not run parallel to his and though I came here mainly to put your mind at rest, at my husband's instigation, I must add, on the matter of his recovery, I cannot talk about the young man in your husband's home. He is recovered. He has employment and that is as far as I can go to set your mind at rest. I have spoken to him when he came to see John—"

"How did he look? Has he put on weight?" A thin, anguished sound escaped from between Abby's lips and Laura Bennett was made to realise what the thin, solemn-faced young man who had been shown into her husband's study meant to this wife of Noah Goodwin. It was clawing her heart to rags, she could see that, and yet bravely she was struggling on with what she saw as her duty.

"My husband would not let him go back to work if he did not think him well enough. Now then" – she stood up and gracefully shook out the full skirt of her gown – "I must go. I have quite a walk."

At once Abby sprang to her feet. She was dressed more finely than Laura Bennett. A plain, pastel-tinted apricot muslin with a wide skirt and a fitted bodice which showed to good effect her splendid breasts and narrow waist. The nourishing food, the softer life she now lived had smoothed her passage from girlhood into a mature woman. "Oh, please,

Mrs Bennett, let me send you home in my grandfather's carriage."

Laura looked bemused, raising her fine, arched eyebrows. "Your grandfather's? I don't understand."

"I know, he's dead but I can't help believing everything still belongs to him. Of course, that's not true. My husband owns it all now. The house, the carriage, the works, even me."

"You mustn't think like that, Abby. Women like you and me . . . all women have rights although the law says not. John is very progressive and allows me to have a mind of my own, which I exercise and you should do the same. I hope you do not think I'm encouraging you to defy your husband but . . . I'm sorry, I should not be talking to you like this."

"No, Mrs Bennett, what you say interests me."

"I hoped you would call me Laura. John and I don't stand on ceremony. We are looked on as oddities amongst our own class, which again is something I abhor."

"Abhor?"

"Yes, there should be no such thing as class. Oh, I realise that every man, and woman, is not able to be employed on the same level but that is where education . . . Oh, Lord, I'm sorry, you have me on my favourite soap box. You have heard of the Chartists and their fight for equality. The Reform Act of 1832 gave the vote to half a million men, but why should not women vote? Tell me that. It is thirty years since then and still we are fighting for equality for all men . . . and women."

Abby's voice was uncertain. She had not the faintest notion what Laura was talking about. "Vote," she quavered.

"Yes. Politics! Have you not read . . . no, I can see you haven't. Can you read, Abby? Forgive me for being blunt."

"Yes, but Roddy can't. My brothers and sisters go to school now that I . . . encourage it."

"Good. All children should have schooling . . ." Laura

stopped speaking abruptly, then began again. "I'm sorry, I'm taking up far too much of your time."

"No, no, you have only to look at me to prove you are right. I could neither read nor write eighteen months ago, now I'm learning French, but I didn't think . . . I suppose . . ." Abby swung round and walked towards the winter garden, the door to which stood open. Like Mr Renfrew she preferred to call it the winter garden instead of the conservatory, for that was what it was. A garden for the winter months when outside it was bare and without colour while in here summer still reigned. She stopped at the door and Laura watched her.

This girl was unusual. She had expected to find some pretty little miss who had married above her but who had once dallied with a man of her own class. She had, it was true, a good heart which had probably saved Roddy Baxter's life and been staunch in her support of him when he was desperately ill, but the luxury and wealth of her husband and her new position in society had drawn her back. That was what she had believed when she left her home this morning, despite John's surprising admiration for Abby Goodwin. But her love for the young man shone through like a steady beacon on a dark night. She seemed to have a sharp mind, wit and intelligence, a quickness of thought that delighted Laura. Laura Bennett was interested in many things that were supposed to be beyond the powers of a woman. It was believed that women would be corrupted and that chivalry would die if they concerned themselves with anything outside their homes, but Laura treated this idea, come from men, with the contempt it deserved.

Abby swung back to her. "I suppose, if I insisted, I could become involved in the business my grandfather left to me but which, of course, my husband runs. I have been married for seven months and have no child and, to tell the truth, the thought of sitting here in this lovely room for the rest of my life, waiting for something to happen, appals me. I even have a governess for God's sake. They want me to learn to be a great society hostess. My job is to entertain my husband's business associates, to run his home, bear his children and do the mindless things women of his, and your, class do. I can't bear it, Mrs Bennett."

"Laura . . . Laura."

"Laura then. What do you do with your time, tell me that?" Abby's face was agonised and Laura was made aware that this young woman was heading for disaster if she did not find some outlet for her . . . what should she call it? Her obvious ability, her brightness, her energy, her mental capacity. In less than eighteen months she had learned to read and write and was learning French. What an addition she would make in the group to which Laura belonged, that is if her husband did not object. So many did. So many husbands were afraid that, should a wife find that she had a brain that worked as well, sometimes better than theirs, life as they knew it would come to an end. The world was a man's world and a woman's part in it was clearly defined as wife, mother, housekeeper. Nothing else.

"Abby, would you care to visit me in Claughton Street tomorrow afternoon? A small group of us have formed . . . well, they are far-sighted women who believe . . ."

She looked somewhat unsure for a moment. This young woman's husband had been given immense power and influence when Bradley Goodwin died and should he be defied might he not turn on the one who had defied him? And the woman who had persuaded her to be defiant? For herself she did not worry, but her husband was very dear to her and she did not want Noah Goodwin as his enemy. There was no way to do this without his permission, not at first, so moves must be made to *court* him, lead him into believing that friendship with herself was a good thing. She would do anything for the cause, the infant cause she so passionately believed in but it must be gone at in the proper way.

"Abby, why don't you and your husband come to dinner next week. I think perhaps it might be wise if we leave your visit tomorrow afternoon until later. I know how husbands can be, not my own, of course, but he perhaps would not care for you to make a friend of a woman he does not know. I have called today, which is perfectly proper, and an invitation to dine with us is not out of place. Ask him. Shall we say next Wednesday? Speak to him about it and let me know."

Claughton Street was in the better part of town, on the fringe of St Helens north towards Denton. It was a street in which the houses were occupied by those with some claim to gentility but who could not afford the out-of-town villas and country houses such as Edge Bottom House. It was a tall, narrow house with a long front garden, a flight of shallow steps to the front door with a fluted, many-coloured fanlight above it. The hall was narrow too and Laura Bennett noticed Noah Goodwin glance round disparagingly, for he was by now used to far grander surroundings than these. There was a thin staircase which led up into the gloom of the first floor but before either he or Abby had time to look about them they were whisked into a drawing-room bright with candlelight and firelight. There were colourful rugs scattered on the polished floor, pretty wallpaper in shades of white and rose, a large gilt-framed mirror over a veined marble fireplace and several comfortable, rather worn armchairs. Plants stood in the window bottom and on the mantelpiece. There were pictures, a porcelain clock above the fire and a couple of Sèvres vases on either side of it. A pleasant, comfortable room, a room warm with something that was lacking at Edge Bottom House and Abby at once understood what it was. There was love here, respect, friendship between husband and wife and when John Bennett strode in, apologising for not being there to greet them, he went at once to kiss his wife, a gentle kiss on her waiting lips.

It had been dim in the hallway with only one lamp at the foot of the stairs but here in the drawing-room Noah Goodwin had his first clear sight of the loveliness of Laura Bennett. Her gleaming hair was dressed in its single massive coil which made her neck seem very supple and long. Her gown was simple, a pale hyacinth-blue silk, the colour bringing out the incredible amethyst of her eyes and she had pinned some flowers on her shoulder.

John Bennett stood with his arm about his wife, smiling at Abby.

"Welcome," he said, "and to you, sir," holding out his hand to Noah, who took it with a great deal more enthusiasm than he had showed when Abby broached the subject of dining with the Bennetts. He had, of course, not then met Laura Bennett.

"That's that bloody man who—" he began.

"Yes, he is," Abby had interrupted, unable to bear Roddy's name on Noah's lips. "But his wife called today and . . . and left her card." She told the lie easily and Noah was led to believe that this could be start of his wife's reintroduction into St Helens society. A doctor was a professional man and though could not be of help to Noah in business, he was a gentleman and his wife a lady. Who knew where it might lead for Abby, and himself, through her, and Noah Goodwin was not a man to overlook any advantage in his climb to glory.

Laura was not a woman to be intimidated by any man, knowing of no reason why she should be, chatting of this and that while she and Abby drank sherry and the gentlemen brandy. She smiled and talked, she dimpled into laughter and it was clear that Noah was charmed by her. Her husband seemed a dry stick but he engaged Abby in some serious conversation, in whose contents Noah was not interested. He could not take his eyes from Laura's animated face. Abby barely noticed. All she wished to do was speak to John, as she had been told to call him, about Roddy, but she could hardly do that with her husband sitting in the room, even if he was flirting outrageously with their host's wife. John didn't seem to mind and she wondered at it, but then she had no conception of the love that existed between these two. He had watched his wife fascinate men ever since he had met her but he knew it meant nothing to her, though they sometimes didn't! He knew she was being deliberately charming and he knew why. She had taken to Abby Goodwin. She was inordinately sorry for the girl stuck in a loveless marriage and she wanted her for her group, as she called it, and to get her she must convince the husband that his wife would come to no harm at Claughton Street.

At the dinner table they ate a decently cooked roast duck brought in by a slip of a housemaid who fumbled her way through serving the meal. Not at all what the sophisticated taste of Noah Goodwin was used to, but Laura seemed to see nothing wrong in the dropping of the serving spoon, the clatter of the soup dishes, the clumsy pouring of the coffee and, besides, he scarcely noticed. His own wife was very elegant in her tawny brocade gown which exactly matched her hair and showed off to perfection the creamy skin of her shoulders and the soft upper swell of her breasts but his easy attention had been captured by Laura Bennett's delicate loveliness. She encouraged him to talk about his business concerns and his coming trip abroad; his plans to extend the buildings at the works and take on more men. She was keenly interested in his experiments in the flattening kiln, as was her husband, and was pleased to hear that he and Abby were to attend the mayoral ball at the town hall in a few weeks' time.

In the carriage on the way home Noah held her hand in preparation for what he would do to her when they were in their bed. He smoked a cigar, the fragrant smoke curling round his dark head and face which wore a satisfied smile. He was well pleased with the evening which he had agreed to reluctantly. She had done well, he told her, as though it were her efforts that had made the evening so successful. And he thoroughly approved of the Bennetts, though he had to admit he could not for the life of him understand why such a . . . a good-looking and charming woman as Laura Bennett could bring herself to marry a dull dog, with no pretension to good looks such as John Bennett.

"I think she loves him," she answered mildly, her mind not on her husband's preoccupation with Laura Bennett but with her own love and the few moments of private conversation she had had with John. He had told her that Roddy Baxter was, this very evening, enrolling at the Mechanics Institute, which had been established ten years ago for the education of young working men.

Noah made love to her as he did most nights, but when it was done he flung himself from the bed and strode naked to the window. He twitched aside the curtain and stared moodily out into the dark night, then, turning on his heel, made for the door.

"I can't sleep," he muttered. "I'm going out for a while. There's gambling in town." And she was made aware that he would find what he needed in the arms of some woman who was more energetic than herself in pleasing him.

16

Harriet Pearson became Mrs Clem Woodruff in September. It was hot, as hot as any summer's day with the voices of wood pigeons throbbing in the trees as they came out of the church.

"September's the month fer 'em," Olly remarked laconically to Ruby who had sat beside him in the pew, doing his best in the conversation stakes. "Wood pigeons, I mean," seeing Ruby's perplexed look. Conversation was not Olly's strong point. "Disappear in October," he continued, searching awkwardly in his mind for some other topic that would interest her, wondering if he dare take her arm. The trouble was he had no small talk and knew nothing except horses and the habits of the birds and animals of the countryside. But he did have a great taking for Ruby. She looked very smart in her "best" outfit, a walking-out dress of rich magenta dimity, a stout twilled cotton, and a saucy straw hat tipped over her eyes with a bunch of violets under the brim. They were all dressed to the nines, Ruby, May, Kitty, Mrs Grimshaw the cook, Nessie, all perspiring freely in the heat, but none was more exquisitely elegant than Mrs Goodwin. Olly himself was stiff and self-conscious in his good suit, which he had inherited from his old dad and which, having lasted his dad's lifetime, would do the same for him.

Harriet was dressed stylishly in a dove-grey skirt and short bodice, her small matching hat bobbing with silk apricot roses and her new husband, in his Sunday suit of dark grey, made a perfect foil for her as he smiled down fondly into her face. Surprisingly, she was quite radiant and Abby felt a pang of envy, for it seemed her friend was to be happy in her new situation. She herself smiled and nodded at them all, gathering with them on the path to throw dried rose petals at the bride and groom, and when they left for Edge Bottom House promised to join the wedding "breakfast" to toast the happy pair.

"Well, don't expect me to honour the company with my presence, my love," Noah had said at breakfast as he attacked the plate of perfectly poached egg on toast that Kitty had put before him. "And I hope you have impressed on them that I expect my meal to be at the usual time this evening."

"Don't worry, Noah. I'm sure by now they all know how particular you are about the smooth running of your home."

He glanced up at her sharply, looking for sarcasm, but she was serenely buttering a small slice of toast, her eyes on her task. She was wrapped in a morning robe of white French lawn tied at the neck and waist with satin ribbons of peach. It was very fine but at the same time modest. Her hair had been brushed by Kitty, for it was felt that the bride could hardly be expected to perform her duties as lady's maid on her wedding day. It was glossy, like a silken shawl across her shoulders and down her back and tied with a ribbon to match that on her robe. She looked splendid and Noah eyed her sourly, remembering the half-hour he had just spent making love to her in his twice daily effort to get her pregnant. Nine months they had been married and still she had not yet conceived and he was beginning to wonder if she ever would. God knows it was not for want of trying. She was compliant in bed, which was all you could say of her, and he wondered if the old man was turning in his grave at the lack of the great-grandson for which he had schemed so assiduously.

She was lovely. She had become polished, the perfect lady and a fit wife for any man, and he realised that it was probably thanks to her growing friendship with Laura Bennett. She had altered in the last two months and he had to admit he was not always sure what she was thinking, or if the words that came out of her mouth had a certain irony in them!

Laura Bennett! No matter how he tried, no matter how he flattered and charmed, flirted and cajoled, though she returned his flirtatious smiles he could not get any closer to her than he had on the first night they had met. He had what he supposed he could call a mistress in Prescot, an easy ride from St Helens, who could be relied on to satisfy his sophisticated physical needs, but Laura was a challenge, a mystifying, irresistible, captivating challenge to his masculine virility and he was not used to having his approaches rebuffed. But then he had never fallen under the spell of a good woman before, what was known as a happily married woman and it was not in his nature to give up. He was not awfully sure he liked his wife being so involved with her, but Abby was certainly becoming the lady her grandfather had wanted her to be.

He turned to Ruby, his face mirroring his thoughts, which were cold and angry for some reason. The house since the old man died had not absorbed his presence lightly, for his wants and needs were definite and precise. He demanded the highest quality in everything from the temperature of the water in which he shaved to the variety and imagination of the food he ate. His linen had to be immaculate in every degree, his trousers pressed to perfection, his boots polished until Frankie, whose job it was to clean them, could see his face in them and if this fell short of his requirements it was Abby who got the blame. She was the mistress of the house, the hostess, his wife, the woman whose duty it was to keep him content and if she could not do it in his bed, and in producing his son, then she'd best see that the rest of his needs were attended to!

She was the only one at the ceremony who could be called "gentry". She wore her plainest gown, since she didn't want to outshine not only the bride but the servants who had been given a couple of hours off to attend the wedding. Nevertheless she stood out in a walking dress of coffee-coloured *foulard des Indes* trimmed with black velvet, a tiny bonnet to match and high-heeled black boots. She watched as Harriet and her husband climbed into the carriage, Olly at the reins, for the short drive back to Edge Bottom House where refreshments were set out in Harriet's old sitting-room and the kitchen, and though she would put in an appearance she would leave them to it, for she knew her presence would inhibit the couple of hours of fun. After the solemnity of the service they liked their weddings to be merry, raucous, with coarse jokes and plenty of drink and she was the mistress, despite her own poor upbringing, and would only hamper them in their enjoyment. They began to troop back to the house with her slightly in the rear.

When she saw him at the lych gate, half hidden behind its stout wooden posts, her first thought was one of thankfulness that the servants were chattering among themselves, discussing the bride and her surprising good looks and the pleased expression of the groom.

Inside her something started to thump and shake as if her heart had come loose and she felt the blood drain from her face. She swayed and, putting out a hand, leaned against the gnarled trunk of an oak tree, praying that none of the servants would look back and notice her, for if they did they would come running. She had endeared herself to them from the beginning, she was aware of that, and their concern would be genuine.

"You go on," she called to Ruby's magenta back. "I want to . . ."

Ruby was eager to get to the entertainment and the admiring

looks of Olly Preston who, despite his own misgivings, she was taken with. She hesitated but her mistress smiled and waved her on and she lifted her hand and ran to catch up with the others.

He took her hand and led her to the far side of the graveyard and behind a tall headstone that proclaimed *Robert Jenkinson lies here in the peace he has earned*, with the enormous horse chestnut spreading its protection over them, he put his arms about her and held her, shuddering, in his arms. They clung together, each one holding the other up, not a word spoken, for there was no need. Their bodies communicated what was in them, which had always been in them since they were children and which would live for ever.

For five minutes they clung together, and gradually the trembling of their bodies eased slightly and they were able to stand an inch or two away and look into each other's faces. Eyes met eyes, probing, seeking an answer to the events since they had been separated, dewed blue-green searching grey, now restored to a gleaming silver as Roddy Baxter regained his full health. He was still thin but his skin had returned to its healthy outdoor colour and his hair gleamed as once it had with glossy brown streaked with honey and cinnamon. He smiled tremulously, ready, she thought, to break down but instead his big hands lifted to cup her face and he bent his head to place his lips gently on hers.

"Sweetheart . . . sweetheart," he whispered. "My Abby, my own."

Olly could have told them that not only was September a good time for wood pigeons it was a good time for butterflies as well. Hundreds of the lovely creatures, golden yellow brimstones, fluttered in the sunshine and alighted on the virginia creeper climbing the church wall, but Abby Goodwin and Roddy Baxter were in thrall to nothing but what was within the circle of their arms.

Their lips met again in a soft and trembling kiss, for both of them were unsteady with the wonder of it. He tucked her head beneath his chin and her mouth pressed warmly, caressingly into the smooth brown skin of his throat. His arms crossed at her back and she arched herself against him, just as she had done eighteen months ago when they had been young and innocent sweethearts. Then he had stopped her, needing in his youthful manhood to take her to her marriage bed virgin but that time was long past. She was his. She was married to another man but she was still his, he knew that, as she did. This would not end here. His body, denied once, would not be denied again. He had been a boy then and was a man now, for though he was still young what he had suffered and survived had hardened him, matured him, strengthened his will and his will, as well as his body told him that this woman belonged to him. His breath sighed out of him as her clear eyes looked luminously into his. He saw the deep emotion in them that softened the bones of him and as she swayed against him his arms held her close.

"Come wi' me now," he said simply. "Don't stop fer owt, just walk away and come wi' me. I've a job over at Denton."

"I know. John Bennett told me. I'm glad."

She could not take her eyes off him, defenceless against the onslaught of his beloved presence. In his own, naked and exposed, was his love for her, his need, which was beyond measuring, his desperation that she might refuse him, which *she* knew she must, and as she looked up into his face he must have read what was in hers, for he began to shake her, not really aware of what he was doing, only knowing that what he saw there he did not like.

Her heart was tripping and hammering and her face was strained, and suddenly the air about them tightened with something that frightened her. Her head lolled on her neck as he became more frantic, for even without the words he knew what she was saying. Her bonnet fell to the back of her neck and she bit her tongue as the ferocity in him strengthened.

"Yer mine," he snarled. "Aye, I know he had yer first but he stole what was mine but I'm tekkin it back, d'yer hear?"

"Roddy . . . Roddy, please." She could barely speak with her mangled tongue and the words came out distorted.

"Don't Roddy me, nor beg me please. Yer mine an' I'll prove it right 'ere in bloody graveyard. I'll not leave yer alone, Abby, never, an' I'm startin' right now."

He bore her backwards until she sprawled on the green hummock of Robert Jenkinson's grave. Roddy Baxter was still virgin but he was a man in love, a man who loved the woman beneath him and though he was untutored in the finer arts of seduction, his love gave him the knowledge of what was needed. He caught the hand that fluttered frantically against his cheek and kissed it. The fingers stirred and then were still as Abby gazed up at him with blind eyes. He turned her hand up and kissed the inside of each finger in turn in an unusual gesture for a rough young man. His manhood throbbed between them, for it cared naught for courtly by-play and in the pit of Abby's belly something stirred and came to life for the first time. Her breasts tingled and she lifted her body to his, and if the grave-digger had come across them at that moment it is doubtful either would have noticed.

His lips rested on hers, soft, sweet, fierce, pressing and folding, and when his hand went to the buttons on her bodice her own went to assist him, for there were a great many of them. He sighed and hesitated at the sight of her rosy-tipped white breasts, the nipples standing out from the areola, firm, proud, waiting for his mouth which took them as eagerly as a baby at its mother's breast. First one tasted and enjoyed and then the other, and as he nipped and sucked his hand went to the hem of her gown and moved up the delicate arch of her foot in its black boot, above the boot to her ankle, the back of her knee and to the inner silkiness of her white thigh. Her drawers were disposed of in one quick movement. She had begun to moan now, her head thrown back, her neck arched until his fingers found the sweet, moist, hot, waiting core of her. With a deft movement which denied his inexperience he was ready, his penis erect, strong, wilful, ready to plunge inside her and when he did she cried out his name so that the grave-digger who was unhurriedly digging the last resting place for the earthly remains of one of the town's dignitaries, lifted his head and glanced about him. The wood pigeons rose from the trees and the grave-digger spoke to himself, which he often did, wondering what had disturbed them.

They lay in a sweet daze, their breathing ragged but slowing gradually to a tranquillity which lapped about them. His cheek rested on her bared breast and his hand smoothed the warm flesh of her throat. Her pulse beat to its normal rhythm and so did his but he knew it would not last, for the nipple beneath his cheek was peaking again. He raised his head and took it in his mouth, smiling in satisfaction, then looked down into her drowsy eyes, the unfocused blue-green of them reminding him of the waters across which he had sailed.

"I'm goin' ter get a cottage, somewhere near Denton. Mr Harrison were tellin' me about it. It's run-down but if I'm willin' ter do it up it's mine fer a few bob a week. It's fer you an' me, sweetheart. Yer could get a job wi' Mrs Hodges. She'd tekk you on seein' as 'ow she knows yer work. We'll start again, you an' me. I know we won't be wed but that don't matter, not ter me, anyroad. Come wi' me. Yer could stay at me mam's until . . . I don't want yer in 'is bed again. Not after this. Yer mine."

She sat up and hastily pulled her bodice together, buttoning frantically the dozens of tiny pearl buttons that ran from the neck to the waist. She reached blindly for something – was

it her bonnet? She wasn't sure but she knew her hair was in
a tangled cloak about her shoulders and she needed to get it
in order, her hat securely holding it to her head. Roddy sat
back uncertainly, his hands on his thighs, but slowly came
the realisation of what she was doing, what she was thinking,
what her next move would be and it was not to go with him
to the safety of his mam's.

"Abby," he said warningly.

"I can't. Dear God in heaven, I can't. Don't you see?"

"No, I bloody well don't. Explain it to me, will yer. Yer
love me, yer know yer do. You'd not have done what we just
done if yer didn't love me." His hands were like claws ready
to grasp her by the forearms and force her into submission
but she clambered to her feet and edged away from him,
from his pain and fury, his desolation, his disbelief that she
could go back to Edge Bottom House and the husband who
waited there for her after the rapturous moments they had
just shared.

Her drawers were draped on poor Robert Jenkinson's headstone and she felt a hysterical urge to shriek with laughter.
And yet in her heart was the same pain, the same fury and
desolation Roddy was suffering. How much harder it would
be to submit to Noah's embraces after what she and the man
she loved had shared. She had *loved* a man for the first time
and he had *loved* her. They had made love together, in the
physical sense and in their loving hearts, and it had nothing
to do with the mechanical act that took place in her bed with
her husband.

But he was her husband. They had been married in the eyes
of God and the law and there was nothing in the world that
could be done about it. She had married him willingly, at least
she thought she had, in the belief that Roddy was dead and
now, as her mam would have said, she had made her bed and
must lie on it. This glory that had happened had come at her

from nowhere, unplanned, spontaneous, thrilling, a miracle she had not dreamed of and had swept her along on a glorious golden tide of love but it must not happen again. She must go back to the house, speak to the newly-weds, prepare for dinner with Noah and resume the life she had painfully made for herself.

Roddy bowed his head, devastated by what he saw in her face. He kneeled in the grass, his furious hatred of her, of Noah Goodwin, of her life with him, draining away from him, leaving him lifeless. "Don't go," he mumbled. "I'm beggin' yer."

"No," she said wildly, afraid of him now, forbidding him to hold her back, refusing absolutely to listen lest she weaken. She turned and began to run, unaware that the grave-digger was watching her with open mouth, for where the devil had *she* come from and what had she been up to? When he saw the young man stumbling towards the lych gate he narrowed his eyes and scratched his head in puzzlement, for what the devil was young Mrs Goodwin, whose servant had just been married, doing dallying in the churchyard with a man?

"Old Dodsworth wants to see us in the morning," Noah announced casually at the dinner table, nodding at Kitty as she placed a dish of whiting *au gratin* in front of him. It was one of Cook's specialities, fragrantly delicious with mushrooms, parsley, butter and a glass of sherry poured over it before it was baked in the oven.

"Old Dodsworth?" Abby picked up a fork ready to make a show of eating, though she felt as though there were a leaden ball in her chest past which no food could go.

"Mmm, the solicitor who dealt with your grandfather's affairs."

"I . . . I can't remember." She couldn't remember anything, for the hour she had spent with Roddy had emptied her mind of everything but him. She had even forgotten to join the merry party in Harriet's sitting-room where the bride and groom were being toasted enthusiastically and had gone straight to the peace and privacy of her room, praying none of them would come looking for her. Her face was set in stone, aching with the effort not to crack up and weep her despair, and her eyes were fixed in a stare which badly startled her when she looked in the mirror. She knew she had taken him to paradise this day, as he had taken her, and then she had crucified him and his pain was more than she could bear.

Noah lifted his head from his meal and looked at his wife. She seemed strange; he could not have said in what way though, and it interested him. Her eyes were burning, like diamonds with a blue-green chip of ice in them, and her face was pale and strained. Her lips were like poppies, red and full, and for a millisecond his male mind dwelled on the ludicrous idea that she had just been thoroughly kissed, or perhaps more; then he smiled. She was his wife!

"Where the dickens have you been this afternoon?" he asked, unconcerned now, for it was not in his nature to be involved with what women did when their menfolk were about their business.

"The wedding . . . Harriet and Clem."

"Ah, of course. How did it go?" Again not interested.

"Very well."

"Everyone behaved themselves?" Nodding at Kitty to let her know he would have another mouthful of the whiting.

"Oh, yes. The party was very . . . correct." She did not see Kitty look at her sharply, for her mistress had not been there. Her absence had been noted and where she had got to was a mystery. It was not like her to stay away from something as important as Mrs Pearson's – Mrs Woodruff's – wedding celebrations, for it was well known that they were fond of one another. She exchanged a look with Ruby then shrugged her shoulders. It was nothing to do with them, was it, but Clem and his new wife had been right disappointed.

They drew up at the solicitor's office at exactly ten o'clock the next morning, Olly bringing the carriage to a smooth halt. The street was busy, for it was the centre, the hub of the business district in St Helens and the traffic was heavy with the equipages of businessmen, bankers, solicitors, all those who were influential in the making of wealth and power.

"Shall I wait, sir?" Olly asked Noah. "Only the road's narrer an' I'm blockin' the way."

"No, go over to the Cock Inn and pull in there, but don't let me smell ale on your breath or there'll be trouble." Just as if the conscientious groom were in the habit of drinking himself into a stupor the minute his employer's eyes were off him!

"No, sir," Olly said sullenly, and for a moment Abby wondered why it was that Noah had this habit of putting down those whom he considered were beneath him.

"I'll send Mr Dodsworth's lad over when we're ready."

"Yes, sir."

"Come, my pet," Noah said to her, taking her unresisting arm and escorting her across the cobbled pavement. He had made love to her this morning and she felt like some painted doll that has passed from its rightful owner into the careless hands of someone who did what he did for his own pleasure only. The sweetness, the gentleness, the fierce passion that true love had aroused, and been given, was known to her now and she could not help but agonise over the difference. She looked quite lovely in the pale delicacy which Noah had noticed yesterday and he wondered hopefully if she was with child. It was cooler today and she wore for the first time a silver-grey skirt and jacket edged with silver fur, of what sort she neither knew, nor cared. Harriet had chosen it, as she did most of Abby's clothes.

He led her through to Mr Dodsworth's office where the solicitor stood to greet them, his florid face beaming, though there was a certain something in his manner which neither of them noticed. Noah was an arrogant man, proud of his climb to importance and determined to get even further, and it was his shrewdness, his skill at reading other men's minds that had helped him. But today he was well pleased with himself, his position, his lovely, well-dressed wife and Mr Dodsworth's slightly hesitant manner went unnoticed.

They signed this and that and discussed this and that, all the talk between the two men, as was only right and proper, and she and Noah both wondered why she had been asked to attend. Women, ladies, left all business matters to their husbands and, before that, to their fathers. She owned nothing. It belonged to Noah so what was she doing here?

The question was answered over coffee which Mr Dodsworth was insistent that they drink. They talked of the weather and the dry summer just gone and it was only as Noah put his cup in his saucer with the evident intention of leaving that Mr Dodsworth cleared his throat.

"There is one more thing, Mr Goodwin," again addressing Noah and not the lady to whom this was relevant.

Noah leaned back in his chair. "Oh yes."

"It is to do with Mrs Goodwin."

Noah turned to stare at Abby in astonishment. "My wife?"

"Exactly."

"Well?" A cold look which might have been apprehension crossed Noah's face, but what had he to be apprehensive about?

"It seems Mr Bradley Goodwin left her something in his will."

"Yes, yes, everything he owned which, as her husband, came to me."

"Not quite, sir. Mr Goodwin left a gift to his granddaughter of five hundred guineas."

Noah laughed. "That is—"

"No, sir, this is a *gift* that only Mrs Goodwin can receive."

17

"I've got five hundred guineas to spend as I wish and, Laura, I've never been so astonished in all my life. My grandfather, who never did anything unless it brought him some advantage, has left me five hundred guineas which Noah can't touch. A gift, it's called. Don't ask me how he did it but it's all tied up legally. Noah is livid. He stamped out of Mr Dodsworth's office as though some personal affront had been offered him. I thought he was going to leave me standing on the pavement and I think if it had not been for Olly he would have done. 'Drive on,' he kept shouting, ignoring the curiosity of the passers-by but Olly . . . well, he just sat there, ignoring him until I had struggled into the carriage. He wanted to hit me, Noah, I mean, and I can't for the life of me understand why. 'Stupid old bugger,' he said over and over again, muttering that he should have known something underhand was going on when old Dodsworth asked him to bring his wife to the office. What's the matter with the man, Laura? He has the house, the glass works, all my grandfather's business involvement with . . . well, I don't know what he was involved in, and yet he begrudges me a few guineas. Dear God, will you listen to me. *A few guineas!* It's a fortune. It would keep my family for the rest of their lives. Mam and Pa, I mean. I can't get over it."

"Which part? The fact that you have five hundred guineas at your disposal or Noah's fury?"

"Both, I suppose."

"You realise why he is so enraged, don't you? It's because your grandfather has given you a tiny measure of independence and Noah doesn't like that. Do you have a dress allowance?"

"No, Miss Beckett sends the accounts to Noah. I can spend what I like and how much I like but I have no . . . no money of my own."

"Now you have and your husband is not pleased. With Roddy Baxter back in St Helens . . ."

They were drinking the hot chocolate that Laura was so partial to, seated in Laura's comfortable but somewhat untidy sitting-room in Claughton Street, the pair of them draped in the shabby armchairs before a pantingly hot fire, for the September days had turned cold. A glossy black cat was curled up on the hearth-rug and beside her two kittens wobbled about in imminent danger of falling into the coals, searching for the friendly teats which the mother was keeping out of sight. The meeting of the ladies who were in Laura's group was over, and they had just discussed the amazing idea that not only should all men have the vote, but ladies too. To be enfranchised, was how they put it, ladies in many parts of the country joining together, moderate groups that met in hope of having a voice but with very little chance of achieving this end. Their cause, they called it, but if they weren't aware that it would be years before even *all men* were enfranchised, let alone women, Laura was. They were ladies, mostly wives or daughters of professional men: Mrs Agnes Holme whose husband was a Liberal and a banker and had himself been enfranchised thirty years earlier with half a million other men, a middle-class gentleman who earned the right to vote alongside landowners; Mrs Ann Dalton whose husband owned a chemical factory; Mrs Adele Drummond, the wife of a teacher at the Mechanics Institute; and, strangely, Miss Florence Tickle whose father worked in the cutting room at Edge Bottom Glass Works and who, because he was financially able to support her, did not believe in his daughter going out to work. One-fifth of all men could vote but women, naturally, were not considered intelligent enough, were in fact too emotional and therefore incapable of making a sound and reasoned political decision, so it was said in Westminster!

In the meanwhile they did sterling work on committees for the relief of the poor. The American Civil War had caused much deprivation amongst the families of Lancashire, many of whom worked in the cotton mills. The shortage of cotton from the southern states of America had closed mills or at least put them on short time and the hardship was only alleviated by the work of women like those who gathered in Laura's drawing-room. They manned soup kitchens and distributed blankets and clothing to the worst hit families, and at their meetings disagreed forcibly about who, among women, should have the vote. Women of property, certainly, spinsters, probably, but not married women, for their husbands were well able to vote for them, to which the married women took exception. A very lively argument was conducted on this hypothetical question and it was not noticed that the lovely Mrs Noah Goodwin, who had just joined their cause, barely spoke a word.

The porcelain clock ticked pleasantly, the kittens mewed piteously and on the table stood a cut-glass vase which, though hideous, Laura admitted, was the only one she had. A wedding present, which held the magnificent arrangement of hothouse blooms Mr Renfrew had sent over for the doctor's wife. It seemed most of the working people in Edge Bottom, and indeed in St Helens knew of Doctor John Bennett and his beautiful, practical wife who did so much to ease the plight of the poor. Both he and Laura had dined at Edge Bottom House and the servants were delighted that their young mistress had a friend of her own age instead of those elderly members of society who usually were guests.

"Laura, dear God in heaven, what d'yer mean?" In times of stress Abby was inclined to fall back into some of the speech of her childhood. "'Oo told yer?" She sat up so abruptly, the startled kittens fell off the fender where they had climbed and the cat turned to stare at her accusingly.

"Told me what, dear girl? Is there something to tell?" Laura leaned forward and took Abby's precariously held beaker from her shaking hand.

"Laura, please . . ." Abby hung her head and it was clear to Laura she was not far from tears. "I can't . . . yer see . . ."

"You've seen Roddy? Is that what you're trying so hard not to tell me?"

Abby sighed deeply. "Aye."

"Do you want to? Tell me, I mean?" Laura put both beakers on to the small side table and took Abby's hands in both of hers. "Your behaviour when the boy came back was a sure indication of your feelings and I think that is what angers Noah. He is not a man to take lightly the thought that his wife might be in love with another man." *Even if he is known for his tomcat ways which I myself have been subjected to!* She did not say this out loud, naturally. It was obvious the girl was in love with the young man who had been treated so appallingly and it was also obvious that with the lad still living in the area they would meet some time. It seemed they had!

"Noah is ruthless," she went on. "A dominant man, strong-willed and strongly opinionated. He has forgiven you for what you did for Roddy, not for your sake but for his own. He needs a wife and he needs a son. I'm not implying that he does not value you but you would be wise not to cross him further." Laura could have said more but she decided against it. If this young woman was to make a success of her marriage she must believe it was worth it.

"Roddy was at the church when Harriet and Clem were married. He . . . he hid and when the others had gone he drew me to a quiet spot . . . we talked . . ."

And something else, Laura suspected, for the girl blushed to a bright hue and would not meet her eyes. Dear God, no wonder, even if he did not know of this meeting, Noah Goodwin was outraged at the idea of his young wife being left money by her grandfather. It wasn't a lot but if she ever decided to . . . Oh, Lord, where were her thoughts leading her? She must stop at once.

"I love him, Laura. I've always loved him and always will. That's the truth and he feels the same."

"What are you to do, dearest?" Laura paid her the compliment of treating her as a woman who could make her own decisions.

"I must stay with my husband, Laura." Abby knew she sounded prim, prudish, self-righteous, which was far from the truth. Perhaps it was her own illegitimacy that made her more conscious of the need to recognise the conventions, the disgrace that would be heaped not only on herself but Noah, her own family and, if she went to him, Roddy, if she should defy those conventions. During the past days and nights, since she had been given the means to be independent, she had brooded on the possibility of doing what Roddy and herself, of course, wanted. To fly in the face of conformity and go with him, live with him as a wife who wasn't a wife, but how would that affect Roddy and his chance of rising above his poor beginnings and the terrible thing done to him? He had enrolled at the Mechanics Institute where he would get the start of a decent education, but none of it would matter if he set up home with a woman married to another man. They would be shunned, not only by those of the upper classes but by those of the labouring class, the decent labouring class who, though they were much lower in the social structure, had standards just as high. Roddy had a job now and was about to start again on his chosen career as a glass-blower, one of the élite in the field of glass-making. There were men who owned small glass-making concerns who had begun as Roddy had, apprenticed to a decent firm and, having been conscientious, hardworking, ambitious, and, most of all, thrifty, had gone on to be businessmen with great prospects for their future.

"It might be difficult for you with Roddy still in the neighbourhood. To avoid him, I mean."

"He says he has been promised a cottage near Denton."

"Leave his mother and brothers?"

The mother cat, as though suddenly aware of her duties, stretched, got to her feet and taking first one wandering kitten in her mouth and then the other, tucked them safely against her where at once they began to suckle. Both women watched them for a moment then Abby rose to her feet and went to the window. She stared out into the street to where the carriage stood. Olly was in Laura's kitchen drinking tea with Laura's cook and maid, since Laura wouldn't hear of him sitting shivering on his coachman's perch for perhaps two hours while the ladies discussed their cause. He was always pleased when Miss Abby ordered the carriage to take her to Claughton Street, for it meant a break from his duties as a groom. He had left Clem, who was made up with his new status as the husband of the former housekeeper, to muck out the stables and Clem was so blissful over the "bed" side of his marriage he made no objection. They all had to smile, the servants, even Nessie who knew nothing much about the married state, on Clem's smug satisfaction with his new wife, and the memory of what she had been to the old master before he died seemed to have been forgotten.

"I think he has it in his mind that if he gets this cottage he might persuade me to go with him. He knows I can't move in with his mam but if he has a home to offer me . . ." Her voice trailed away and Laura sighed in sympathy. She was so ecstatically happy with her John, so lucky to be married to a man who adored her and whom she adored in return; a man who shared her ideas, her values, her beliefs, Abby Goodwin's predicament filled her with sadness.

"But you won't?"

"How can I? I have a husband, a house to run, people who depend on me. Mam couldn't manage without the few shillings I give her and should Roddy leave Edge Bottom Row, Dorcas would have to bring the boys away from school and put them to work. They all rely on me, you see."

"You don't mention Noah in your—"

"No," Abby interrupted harshly. "I have no feelings for Noah and he has none for me. He married me to get the glass works. He has them now and all he wants is a son. So far I have failed him in that direction but, dear God in heaven, it's not for want of trying on his part. Now, I must go or it will be dark before we get home."

Though Olly protested vigorously, she insisted on riding alone the following week.

"Maister'll not like it, Miss Abby," he grumbled as he saddled Poppy. "Miss Goodwin" – meaning Joanna, Noah's sister – "were only sayin' t'other day it weren't right fer yer ter go out alone. She must've seen yer from 'er winder goin' along Croft Bank."

"I was walking, not riding," Abby said sharply. "And anyway when did Miss Goodwin talk to the master about me and, more to the point, how did you overhear the conversation?"

Olly looked abashed but then it was not his fault if his employer talked to his sister in front of him, was it? That's what masters and mistresses did, just as though servants were not only deaf but daft.

"Maister were givin' Miss Goodwin a lift inter town in't carriage. She were goin' ter't dressmaker's in—"

"Yes, yes, very well but I'm still going alone."

"'E won't like it." Olly shook his head.

"He won't know unless you tell him, Olly. I shan't go far. Only up to Old Fellows Edge and back." Old Fellows Edge was where Noah and she had once walked when he was courting her last year. They had sat on a mossy stone and looked out over the shallow bowl in which St Helens lay, talking, laughing sometimes, for he had made an effort to please her, to win her confidence and trust, she realised that now. And he had, but those days were over, for she and the glass works were his and he had no need to woo her as he had then.

There was a mist on the top pathway, shifting and mysterious, but she knew the way having ridden up here many times with Olly. She had become an adept horsewoman in the six months that Olly had been training her and when, as she reached Old Fellows Edge, the mist had cleared she saw him at once leaning against the pile of rocks and she wondered at her lack of surprise. There was ill temper in his face, once so engaging and merry, his mouth tightly clamped, his eyebrows drawn down in a scowl.

"I've bin waitin' fer hours." His voice was sharp and yet there was a ragged pain in it that closed round her heart like a fist.

"I didn't know you'd be here. I wouldn't have come if I had."

"In a way I were hopin' yer wouldn't. It would've bin easier."

"Yes, yes, you're right so I'd best turn round and go."

"Lass, hopin' yer wouldn't come's got nowt ter do wi' wantin'. I come every day I'm off shift, waitin', sittin' here all day long sometimes. I can't see beyond yer, Abby. I can't get on wi' me life 'cos you *are* me life. Can yer understand that? All I do is go ter work an' school; oh aye, I'm betterin' meself ready fer the day when you an' me'll be tergether. I'm learnin' ter read an' write an' it's all fer you. Won't yer get down from that bloody horse an' sit a while? Talk ter me. Tell me why yer stoppin' wi' that bugger. Yer don't love 'im, I know that, fer it's in yer face. Yer love me. Yer mine. Mine! An' I won't let yer go."

She turned Poppy, her eyes unseeing, the mist, which had begun to thicken and drift, coiling round her so that it seemed to be in her mind, muddling her clear common sense, her reason which had told her a thousand times what her life must be. He sprang forward and grabbed the mare's reins, then dragged Abby from her back, pulling her roughly into his arms. He had almost regained his full strength and when he placed her body along the length of his she could feel it surging through him, conveying itself to her. His mouth came down on hers, fierce and passionate, and at once her loving, treacherous body responded. Her mouth opened and she moaned, her breath mingling with his, from her mouth to his, sweet, as his was. He drove her back into the shelter of the rocks, straining her to him, his hands, no longer needed to contain her, smoothing her face and jawline, the arch of her throat, the curve of her breast.

"I love yer, Abby, my Abby. I love yer, don't leave me. I want yer. Let me love yer again."

And she did. It was trickier than last time, for she wore her riding breeches but in the damp shelter of Old Fellows Edge he made love to her as fiercely, as passionately, as possessively as he had done in the churchyard and she had no defences to stop him. Had she wanted to.

Afterwards she put her hands carefully about his cheeks and kissed him softly, gently, her mouth lingering to retain the odour and texture of him in her mind, to cherish, to sustain her lest she never see him again. He smiled up into her face, his expression peaceful, calm, his eyes dreaming, she knew, of the day when they would be together, not like this, but in the place he was making for her.

"I've got cottage, sweetheart. Mr Harrison's right pleased wi' me, an' he's paying me wages I would've got if I'd stayed in me apprenticeship wi' Goodwins. I earned fifteen shillings last week which is what I were gettin' before . . . before I were took." He gulped, for the memory of those months was something that would always haunt him. "But if I work another two years, finishin' me apprenticeship, Mr Harrison's promised me a job as a glass-blower. If I shape, that is. I still give me mam a few shillings a week but I'm savin' an' every minute I got spare I do up cottage. I'm livin' in it." He laughed. "It's a right bloody mess but I'm makin' it right for yer. Will . . . will yer come an' see it, sweetheart? Tell me what yer want doin'." His eyes, which had changed to a clear crystal grey were filled with longing, and yet in them was a shadow which said that he was not certain of her. Oh, she loved him, there was no doubt of that in his mind, for hadn't she just proved it in the only way a woman can, for his Abby was honest and would not pretend a feeling she did not have. And yet, the disturbing thought came to his mind, a disturbing and *terrible* thought, which was that every night she got into bed with another man and presumably did with her husband what she had just done with him. Not with love, of course, but because it was her duty as his wife.

He saw it in her eyes before she spoke, her refusal. He sat up, pushing her away roughly, sorry as he did it but his fear and pain and jealousy turned him away from the kind, fair-minded lad he had once been.

"Yer won't do it, will yer? Yer'd rather stay wi' a man yer don't love than come wi' me. Yer can't bear ter give up silk gowns, jewellery an' such—"

"Don't, Roddy, please, my love."

"I'm not yer love. Yer might like this . . . this what we've just done but—"

She sprang to her feet, forgetting she was tangled up with breeches, riding skirt and all the paraphernalia that women are forced to wear and with an oath that might have come straight from the stables fell in a heap across his knees. His arms went round her instinctively and his hand fell on the satin smoothness of her exposed thigh and with an oath to match hers he flipped her on to her back and thrust his body into hers. She wept, not with joy but with passion and fear and fury and then her voice rose into the air in rapture.

"Roddy . . . Roddy, my love, how can I . . . I love you so much . . . and this . . . yes, and this . . . your body was made for mine. I have never . . ."

"Not with him?" His voice was a snarl. He ripped open her bodice and turned it back to expose her breasts. Bending his head he kissed each one, touching the nipples delicately with his tongue so each one peaked as though by magic, a swelling rose pink against the white skin of her breasts.

"Jesus God, you're so lovely."

He sighed then and lay back to stare into the grey mist above them while she slowly pulled her clothing modestly about her, then hitched himself up from the wet grass to do the same with his breeches. It was turning colder and neither had noticed as they were swept on a sea wave of passion but now, their bodies parted, they began to shiver. Abby stood up and so did Roddy, making no move to touch her again. He knew that this time he had lost her, but he wouldn't give up and it was this that gave him the strength to stand away from her.

"Olly will be sending out a search party if I don't go."

"Right."

"You know I must go."

"No, I don't but I'm not stoppin' yer. An' everythin' I've said terday will be't same termorrer an' every day after. I'll come after yer, my lass, an' one day yer'll say yes."

He watched her gracefully mount her mare which had stayed placidly by the outcrop of grey stone, grazing on the sweet grass. She didn't turn to look back and he sighed as he turned in the direction of St Helens and Green Lane to the north which would take him to his cottage at Denton's Green.

"Did yer come off, lass?" Olly asked her anxiously, eyeing the damp stains that marked her smart riding habit. He had run out into the yard when he heard the mare's hooves on the cobbles, leaving Clem to his daydreams about his new wife, who had just winked at him as she crossed the yard to the kitchen.

He took Poppy's reins as Abby dismounted. "Yer all wet. She didn't throw yer, did she?" smiling at the very idea of the gentle mare doing anything so foolish.

"As a matter of fact, she did," Abby replied, sad to be saying such an awful thing about her beloved horse, then smiling a little at Olly's consternation. "Well, no, she didn't actually throw me, Olly. I set her to a jump – a wall up at the top. She refused and I fell off."

"Set 'er to a jump!" Olly was outraged. "She's not a bloody jumper, my lass, an' yer'd no right to try 'er. Poor little girl . . ." His concern was for the animal rather than his mistress which was just as well, for it gave Abby the perfect reason for being in such a tousled state. It would be all round Edge Bottom House and its environs within the hour that the young mistress had come off her horse and when it reached its master she would probably be in for a tongue-lashing, but as she climbed the stairs to the bedroom and the hot bath she had ordered, her face was flushed and dreaming and her eyes misty and unfocused. If Noah Goodwin had been about and looked into his wife's face, being the experienced man he was, he would have known at once that the fall from her mare had not caused that look.

There was someone who was just as experienced as he in such matters and as Harriet picked up her mistress's riding habit to take it downstairs to be cleaned and brushed, and gathered up her scattered undergarments she watched as Abby languidly lifted a leg from the hot water and smoothed it with the jasmine soap she favoured. The girl was in a trance-like state, half smiling, slow and graceful in her movements. Harriet folded the riding habit over her arm and as she did so she was transported back in time to nearly thirty years ago when she had been a pretty young housemaid in love with the master's son. She had looked like that then, not in a bath, for such things were not always available to servants, but in the cracked and peeling mirror in her room as she brushed her long silky hair which her lover, half an hour since, had spread over her naked breasts.

Jesus God, not . . . surely she hadn't. He was back, and she had just come from riding the moor, returning with her clothes wet and crumpled. Dear God, not that!

18

She and Noah had been married for exactly one year in December and soon it would be Christmas and the start of the seasonal festivities. There were to be dinner parties, luncheon parties, balls, musical evenings where Christmas carols would be sung, and she and Harriet had been busy for weeks making arrangements for a party Noah had decided they would have, a party to which would be invited everyone of importance in St Helens. Harriet, though she did not speak of it, thought it was to show all his friends and acquaintances, gentlemen with whom he did business and their wives, how well Noah Goodwin had done for himself, what a success he had become, his steady advance in the world of glass-making enabling him to deck his young wife with jewels of the highest quality, which he did. And, more importantly, that he and his lovely but somewhat unconventional wife were a happily married couple. To scotch any remaining whispers or rumours that might have arisen during the early part of the year. That he had not been cuckolded by a lad of seventeen! To put on display the true accord between himself and Abby. That she was not yet with child when, by all the law of averages, she should already have one in the cradle was a stumbling block which he did his nightly best to overcome but he was not a man to give up hope.

"It comes of riding too much, Noah. She should not be up on that horse of hers at all, in my opinion. Shaking her insides about like that can only be harmful. I see her several times a week going past Croft Bank."

Noah and his sister were sipping their after-dinner coffee in the drawing-room. Abby had retired to bed as she often did when Joanna dined with them, as soon as it was politely possible to do so. Joanna was a good woman, much involved with the church and with Sunday school and with no man of her own to order about had taken over the parson to whom she made suggestions, which he carried out. She was staunch and true and extremely fond of her brother and had from the first made it plain that she did not approve of her brother's choice of wife. It had, of course, given Noah a great deal of wealth and influence and had made her own finances immeasurably easier, but nevertheless the girl's behaviour could only be called unorthodox.

"I would like a child, Joanna," Noah answered stiffly, "but there is nothing I can do to make her pregnant other than what I am already doing."

Joanna averted her gaze, her face showing her disapproval of her brother's forthright remark. Joanna would have liked a husband, and children, but what must be done to bring this about was not something she could bear to contemplate, let alone act on.

"And I am of the opinion that she sees far too much of that doctor's wife. Do you know what their aims are, that group that gathers in her drawing-room? *Enfranchisement for all!* Even women!" She sat back in triumph as though she had just described an act of such depravity her brother would at once refuse his wife not only the company of Laura Bennett but would never allow her out alone again. Especially on a horse.

"I can see no reason to forbid it, Joanna," Noah said mildly. "They are harming no one and the likelihood of women, or even the lower working-class men of this country ever having the vote is too ludicrous for words." *Besides which it keeps her busy and in the company of the woman whom, above all others, I would like to seduce.*

"Perhaps all this dashing about is having an adverse effect on Abigail's chances of having a child. Have you thought of that?"

"Well, if it will allay your fears I will forbid her to ride. Oliver always goes with her."

"He's not with her when she passes Croft Bank, Noah."

Noah sat forward and slowly put his cup and saucer on the side table. From being relaxed and patient with his sister's complaints about his wife, his face became set like stone, his jaw clamped and rigid. There was visible menace in his eyes and his sister reared back in alarm.

"She goes out alone?" He spoke as though he had a stone in his mouth that was impeding his speech.

"Yes, she does, and it's not proper that a lady of good class should roam about without a groom in attendance. Of course, we all realise that she is—"

"Not a lady of good class."

"Well, yes. She has been trained by her grandfather, by you and by that governess but she is still—"

"Not one of us? Is that what you're saying?"

"Yes, I am, Noah, and you should watch her more closely. She made a fool out of you when she stayed at that—"

"Thank you, Joanna. I believe I have the picture and, believe me, she has had her last ride, with or without the groom."

She had not been back to Old Fellows Edge since the last time she had seen Roddy. She still took Poppy out a couple of times a week but she rode in the other direction towards Burton Wood. She was doing her best to come to terms with her sense of isolation, desolation, loneliness, which were strange words to use, for she was surrounded by friends, servants, but the barren years ahead of her sickened her and turned her cold. In the depth of her soul a miserable creature wept for the man she was forced to turn away from, but he invaded her thoughts, day and night, and she wondered how long it would be before she could get on with this life she had chosen with Noah. She was only seventeen but she felt as though her life were over. Nightly she prayed to a God she found hard to believe in that she would become pregnant but it did not happen. A child would have made their life worth while, given her a reason to believe she had made the right choice, but Noah was strangely truculent as Christmas approached and the sad thing was she could not really bring herself to care.

It was a week before the dinner party which she and Harriet were so busy with when it happened. She had pored over menus, table decorations, supervised the washing of the best china, the cleaning of cutlery and silver, had long discussions with Mr Renfrew about the flowers, planned the arrangements for those who would stay the night, for some were to come from as far afield as Carlisle and Leicester, made decisions on her gown and the dressing of her hair and a hundred and one things which would make an evening such as the one Noah wanted a success. He had left early for the glass works and when she herself rose to her breakfast tray brought by Kitty, who pulled back the curtains, the sunshine streamed in across the carpet.

"A lovely day, Miss Abby. Yer should see the frost. White over as far as the eye can see. I'd best mekk up this fire for yer. They're all lit downstairs and Cook's got kitchen fire halfway up chimbley."

"Where's Ruby today? Is she not well?" For it was Ruby who usually bustled in first thing in the morning.

"No, Miss Abby."

"What's wrong with her?"

"Summat an' nowt," Kitty answered shortly, and without another word left the room, banging the door behind her.

Abby raised her eyebrows in surprise but ate her breakfast, washed and dressed and went down to the kitchen. She had decided to have a last ride out before she became too busy with the remaining preparations for Christmas, but as she went through the kitchen, greeting the servants pleasantly as she usually did she was bewildered by their strained expressions.

Olly was nowhere about and when she popped her head into the stable it was Clem who came forward, wiping his hands on a wisp of straw.

"Will you saddle Poppy for me, Clem? I thought I'd ride over to Burton Wood while I can."

"Well, I'm not sure whether . . ."

"Whether what? Is something wrong?"

"It's not fer me ter . . ." He hesitated and Abby became impatient.

"Oh, for goodness sake, Clem, saddle Poppy."

"Yes, Miss Abby," he said, turning back to the stall where Poppy was whickering a welcome to her mistress.

"Where's Olly?" Abby asked casually, glancing round the stable expecting Olly's grin to pop up over the stalls.

"'E's not 'ere, Miss Abby."

"Oh, where is he then?"

"'E's . . . 'e's bin turned off, Miss Abby."

Clem threw the saddle over Poppy's back, his own turned towards Abby and so he did not see Abby's jaw drop nor her eyes widen. She stood for several seconds in total amazement, for Olly was the best horse man in the county, Noah had always said so. He was hardworking and conscientious and had worked at Edge Bottom House for many years. He was cheerful and willing and, unless he had done something so criminal it could not be ignored, was the last man on the estate to be fired.

"Turned off?" she managed to blurt out. "What the devil for?"

"Nay, 'tis not fer me ter say, Miss Abby. Master 'ad 'im in the 'ouse last night an' told 'im ter get his things an' go."

"But there must be a reason."

"I reckon there is but yer'd best ask 'im. The maister."

"I believe I will." And she whirled about, stamping into the house and going to the only person who would tell her why Olly had been sacked.

They all eyed her apprehensively as she marched through the kitchen to the small sitting-room where Harriet was bent over the account books on the table. Harriet lifted her head and sighed, a long sigh, for there was trouble ahead. She and Clem had found a late happiness together, an unexpected happiness and if this young woman caused trouble, *more* trouble, who knew where it might lead for any of them. Noah Goodwin was not a man to be defied, which Olly had found to his cost. He was touchy where his young wife was concerned and with reason, so Harriet thought, and his pride would not allow her to rebel against him.

"What's happened?" Abby said without preamble.

"Well . . ."

"Don't quibble, Harriet. I had enough of that with Clem. Why has Olly been sacked?"

"Right, the truth. He allowed you to ride out on your own. All these months you have been galloping off on that animal, leaving Olly behind, which he knew was wrong. The master found out from someone. So he sacked him."

"The sod!"

"Maybe he is but Olly should have let him know what was happening, he knew that; instead he let the master's young wife ride unaccompanied and for that he has been fired."

"We'll see about that." Abby whirled her full riding skirt dipping like the full bloom of a dark summer rose. Her chamois trousers were revealed and her shining boots. She wore her top hat with the small face veil but, as though in preparation for a battle or perhaps in full rebellion to her husband's wishes, she tore it off and flung her head back, allowing her glorious cape of hair to fall to her buttocks.

"Abby, don't, I beg you," Harriet cried, getting to her feet and running after her while the servants stood and gawped.

Clem had Poppy in the yard, holding her by the rein while she jinked and turned in her eagerness to be off. He had already opened the yard gate and nearly fell on his back as Abby burst from the kitchen, tore off her riding skirt, threw it at him, leaped agilely on to the mare's back and broke at once into a gallop towards the gate.

"Jesus ternight!" he gasped as his wife flung herself from the kitchen, the maidservants at her back. "Where's she off?"

"To see her husband."

"What, at works!"

"Where else would she find him?"

"Jesus ternight!"

The office block was in a corner of the yard furthest from the gate and, besides, there was so much din in the yard he did not hear her clatter in and, still at a gallop, cross the yard to the office block doorway. But all the men did, and saw her in her skin-tight chamois leather riding trousers. They were a pale coffee colour and from a distance she appeared to have nothing on her lower half, and every man in the yard stood like a figure carved in wood to watch her. She leaped from her horse, throwing the reins to a man who had just emerged from the office block and so great was his stupefaction, though he was on an important errand for his employer, he took them, watching her as she took the stairs that led to the offices two at a time.

He was at his desk, a clerk standing at his elbow as they

bent over a ledger. She had never been up here before but though it was a magnificent room with the best of everything in the way of furniture, paintings, thick, thick carpet, and an enormous coal fire in the mahogany fireplace, she didn't even glance round but marched over to the desk and, ignoring the open-mouthed clerk, attacked her husband whose mouth also hung open.

"What the devil d'you mean by sacking Olly Preston? If any wrong has been done I'm the one to blame. He was only doing his job and obeying orders which is surely all that is demanded of him. Why didn't you come to *me*? It wasn't his fault that I rode alone. *I* told him to stay behind and—"

Noah stood up and the clerk recoiled, released at last from the same frozen state the men in the yard had been in. Without a word or a backward glance he scurried from the room and closed the door quietly behind him.

"What the bloody hell's the meaning of this intrusion?" Noah snarled, his glance going up and down her figure in total disbelief. His eyes had deepened until they were almost black, his scorching anger burning a tiny flame in the centre of each one. He brought the flat of his hand down on the table with a mighty slap, setting the coffee cup and saucer that awaited his attention jangling. "And may I ask why you are riding – I presume you have ridden over here – in that indecent outfit? You look half naked."

"Don't try to change the subject, Noah. What I wear is not in question here."

"Is it not? Then let me beg to differ, madam. As my wife I expect you to be properly dressed at all—"

"Stop it, *stop it*. I'm sorry if you're offended by . . . I was in a hurry and . . . but you haven't answered my question. Why have you sacked Olly Preston? I was in no danger when I rode out alone, for who in these parts would dare to offend the great Noah Goodwin's wife? Besides, I like to be alone sometimes and I'm sure Olly has better things to do than follow at my mare's tail."

"Will you never learn that as my wife you will do as *I* say? I bought you that mare so that, as a gentleman's wife, you could ride in a circumspect manner about the countryside but not alone. God knows who you might meet."

"Rubbish!"

His face was a livid mask of rage. He got up and strode to the fireplace where he took a cigar from a silver box on the mantelpiece, lit it with a taper from the fire and blew the fragrant smoke into the air. And it was fragrant, for nothing but the very best was good enough for Noah Goodwin now.

"I wish you to go home now, Abby, where you belong. I shall sell your mare and from now on you will go nowhere unless it is in the carriage and you are accompanied by Joanna. Is that clear?"

"So, she was the one who ran to you with tales of my misbehaviour?"

He strode across the room, bringing his leashed, snarling anger with him until they were face to face, no more than inches between them, but she did not back off.

"My sister has only my interests at heart. She knows the damage this kind of thing can do."

"What kind of thing? I have done nothing wrong, and neither has Olly, so unless you reinstate him I shall leave you and you know I can. My grandfather gave me the means to be independent."

He laughed then but his mouth was hard and cruel and sarcastic.

"What, with five hundred guineas? That will hardly keep you in the way you have become used to."

"You forget, Noah, I was brought up for the first fifteen years of my life in a labourer's cottage. My father earned ten shillings a week and five hundred guineas is a fortune to the likes of us. And I'm strong, used to hard work and *childless*."

His face lost every vestige of the colour his anger had introduced. His lips thinned into a white line. "Don't make an enemy of me, Abby. I warn you I can be very dangerous to those who cross me and there are others involved in your life who might be . . . hurt by your disobedience. I have a strong urge to hit you but a woman with a cut lip and a black eye is one that will be wondered at and I want no further gossip."

"Then you'd best give Olly his job back or I shall create such a scandal you'll never live it down. I know you can hurt me and those I love but if you do this thing for me I will never go out alone again, I promise you."

He had time in that part of his livid brain uninvolved in this drama to wonder from what ancestor this girl inherited her proud carriage, her fearless courage, her strength of will, her beauty. They were both Goodwins, descended from some shared predecessor but not one of the women he had known had what she had. His own mother had been meek, plain, mousy, and Bradley Goodwin's wife, this girl's grandmother, he could only remember as plump, short, motherly, obedient to her husband's wishes and concerned only with the affairs of her household. Of course, Abby had, as she had just told him, led a far different life before her grandfather took her but, by God, if he wasn't so bloody wild and if they had been in their own bedroom, he would like nothing better than to throw her on her back and take her right now.

They stood for several long seconds then he turned away so that she would not see his smile. In a strange way he was pleased with her, despite his outrage at the way she was defying him, but really, the groom had learned his lesson and she would be so grateful that he had done as she begged . . . no, not begged, demanded, she would make their life together increasingly pleasant. He knew she did not love him, her submission in his bed told him that, and though he had grown fond of her in the past eighteen months or so, she did not quicken his heart, only his loins. Perhaps, with a degree more closeness they might make a child.

He turned towards her, his face cold now. "Very well. I believe the man will do as he's told from now on and so will you. You have seen where your wilfulness has led you and I hope you have learned a lesson from it. You must conform, Abby. You are the wife of a prominent citizen, a man of wealth and influence and I will have no more talk, d'you understand?"

"Yes."

"Then go home, not on that mare but in the carriage which I will send for and get into some decent clothes. You'll not be requiring your riding habit again. Perhaps my sister is right and a few months without riding will increase the chances you will conceive—"

"Please, please, Noah, don't get rid of Poppy," she could not help saying. "I have grown very fond of her and I would hate to think she was with someone who did . . . did not care about her as I do. I have given my promise. I won't ride her again until you say I may but I beg of you, don't get rid of her."

The mare had cost him a pretty penny and he knew he would not get his money back. His wife, though she was still flushed with indignation, had a look of contrition about her, whether real or assumed he could not say, but he thought she had been taught a lesson. The threat to Olly, to her family and to the Baxters in their Edge Bottom cottage, which should by rights have been taken from them since it was supposed to be occupied by a man who was employed at the glass works, was sufficient to keep her in line. She was learning, he persuaded himself, to be the lady his wife should be and from now on would take her exercise in her carriage as other ladies did. Calling on other ladies of the same class; that group of Laura Bennett's, for the last thing he wanted was to lose the Bennett's friendship; a walk about the acres of Edge Bottom House in full view of the outdoor servants would be enough for her and if she stepped out of line, did not conform to polite society's idea of a gentlewoman, she would be punished.

From his window he watched her as she climbed into the carriage which had hurriedly been fetched to the door of the office block. Her head was high and her magnificent hair swung in defiance as she turned to stare at all the men who were staring at her. She lifted it into an even haughtier position and straightened her back so that it did not touch the cushions of the carriage and, for some reason, though he had won her obedience, quelled her defiance, made it clear to her who was the master of their household, and her, he did not feel the triumph he should have done. In some way he felt she had won! Clem was driving and the carriage threaded its way through the wagons and crates of glass waiting to be loaded, disappearing through the gates and out into Bamford Street.

He was pleased when he returned home that evening to find her dressed for dinner in one of her new gowns, one of those she had bought for the season's festivities. She had begun to choose her own garments now and her taste did not, as one might have expected, run to the bright and frothy. This was of heather blue, a rich shot silk, the bodice cut very low off her shoulders, the sleeves tiny. The wide skirt had a short train and was looped up at one side and trimmed with blue ribbons to match the colour of her gown. It was perfectly plain, almost severe, but it suited her rich colouring. Her hair was arranged in an artfully careless knot of curls looped with blue ribbons and she wore the exquisite and very expensive diamond earrings and necklace which were his Christmas gift to her.

"Very nice, my dear. *Very* nice indeed."

They ate the superb meal Harriet had planned and Jane Grimshaw had cooked. The wine was excellent, chilled to the correct degree, and Noah Goodwin sighed with great content as he led his obedient wife up the stairs to their bedroom where he proceeded to make love to her, determined this night to make her cry out in passion.

She did cry, but not with passion and not until he had fallen asleep.

19

The Cavalry Ball was held on New Year's Eve at the town hall. The impressive building, which was erected by public subscription, was situated on the west side of New Market Street, its courtroom furnishings being designed to vanish below floor level in the most magical way to turn it into an assembly room. In addition to the courtroom there were rooms for the magistrates, a bridewell and a house for the constable. It housed the Mechanics Institute and the first ever public library. A truly wonderful achievement of which the people of St Helens were justly proud. Along the length of its frontage were wide steps with a terrace at the top overlooked by eleven arched windows, matched on the first floor where the ball was to be held, each one a blaze of light shining out on to the light fall of snow which had begun as dusk fell. It was rumoured that their manorial lord, Lord Thornley, was to bring a party and the excitement was intense, for His Lordship was not often at home on his vast estate but preferred to remain at his hunting box in Leicestershire or his town house in London.

Abby wore a dress of cream-coloured gauze over a foundation of embroidered silk, cream on cream with a low neckline and tiny sleeves and a skirt as wide and as light as a summer cloud. Her satin slippers were cream as was her silk fan and even Noah was impressed by her style. Over her gown she wore a dove-grey velvet evening cape lined with chinchilla and the servants crept to the front of the house to see her go, for Ruby had reported that she looked a picture. Harriet had dressed her hair into a heavy, intricate coil threaded with cream rosebuds and as she climbed into the carriage driven by Olly they were proud of their young mistress, who not only looked the part of a great lady but had acted like one in the matter of the reinstatement of Olly Preston.

They were received at the head of the stairs by Sir Robert Gerard, Lord of the Manor of Windle, and his wife. They arrived at the same time as Laura and John Bennett and mounted the stairs together. Laura was in the palest blue, almost white, a simple gown adorned not with jewellery but with a small spray of wild snowdrops which she said John had found for her in a sheltered part of the garden. There was a magnificent chandelier above them, a donation from some earlier St Helens worthy when the imposing building was built over twenty years ago and the dazzling light fell on the two lovely women who complemented one another perfectly in their colouring, not just their hair but their gowns. Bronze and gold and cream set beside warm brown, the palest of blue, and white. They caught the attention of the many colourful cavalry officers who hung over the banisters to watch the ladies before they entered the ballroom. The officers were even more spectacular than the ladies in their full dress uniform of the East Lancashire Cavalry Brigade which had fought so valiantly and died so disastrously in the Crimean War ten years ago. Scarlet tunics with collars so stiff and high their chins were lifted into a proud and challenging manner. Each had a chest of brilliant buttons and medals, all a-glitter, a cross belt of rich blue satin and a sword belt of white enamelled leather though naturally none of them carried a sword, for this was a social occasion and a sword could impede their dancing. Their tight trousers were dark blue with a red welt down each outside leg and on their shoulders were the insignia of their rank. Even before they reached the top of the stairs Laura and Abby were being quarrelled over!

"Dear Lord, Abby, I hope you've the stamina for this. I have the feeling you'll not be sitting down for a long while. These . . . these vultures are ready to descend on you the minute you enter the ballroom."

Abby laughed in disbelief. "It's not me they're after, Laura Bennett. You must realise you are the most beautiful woman here."

"Rubbish, my dear. I'm too old for these youngsters. I shall have a couple of waltzes then my husband and I will retire to the sidelines with all the other elderly folk."

"We'll see."

The hallway, the stairs, the landing, the ballroom were like a rose garden, dozens of hothouses, including Edge Bottom House, raided that morning for the choicest blooms, with vast arrangements of pink and white twining themselves about the banisters, while every wide shallow step was edged with a basket of flowers. The ladies' room behind the ballroom was staffed by a half a dozen maids who took their capes and were there should a hem need a stitch or a lady a whiff of smelling salts.

The orchestra was playing and about the huge room was placed a row of blue and gold chairs for the comfort of those ladies who were not dancing, but the minute Abby and Laura entered they were surrounded by tall young officers begging to fill their dance cards. Abby raised her eyebrows at Laura as though to say, "There you are, what did I tell you?" And before she knew where she was her dance card was full and two officers were bristling up to each other for the honour of taking her into supper.

Noah shrugged at John, smiling good-naturedly, then promptly vanished, presumably to a side room where card tables were set out. John sauntered over to the table on which refreshments were laid out, champagne, wines, brandy for the gentlemen, a punch bowl and crystal glasses, and with a glass of champagne in his hand he did the rounds of the ballroom, talking to acquaintances, bowing to this one and that, watching his wife resignedly as she waltzed by. He was used to men commandeering Laura, well aware that though many would try, and had done so many times in the past, she would laughingly decline all offers of any sort and within half an hour, duty done, would be in his arms for the rest of the evening.

Not so Abby! She waltzed, she performed the quadrille, the lancers, the polka, all taught her in the nursery with a great deal of hilarity by Holdy, with a verve and grace and confidence that seemed to say she had been used to this sort of occasion all her life. She laughed and chatted to her partners who were enchanted with her, though the tall, slender, bewigged young footman who stood inconspicuously by the door of the card room, almost hidden by a palm tree, should anyone have noticed, which they didn't, frowned fiercely, never taking his eyes from her.

Lord Thornley and his party arrived late. A breathless lad, posted to keep a lookout, came racing up the stairs to herald the arrival of His Lordship's carriages. They were a large group of all ages, the most conspicuous being his tall, handsome son, arrogant, overbearing, land rich, or would be when his father died, who looked about him with an amused smile on his face as though to say how quaint were these manufacturing folk in their play! Amongst others there was a young woman, very pretty and smart, who was not the wife of Lord Thornley's son but a Mrs Carruthers, her husband being one of the tall cavalry officers who were dancing attendance on Abby and Laura and every other young lady with a pretension to looks in the room. Mrs Carruthers looked about her openly and when Noah came from the card room she smiled brilliantly as without a word he led her on to the floor, took her in his arms and whirled her about the room, his head close to hers, and by the expression on her delighted face she was evidently well pleased with what he was whispering to her.

The young officer who was dancing with Abby, as though at some signal from the Honourable Miles Thornley, came to a gliding halt in front of him. He held her arm but it was evident that the older man cared naught for a young captain or his feelings.

"Charlie, introduce me to your lovely partner," he drawled, holding out a hand to her and gazing down insolently into her face with the most beautiful blue eyes Abby had ever seen. They were set in a fan of dark lashes in a face that was as beautiful as his eyes, except for the mouth which had a cruel twist to it. A mouth that could turn nasty if its owner's wishes were not immediately gratified. The young captain did his best to hold on to her and at the same time be polite to Lord Thornley's son.

"This is Mrs Noah Goodwin, Miles. Her husband is—"

"Charlie, be a good fellow and don't bore me with details of Mrs Goodwin's marital status. Instead go and fetch a bottle of champagne for this delightful young lady and myself. We'll be in the—"

"Sir, do excuse us but the captain and I are in the middle of a waltz and I'd like to continue, wouldn't you, Captain." She smiled at the bemused young officer, turning to lead him back on to the floor. Miles Thornley was, for a moment, totally stunned, for he was a man who was used to getting his own way; then he grinned, for he was also a man who liked the chase whether it be on the hunting field or leading to the bedroom. The footman, who was about to step out on to the floor from behind the potted palm thinking there might be trouble, for he had overheard the conversation, slipped back into his hiding place. He fingered the note in his pocket and waited.

She managed to excuse herself from the enthusiastic clutches of a major, the young captain and an impertinent lieutenant who, in the eyes of his superior officers, should know his place and not importune Mrs Goodwin for further dances. She was breathless and flushed, though she could not help but admit she was enjoying herself, but some apologetic gentleman had put his heel in the hem of her gauze skirt and it needed a stitch before it tore further.

She was making her way through the chattering, colourful, constantly moving crowd of guests who stood at the edge of the floor, nodding now and again at a face she knew, smiling at others, when she was startled by a hard hand on her arm. She turned and those about her became still and silent, for it was very evident that Joanna Goodwin, whose hand it was, had something to say to her sister-in law. Joanna had shared their carriage to the town hall, sweeping in and up the wide staircase believing herself to be regal, a grand personage who deserved great respect and though she might have earned the respect, for some reason she was not invited to dance, at least by any gentleman of consequence. Her face was rigid with displeasure and something else that might have been jealousy. She was dressed in a rich velvet gown in a shade of dark green, and her eyes snapped with annoyance.

"And where are you off to might I ask? An assignation, I'll be bound, knowing your liking for the opposite sex. I've seen you flirting with every man with whom you danced . . ."

"Joanna, what on earth?" Abby managed to gasp but Joanna was not yet done.

"Don't you realise what a fool you are making of yourself and of my brother? And now you are making up to the aristocracy as—"

Those about them stared in horror at this grave breach of

good manners, for no matter what dirty linen a family might have in its laundry basket one did not wash it in public.

"Take your hand off me, Joanna, and if you have something to say might I suggest you wait until we are at home. I'm sure Noah would not be—"

"Noah is a fool and knows nothing."

But Abby wrenched her arm from Joanna's grasp and made for the door, all eyes following her, and then glancing back to Joanna who, head high, colour high, turned away imperiously.

Somehow, she was not quite sure how she did it, she ran up another flight of stairs and found herself, obviously lost, in a long, wide hallway on the floor above the ballroom. It was dimly lit and at once she realised her mistake, for this did not lead to the ladies' room where she was headed. She turned and it was then she heard a woman's soft laugh. It was throaty, attractive, seductive, Abby would have said, and at once she began to hurry away, for she had no desire to interrupt some lovers' assignation. Then a man's voice murmured something and her skin prickled, for she had heard that tone, that note of desire, in her own bed almost every night since she had married Noah Goodwin.

The couple were leaning together at the end of the dim hallway. Noah was kissing her shoulders and the woman – she had not been introduced to her so did not know her name, only that she had come in with Lord Thornley's party – arched her neck and moaned slightly. Noah's hands reached for the neck of her already low neckline and pulled it down, exposing her peaked breasts. His hand fondled first one then the other, then his head bent and his lips took one of the rosy nipples into his mouth. When his hand reached for her full skirt and began to pull it up towards her waist, Abby silently fled, running so quickly she almost fell down the stairs. There was a footman at the bottom, his hand outstretched and instinctively she took it, for she had a feeling she was going to fall. It was not that the sight of another woman being made love to by her husband distressed her unduly, for she had long suspected he was unfaithful to her but the shock of it, of actually stumbling across it in such a public place humiliated her and made a mockery of their marriage. It was as though he were saying to the world she did not matter. He had no need to be discreet about his mistress, which most men were, for his wife did not matter. It was a bitter blow and she clung to the young footman's hand as though it were a lifeline in a stormy sea.

It was when the man began to lead her towards the back of the building, going deeper and deeper into the bowels of the town hall, into the darkness which was lit only by the light they had left behind that she stirred from her shock and began to struggle.

"Abby, sweetheart, it's me," a familiar voice whispered and against her ear she felt a breath, again familiar as was the hand that held hers. "I'd a note ready ter give yer but when I saw yer go upstairs I reckoned—"

"*Roddy!*"

"Aye, lass, it's me. I bribed a lad ter lend me this bloody outfit. He goes ter Mechanics Institute wi' me an' does this ter earn a bit of extra cash fer his family. See, it's me." He lifted a hand and whipped off his wig and there he was, her beloved Roddy, his hair all over the place, sticking up in tufts at the back and stuck to his forehead at the front. His eyes were velvety grey in the dark and his teeth were white as he smiled down at her.

"Roddy . . . Roddy, my own love." She swayed with the shock of it on top of the one she had just suffered, but he held out his arms to her and she stepped thankfully into them, into the sweetness, the gentleness, the clean goodness, the steady, honest goodness of him. The sickening sight of her husband stripping another woman barely yards from the ballroom was wiped away as her Roddy held her to him in love, a love that had never faltered through all that had happened to him.

As naturally as the sun touches a flower, he put a hand to the back of her head. Bending, he placed his lips softly on hers, his mouth slightly parted. Hers opened beneath his and they both knew that nothing had changed. Again he put his lips on hers and this time the touch was more demanding, warm, soft, sweet, eager, moist and his arms about her drew her so close he could feel the fullness of her breasts and she could feel the fullness of his erection, then he pushed her gently away, still holding her but pressing her face into the hollow of his shoulder.

Sighing, he put her gently from him, holding her arms out, allowing his eyes to roam over her. "Look at yer. Yer like a princess. Abby, my Abby, yer so beautiful. I've watched yer fer months . . . oh aye, waiting at corners, hidden away so yer wouldn't see me. Up on't moor behind Old Fellow an' then up by Burton Fold when I realised you were avoiding me. I knew why. I knew yer were trying ter be a proper wife to him but I had ter see yer, lass. I couldn't manage without yer somewhere in me life. I was going ter get a note to yer. Aye, I can read an' write now, my darlin'. I needed . . . just once ter talk to yer, yer see, ter tell yer about meself but now . . . Oh, Jesus, Abby . . ." His face creased in agony and she cupped her hands on either side of his cheeks, her own eyes filling with tears. "I've watched them bloody officers dancin' with yer and it were all I could do not to stride across an' smash me fist into their faces. I can't stand it, my love. Come with me. Come with me now. I've got me cottage an' a job . . ."

His arms rose to enclose her again and she pressed her face closer to his shoulder once more so that he would not see the longing in her face. The longing to leave behind all this . . . this artificial life of wealth and false gaiety. Oh, she could not deny that she was enjoying the attention, the laughter, the handsome young officers who fought over her. She was young and loved to dance and, when Noah allowed it, which he surely would soon, to ride out on Poppy; the lovely gowns, the comfort and warmth of her home, but there was no love in it or in her heart. Noah was not unkind to her. He was generous and when they were alone was good company with a dry wit that made her laugh. But where was the warmth and gentleness, the passion, the tenderness she had found with only one man?

With Roddy Baxter!

"Roddy . . . oh, Roddy, I can't, not now . . . not yet."

He seized on her words eagerly. "Then soon? Yer'll come ter me soon. Oh, my lovely girl." His lips took hers fiercely and his body pressed hers against the wall, deep in the shadow of a huge cabinet and this time his hands reached for her, for the soft swell of her half-exposed breast and then to her skirt in a manner so exactly like that of her husband with the woman on the floor above, she recoiled. The heat of Roddy's passion surrounded her but she could not respond, not after what she had seen upstairs. She began to struggle and at once he let her go but his face, deep in the shadow of the cabinet, was so devastated she fell against him in loving sorrow. She dared not tell him what she had witnessed upstairs or he would use it as a lever to free her from Noah.

"My love . . . my love, please. I love you but I can't, not here. Let me go. If you love me let me go." His arms remained at his side with no attempt to hold her to him and his voice was bleak.

"Go then, go."

"Not like this, Roddy, not in anger."

"I don't know what ter do, love." He shook his head and slowly his arms rose to hold her. His cheek rested on her carefully arranged hair and he mumbled into it, making no sense but she understood and her heart became peaceful as her decision was made.

"Where's your cottage? Tell me how to get there."

Olly and Clem watched her as she slipped silently along the side of the house, and across the back of the stables to the hedge that surrounded the vegetable gardens. As she vanished from their sight they looked at each other and shook their heads sadly. Olly would never forget how she had got him his job back, and neither would Ruby, for it had brought to a head their affection for one another and in the spring they were to be married. But would you look at her, still defying the master, though the way she did it ensured that nobody but herself would get into trouble. At least in this household.

She was dressed in her usual outfit of good quality grey woollen skirt, knitted stockings, clogs, a warm grey bodice and a woollen shawl, the ones she had exchanged the year before last on the market for one of her lovely gowns. She had kept them, unknown even to Harriet, stuffed at the back of her wardrobe, she didn't know why, or at least she didn't then, but now, as if she had been waiting for this day, there they were to her hand. Without them she could not have walked the fields about St Helens without causing talk but now, dressed as all the working women were, she moved effortlessly between Edge Bottom House and Denton's Green without a second glance from anyone she met. Her shawl was fastened tightly about her head and face and if her own husband had passed her he would not have known her.

This was not the first time the two men had seen her slip from the house and head for the wall that divided the property of Edge Bottom House from the fields behind it. There was a wood at the rear, not very big, with a small pond in the centre where water birds roosted and on the far side of the wood a high wall with a gate in it. The gate led on to a track encircling the field in which cows grazed and, as usual, the moment they became aware of her they began their slow, inquisitive plod in her direction. She ignored them, turning to the right and the fields she had to cross to reach Roddy's cottage south of Denton's Green.

She passed the end of Sandy Lane, bowing her head in case her mother or one of her mother's neighbours might be about, but it was a bitter February day, the sort of day when the damp entered the bones and made the teeth chatter and there was no one in sight. Across another field towards Little Dam and Big Dam where once, long ago, a young boy and girl had skated, unaware of the disaster that was to befall them. She began to run as she entered a strip of woodland that ran beside the dams, for there was no one about to wonder why a woman should be making haste through a deserted wood. Across Works Lane and keeping in the shelter of the dense thorny hedge, which in summer would be laden with blossom, she walked quickly along the lane until she came to Eccleston Lane on the corner of which was Roddy's cottage.

It still looked dilapidated despite the work Roddy had put in since Jack Harrison, knowing his story and feeling sorry for the lad, had told him he could have it without rent if he knocked it back into shape. It was no good to him standing empty, he said, and though he could let it to some labourer who was to say the man would not allow it to fall into further ruin? Roddy had mended the roof, for it seemed only common sense to keep the rain out, and had renewed old window frames and the front door. There was always wood lying about at the glass works and since he had finished his studying and was not on shift, had visited his mam and put a few shillings in her hand, he had worked on it for the better part of six months. It was sturdily built though a coat of paint was needed and the garden, which he meant to tackle as soon as spring came, was a wilderness.

He had little money to spare for even the essentials. There was a table, knocked up by his old friend Jos Knowles, the joiner at Edge Bottom Glass Works, a chair with a leg that needed mending, and upstairs a bed which Abby had made up with warm blankets, a pretty quilt and clean cotton sheets, purchased with her own money at the market, for, as she told Roddy loftily, she did not mean to lie on a bed that had nothing but a flock mattress and some old sacking to throw over them. In the tiny scullery there were a few pots and pans, again purchased in the market, two cups, two plates, two knives, two spoons, two forks: a pair of everything necessary for them to prepare and eat a meal.

Not that they did much eating, for the short time they could manage together was spent in the bed upstairs where they made love as though, in their hearts, they were afraid each time might be the last.

Roddy's needs were more urgent than hers. He was a man in love with another man's wife and her naked body was a gift he had never, since he came home, expected to receive. He would strip her almost savagely, his will mastering hers, his male body needing to dominate as though it was only in this way that he could call her *his*. For just this hour she belonged to him. He moved within her and she was filled with *him*, not that bastard who called himself her husband. He pounded into her until she cried out, whether in pain or gladness neither of them knew, and afterwards when they lay peacefully in one another's arms he would laugh and murmur that it was a bloody good job the cottage stood in such isolation, for the sound of her voice would certainly come to the attention of any neighbours they might have.

"Abby, my Abby," he would say again and again, his voice becoming ragged and choked, for he realised that she had, so to speak, one eye on the clock. If she was away from the house for longer than an hour or so someone might be looking for her, and then again, he must get ready to go on shift for he didn't want to lose his grand job. He was doing well. Mr Harrison was pleased with him and there was talk already of a promotion. He was at the moment doing the job of a lad. He had ten hours on and twenty-four off, as all apprentices did and it was this shift work that allowed him to meet Abby at his cottage. But the apprentice boys always got called out about three hours before the men, for they had to sweep up and get the furnace room ready for them. The boys were so much younger than he was and liked to lark about, which irritated him who longed to get on. The work was hot and exacting and each glass-maker constantly moved about in the firelit gloom, with his band of assistants, of whom Roddy was one, scurrying about him, fetching and carrying. Heat, bustle and dexterity, Mr Harrison often remarked, for they were the characteristic features of the pot furnaces.

Sometimes, if he had several hours to spare, he would persuade her to sit at the solid table old Jos had made for him and eat the rabbit stew he had cooked in the old blackleaded oven set in the wall. He kept the place spotless, a leftover from his life aboard ship, he told her, for it was the cat-o'-nine-tails for any infringement, or at least a hefty cuff about the head.

They would cling together when they parted, their flesh hurting from the pain. His heart strained to free itself of his love for her, to pour it over her in endless waves, to wrap it about her, to hold her within it, with him, for the rest of their days, but in his eyes as they looked deep and anguished into hers he knew it was not to be so. She belonged to Noah Goodwin.

20

"'Eh, chuck, come in, come in. It's weeks since we've seen yer. We was beginning ter think yer'd forgot all about us though the money were a godsend. That there Olly's a grand lad, the way 'e fetches it over. 'E thinks the world o' you. Eeh, will yer listen to me goin' on wi' you standing on doorstep in't cold. See, give us a kiss." And Abby was pulled fiercely into Betty Murphy's loving arms. She was held protectively against the bump of her mother's new pregnancy, her cheek kissed, her hair smoothed and patted before being pulled into the warmth of the kitchen and pushed into Pa's chair in front of the enormous fire whose flames leaped up the chimney.

"Mam, I kept meaning to come over but there always seems so much to do at the house, which sounds daft with all those servants but Noah's so damn fussy."

"Lovey, I weren't criticising yer." Criticising was a word Betty had learned from their Cissie who was turning out to be a bit of a scholar at that grand school their Abby sent her to. Sara-Ann went as well but she was not so bright nor so enthusiastic as Cissie and, of course, the two eldest lads being lads and already in work when Abby left, they refused to go. Freddy attended now but Dick, who was still a bit young, was to be sent at the beginning of next year, for it seemed their Abby meant her brothers and sisters to have what she missed. So Betty would only have their Georgie and the new one under her feet. Well, under her feet was not the way she would have put it, for her children were dear to her and if they were all eventually to go to school she'd be right lonely without them. Still, she couldn't deny them their chance, could she, not with the example of their Abby before her.

She bustled about the untidy and none too clean kitchen, putting the baby, as Georgie was still called, on Abby's knee, unmindful of the smelly napkin that hung about his baby hips and lifted Dicky on to her own lap. God knew where Freddy was, for the lad had a mind of his own, despite his young age, but she did not let it stop the flow of conversation concerning her neighbours and their doings which she kept up. The kettle was on the boil and she would heap two good spoonfuls of tea into the pot in celebration of her daughter's visit, for she and Declan could afford to be a bit extravagant now and again what with the pair of them in work, the two eldest boys bringing in a few bob a week and the money their Abby sent over regularly.

"No sign of a babby yet, chuck," she said diffidently, eyeing her daughter's slim figure. Though Betty loved this first child of hers, her *love child* as she undoubtedly was, at times she felt a bit awkward with her, for it was like sitting down to a cup of tea with one of the gentry. Abby was so . . . so ladylike, so well-spoken and though she was always affectionate and concerned for her family it was not the same as the old days. Two years now since she had been taken from her and taught to be a proper granddaughter to that old bastard. She had married a gentleman and from what she had gathered from Abby's conversation mixed with the finest in St Helens.

"No, but we've only been married a few months, Mam. Give us time." Abby smiled at her mother, hoping she'd get off the subject of babies.

"A few months! It were a year last December, lass. I swear ter God Declan only 'ad ter look at me an' I were in't family way. I don't know 'ow yer do it," she added enviously. "Not that I'd be wi'out any of yer, even you 'oo give me such grief at first an' if Declan 'adn't bin such a grand chap I don't know what I would've done. But there, yer get what the good God give yer an' the strength ter bear it."

She stared reflectively into the flames of the fire, sipping her tea which was just as she liked it, thanks to the good girl who sat opposite her, hot, sweet and strong.

She stirred herself presently, looking at her daughter. "Why are yer wearin' them old duds, our Abby?" she asked. "Where's that lovely outfit yer wear on yer 'orse?" For Abby had ridden over a time or two on Poppy, tying the mare to the gate in the lane. It had caused a small sensation among the occupants of the cottages who had all come out to stare and whisper among themselves. Betty had not been told that Noah had forbidden her her mare.

"I walked over, Mam and I can't do it dressed in . . . in what I wear at home, surely you can see that." Neither of them noticed the use of the word "home"!

"I suppose not but what's wrong wi' that there carriage? We all enjoy seein' it standin' in't lane."

"I wanted to walk, Mam, it's not far across the fields and would it be too much trouble to ask you to change our Georgie? He's filled his pants by the smell of him."

Betty looked surprised. "Well, yer never used ter be so fussy. Put 'im on't floor if yer don't like it."

"Mam, for goodness sake, it'd only take a minute. Anyway, I can't stay long. I've an errand to run."

"An errand? What sorta errand? You wi' all them servants an' they've got yer runnin' yer own errands."

"Now, Mam, don't be daft. It's summat an' nowt," reverting to the vernacular of her young girlhood. "I just get the longing to walk, sometimes, to be free and—"

"Free. That man o' yours don't keep yer locked up, do 'e?"

"No, of course not but . . . well, I'd look a right fool

squelchin' through Smithies Field in a silk frock, wouldn't I. That's why I keep these things," looking down at herself. Her mother had taken the baby and was busy changing him on the kitchen table where the remains of the family's breakfast still lay. The napkin was slung into the tiny scullery, its contents leaking somewhat, where it was left to stink against the back door and Georgie was cuddled to his mother's enormous bosom as though Betty Murphy were highly offended by her daughter's attitude to the baby who was, after all, her own brother, and was reluctant to chance him on Abby's knee again.

"Is everybody well?" Abby asked, wondering, as her mother had done minutes before, why it was becoming so difficult to talk to her own mother. She loved her and she knew Mam loved and was proud of her, but the division between them was growing with every month they lived apart. She had become used to the clean comfort, the smooth running of her own household, thanks to Harriet, the cheerful, immaculate servants, the fragrance of fresh flowers every day, the endless supply of hot water and thick white towels, the scented soap, she supposed, and her mother's careless ways, which once she had hardly noticed, were becoming onerous to her.

She had not been to Sandy Lane for weeks, preferring the lively conversation, the heated debates on women's rights, the plight of female factory workers in which Laura was involved, the question of education for every child, the evil of prostitution, female suffrage and even the subject of birth control as advocated by Annie Besant and enlightened members of the medical profession. In fact she had meant to bring up the matter with her mother who had suffered more than a dozen pregnancies of which nine had survived, but it seemed there was another on the way so perhaps she would leave it for now. She herself had been a little shocked when the ladies had discussed the subject as though it were merely some medical matter to which their philanthropy might be applied. They talked of so many things with the utmost candour that she had begun herself to see that these women were working towards a better life for other women and she found herself becoming more and more involved. She enjoyed the sharp minds and pleasing company of women like Laura Bennett, sending Olly with the money she gave to her mother each week instead of bringing it herself. Any moment she could manage was spent in Spring Cottage with Roddy and her own family had been neglected. Her life was full and busy.

She felt ashamed at times when the thought occurred to her that she had outgrown her own family, finding the cottage squalid and her siblings coarse and untutored, which they were. The boys were hopeless cases, seeing no benefit in the ability to read and write and Sara-Ann attended school only because she was made to. Only Cissie was showing promise and sometimes Abby wondered why she bothered, for the girl would probably end up in the kitchen or laundry of a big house, or in the dairy at Updale Farm. Perhaps something could be done. Perhaps her sister, who was nearly ten and in Betty's opinion ready for work, could be kept on at school, or . . . or put to some work that would be more suited to her abilities, but in the meanwhile she herself must be off on her *errand*.

The thought had suddenly come to her as she walked across the fields this morning that a visit to her mother's cottage in Sandy Lane was the ideal excuse she needed to slip up to Denton's Green and Roddy's cottage on a regular basis. Mind, Noah would object to her even going to Sandy Lane, never mind walking there, but if she must go, he would say, hardly able to forbid it, one of the grooms would take her in the carriage. But if he didn't know, if she could keep it from the servants, when he did become aware of it, for he surely would, she would at least have the innocent excuse that she had been to visit her family.

She was just about to leave, smoothing down her woollen skirt and wishing she didn't feel quite so . . . *soiled*, especially as she was going straight from here into Roddy's arms, when the door was flung open and her two sisters entered the kitchen bringing the blast of cold air with them. Their little faces were chapped and though Abby had told her mother to get them some warm mittens she noticed they weren't wearing them.

"Come ter't fire," their mother cried, once again thrusting Georgie into Abby's arms, bundling the girls towards the warmth and, after taking their shawls from their shoulders and throwing their books contemptuously on to the littered table, put a cup of the tea into their hands, wrapping their chilblained fingers about the cup. Abby knew that her mother loved and cared about these children of hers but she was slipshod, careless, enjoying the kudos among her neighbours of having daughters who could read and write but unable to see where it would lead them.

Abby spoke from the doorway as she placed Georgie on his feet, for she could see no good reason why he had to be nursed. His mother at once snatched him up and Abby wondered what the toddler would do when the new one came. What they had all had to do, she supposed. Move over and let the newcomer take its place!

"What did you learn today, girls? I see you've got a picture book with animals in it. See, Sara-Ann" – moving over to the fire where the child huddled – "what's this?" opening the book at a random page.

"Er, well . . . a hanimal," the girl floundered, frowning, not with determination to master the picture, but with annoyance at being bothered with it here at home.

"But what sort of animal? What do the words say?"

"Nay, don't ask me." Sara-Ann's voice was indifferent.

"It's a camel, our Abby," Cissie piped up.

"That's right, love, and can you tell me what it says underneath?"

Cissie leaned against Abby and her eyes devoured the page.

"Camel, patient, kind and mild, teach me, though a little child, that obe . . . obed . . ."

"Obedient."

". . . obedient I must be, patient, willing, just like thee."

"That's wonderful, love. You read so well and I'm proud of you."

The child preened, Sara-Ann sulked and their mother looked from one to the other as though the whole thing was a mystery to her. She had the strangest feeling that their Abby was up to something and she didn't like it but her brain, concerned for so long with nothing more than how to keep her family warm and fed and clothed, couldn't quite get to grips with it.

"Well done, sweetheart," Abby told her again, bending to plant a kiss on the little girl's cheek.

Cissie was a pretty child. All Betty's children had some claim to good looks but Cissie was more . . . well, a bit like Abby who was the beauty of the family. Cissie, of course, was the child of Betty and Declan without the strain of breeding and comeliness of Abby who had inherited her features from the Goodwins.

Georgie began to whine and at once Betty opened her bodice and brought out her sagging breast. He bent his head and fastened his mouth on the nipple. Betty had hoped if she fed the child herself, as she had done with them all, Declan would not get another baby on her, a common belief among the poor but it had done no good. She'd have to get Georgie off soon, for the other one would need all the sustenance she could give it. She sighed and pushed her hand through her untidy hair, for it seemed she would never get shut of these constant burdens, not until she reached that stage all women come to in their lives.

Abby put her arms awkwardly about her mother and the little boy, then let herself out of the house and stepped swiftly along the lane until she reached the lodge that lay to the south of Little Dam. She looked about her and, seeing no one, slipped through the hedge and began to run through the stretch of woodland beyond. Within ten minutes she was in Roddy's arms and within five more, in his bed.

"I want to bring my sister to live with me," she said baldly at dinner several weeks later and was not surprised when Noah's mouth fell open in consternation. Joanna was dining with them and her expression, which like Noah's had been one of amazement, changed to a look of utter disapproval. She turned to look at her brother, waiting for the explosion which, naturally, would come.

It did!

"What the bloody hell are you talking about? Your sister! I never heard anything so preposterous in my life. Have you taken leave of your senses?"

"I agree with Noah. My goodness, are we to have your entire family?"

Abby turned on Joanna like a tigress defending her cub. "This has got nothing to do with you, Joanna, and I'd be obliged if you would mind your own business."

"This is my business. Noah is my brother."

"And *my* husband. He is the master of this house."

"I'm glad someone recognises it," Noah said mildly, for after the first shock of his wife's statement he felt like smiling, since who but Abby would have such a daft idea and who but himself could put an end to it? He was surprised that she had not made more fuss over his refusal to allow her to ride. Every day as he rode into or out of the yard he could see the pretty little mare grazing in the paddock or throwing up her heels in that flighty way she had, and though he knew Olly or Clem exercised her Abby had made no fuss about it. She seemed to be behaving herself, though he was not really sure he approved of her constant visits to Laura Bennett and the somewhat progressive and growing group of ladies she met there. Miss Tyson and Miss Bowman who were well known for the views voiced by what was called "the women's movement" such as universal suffrage, Mrs Holme and Mrs Sheen, among others, wives of prominent gentlemen, certainly, but he had heard some of them had very peculiar ideas. Still, he hoped that at last she was settling down, though there was still no sign of a child. It was about four months since he had banned her from riding but perhaps these things took time. They had been married for over a year now and he had the niggling feeling that other men were talking about him behind his back, knowing of his experience with the ladies and speculating on when he would get his wife with child!

"Well, I am appalled at the very idea—" Joanna began, but Noah lifted one hand to silence her.

"I'm sure you are, Joanna, but the matter is no longer under discussion. Abby's sister is not to take up residence at Edge Bottom House."

"I should think not. We'll have them all coming over to dine next."

"That is enough, Joanna. I have told Abby what I think."

"Besides which it is nothing to do with you, Joanna," Abby hissed. "You will keep involving yourself with my affairs and I must tell you it is beginning to irritate me intensely."

"That's enough, Abby. We have finished—"

"No! You may have finished but I haven't. Joanna and I don't like each other and if I said black she would say white.

It is through her meddling that Olly was dismissed and I was forbidden to ride Poppy and I can't forgive her for it."

"Oh, for God's sake, Abby, ride your bloody horse if you insist," Noah snapped.

"Well, really, Noah Goodwin, your language at the dinner table is beyond believing and I can only say I am astonished that you should let this . . . this . . ."

"Be careful, Joanna. Abby is my wife and you must realise I will take her side."

"*Take her side!* I am of the opinion you are far too lenient with her as it is and now you say that not only are you to allow her to ride out again, flaunting herself in that . . . that outfit she wears, but are to ignore my advice in the matter of the company she keeps."

Abby sprang to her feet and both Kitty and Ruby squeaked and huddled together against the sideboard wishing, or so it seemed, to become invisible, at the same time committing every word to memory in order to repeat it all to the others in the kitchen.

"*The company I keep.* And what does that mean, Joanna? Are you by any chance referring to my friendship with Laura Bennett and the other ladies, yes, they are all ladies, who meet to discuss—"

"That woman and her husband, or so I have heard, take common prostitutes into their home and keep them there for some purpose."

"Yes, they do but he is a doctor, Joanna and some of those women are badly injured by men who care naught for—"

Joanna lifted her lip in distaste. "How can you talk in such a disgusting manner when—"

"*That is enough!*" Noah thundered, considerably disgusted himself, and the two maids cowered even further, wondering if the subject of prostitutes would be considered a matter for a gossip in the kitchen. "I will not have this turmoil when I am trying to eat my evening meal. Nor at any other time, come to that. I have said Abby may ride again providing she has a groom with her, but let me make it quite clear that her sister will not take up residence in my home. If Abby wishes the girl to live in good society let her take her to Laura Bennett's where she will mix, as my wife points out, with ladies. Now, let us get on with our meal. Kitty" – turning to the paralysed maid – "refill my wine glass, if you please, and you, Abby, sit down and eat your meal. No, Joanna, not another word," as Joanna would have continued with her complaints against his wife. "Thank you, now pass the salt and let us talk of—"

But whatever he had in mind, perhaps a progress report on his plans to build a brick works on the spare ground at the back of the glass works, was rudely interrupted by the door swinging wildly open and the abrupt entrance of May who seemed to have been flung into the dining-room by force.

"Confound it, what now?" he snarled, throwing his napkin to the table and upsetting his glass of wine which Kitty had just filled. Kitty didn't know what the devil to do. Rush forward and mop up the wine or turn to May and ask her coldly what she thought she was up to, entering the dining-room so rudely. Ruby had her hand to her mouth, ready, it appeared, to burst into tears, for really, what with one thing and another, she had half begun to believe she and Olly would never get wed. Why she should think that was a mystery, even to herself, but as that was the subject on which her mind dwelled the most any small thing upset her.

"Oh, madam . . . Miss Abby . . . Oh, please, miss, can yer come at once. We don't know what ter do."

"I swear to God every woman in this house has lost her mind," Noah bellowed. "First we are to have visited on us . . ."

Abby had risen to her feet, her own thoughts plagued with pictures of Roddy at the back door, her mam come to tell her of some dreadful accident, Dorcas Baxter, perhaps Laura but then she would not come to the back door.

"What is it, May?"

"Can we not eat a meal in peace, Noah. Your servants are—"

"Shurrup you old bugger," Abby said almost mildly, shocking every occupant of the room as she reached out to May and took her hand. "Tell me, May."

"It's Mrs Woodruff, ma'am. She's bin took badly. Oh, Lord, there's blood an'—"

"*Blood!* Has she cut herself?"

Incensed by her sister-in-law's language, which she supposed was only to be expected considering her upbringing, Joanna sighed deeply and looked at her brother, shaking her head. "Noah, your household seems to need organisation, to say the least."

Abby was leading the somewhat hysterical maid through the open door, turning to summon Kitty who was the most sensible of the lot. "What has happened to Mrs Woodruff?"

"It's babby, we reckon, though it's not due for weeks yet. Well, they only wed in September and it's only April."

"What are you babbling about, May? What baby is this and why—"

"Nay, Miss Abby." May's voice was reproachful. "Don't tell us yer didn't know."

The kitchen was a scene of chaos and Abby had time to wonder when Noah and Joanna would get the rest of their meal, if indeed they ever did. Harriet lay on the kitchen floor, her head in Nessie's lap, her arms waving feebly as though trying to rise or as if she were doing her best to get the kitchen servants back into some sort of order.

"Really, Abby, such a fuss."

"A fuss. Such a fuss! Why wasn't I told about this and why in God's name didn't I guess? Jesus tonight, I'm the eldest of the family and I've seen my mam in this condition that many times, aye, and helped her to give birth and yet I didn't know. See, May, run for Olly or Clem. No, not Clem, he'll want to be with his wife, send Olly for Doctor Bennett. Off you go and you, Kitty, mop up this floor or someone'll slip in the blood. Now then, Harriet, we're going to lift you into your sitting-room for the moment. You can't give birth on the . . . Why didn't you *tell* me?"

"I'm not giving birth, Abby," Harriet hissed through clenched teeth. "It's not due for another month or two."

"A month or two, which is it?"

"I don't know. I've never had a baby. I thought it was, you know, what women have in their . . ." Harriet began to pant, arching her back and then there was Clem in the doorway, fetched by Jacko who slept over the stable and had been roused by the commotion. Clem's seamed and weathered face was as white as Cook's apron and he seemed to leap across the floor, kneeling at his wife's side. He took her from Nessie and gathered her tenderly into his arms, smoothing her, patting her, murmuring to her as he did with the horses in his care.

"Now, lovely girl, steady, steady, I'm 'ere and doctor'll be along soon an' if not then there's enough of us ter see yer through it."

"It's not due, Clem," Harriet pleaded.

"Aye, my lass, whether it is or whether it's not us'll manage."

The bell on the wall jangled persistently, calling for attention from the dining-room but nobody took any notice as they watched the miracle of Clem Woodruff deliver his wife of a small, but perfectly healthy boy.

21

Why wasn't she told? Why hadn't she seen it? How could she have been so blind? Dear Lord, hadn't she had enough experience in the first fifteen years of her life to recognise a pregnant woman when she saw one, and she really thought Harriet had been most unkind not to tell her. She hadn't even noticed Harriet putting on weight, she complained, and on and on until Harriet laughingly stopped her.

"Here, hold the boy and stop berating me. I must admit I didn't know myself until I was well on into the fourth or fifth month. I couldn't believe that a woman of my age could conceive, Abby, especially after, well . . ." – she hesitated and her face became flushed – "after the life I have led. I've never hidden it from you what I was, what I did with your grandfather and with many other men, and not once did I become pregnant." She paused again. "That's not quite true. There was one time, when I was loved by the son of the family I worked for. Mind you, loved is not a word that really describes what he felt for me. The moment it was disclosed I was with child, they threw me out and left me to starve for all they cared. Me and the child I was expecting. But . . . I got rid of that baby, Abby. I had no choice though I loved its father. He was called Todd," she finished simply.

"So the boy is named . . . ?"

"Do you think it strange after what he did to me?"

"Well . . ."

"He was my first love, Abby. A woman never forgets her first love, you should know that, lass."

Abby looked up sharply, but Harriet was gazing dotingly into her baby's face. The child lifted a tiny hand and waved it experimentally in the air, fixing his strange, troubled eyes on Abby, frowning as though he knew something that worried him and was wondering whether to tell her, then he yawned and his eyes closed. Abby felt her heart tug painfully, brooding on why it was that she did not conceive a child. For God's sake, she was making love to two men, one of them for over a year, and yet neither of them had made her pregnant. Which was just as well, her aching heart decided, for she would then be faced with the dilemma of wondering who the father was, Noah or Roddy.

"Well," she said lightly to cover her thoughts, "this one was an early arrival so am I to believe that you and Clem . . ."

"Trust you, Abby Goodwin, to say what all the others are thinking. Married in September and a mother in April. A seven months baby which we both know is not so. Doctor Bennett confirmed it with Kitty standing at his elbow and she will no doubt have passed it on to the others but frankly, I don't care. Clem and I are married, happily married, let me add, and this son of ours is not a bastard. Oh, dear God, I'm sorry, my love, I didn't mean to . . ." Harriet had her hand to her mouth in dismay but Abby shook her head and smiled, then placed Harriet's son in her arms.

"When you are in love how can you turn away from . . . from it, Harriet? You and Clem . . ."

"Dearest, I'm sorry. You still think of him?"

"Of course. He will always be in my heart."

"And how is the new mother, my pet, and her son? Thriving, I trust?"

Noah smiled at her through the candlelight and she was

struck by the expression of sadness in his eyes. She knew he was thinking that a man and woman in their forties could get themselves a son and yet he, a man in his prime with a young and healthy wife, no matter how hard he tried, could not impregnate her. It must be her fault, she supposed, for surely *two* men could not be incapable of fathering a child. It was probably this preoccupation with her own dilemma, that of being in love with a man who was not her husband, and how to see him as often as possible that had blinded her to Harriet's condition.

"They're both well, Noah. John is pleased with them and has allowed Harriet to be carried back to End Cottage. I've been over today to see she has everything she wants. I've lent her Nessie."

"Nessie?"

"The scullery-maid."

"Ah."

"She needs someone to help her until she's on her feet."

"Of course."

"You don't mind?"

"Why should I mind, my love? This is your household and you have the domestic arranging of it and the servants. If you can manage without . . . ?"

"Nessie."

"Without Nessie, then that is for you to decide. You realise you will have the full running of the household now, with Harriet taken up with her new role. Good God, old Clem and Harriet who used to service your grandfather . . ."

"*Noah!*"

"It's true and you knew it. She must have been terrified at the prospect of losing her livelihood when he died and yet you kept her on."

"*I?* I had nothing to do with it. You were well aware that without Harriet this house would have ground to a halt and you would not have liked that, Noah. I was incapable of being the mistress of a house like this when we married and had it not been for Harriet—"

He held up his hands in mock dismay. "Please, my pet, I was paying you a compliment. But Harriet has trained you. You were an apt pupil and now I think you are ready to take over. You will, I'm afraid, have no choice, for I do believe Harriet is to be a doting mother with no time for any other role. I think you will manage, my pet. You have proved it in the past year and I applaud you for it. My only criticism is your . . . leanings towards this women's thing in which you and Laura Bennett have such an interest. But I suppose as they are all ladies, those involved, there can be no harm in it."

She was surprised by the quietness of his tone, his unruffled belief that she was ready to take over the running of his household. By his acceptance of the situation and his . . . yes, his understanding. She had never thought of Noah as an understanding man, or even a very moral one. He had his mistress, she knew that, for he had been seen with Mrs Carruthers on his arm in some gambling house in Liverpool, but she thought he would not approve of the topics discussed in Laura's drawing-room. This was a man's world and women belonged in it only for the purpose men decreed. It was Laura who had spoken to her of the male middle-class ideology which stressed that the role of decent women as wife and mother was the only function of which they were capable. Under the law married women had no rights or existence apart from their husbands.

"Have you heard the popular maxim, 'my wife and I are one, and I am he'. It means that a married woman has no legal right to her property, her earnings should she be in employment, her freedom of movement, her conscience, her body or her children."

"Dear God, I had not realised," Abby had answered, aghast.

"No, but something must be done about it, Abby. We are nothing but sexual objects to—"

"Not you, Laura."

Laura had smiled. "No, not me, dearest. I am one of those strange creatures who enjoys the love of my husband but for heaven's sake tell no one, or they will think me a freak. Even the enlightened married ladies who are in accord with my views."

Noah would be appalled if he knew of the subjects discussed at Laura's house. There were women in many parts of the country who were ready to rise up and rebel against this male dominance and Laura was one of them, even though she herself was not one who was dominated. There were women whose names were to become increasingly familiar to Abby: Lydia Becker, Josephine Butler, Barbara Bodichon, Emily Davies, Elizabeth Garrett. Lydia Becker, Laura told her, had already formed a group who called themselves the Ladies Institute and if Abby cared to read it, had published their *English Woman's Journal* which was to be the voice of the women's movement in Manchester. Many of these women wished to become doctors, lawyers and members of other professions, making careers for themselves as men did and they were prepared to fight for their aims, amongst many others to do with bettering the lives of women.

But Noah, like all gentlemen, had no idea of it, believing that Abby, Laura, Miss Tyson, Mrs Drummond and the others who took tea at Claughton Street were doing nothing more than interfering, in a benevolent way, of course, in the way the poor ran their lives.

Roddy knew and she thought he might have told Dorcas, for she had a feeling that Dorcas would approve of the things Abby and her group, and indeed women from many parts of the country, were trying to do for their sisters. She supposed Dorcas was aware that she and Roddy were lovers early in their relationship though she never once voiced her disapproval, or even opinion. Dorcas was like that. One day early in the year, a few weeks after Roddy had moved into Spring Cottage, Abby had burst into the kitchen, her face rosy with running, her arms already stretched out to fold herself against Roddy's waiting body, only to find his astonished mother sipping tea by his fireside. Roddy sprang up, overturning his own mug of tea and did his best to pretend surprise, eager, she supposed, to protect her own reputation. Not that his mother was likely to spread it about the village that Noah Goodwin's wife, dressed like a field woman, was visiting her bachelor son, but her eyes, so like Roddy's in colour and shape, had become hazed with fear, for the consequences to them all would be catastrophic should the owner of Edge Bottom Glass Works know of this visit.

"Mrs Baxter," she had stammered, looking no more than about twelve in her confusion. "How lovely to see you," she had continued in that polite, well-bred manner she had learned in the past two years.

"Abby." Dorcas nodded regally and also rose to her feet and folded her arms across her chest, ready to speak her mind, which was her way, but something crossed her face and her eyes softened, for hadn't this lass defied her husband and saved the life of Dorcas Baxter's son.

"Come in and get ter't fire, Abby," Roddy babbled. "This is a grand surprise. See, 'ave a cup o' tea. It's just brewed."

But Dorcas passed between them, moving towards the door. "I'll be on me way, our Roddy. Come fer yer dinner on Sunday if yer can."

"I will, Mam."

"Good-day ter yer, Abby," Dorcas murmured, giving Abby a steady look, which told her that if hurt came to Roddy

Baxter through Abby Goodwin, Abby would have Dorcas to contend with.

At once she fell into his arms. "Oh, God . . . Oh, God. I never thought . . ."

"She just turned up. I didn't know yer were comin'. Abby, my Abby . . . Dear sweet Jesus, I've missed yer." His voice shook as he lifted her hand and kissed it reverently so that her heart almost broke with love for him.

"Does she know about us, Roddy, your mam? Have you told her we are . . ."

"No, I haven't, but she's not daft, lass." He wrapped his arms tightly about her, as though afraid that this confrontation might somehow tear her from him and though she could scarcely breathe she did her best to get even closer, burrowing her face against his chest, her cheek to his fast-beating heart. It was as though they had believed themselves to be invisible, that their love and their meetings were a secret which, as long as it was not discovered, was impregnable. They were both aware that Dorcas Baxter was not a gossip about anyone or anything, let alone her own son's personal life. Put to the torture she would remain silent but it put a different slant on the relationship which they had thought was shared by no one but themselves.

"I should've gone away months ago," he said bitterly. "God knows what he'd do to yer if he found out. I should leave yer in peace now but it seems I can't." He spoke as if his heart were being torn from his body in pain.

"No, don't say that, my dearest love." She smiled lovingly into his face, combing his thick waving hair back from his forehead with her fingers. "Of course, we should leave one another in peace but it's a peace I don't want. It would be like cutting off a part of me that's essential to life and though I could stumble on, injured and ready to die, I would never be whole again."

"Then leave 'im," he said eagerly. "Come ter me. We could go far away, to another country perhaps. They have fine glass works in France and Belgium and I'd find work. Sweetheart, I've no wish ter upset yer but it seems yer not to have a child. I know you must—" He stopped speaking abruptly, his throat working convulsively. "I know yer must let 'im . . . he's yer husband an' . . . and then there's you an' me an' yet yer don't get with child. Now's the time ter make the break before yer do. What keeps yer?"

She put her hand to his lips, then kissed him carefully, as one would a sleeping child and when she stopped his head fell slowly to her shoulder in despair. He held her gently now, not clutching her body to him as he had done earlier. When he looked up at her she saw for the first time the fine grooves on either side of his mouth, the smooth skin creasing at the corner of his eyes and his eyebrows dipping in a frown. He looked thinner, older, his eyes a paler grey than once they had been as though they were washed by fatigue. She was doing this to him. He was a young man, not yet twenty. He should be merry, spritely, perhaps courting some comely lass who would make him a fine, strong wife and give him strong healthy children. She knew he was doing well at Mulberry Glass Works and that Mr Harrison thought highly of him. He had this cottage which he intended to turn into a snug little home of which any woman would be proud. And it was *she*, Abby Goodwin, who was preventing it.

"Should we . . . give it up?" she asked tentatively.

"Give it up? What? Give what up?"

"This. You and me."

"Oh, Christ, Abby," he said, his voice no more than a whisper, his eyes closing briefly as if, suddenly, he couldn't bear to look at her. "Don't do this. Don't say it. I can't bear the thought. It would hurt you, I know that, but it would crucify me."

They sat down abruptly on the bench that lay to the side of the table, both trembling in terror at the very thought of being parted again. She cradled him to her, for of the two of them he was the worst affected. She soothed him wordlessly, pushing his hair back, kissing his brow, his cheek, his closed eyes. She had loved him for perhaps ten years, ever since as children they had discovered a liking for one another. She loved him without question. She desired him, her body's sheer basic need to possess him governed her, to give herself into his possession. She would never alter. Her love of him would never alter, for it was fused into her body, her mind, her heart, the very soul of her and would never die. So why, as he begged her to do, could she not leave Noah and simply walk away with the man she truly loved? As he had said, she had no children to hold her to her marriage vows so what was it that kept her to her husband? Surely it could not just be the material things she possessed as Mrs Noah Goodwin, but even as the thought slid into her mind another thought followed it and in the centre was the determined but kind and smiling face of Laura Bennett.

She could hardly believe that what she had been told only a couple of days ago could influence her but it seemed it had wriggled into her consciousness and taken root. The ladies had been discussing another lady, Josephine Butler, who had for many years been crusading for the repeal of the Contagious Diseases Acts which required any woman in a garrison town or a port who was suspected of being a prostitute to be examined for venereal disease. If found to be infected the prostitute was locked up in a hospital treating venereal disease until she was deemed to be disease-free, at which time she was given a certificate. This then meant that she was *clean* and available to any disease-ridden male to infect her again and, according to Josephine Butler, gave an unthinking acceptance of male sexual licence. These *fallen* women were a necessary part of society in order that *pure* women, wives and mothers of children, the protected, privileged ladies married to gentlemen, could remain untainted. There was more to it, much more, Laura had told them, regarding the inequality of men and women. She later asked if Abby would care to come with her to Manchester where a group had been formed and where a lecture was to be held. She would hear things that might incense her. Had Abby been aware that children were sold . . . No, no, she would not go any further, she said, at least not at the moment, for the look of horror on Abby's face had told her that her new friend was as ignorant of the vices of the time as were most women.

But surely this . . . this crusade that the women of the country were starting out on could not be holding her back from leaving Noah and living with Roddy? There was something deeper than that and she was not at all sure what it was. Something to do with Noah himself, she supposed, for the thought of the scandal that would explode if she should take such action did not frighten her. He would not sit still and accept it, she knew that, and in the battle that would ensue, for he had the law on his side, there would be wounded, those more badly affected hers and Roddy's family. She was not afraid for herself but for them.

"I love you, Abby."

"And I love you."

They drifted up the stairs and slowly, one by one, he removed pieces of her clothing, his mouth smiling and tasting, his nostrils inhaling the fragrance of her, shaking loose her hair and burying his face in it. She raised her arms to display her naked body, the pale spring sunlight falling on her bare shoulders, the contours of her breast, the proud peaks of her rosy nipples. Her young body was smooth and firm, her legs long and slender. He shed his own garments and for a long while they simply gazed at one another, then began the touching, with fingertips on the outline of an ear and throat, the hardness of chest and thigh until they were both sighing languorously as his body flowed over hers, hers dissolving like a rich, unhurried stream as he entered her.

Later their bodies were entwined in the aftermath of loving so that neither was aware where one ended and the other began. Two bodies made into one, flesh cleaving flesh as the Bible said, then the sweet confusion as they became two again. To be loved, to come back from heaven and find heaven is still beside you was the wondrous miracle of the love in Roddy and Abby and she felt like weeping, for she knew though it could be hers for the asking until death ended it, something held her back. She was bemused with adoration and yet her mind was as sharp and as clear as the ice that had tinkled from the frozen trees in the garden in winter.

They lay for ten minutes, quiet, slowly returning to their own separate worlds and for some reason, she didn't know why, she began to talk to him of the meetings at Claughton Street. He listened, his chest rising and falling slowly beneath her cheek, his heart beating with his love and admiration for her, because he knew, as many another man would not, that what she and the ladies were quietly striving towards, freedom and equality for all men and women, was a good thing. He himself did not have the vote since he had no property. Only one and a half million men were enfranchised, and that brought about by the Reform Bill of 1832.

"Are there any lads involved in this . . . this thing the ladies talk about?"

"I think there might be. John Bennett for one. I've heard him say Laura's got a brain as good or better than a dozen men he knows. D'you know, she wanted to be a doctor?"

"What, a lady doctor?"

"Don't be so bloody scathing," rearing up and glaring into his face. "Why shouldn't women be doctors, or anything else that men can do? Look at us, you and me. Two years ago we could neither of us read nor write, now we can do both. You're learning all sorts at that Mechanics Institute and I only wish I could go there. All I've been taught is how to be a lady. I can play a bit on the piano, speak a word or two of French, paint though I'm awful at it and I've learned where countries of the world are. Now Laura is teaching me a lot of other things I'm not supposed to know. Politics and this . . . appalling inequality which affects not just women, but men too. Why shouldn't *you* have the vote, like other men? Your brain's as good as Noah's and yet, just because he is a property owner he—"

She felt him stiffen in her arms and knew she had broken the cardinal, but unspoken rule that her husband's name was not to be mentioned in this cottage. Roddy couldn't cope with it and so she did not speak of her life apart from his. Except this, this new ideal she was learning from Laura. This idea of the emancipation of women. She was not and never would be a free woman, for Noah would be totally against her fighting this war, this so far silent, domestic revolution; the idea that men and women were equal. He would laugh at the notion of women having "rights", at social reform, at all the other wonderful campaign ideals Laura and the others discussed.

But Roddy might. Roddy was a man who had suffered and won through. He was a man who respected his mother, and other women, and felt great compassion for those women who were exploited to make "gentlemen" wealthy.

But it seemed today was not to be the day Roddy Baxter could be encouraged, like some other men were, into helping in this cause that was becoming so dear to Abby's heart. Roddy knew her better than she knew herself, she thought, and instinctively, perhaps subconsciously, he was aware that it was part of the reason why she could not simply pack her bags, leave Noah and move in with him.

"I'd best be off," she murmured. She shrugged into her clothes, watched from the bed by Roddy. She wound her hair into a plain knot and tied her shawl closely about it. She had committed adultery, a crime before God and the law. It was not the same law for a woman as it was for a man. Society excuses a man but an adulterous woman is worse than a leper and Noah, if he found out, would hurt her badly. Which made even more worth while the cause she was drawn to fight for.

Roddy held out his hand and smiled and when she took it drew her down next to him.

"No, if I'm late . . . please, Roddy, if you love me . . ."

At once he let her go and, leaping to his feet, threw on his clothes and followed her down the stairs to the kitchen. He wore no shoes but hand-in-hand they walked down the overgrown path to the rickety gate, caution thrown to the wind, for their love blinded them. It was not a busy lane but the occasional wagon creaked past on the way to the farm.

"When?" he asked her, his mind filled with the days when he would be alone and she with her husband.

"As soon as I can."

"Promise."

"I promise, my dear love."

"I might join this 'ere group an' fight for me fellow man if it meant seeing yer more often."

He smiled, his face gentle with his love and as she ran back through the trees beside the Big Dam tears flowed across her cheeks with her sorrow.

22

In 1867 the first women's suffrage society was formed. It was in the beginning named the National Women's Social and Political Union and a month after its inception Abby Goodwin realised she was pregnant. She had been married for almost four years, accommodating her husband in their marriage bed almost every night and sometimes in the morning as well and for almost three of those four years she and Roddy Baxter had been lovers.

It was Midsummer day, June, and her birthday. She was twenty years old and her husband had given her an exquisite bracelet, diamonds linked by a lacy chain, light and delicate, fastening it to her wrist that morning as they lay in bed. She had been totally naked, calm, peaceful, smiling after he had made love to her, for she had long come to terms with this husband of hers who went his own way, as she went hers and which he allowed providing she was circumspect about it. There was to be a party that evening to which not only his friends, well, business acquaintances really, but also hers from her group were all invited. Laura Bennett and John, first and foremost, Emmeline Tyson and her brand-new fiancé, Charlie Hardwick, who had once had hopes of Abby herself, Jane Bowman for whom an extra man had been invited to balance the numbers, Agnes Holme, Faith Sheen, Ann Dalton, Adele Drummond and their respective husbands, and Miss Florence Tickle whose father worked on Noah's cutting-room floor.

"Nay, I can't come to a party with all them posh folks there, Abby," Florence had declared emphatically, shocked, her plain face screwed up with differing emotions: delight at the thought of her friend and fellow suffragist including her, and fright at the thought of being included.

"Nonsense, Florence, you and I are the best of friends. All the others are coming so why should you be left out?"

"But they're gentry, Abby. My pa works for your husband."

"Florence, you and I are not only friends but sisters in our cause and I wouldn't dream of excluding you. Bring someone, a young gentleman, if you wish. I happen to know that you and that young glass-blower have been seen walking out on certain occasions. I know it's not some light-hearted thing, for your father wouldn't approve."

Florence blushed to the roots of her plain brown hair. "Abby, I couldn't; he wouldn't . . ."

"There will be over a hundred people there, Florence and you and he will be able to hide yourself amongst them if you so wish. All your friends from the society will be present, not to mention dozens from Noah's circle. I shall be upset if you don't come, Florence." Florence had reluctantly agreed.

It was pandemonium in the house as all the servants prepared for the party, even the outdoor men fetching and carrying half of Mr Renfrew's garden into the house, or so he grumbled. She and Harriet had spent the last few days arranging menus, overseeing and even helping with the vast amounts of cooking, baking, roasting and mixing, stirring and whisking that had gone into the magnificent buffet she and Noah had decided upon. There was to be a boar's head garnished with aspic jelly, mayonnaise of fowl, hams, chicken pies by the dozen, roast pheasant, decorated tongue, veal and larded capon. Dishes of prawns, oyster patties, lobster salad, and to follow trifles, iced Savoy cake, tipsy cake, which was a masterpiece devised by Cook, who had declared she would finish up in the lunatic asylum if one more thing was asked of her, but still managed blancmange, fruited jellies, custard and cream topped with almonds and charlotte russe. Enough to feed a bloody army, she had whispered inelegantly but smugly in Kitty's ear. There would be tea or coffee for those who required it, wines, liqueurs, spirits for the gentlemen and bottles and bottles of the best champagne money could buy, for there was no doubt that Noah Goodwin was a wealthy man and becoming wealthier by the month. His new brick works had, from the moment the building was finished, done a roaring trade, for as Noah remarked, bricks and glass went together, it was only common sense!

Abby and Harriet were taking a breather, pressed by Kitty who insisted there was nothing more they could do. All that needed to be done was done and why didn't they sit in the garden under the oak tree and she'd get Ruby to bring them out a tea tray. Though Mrs Woodruff was merely the wife of a Goodwin groom, she was also Mrs Goodwin's friend and companion and the mother of the little lad every servant in the house and garden adored. Such an engaging little chap, mischievous but with the sweet nature of his pa and he was the spoilt favourite of them all, but the best part was it didn't *spoil* him.

Ruby, the mother of a fine son herself, was neat and pretty, rosy and plump, her happiness, which was all thanks to Mrs Goodwin, she said a dozen times a day, shining in her eyes. She had married her Olly and she and Mrs Woodruff were not only neighbours in their cottages at the back of the stables but their two lads were in the care of the woman who had once been Mrs Goodwin's governess. They all called her Holdy though her name was Miss Holden. Mrs Goodwin's present to Ruby and Olly when their Harry was born was a brand-new perambulator, a large, high-backed, three-wheeled vehicle with a hood which was Ruby's pride and joy. No one in her world had ever owned such a thing and with Mrs Goodwin's insistence that Ruby could leave her baby in Holdy's care and come back to work at Edge Bottom House when she was needed, Olly and Ruby were made up.

Mrs Goodwin had also given Ruby something she dared not tell Olly about, not yet at any rate, though he thought the world of Mrs Goodwin, and that was a method to restrict the family Ruby and Olly would have. Harry was a year old now and Ruby thought she and Olly might try for another soon but had not Mrs Goodwin revealed this rather frightening secret, frightening in as much as it was so daring, so controversial, though Ruby did not use the word, Ruby would have probably had more children by now, at least one on the way, and would certainly not be in the fine position she and Olly now enjoyed. And it was all down to Mrs Goodwin and that group of ladies they had heard were doing their best to make a woman's world a little easier. All the servants called their mistress Mrs Goodwin now and if you were to ask them it is doubtful if one of them could remember the exact time when they gave up "Miss Abby". She was a woman, mature, confident, capable of running her household without Mrs Woodruff to guide her, though the former housekeeper was still involved, for so much of Mrs Goodwin's time was taken up with that society of hers. They were amazed that the master allowed it but as long as his home ran smoothly and Mrs Goodwin was at the dinner table when he was, he seemed not to mind.

The two women sat without speaking for a while, the silence broken only by the children's voices from the side of the house where Todd, Harry and Holdy were exploring the stand of trees. Holdy would be trundling the perambulator behind her, allowing the toddling Harry to jump out and join in the fun, and the sound of childish laughter was a joy to the ear. A skylark, no more than a dot in the sky, was singing its heart out and pollen-laden bees blundered from flower to flower. And what flowers! The scent from Mr Renfrew's roses was heady and the colours, from the creamy yellow of Rosa *Mme Hardy*, to the deep scarlet of Rosa *Alice Goodwin* which Mr Renfrew had grown and named after his last mistress, with every shade in between. Hollyhocks stood against the stone wall, red and vibrant, mixed with the blue of delphinium and in between, low-growing, the edges of the beds were lacy with thrift and alyssum. Verbena jostled with calceolarias, geraniums, petunias, spilling against one another in the rich, well-fed soil that Mr Renfrew insisted upon. The grass was as green and as smooth as the billiard table Noah had put in the new room built on to the side of the house, grandly called "the games room" where he and his male guests went to smoke their cigars, play cards or billiards, leaving the ladies to do whatever it was ladies did when gentlemen were not present.

Mr Renfrew was nowhere to be seen today, for he and his lads were overseeing the distribution of the blooms he himself had cut a couple of hours since in readiness for the party. He had mown the lawn himself at daybreak and Abby viewed it with trepidation, for if the two youngsters took it into their heads to run across it there would be hell to pay!

"Will you and Clem have another child, Harriet?" she said lazily, leaning back in the white wicker chair, her shoulders comfortable against the bright cushions.

"Heavens, what on earth made you ask that?" Harriet laughed. "And the answer is no. I'm afraid my childbearing days are gone, if you know what I mean?"

"Ah, I see."

"What do you see?"

Abby sat up abruptly and placed her cup and saucer on the white wicker table. "No one knows yet, Harriet, but I'm pretty sure . . . I'm pregnant."

Harriet nearly threw her own cup and saucer over her shoulder in delighted astonishment. She stood up and drew Abby to her feet, throwing her arms about her and hugging her close. She kissed her cheek and May, who happened to be dusting, for the third time, the windowsill in the drawing-room, stared out in amazement.

"Sweetheart, oh, Abby, how lovely. Oh, dear God, I couldn't be more pleased if I was to have another myself though at my age one is enough. When . . . when is it to be? How long have you known and . . . Dear God, Noah will be jubilant. And after all this time. D'you know, nature is the strangest, the . . . Abby, what is it?" For the figure she held in her arms was like a rag doll from which the stuffing is fast running out. Harriet stepped back, unaware that May was watching the pair of them with bated breath, wondering what the devil was happening.

"Sit down, dearest," Harriet murmured to Abby, then, when they were both seated, pulled her chair so close to Abby's they were knee to knee, while May watched avidly.

"Tell me why you aren't pleased."

"Oh, I'm pleased, Harriet. It's what I've always wanted but . . . oh, Harriet, how can I tell you? How can I?"

"If it's about Roddy Baxter I already know, my love." Harriet's face was compassionate and she held Abby's hands tightly in her own. "Clem and Olly knew years ago that you were slipping out of the house dressed in your old skirt and shawl, but until Clem and I were married he told no one. Olly hasn't even let on to Ruby, for though she's a good, kind girl, she could never keep it to herself. I'm not even sure that Clem and Olly . . . well, they pretend to each other that you are going to your mother's and like to walk there in your old clothes but Clem and I realised that you were . . . meeting someone. God only knows how Noah has missed it. I was frightened for you. I was convinced that someone would see you and tell him and I suppose you could have said you were visiting your mother but he wouldn't have liked even that. Not dressed as you used to dress. Stop me, sweetheart, I'm babbling, I know, but you look so . . . Oh, dear God in heaven, you don't know who the father is." Harriet sat back, appalled, the realisation of how Abby must be suffering shocking her into speechlessness.

"I love Roddy, Harriet," Abby mumbled as though that was all that concerned her in these dreadful circumstances, as if all that mattered was her love for Roddy Baxter, which had been torn from her, trampled on and injured years ago almost beyond mending. But it had mended. It had recovered and flowered in beauty all these years and now she was to bear a child, perhaps his, perhaps her husband's. "I want a child, Harriet. I have wanted a child for so long and yet at the same time when each month brought proof that I wasn't to have one I was relieved. I have been facing this moment for almost three years, ever since Roddy and I . . . But now, how am I to tell him, either of them?"

"Abby, oh, Abby."

"I can't imagine the world without him in it, Harriet," she ended simply and Harriet knew she did not mean her husband.

"What will you do, my love?" she whispered, looking about her as if afraid they might be overheard, which was ridiculous for the whole world would soon know that Noah Goodwin had at last got his wife with child!

May watched, idly swishing her duster back and forth on the windowsill and when Kitty entered the room, somewhat fretful at May's long absence, May hissed at her to come to the window.

"What's the matter with—"

"Ssh, be quiet, there's summat up."

"What you talking about?"

"Them two," pointing from behind the curtain at the two women who had their heads together in the garden.

"I can't see nothing."

"You mark my words. Mrs Woodruff was huggin' the mistress an' the mistress looked as if she was goin' ter cry."

"Don't be daft, May Jenkins. What's the mistress got ter cry about, tell me that? It's her birthday and the master's havin' a big party for her. And have yer seen that bracelet he give her?"

"You wait an' see. Summat's up."

Their eyes were drawn to the sudden appearance of the two little boys who ran round the corner of the house screaming as though the devil were after them. Behind them, still pulling the perambulator, was their governess and nursemaid, but a far different young woman to the one who had sat stiff-backed and waiting for the granddaughter of the master to be brought to her. She was growling, her hair falling about her face and neck, her face flushed and her eyes filled with lovely laughter.

"Mama, Mama," Todd Woodruff was shouting, "there's a wolf chasing us. Hide us, hide . . ."

"Hide, hide," echoed young Harry Preston and the moment was filled with excited screams and laughter. Abby took Harry on to her knee, putting her face against his fair curls and over his head exchanged looks with Harriet.

The party was an enormous success, the two totally different sets of guests mixing well together. After all, except for Miss Florence Tickle and her tongue-tied gentleman friend, they were all of the same, middle class and even Florence and her Albert timidly enjoyed themselves when they realised that not one guest was taking the slightest notice of them in the crush. The only bugbear was, as usual, Joanna's high-handed belief that as Noah Goodwin's sister she was entitled to interfere with the running of his household. Everyone knew the dreadful upbringing and consequent actions of his lowly-born wife and she felt it her duty to put right things that she believed were wrong.

"Really, Abigail," she was heard to whisper in a voice loud enough to be heard, "I hardly think it necessary to invite a man who works at my brother's glass works. I know that Miss Tickle is a member of that group, which I'm amazed my brother has allowed you to join, but that does not mean you must ask them to Noah's home."

"Noah does not seem to mind, Joanna," Abby said through clenched teeth, doing her best to signal to Miss Holden to rescue her before every guest in the room should hear Joanna's spiteful words.

Miss Holden recognised the hint. She was a gifted pianist and was to play the piano for those who wished to dance in the large conservatory, which had been cleared of its tables and chairs and many of its standing plants. She was happy to accompany any lady or gentleman with pretensions to a voice and as the champagne went round and round, the laughter and music rose, candles glowed in every window and the man lounging quite openly at the edge of the small stand of trees where earlier two children had played, sighed and spoke to the small, wriggling little creature in his arms.

"They're havin' a good time, lad," he murmured into the puppy's rough fur, "so I reckon you an' me'd best get lost. We'll have ter wait. I would have liked ter see her on her birthday though."

His quiet whisper in the puppy's ear was suddenly interrupted by the sound of the door of the conservatory being flung open and a female voice declaring she was so hot she must have a breath of air and was anybody else to accompany her. It seemed no one did and Abby Goodwin moved down Mr Renfrew's immaculate lawn, clearly visible in the blaze of lights from the house. As she sauntered further down the garden she began to disappear into the shadows and Roddy moved with her, keeping to the shelter of the trees. When she reached the wrought-iron bench beneath the sheltering shade of a magnificent hawthorn, still burdened with the flowers that bloomed in May, she sat down. Its branches almost reached the ground and when Roddy Baxter slid beneath them and whispered her name she let out a little squeak of alarm.

"Dear God, you gave me a fright, Roddy Baxter. Don't you know we can be seen from the house? But I'm glad you came."

"Nobody can see us under the branches so give me a kiss. Happy birthday, my lovely," he murmured in her ear before putting one arm about her and reaching for her mouth. Her lips were waiting, eager, warm, moist and he wanted nothing more than to take her right here beneath the lovely tree. But though he needed to make love to her he had come here for another reason.

"I've brought yer birthday present. If yer'd not come out I would've given it yer when yer came to the cottage but now yer can have it on yer birthday. Look, I got him from a chap I know. Jesus, don't let him escape," as the little bundle of fur struggled valiantly to get to the ground. He had been held tightly by the man for a long time and it was in his nature to be active, not nursed!

He leaped from Roddy's knee to Abby's, a cold, damp nose, a frantically licking tongue, wicked little baby teeth and a personality that promised to be lively and loving.

"Roddy, he's lovely. I love him, but . . ."

"I knew yer would," Roddy said with great satisfaction, ignoring her uncertainty.

"But how can I explain him?" arching her face away from the loving attentions of the puppy.

"Yer mean yer don't want him?" Roddy's voice was cold and hurt.

"No, no, I would love him, but I have to say where he came from and I can hardly tell—"

"Your husband."

"Everybody, the servants . . ."

He stood up and reached for the puppy and in his stance was the familiar jealousy, pain, the venomous, poisonous pangs of a love that had to be shared with another man. He had given up trying to persuade her to leave Noah Goodwin and though it crucified him to lie in his bed at night and imagine her in her husband's, he had been forced to accept it. It had soured him though. He was becoming successful and there was talk of him taking over the running of Mulberry Glass Works. He dressed in good, unpretentious clothes and was seen to be the catch of the district amongst girls of his own sort, but he was in that precarious position of being in neither one class or another. He still attended night school at the Mechanics Institute. He took history, geography, mathematics, English literature, chemistry and philosophy, more for something to occupy his time when he was not with her, Abby suspected, than for a thirst for knowledge. He was, in fact, better educated than many of the middle-class gentlemen who were at this moment drinking Noah's champagne, or even Noah himself. He could almost pass as a gentleman, for even his speech had improved.

She reached for his hand and drew him down to the seat, then, lifting his arm about her shoulder, leaned against him, the puppy settling for the present as though even at such a young age he knew a serious moment when it came up. Abby lifted her face and offered her lips to this man whom she loved, *had loved* for as long as she could remember more than anyone in the world. She hurt him desperately, she knew that, but there was something else in her life now that must be considered, even against this man, this good man who loved her and because of it was willing to step back and allow her to be part of it. He knew, for she talked to him about it, and he had even accompanied her, not *with* her, naturally, for she went with Laura and John, to several meetings in Manchester where the speaker, Barbara Bodichon, had read a paper before the National Association for the Promotion of Social Science. He, like John Bennett and many other gentlemen, supported women's suffrage. He had signed the petition last year, as she had, to demand votes for women, and on that petition were names such as Florence Nightingale, Harriet Martineau, women of high profile, and John Stuart Mill, who was a Member of Parliament, had presented it to the House of Commons. Unlike Noah, who thought the whole thing was nothing more than a hobby to keep women safely occupied in a movement that would come to nothing.

"Roddy, please be patient with me. I love you, that is not in dispute, for would I take such chances—"

"I bloody wish yer would then if he found out yer could come ter me."

"Sweetheart . . ."

"I often wonder how much longer I can stand it, Abby," he said musingly. "I'm twenty-one years old and for most of those years I've loved you. And yet I'd dearly like a wife and children. A family . . ."

"Dear God in heaven, don't you think I don't know it and pray that—"

"That I'll hang about like this for the rest of me life?"

"No, oh no, my love."

"Then come with me."

She was weeping now and the puppy whined unhappily. From the doorway of the conservatory a male voice called her name.

"I must go. Please, my darling, let me go. I love you, only you."

He stood as though turned to stone, watching as she hurried up the garden from the shadows into the bright lights that spilled on to the garden. She was wearing some transparent lacy green dress, apple green lined with some material which he did not know was silk. It seemed to float about her as she ran. Laura and John stood just outside the conservatory door and Roddy watched as Laura, obviously seeing something in her friend's face, held out her arms and folded her in them.

"What is it, dearest? And what have you there?"

"Blow me down, if it isn't a puppy. But, Abby, where . . . who?"

Roddy turned away and broke into a desperate, disjointed run, letting himself out through the wrought-iron gate in the high wall. He didn't want to hear any more.

"Help me, Laura," Abby murmured against her friend's shoulder. "Help me," for the tears still poured across her cheeks.

John took the puppy from her arms, his face bewildered, and his wife shook her head at him. It is said that a happily married couple have some sort of telepathy moving from one mind to the other and as Laura reached into her reticule for the scrap of lace she called a handkerchief, John seemed to read hers and went inside holding up the small, delighted animal.

"Look what we've found in the garden. Caught in the brambles beside the gate. Goodness knows where it came from." He studied the puppy's anatomy then told them, "We shall call him Bramble, what d'you say, Miss Tickle?" For Florence, who had a small dog of her own, was petting the dog's head.

"But where *is* Abby?" someone asked, and it was noticed that it was not her husband who asked the question.

"Here I am," a cheerful voice said from the doorway. "I've been making a few repairs to my person. He's a very lively young dog with sharp teeth but isn't he beautiful. And what a wonderful birthday present to receive at the end of the day. The very best."

As she reached for the puppy, who greeted her like an old friend, her husband's diamond bracelet sparkled unnoticed.

23

She and the puppy were becoming bigger together and as no one had noticed it, or at least mentioned it, she took it that Harriet was the only one to know of her condition. She was slender, her waist narrow and her stomach flat but the small bulge, which was beginning to show, could not be detected when she lay on her back, or when she was fully clothed. *It soon would be!* Each night she lay awake hour after hour beside her husband, and in the morning wondered why on earth no one seemed to remark on the circles beneath her eyes or her pallor. Harriet watched her, she could sense it, and the questions that her friend longed to ask but didn't, and she brooded on how long she could keep this from Noah, who would, of course, be delighted, and from Roddy, which was even worse. Both men would believe that the child was theirs, Noah legitimately, unaware that Roddy was her lover, and Roddy because it would give him a lever to pry her free of her husband.

She knew that Noah would at once put a stop to all her activities, the riding he had allowed her to continue accompanied by either Clem or Olly, the walks she took up on to the low moorland as far as Old Fellows Edge with the puppy, her trips with Laura to Manchester to meet Lydia Becker, who was secretary to the National Society for Women's Suffrage, to speak with Mr and Mrs Jacob Bright, and Mr John Thomasson, all passionate campaigners in the cause. With the other members of the Claughton Street group she went to public meetings in different parts of Lancashire to hear visiting speakers. Manchester was an important centre for women's suffrage societies and the great reformer Richard Cobden was a firm supporter of the cause and alongside other men and women worked hard to remove what was called the electoral disabilities of women. Feminists, as they were called, among them Laura Bennett, published pamphlets, wrote articles in periodicals, collected signatures to a petition to be sent to London and wrote to local Members of Parliament to support them.

Though Abby did no more than address envelopes, go to meetings, listen to other women and read the articles – over which gentlemen guffawed – that appeared in the periodicals, it would all come to an end when Noah was told of her condition. He would keep her at home, allow her only carriage exercise or short walks about the garden on his arm and sit her by her fire with her feet on a stool. She would be a prisoner and there was not the smallest doubt in her mind that Roddy would play havoc with her life if she was no longer in his. For the past three years he had simmered beneath the surface, loving her, hating her at times, reluctant to disturb the already rocky tenor of the life they led, afraid he might lose her altogether, but should she vanish from his life he would set off such an explosion it would be heard and felt all over St Helens. She would be pulled between the two men should he find out she carried a child that might be his and she really didn't think she could deal with it and what would follow with Noah. She felt well, no sickness in the morning, which she knew from her own mother could be weakening and the first indication to others of her condition. She was tired but that was more from worry and lack of restful sleep and she knew she was beginning to look gaunt with the constant gnawing anxiety. If only she could escape for a while. Have some peace in which to think, leave them all behind, all those who loved her and would do anything they could to help her, but at the same time would pull her this way and that in the direction they thought best for her. She needed a retreat where she could rest and decide what was best for herself and her child.

She was brooding before the bright fire that burned in her bedroom grate, Bramble curled up at her feet. Though it was July and high summer the rain lashed against the windows and the heavily leaved branches of the tree beyond them swayed with the power of the wind. She was drinking hot chocolate just brought up by Harriet, who had hovered for a moment as though letting her know that should Abby want to talk she was available then left quietly, shutting the door behind her.

Abby finished the chocolate, stood up and wandered to the window, staring out blindly at the sodden garden. Mr Renfrew would be furious when he saw the state of his splendid display of flowers and shrubs, she thought absently, bending down to fondle Bramble's ear, for the young dog had followed her to the window. He was as high as her knee already, his legs long and gangling and though when he had been found he was thought to be a terrier, perhaps a Cairn or a Norfolk, Bramble had grown taller and taller until it was obvious, despite his rough coat, he was to be neither. Noah would not allow him into the bedroom and at night he slept on the kitchen mat before the fire, curled up with the cat, of whom he was passionately fond. The cat, being old, suffered his presence with a sigh of resignation.

Scarcely aware of what she was doing, Abby crossed to the wardrobe and rooted about in the deep drawer at the bottom. She found and withdrew a tin box. She took the box to the bed and opened it. Inside was a small velvet bag that chinked cheerfully when she lifted it out and almost as though she wasn't sure what she would find she opened the bag and allowed its contents to spill on to the bedspread. A stream of golden guineas fell in a glittering, scattered pile and the dog, who had jumped on to the bed thinking there might be something tasty involved, sniffed at the coins, then jumped down again and wandered off.

Abby kneeled by the bed, remembering the scene in old Dodsworth's office after her grandfather died. Noah had been almost abusive and would, if he could, have ordered her from the office as though she were a child who did not understand an adult's world, but Mr Dodsworth very apologetically told him that that was not in order.

"You see, it is here."

"What is here?" Noah asked rudely.

"The money. Your" – he turned to Abby since he was not sure of the relationship between Bradley and Noah Goodwin – "your grandfather was most insistent that I put this into your hands, Mrs Goodwin. It is not strictly in the will, which would then have made it your husband's property, but a . . . a *gift* from him to you. I have kept it here in my safe until you came."

He had placed a velvet bag heavy with coins in Abby's trembling hands and now, here it still was, forgotten for the most part, waiting for the right moment when it would be needed.

Abby gathered up the money and replaced it in the bag, then stood for perhaps half an hour by the window, weighing it in her hands, then she reached for the bell and rang for Ruby.

She stepped from her carriage, taking Olly's outstretched hand as he leaped to help her down. It had stopped raining and the sun was doing its best to escape the drifting, golden-edged clouds but the rainwater, which gathered in the many rutted pools between the carriage and her mam's front door, flooded over the tops of her dainty boots and wet the hem of her skirt. She knocked at the door, for though this had once been her home it was no longer nor had it been for over four years.

It was as though it was meant to be. As if the gods were in favour of her decision and were giving her a helping hand. Cissie opened it, gawping in astonishment at the sight of her lovely, fashionable sister standing on her mam's mucky doorstep, then stepped back hastily and if Abby hadn't put out a hand would have bobbed a curtsey.

"No, sweetheart, don't do that, after all we are sisters. Now then, put the kettle on and make a cup of tea." Though the idea of drinking out of one of her mam's carelessly washed mugs was not a pleasant one. "I have something to discuss with you."

It did not take long and when she left twenty minutes later, thankful that they had not been interrupted by any other member of the family, Cissie was flushed and wide-eyed with excitement. Abby had brought a basket of food from the kitchen as an excuse for the unannounced visit, which Olly carried in, glancing about him as though scarcely believing that his ladylike mistress had once lived here.

Ruby and May carried the old trunk down from the attic, giving it a good clean before taking it into the mistress's bedroom, for the thing was covered with cobwebs. It had been found to hold clothing which must have belonged to Mrs Goodwin's grandmother or even great-grandmother and which Mrs Goodwin carelessly told them to dispose of, for it was no use to anyone, she added. There had been a bit of a tussle in the kitchen, since there was some lovely stuff there, velvet and silks and brocade which anyone with a bit of sewing in their fingers could soon transform into wearable gowns, and they had squabbled over who was to have what. When any one of them would wear silk or velvet or brocade did not occur to them.

Then, to their surprise, Mrs Goodwin started to fill the trunk up again with what she called her *old things*, as if the lot she was chucking out wasn't old, and which she meant to send to some charity which the group she was in supported. They never saw what it was, for she packed it herself and even had Clem put a padlock on it and then deliver it to St Helens Station where he was to leave it and where it would be picked up.

"I can deliver it where yer want, Mrs Goodwin," Clem protested, but she was most specific that it was to be dropped off at the railway station where one of the members of the society would collect it. He was to get a receipt, of course, otherwise her friend would not be able to retrieve it.

It all sounded a roundabout way to Clem and Olly, who discussed it but then who were they to interfere with this lot the mistress had got herself mixed up with?

The two young women, one merely a girl, both dressed in mourning black and draped with enveloping shawls despite the season, their faces barely visible, were decent working-class women who booked two third-class tickets to Manchester. The shorter of the two had a lively young dog on a leash.

"Straight through ter Manchester, missis, stoppin' at Newton in Makerfield, Patricroft, Salford and inter Victoria."

"Yes, thank you. How much will that be?" The woman spoke in a low voice as she opened her deep black bag and withdrew her purse, and the clerk wondered sympathetically if she was a widow, and her so young, her voice told him that. Her companion hung her head, the edge of her shawl well down over her forehead.

"All the way to Manchester."

"Yes, please, and would someone help us with our trunk? I believe it's been left here. I have the receipt."

"Right, missis," turning to someone in the office whom he

addressed as Fred, handing him the ticket. "Fetch this trunk for the lady. She's to take the train ter Manchester. Yer'd best put a label on it."

"Rightio," a cheerful, disembodied voice shouted, and the two women moved to the edge of the platform awaiting the train which was due shortly. The booking clerk did not see them board the train.

Cissie had never been on a train before and the sight of the monster that steamed angrily into the station and came to a hissing, whistling halt in front of them had her clutching at Abby, who had made the journey several times with Laura and John. They were not even on the thing yet and she was terrified, but the other passengers didn't seem to be afraid to climb aboard, or even to give her and Abby a second glance. It seemed Abby had noticed that men seldom took any interest in a woman who was in mourning which was why she had decided on it for her and Cissie.

The compartment was half empty, the other passengers studiously avoiding one another's glance and when the train got up steam and began to move, going faster and faster, so fast indeed that Cissie grabbed Abby's hand and turned her face into her shoulder, the three other passengers, all men, shook out their newspapers and began to read. What sort of men were they? Abby wondered. Of the same class as herself but able to read! Respectably dressed but not gentlemen. As they left the town and clattered into the countryside Cissie ventured a peep through the window from under the edge of her shawl and out into the fields and woods which went by at a frightening speed.

"Oh, Abby," Cissie breathed, her shadowed face, which Abby had insisted she must keep hidden, pink with excitement, and as her fear of being flung from the train lessened she was like a child, begging Abby in a whisper to change places with her so that she might sit next to the window. Bramble fell asleep on Abby's lap, not at all nervous of this strange adventure.

Their next crisis came when they reached Newton in Makerfield where they were to get off and sit in the ladies waiting-room for the train to Warrington. Cissie was in such a state of excited terror she failed to ask her sister why, having booked tickets to Manchester, they were going to Warrington. Again they were unnoticed by the alighting and boarding passengers. Abby had not begrudged the fare she was forced to pay, much of it wasted since they never went the full distance she paid for, but if she was to find peace and quiet for a few weeks she must throw off those who would search for her. Her money was sewn into the hem of her petticoat but for a guinea or two in her purse to get her to her destination and a hotel until they were settled, and she and Cissie must manage on it.

She had written to no one but Laura, posting the letter at the post office in St Helens.

They changed trains six times that day, resting when they could in the ladies waiting-rooms, eating and drinking nothing, for Abby was reluctant to draw attention to themselves. They passed through Wigan, Bolton, Chorley, Preston and Ormskirk until at last the train drew into Lime Street Station in Liverpool and the end of their journey. The trunk was, presumably, sitting on the platform at Victoria Station in Manchester waiting to be picked up and she had nothing but the deep portmanteau in which were a change of underwear for her and Cissie.

They had thought the forecourt of the railway station at St Helens was bedlam, but when they had struggled through the crowds to the top of the wide, imposing steps at Lime Street Station in Liverpool they felt their senses, all five of them except their sense of smell, reel and flee away. It was pandemonium, alive and teeming with men and women all bent on getting to some important place with no thought of who might be in their way, some coming up the steps, others going down. Porters trundled by with trolleys on which luggage teetered, shouting, "Make way there," but not caring overmuch if they were ignored. There were dozens of hansom-cabs, smart carriages disgorging ladies and gentlemen in fashionable garments, street urchins, street hawkers, street entertainers, and at their back the shrieks of train whistles, hooters and the angry hiss of steam.

"Oh, Abby," quavered Cissie, huddling up to her sister, wishing she was back with her mam.

"Come along, Cissie, we can't stop here. We have to find a decent boarding-house close by and get a good night's sleep, for tomorrow we must start the search for our own place."

They didn't miss her until the master rang the bell from the drawing-room and when May entered demanded of her where her mistress might be.

"The mistress?" May looked puzzled as though she were not sure who the master meant.

"Yes, you remember your mistress? My wife. Mrs Goodwin, the lady who should be here ready to dine with me."

"Sir?"

"Bloody hell, girl, have you lost your mind? I have been waiting ten minutes for her to show her face. I supposed she was closeted with Mrs Woodruff or even over at the woman's cottage admiring that lad of hers. Well, wherever she is, tell her her husband is waiting for his meal and to look lively."

"Sir," May said again, her face becoming pink and anxious. "We was told she was ter spend the day wi' Mrs Bennett and may not be home to dinner."

"Dear God, why was I not told?" her master thundered.

"I seem to be the last one in this house to be informed of its mistress's movements. When did she leave?"

"I'm not sure, sir." For the strange thing was that when Kitty had gone up to enquire of Mrs Goodwin whether she would like a breakfast tray in her room she had already gone. No one had seen her leave. She had summoned neither Olly nor Clem to get out the carriage so they had just presumed she had decided to walk to Claughton Street. There was a note addressed to Mrs Woodruff with the message that May had just conveyed to her master.

"Well, you'd best serve dinner then, and be quick about. It seems I'm to eat alone."

May hurried back into the kitchen and broke the news to the rest, who were just sitting down to a nice leg of pork with all the trimmings, pleased to have an evening off, that the master was expecting a meal.

"Dear God in 'eaven," Cook shrieked, whipping the plate from under poor Nessie's very nose. "Get them sprouts off the plates. May, put tureens inter warm and stick the gravy in the oven. Them roast potatoes, put them in too, an' do something with the parsnips. Nessie, run ter't dinin'-room and set table fer one. I know, girl, yer not parlour-maid but surely yer can manage a knife an' fork an' napkin. See, carve some more meat, Kitty, an' . . . Dear God, what can we give 'im fer a dessert?"

For five minutes there was pandemonium in the kitchen while in his drawing-room Noah poured himself another brandy and brooded on his wife's disregard for his own comforts and need of her. He had had a bad day at the glass works where some children employed grinding the smooth surfaces of mirror glass, left unsupervised for five minutes, had managed to damage several, which would not have been unduly worrying, but in the process three of them had been badly cut and had to be taken to the infirmary. There was talk of one losing a hand and Noah knew he would be in for a hard time of it from those who did not believe children should work twelve hours a day but should be in school! His wife would probably be one of them, but at least he could argue and bellow at her and relieve his own guilt. Now she wasn't here and neither was his dinner and if those lazy sluts in the kitchen didn't put his meal on the table in the next two minutes he'd sack the lot of them.

He ate his meal and drank several glasses of wine, turning up his nose at the special Swiss cream Cook had hastily whipped up for him with macaroons, sherry and a pint of cream, which didn't please her, and the rest of them had to eat almost cold leftovers.

They were once more beginning to relax, their boots off, their feet up and thinking of making their way to their beds when he came storming, one could use no other word, into the kitchen and demanded to know where the bloody hell his wife was, as if it was anything to do with them, for pity's sake!

They had all jumped to their bootless feet, doing their best to hide them in the folds of their skirts, exchanging glances, for it *was* getting late and none of them liked the idea of their young mistress coming home in a hansom on her own. Mr and Mrs Bennett did not own a carriage. The doctor did his rounds on his bay and Mrs Bennett either travelled with other, wealthier ladies or walked.

"You" – pointing at the trembling Nessie who was still in a state after setting the dinner table – "go and get either Olly or Clem and tell them to get round to Claughton Street and fetch my wife home. Look sharp, girl, if you want to keep your job."

It was after midnight and they were still hanging about the kitchen when it was finally realised that their mistress was missing. Doctor and Mrs Bennett had been tucked up in their bed when Olly's thunderous knock brought them out of it.

"Who the dickens . . ." Laura had protested.

"It will be Mrs Mead's baby. She had a bad time with the last and I promised her I'd go immediately."

They were astonished when the Goodwins' groom stood gasping on their doorstep, white-faced and trembling, for the dark house without a vestige of light showing had badly frightened him. It was very evident that no entertaining was being done here!

Mrs Goodwin! No, they hadn't seen her all day . . .

"But she left a note fer Mrs Woodruff ter say she was spending day 'ere wi' you." Olly was ready to push his way into the Bennett's narrow hallway as though he were not prepared to believe that his mistress was not hiding somewhere.

"She's not here, Olly. We haven't seen her all day."

"Jesus ternight, master'll be . . ."

"Come in for a moment while . . ."

"Eeh, no, sir, I'll 'ave ter tell 'im."

"I'll come with you, Olly. Just let me put on something warmer." For Laura was wearing only a robe thrown hastily over her nightgown.

"Bless yer, Mrs Bennett." Olly was vastly relieved at the thought that someone other than himself was to break the news to his master that the mistress had not been seen since . . . well, it'd be last night when he and she had gone to their beds. The master had breakfasted and gone to work at his usual time this morning and when Kitty had later entered their bedroom Mrs Goodwin was already gone, leaving only the note for Mrs Woodruff telling them she was at Claughton Street.

They none of them knew what Mrs Bennett said to Mr Goodwin in the privacy of the drawing-room. They huddled together, doing their best to draw comfort from one another's presence, even Mrs Woodruff who had shown the note to the master, her face ashen, her hands trembling. She sat at the kitchen table, then, startling them all with the violence of her movement, she stood up and almost ran from the kitchen and along the passage to the main hall. They stared after her, watching as she burst into the drawing-room without knocking on the closed door.

Two minutes later the master's roar echoed through the house and they all cowered, for surely he would blame them for not watching out for Mrs Goodwin who was known to be wayward. His voice could be heard, so loud and abusive Clem moved towards the kitchen door, his face set like steel as though he were prepared to defend his wife, who seemed to be at the mercy of his master.

It was Mrs Bennett who came in to tell them that the master wanted to see every one of them separately, even the gardener's lads, in the drawing-room.

Nessie began to weep.

24

The letter was delivered to Claughton Street the next day.

Dear Laura

I am leaving you all for a short time but I know I could not simply disappear without word. You are the only one who has the courage to stand up to Noah so I am trusting you to let him know I am safe and well. He won't accept it, of course, but he won't find me until I want to be found, for I shall cover my tracks well. And if you can get her alone would you ask Harriet to tell Roddy Baxter and do her best to keep him away from Edge Bottom House. She will know what you mean. I am not alone, for I have taken my sister, Cissie, with me so, my dear friend, that is another favour I must ask of you. Tell my mother she has lost neither of her daughters for good. I am so sorry to burden you with this but I must get away. I am quite desperate.

My dearest love to you and John
Abby

Laura passed it to John. They were breakfasting late, for not only had Laura spent a good deal of the night at Edge Bottom House but the infant Mead had decided to put in an appearance and John was as exhausted as his wife. The little maid hung about at her mistress's elbow, her cap askew, her apron not quite spotless and her face anxious, for she did love Mrs Bennett and wanted to please her. She had lived at the local orphanage and had been passed over a dozen times by prospective employers before Mrs Bennett had smiled at her and given her this wonderful chance at the age of twelve.

"I'll have to go," Laura sighed, pushing her hand through her glossy brown hair, then reaching half-heartedly for a slice of toast which she began to butter. "The revelation that Abby was pregnant which Harriet felt *must* be disclosed to him was like a bombshell exploding," she went on. "His face lit up, John, and for a moment I thought he was going to grab poor Harriet and waltz her round the room in his joy, then from joy he became white and livid with anger and for a terrible moment it was touch and go whether he was going to strike her. I actually stood up and moved towards her but he stepped back from it and roared like a wounded bull instead. Dear Lord, after last night I feel I never want to see Edge Bottom House again. He was quite out of his mind and reduced every one of the maidservants to tears. Even Cook! I thought Olly was going to hit him when he as much as accused the poor man of neglecting his duty. Harriet sat in a corner and wept until Clem was summoned. 'And you can leave that woman alone, Clem Woodruff, for she has stabbed me in the back and I'll never forgive her for keeping this from me,' Noah snarled, just like a beast at bay. 'That woman's my wife, sir, and I'll not have her spoken to like that,' Clem said. 'Then the pair of you had better pack your bags and bugger off because you're obviously not to be trusted. If anything happens to my wife and child I'll see the pair of you in gaol.' I wanted to leave then and there but I was forced to sit through his interrogations for another hour or so and then when Olly brought me home you weren't here."

"I'm sorry, my darling, but baby Mead was a—"

"I know. It couldn't be helped. Oh Lord, John, what am I to do?"

"What can you do, dearest, except take the letter to Noah and—"

"But she might not want him to see it, don't you understand? That's why she sent it to me. This reference to Roddy Baxter might make further trouble. Only Harriet seems to have Abby's full confidence. Am I to go to Noah and say I've heard from Abby and she's quite safe but doesn't want to come home just yet? He'll demand to see the letter."

"It's your letter, Laura, and if anyone can stand up to Noah Goodwin it's you. Just refuse to let him see it. Leave it here when you go. I will, naturally, come with you, for I won't have my wife berated for something that was not of her doing. Come, my love, eat a little" – for Laura was doing no more than toy with the slice of toast – "and drink your chocolate then we'll get dressed and beard the lion in his den."

But the lion was not in his den, nor indeed anywhere in the house or grounds. His horse was gone from the stable and Olly and Clem were standing in the stable doorway scratching their heads as they stared disconsolately at the empty stall which Lysander usually occupied. From the look on their faces it might have been thought that someone had kidnapped one of their sons!

"'E must've saddled Lysander 'imself, Doctor, some time in't night. Me an' Clem were in our cottages . . . not that we slept, yer understand, but Frankie and Jacko 'oo sleep above the stable, bein' no more'n lads and not so upset as the rest of us, never 'eard a thing, they said. God knows where 'e's gone, the master, I mean. Well, where would yer start ter look, I ask yer? An 'er wi' child all on 'er own."

"No, Clem, not on her own. Mrs Bennett has had a letter."

The faces of the two grooms lit up and they turned to one another in relief. Though the master had given them both a good tongue-lashing last night, unfairly in their opinion, he had had good reason to lose control and they had forgiven him. They both had wives of whom they were inordinately fond and so they could imagine how he felt, though they were wondering if they – and their wives – still had employment!

"Where is Harriet, Clem? I must have a word with her and let her know Abby is safe and not alone."

The grooms would have liked to question Mrs Bennett on the identity of the person who had accompanied their mistress but it had occurred to them that it might be that lad she was so fond of. The one she sneaked out a couple of times a week to meet, though neither of them would admit that that was where she went, even to each other.

"She's in't kitchen, Mrs Bennett, an' little lads wi' 'er." A fond expression crossed Clem's face. "Them lasses love the bones of our Todd an' young Harry, an' all. She thought it'd tekk their minds off the worry of where the mistress might be."

"That's kind of her, Clem. I'll just go and have a word with her and then . . . if you or Olly could fetch a cab I have another task to perform." It was her duty to go to the Murphys' cottage in Sandy Lane and tell the mother that her missing daughter was safe and well and that somewhere she and her sister, Abby Goodwin, were in hiding. Betty Murphy would be frantic by now with her Cissie gone overnight, but it might allay her terror if she was to be told the girl was with Abby even if no one knew where that might be.

"Nay, yer'll not need a cab, Mrs Bennett. Me or Olly'll tekk yer wherever yer want ter go. I'm sure master wouldn't mind, especially if it were ter do wi' Mrs Goodwin."

"That's kind of you, Clem, but I couldn't possibly take Mr Goodwin's carriage without his permission."

"Lass, he'd not mind," Clem protested, forgetting as he did when his emotions were involved that he was talking to a gentlewoman, but Laura was adamant and, after speaking with Harriet in the privacy of the housekeeper's sitting-room, left with her husband in the hired hansom.

The clerk in the booking-office at St Helens Railway Station eyed the gentleman who had his face pressed against his window with some alarm. He was a tall man, lean of waist and belly and hip but with strong muscled shoulders which filled the roomy-sleeved riding cloak of navy cashmere he wore. Not that the clerk could see the man's figure on the other side of the booking-office window but he got the impression of great strength and a formidable willpower. He wore no hat and his hair was thick and a rich, dark brown, ready to curl vigorously over the collar of his cloak. He was amber-skinned, handsome, but the clerk noticed he needed a shave and his eyes were set in deep, mushroom-coloured circles. They were a menacing, mud-coloured brown with no light in them and his voice was flat as he glared through the window.

"I'm looking for a lady," he proclaimed in a tone that allowed for no nonsense. With another man, a man of his own class, the clerk might have made some witty remark such as "You're not the only one, lad," but not with this one.

"A lady . . . ?" he stammered, for the man's manner was hazardous.

"Yes. A lady, dressed well, handsome and . . . have you seen her?"

"Well, sir, we have a lot of passengers through 'ere every day, it bein' such a busy station an' I can't be expected ter remember every one."

"You would remember this one. She is tall with the most . . . with hair the colour of a fox's pelt."

"*A fox's pelt!*" The clerk looked astonished.

"Have you or have you not had a lady of that description through here?" the man hissed through gritted teeth, and behind him several people wishing to purchase tickets for the next train, which could be heard in the distance, shuffled restlessly.

"When was this, sir? Not this morning or I'd a' remembered. An' please, sir, if yer don't mind there's folk wantin' ter buy tickets fer the seven fifty ter Manchester which is due any minute so if yer'd—"

"When I have finished I will move away but until then answer my questions. It would be yesterday some time, I'm not sure exactly." His face lightened suddenly. "She would have a dog with her and—"

"A dog, sir, well, there was a lady with a dog. Two ladies actually. Well, I call 'em ladies!" He smirked but the man reached his hand over the counter and grasped his wrist, dragging him closer to the window.

"Two ladies?"

"Females, sir, working women wi' shawls on their 'eads but one of 'em had a dog."

"Excuse me," a distinctly irate male voice said from behind the tall man. "I am to catch the train to Manchester and I'd be obliged if you would finish your conversation and allow me to buy a ticket. Some of us have—"

The tall man turned slowly and before the fierceness of his expression the second gentleman fell back. "I beg your pardon," the tall man said dangerously. "I am speaking to this . . . this dolt here and I'd be obliged if you would not interrupt."

"But the train is drawing in, sir—"

"Sod the bloody train, sir, and sod you."

"Sir, how dare you and with ladies present. Your manners are quite appalling and I've a good mind to—"

"Yes?"

"Report you to the station-master."

"Don't trouble yourself. I shall speak to him on your behalf.

I have never in my life seen a more badly run concern than this," he said unfairly. "As for you" – swinging back to the booking-clerk who recoiled fiercely, obviously wondering if the tall man had escaped from a lunatic asylum his manner was so erratic – "I shall report you for dereliction of duty if you know what that means, which I doubt." The clerk didn't but suspected it was not a compliment!

Noah Goodwin swung round, glared at the queue of people cowering at his back, women amongst them and stamped off in the direction of the sign that said "Station-master's Office".

It took half an hour of heated questions and placating answers on the part of the station-master; the search to find Fred who was off duty today but who had yesterday seen to the ladies' trunk, before Noah Goodwin was satisfied that he had pried every scrap of information there was to be had about the two ladies and the dog. They had boarded the train for Manchester and Fred had personally stowed the trunk in the luggage van, and though they racked their brains to think of something to tell the coldly strung-up gentleman that might help in his search no more could be found.

"I'll take a first-class ticket to Manchester, if you please," he told the station-master, and the man hurried to do his bidding, breathing a sigh of relief when the gentleman arrogantly ordered poor, bewildered Fred, who was not even on duty, to run to Edge Bottom House and tell one of the grooms to fetch his horse from the station yard. He then boarded the next train for Manchester.

The scene was played out again in the frantic bustle of the glass-domed splendour of Victoria Station where Noah demanded not only that the station-master be summoned to attend him but every porter who might have handled a trunk the day before. No, he didn't know what the bloody thing looked like, never having seen it but a trunk was a trunk, surely, and if there was one waiting to be picked up in the left luggage office he would like to inspect it.

"What name would be on it, sir?" the station-master asked politely, keeping several of his men about him, for the gentleman looked as though he could turn nasty.

"How the hell do I know?" he snarled, for he was pretty sure that his wife would not have used her own name in this lunatic business.

"Then you must see I cannot help you, sir. There were several trunks waiting to be picked up but—"

"They've all gone, sir," one of the porters piped up. "There's none in't left luggage office. Just some packing cases an' a leather 'at box some lady left in't compartment."

"Then where's the trunk I was told at St Helens was sent here? The man was most insistent he put it in the luggage van on a train to Manchester."

"Nay, sir, don't ask me," the porter said unwisely.

"But I am asking you, you fool. If you did your job properly there would not be this bloody muddle. God in heaven, it's a wonder the damned railway system doesn't grind to a halt with the service it provides. Oh, never mind."

Noah Goodwin strode along the crowded platform, pushing his way through groups of passengers just alighting from the train, ignoring the muttered complaints and the haughty tones of one lady who said she had never seen such appalling behaviour in her life. He strode on, unaware of them all, coming out into the station yard and looking about him. There were hansom-cabs with their drivers looking hopeful of a fare but each one, when questioned, told him that they had seen no one answering the description of the two ladies, nor even a dog. For an hour or two he hung about, not knowing why, since it was evident there was nothing to be found here, then moved back to the concourse where he purchased a ticket for St Helens.

* * *

The woman he searched for rented a small, clean and plainly furnished bedroom in a boarding-house in Bolton Street which was no more than a step or two from the railway station. The porter who had seen them hovering at the entrance to Lime Street Station had told them he often sent respectable-looking folk there, for Mrs O'Neill was fussy about who she took in. It went without saying, no drunks, layabouts or sailors and if Mrs O'Neill asked, Abby was to tell her that Wally had sent them. Now they were not to worry about their trunk, which was in the luggage van, she had told him. He would see that it was delivered to Mrs O'Neill's in an hour or two and it was no trouble but *ta* very much for the splendid tip she gave him. She was such a pretty, gracious lady he would have done it for nothing, wondering why it was, her being such a lady, she was wearing a shawl. The lady in question was brooding on how many times the large piece of luggage had been hefted on and off the numerous trains they had travelled on in their tortuous journey between St Helens and Liverpool.

Mrs O'Neill appeared to be satisfied with them but she was not too sure about the dog, she said, but she reluctantly allowed it as long as Mrs Brown and her sister kept it from under her feet. She charged five shillings a week for the room and was prepared to cook them an evening meal. Did they have no luggage? she asked suspiciously. But Mrs Brown explained that they were expecting a trunk which Wally – was it? – would be bringing round directly. In the meanwhile they had a change of underwear in her portmanteau. Satisfied, Mrs O'Neill let them over her well-scrubbed doorstep. Only clean and decent young women carried a spare set of clean underwear!

Mrs O'Neill had no complaints about her two lady lodgers who were, Mrs Brown explained to her, looking for a small house or cottage to rent. If Mrs O'Neill knew of such a place she would be most grateful. That was how Mrs Brown spoke, very ladylike, though her sister never opened her mouth. The dog was no trouble and as the pair of them were out most of the day with it, looking for this cottage Mrs Brown seemed set on, she supposed, the thing bothered no one.

They spent the first few days in St John's Market buying household goods, bedding, cutlery, crockery, pans, not quite sure how much they would need until they had found the property Abby was looking for, not even sure what that might be. If it was unfurnished they would need a couple of beds, chairs, a table, perhaps rugs and so they scoured the market where such things might be had for a reasonable price. The small stuff, the pans and such could be stored under the bed in their room at Mrs O'Neill's, with her permission, of course, but in the meanwhile they studied the furniture in the market and even the rather grand and extensive Furniture Mart which went by the name of *Samuel Cutter's* in Bold Street where everything for the home could be bought. It was rather more expensive than the second-hand goods to be had in the market, and though Abby would have liked to buy the sort of furniture to which she had become accustomed in the past four years she reluctantly decided against it. She had no idea as yet how long she and Cissie might remain in Liverpool. Indeed she had no wish even to think of it. She looked no further ahead than tomorrow or the next day when she hoped to install them both, with Bramble, in their own little home. But she must conserve her money, so they left the Furniture Mart and headed back to St John's Market. Mrs O'Neill, though she had asked around, even questioning Wally who knew everything that went on in and around Liverpool, had drawn a blank on the question of a cottage for Mrs Brown and her young sister.

They were standing in front of a stall piled high with feather beds, the stall-owner eyeing them impatiently, for this was the fourth or fifth time the shawled women had fingered his goods, when Abby turned to Cissie and found herself looking and stepping into a large black hole. Cissie's face was blurred and though Abby put out her hands and did her best to steady herself on her sister's sturdy frame, she went down like a felled tree. But for the fact that a feather bed went with her, cushioning her fall, she might have done herself an injury.

She came to with her head in Cissie's lap and a crowd of sympathetic women about her. The stall-holder was doing his best to retrieve his feather bed which the fainting woman appeared to be lying on and Cissie was crying noisily. Cissie was finding it difficult to cope with this life their Abby had led her into, for she had never been more than a mile from her home in Sandy Lane in her life. The crowds, the busy markets, the bustling streets, the hustle and noisy energy of the large seaport where sailors eyed her admiringly and there was a constant commotion day and night was hard to get used to, and now, their Abby, who was the one sure cornerstone in this new world of Cissie's, was sprawled in the aisle of the market and Cissie didn't know what to do.

"Best send fer Doctor Tom, queen," one woman advised. "'E's only in Duke Street. See, Archie" – beckoning to one of the many barefoot urchins who hung about wherever there was a crowd in the hope of earning a farthing – "run ter Doctor Tom's place an' tell 'im 'e's needed in't market."

"No, really," Abby protested, doing her best to sit up, but the woman who seemed to have taken charge was having none of that. "You lie still, my lass, an' wait ter see what Doctor Tom ses. 'Ow far gone are yer?"

"I beg your pardon?" Abby said faintly.

"Four, five months, I'd say, so you just lie there, chuck. Yer don't want ter lose it."

"Please, Cissie, get me up," Abby pleaded, but the woman in charge kneeled down and, despite her belligerent tone, held Abby gently, smiling at Cissie to tell her there was nothing to worry about. When the tall, dark-haired young gentleman with the kindest, bluest eyes Abby had ever seen kneeled down beside her she felt a great peace come over her. This was a man to be trusted, she decided. If she could have had him, John Bennett would have been her choice of a doctor to see her through this ordeal but something in this man's face reassured her and she returned his smile.

"Let the dog see the rabbit, ladies," he cried cheerfully, smiling humorously at Abby to take away any affront she might feel at the words. "No, don't get up, madam. You seem to be recovered from your faint but I shall take you back to my surgery just in case. This young chap will call us a cab. This must be your sister," turning to smile at Cissie who felt inordinately better and amidst cries of good wishes from all but the stall-holder, who was glad to see the back of them, they were whisked into a hansom-cab, the doctor beside them, his horse being taken care of by the same boy who had fetched him. The cab drew up in front of a tall house in a rather run-down crescent with railed gardens in front, and when the door was opened by an elderly, grey-haired woman, Abby was led into a room shabby and cheerful but comfortable. It reminded her of Laura's parlour and at once she was at home. There was the sound of a dog barking at the back of the house and Bramble, who was on a leash held by Cissie, lifted his head and growled.

"Oh, don't bother about old Blaze, fellow," the doctor told him cheerfully. "He's harmless. Now how about a cup of tea. I'm Tom Hartley, by the way. And you are?"

"Abby . . . Brown and this is my sister, Cissie."

"Right then, Mrs Brown, while we're waiting for the tea I shall ask you one or two questions and, if I may, examine you. You're pregnant, aren't you, of course, I can see that but we don't want you fainting all over the place, do we? No, please stay, Miss Cissie," who was trying to edge her way from the room, her small face white with shock. It was not that Cissie was unused to a pregnant woman. Her mother was more often pregnant than not but the fact that Abby was in the same condition was not only a shock but cause for amazement after all these years of marriage.

They drank tea and Tom Hartley, who was known for his good heart and his predisposition for doctoring not his own class, but the poor of the city, soon had them at their ease. They were both reticent about their reasons for being in Liverpool, though he thought the younger one might have been persuaded to open up had not Mrs Brown thrown her several warning looks. There was some mystery here, but having determined that she was a healthy woman in her fifth month of pregnancy he let the matter drop.

"Let me call you a cab to take you home," he said, standing up and moving towards the door. "Where do you live?"

"We are temporarily staying in a boarding-house in Bolton Street," Mrs Brown said in her faultless English and Tom Hartley was once more to wonder at the difference in the two sisters, for the younger one, when she could be persuaded to open her mouth, spoke with the clipped and broad Lancashire accent of the working-class woman.

"Temporarily?"

"Yes, we're looking for a small cottage to rent." Abby's face brightened, for perhaps a man of the doctor's class might have more information on such a thing than a man like Wally. "You don't happen to know of such a property, do you, Doctor?"

Tom Hartley was curious about this lovely, pregnant woman, as who would not be, and her pretty young sister but it was not his nature to pry. Where was her husband? She wore a wedding ring but that could mean nothing. She was so obviously well educated, well spoken and her clothes, though those of a woman from the lower orders, were of good quality and cut.

"Well, I know a lot of people, people with property. I could ask around for you, Mrs Brown. Give me your address and I'll let you know. And, if you don't mind, I'd like to keep an eye on you." Though he did not mention it to the expectant mother he was mystified about several aspects of her pregnancy.

"That is most kind of you, Doctor." And with the gracious ladylike manners that Holdy had taught her, she passed through the door he held open for her, swept across the pavement and into the waiting cab.

25

Roddy Baxter was turning over the rich, dark soil to the side of his cottage when the couple, the man carrying a small child, opened his garden gate and moved hesitantly inside. When he heard the squeak of the hinges, which he had not yet got round to oiling, he turned eagerly, hoping that it was Abby, Harriet knew. When he saw it was not her his bright face sagged with disappointment.

She and Clem moved further into the garden, Clem looking round with approval, for though he was not a gardener he had seen what Mr Renfrew did and he recognised one that had had hard work spent on it like this one. There were rows of potatoes, their leaves a bright and healthy green, cabbages, the stems about eight or nine inches high, cauliflower, with heads a delicate yellowish-white, carrots which would not be ready until October and others which Clem, despite Mr Renfrew's ruminations about his own vegetable garden, could not identify. He wondered who was going to eat this bounteous crop, then he remembered that the lad had a mother and two younger brothers so they would not be wasted. And from what Harriet had told him about this Roddy who was so closely connected to Noah Goodwin's wife, he probably worked his garden for want of something better to do while he waited for her to visit him.

"Roddy," Harriet called. "Roddy Baxter?"

"Aye," the young man said uneasily.

"You won't remember me, Roddy. I may call you Roddy, mayn't I?"

"Aye," he said again, clearly mystified.

Harriet did not remind him that it was she who had directed him into the spinney and the clutches of Paddy O'Connell all those years ago. "When you returned and were ill I came from . . . I helped Abby with a few things to aid your recovery. Not a lot, just blankets she asked me to bring and other things. You were so ill and she . . . you look completely recovered now but . . ."

Harriet knew she was babbling in order to put off what she and Clem had come here to tell this wary young man. Well, Clem wouldn't say a word but she had insisted he came to give her support, for who knew how this Roddy would react when he was told that two days ago Abby Goodwin had vanished off the face of the earth. Please God he wouldn't go tearing off to confront Noah Goodwin, demanding to be told where his Abby – for he would consider Abby Goodwin belonged to him – had got to. What had Noah Goodwin done with her? What had he done *to* her to make her run away? And if he got to know that Abby was pregnant the consequences would be dire. She knew how things were between this lad and her young mistress and the child could be his, there was no doubt of it. Oh, God, she wished there was someone else who could do this for her but there wasn't. Abby had entrusted her with this task just as she had entrusted her with the one she had just carried out. That had been difficult but not half as difficult as this one was going to be.

Despite the earlier visit of Laura Bennett Betty Murphy had been in a state of near hysteria when Harriet and Clem had knocked on the door of the tumbledown cottage in Sandy Lane. Her husband, his own face white and strained was almost as frantic, for Cissie was the eldest of his daughters, his own blood and was very dear to him.

When he opened the door to them they could see by his expression that he had believed it was to be bad news. Cissie murdered in a field somewhere, or set upon by a gang of youths and raped and when, at once, Harriet gasped that she had news of Cissie, good news, Clem had to put out a hand to him to stop him from collapsing.

"Where is she?" Betty Murphy shrieked from the depths of the muddled kitchen. "Where's my baby? Oh, dear Mary Mother of God" – using one of the phrases she had picked up from her husband – "what's happened? Where is she?"

"She's well and safe, Mrs Murphy, if we might come in." Though Harriet was not sure she wanted to put her lovely son on the floor with the rest of the urchins who seemed all to be howling with the same fervour as their mother. Three older boys, the youngest about fourteen, leaned against the mildewed wall, their arms crossed defensively across their chests, longing to be away from this drama, she could see, but at Harriet's words they straightened up in great relief and made ready to leave.

Betty Murphy howled even louder when Harriet informed her that not only was their Cissie lost somewhere – only the Blessed Virgin Mother knew where – but their Abby as well. Not that Abby had been hers for a long time now but she was still Betty's daughter.

"But where've they gone?" she begged. "An' why? I can't understand it, really I can't. Can you, Declan?" Declan said he couldn't and they both looked, tearfully bewildered, at Harriet. She had passed Todd to his father, though the lad was wriggling to get down. He was an active, healthy child and did not care to be held like a baby but Clem, following his wife's lead, kept the small boy firmly in the safety of his arms.

"I'm sorry, Mrs Murphy, but I can tell you no more than that. Abby wrote a letter" – she didn't say to who – "telling us she was safe and that Cissie was with her. I came at once to let you know. I have nothing further to add."

"I can't understand it, really I can't," Betty repeated. "What's she got ter run away from? A good 'ome an' 'usband an' she's no right ter tekk our Cissie. She's a wicked girl an' I'll tell 'er so when she gets back."

"I'm sure you will, Mrs Murphy, but my husband and I must get on now. Mr Goodwin kindly gave us time off to walk over here." Which was a lie but she had to say something to get herself, Clem and her precious boy away from this insanitary hovel where she was sure all sorts of undesirable horrors might lurk.

"Yer'll let us know if yer 'ear 'owt?" Betty pleaded, for there was no point in hoping their Abby would write to her. The only one in the family now with a bit of learning was their Sara-Ann and she hadn't kept it up like their Cissie.

"I promise I'll send word at once." With great relief she and Clem and the wailing child who had begun to cry in sympathy with the rest, left the cottage and headed towards Eccleston Lane where Roddy Baxter lived.

And now she faced the young man whose whole life had been totally absorbed in the wife of Noah Goodwin; who had loved her and been loved by her ever since they were children and who would not be as easy to comfort as Betty and Declan Murphy.

"I came to tell you, a letter has been received . . ." Her voice dwindled away and her hand crept into Clem's, for Roddy's face had drained of every scrap of healthy colour as though he knew she was about to tell him bad news. Well, she wouldn't be here if it wasn't, would she? He swayed a little and leaned heavily on his spade, swallowing frantically as he tried to speak.

"Abby?" he croaked at last. Todd, who had been allowed to run on the walk over to Roddy's cottage but had been picked up again as they approached it, struggled with Clem and reluctantly his father put him down on the uneven flagged path. At once he began to poke about among the vegetables, picking up a snail and regarding it with great interest. Something on the ground caught his attention and squatting down he pulled a worm from the soil, holding it up in triumph for his parents to see.

"Look, Mama, Dada, a worm. Will it eat the snail?" And without waiting for an answer he put the two together and watched to see what would happen.

"Tell me, for God's sake," Roddy whispered, so low they could barely hear him and at once Harriet crossed the rows of potatoes and went to him. Clem stayed on the path to keep an eye on his boy who had put both the snail and the worm in his pocket and was wandering about looking for further treasure.

"She's gone away, Roddy."

"Gone away? Gone away where?"

"We don't know. She and Cissie—"

"Cissie's gone with her?"

"Yes. The day before yesterday when we went to her room she wasn't there, so naturally we thought she must be with Mrs Bennett. You know Mrs Bennett?"

"*The day before yesterday an' no one thought ter tell me?* What's been done ter find her? What's that bloody husband of hers doing? Sweet Jesus, someone could've taken her."

"No, Roddy, she wrote a letter saying she was going away, as I told you; for a while, that's what she said." Harriet put a hand on the young man's arm in an effort to calm him, for he was beginning to fling himself about in great agitation as though he needed to be doing something but didn't know what.

"I'll start up on the moor," he said as though to himself but Harriet clung on to him.

"It's no use, Roddy. She's not up on the moor. *She sent a letter to Mrs Bennett.* Mrs Bennett came over to Edge Bottom House to tell Mr Goodwin. He has been to the railway station and was told two women answering the description of Abby and Cissie got on a train to Manchester. They remembered them because of the dog."

"She took Bramble?"

"Yes. She had a trunk; they remember that, the booking-clerk and another chap. It was put on the Manchester train but it didn't arrive there and neither did she."

"Oh, dear God," Roddy moaned. "I don't know . . ."

"She told Mrs Bennett to ask me to tell you so that you . . ."

"Jesus Christ, I must get over there." He didn't elaborate on where "over there" meant, Laura Bennett's home in Claughton Street or Edge Bottom House. He swung away from Harriet, knocking her hand off his arm, making for the gate, but Harriet hurried after him.

"Mrs Bennett knows nothing, Roddy. Mr Goodwin has been to Manchester and is still searching. He thinks she must have got off somewhere along the route to throw us off the trail."

Roddy stopped for a moment by the gate. It was a lovely summer's day with the sky arching, cloudlessly, from horizon to horizon. There was a faint mist waist-high in the meadow beyond Roddy's garden but the sun was drawing it up and dispersing it. There were narrow ranks of larches surrounding the cottage and the sunlight struck through the pale green shimmering leaves and from them the song of the blackbird and a thrush rang out. The hedgerows were dressed for summer, black bryony sturdily protecting traveller's joy, wild clematis, lady's slipper and purple tufted vetch. Common bumble bees moved among them and a red admiral did the same but the couple at the gate saw none of it.

"Why? Why should she run away like this?" His voice was high, near to breaking like a boy who has been unjustly punished, but with a great effort he pulled himself together. "I can't just bloody do nothing. I've got ter look for her. I've got ter find her."

"Mr Goodwin is looking."

"Bugger Mr Goodwin. He doesn't love her like I do. An' she doesn't love him, but I still can't understand why she'd run away. She could've come ter me." His voice was anguished. "But I can't just stand here or I'll go mad. I'll go an' see Mrs Bennett and then if I get nothing from 'er I'm coming over to see *him*."

"Him?"

"Aye, bloody Goodwin."

Tearing his arm away from Harriet who had not been aware that she had hold of it again, he began to run along Green Lane in the direction of St Helens.

Harriet sighed and turned to her husband, who put a comforting arm about her. "Dear Lord, Clem, what is to happen? Surely she knew her disappearance would create such chaos things would never be the same again. And what of the child she carries? Noah Goodwin will not rest until he finds her. He has wanted a son ever since they married and he will not give up until he has her back home."

"There's nowt more yer can do, lass. Come on, let's get back afore that child digs up the lad's vegetable garden."

Abby was surprised and alarmed a few days later when Mrs O'Neill knocked on the door of the room she and Cissie shared and told her there was a visitor for her. Dear God, he'd not found her already, was her first thought, for she knew how thorough her husband was. He was rich and influential and could command the help of not only the police but private detectives to follow her trail.

"Who . . . who is it, Mrs O'Neill?" she quavered.

"It's that doctor chappie what brought yer 'ome t'other day. Come ter see 'ow yer are, 'e ses."

"It's Doctor Tom, our Abby,' Cissie whispered in relief, though to tell the truth what had seemed like a wondrous adventure when Abby had put it to her had become rather frightening to country-bred Cissie and she had half hoped it was Mr Goodwin come to fetch them home.

"I'll be right down, Mrs O'Neill. If we might use your parlour I'd be very grateful."

Mrs O'Neill had quite taken a fancy to the ladylike Mrs Brown who, it turned out, was a widow expecting her first child. Mrs O'Neill had never had such a genteel boarder before, though Mrs Brown's sister was a bit of a puzzle. Nice little thing who rarely opened her mouth but when she did spoke with a broad northern accent quite unlike her sister. They were both quiet and even the dog was no bother. They never went anywhere without one another, even on the nightly visit to the bit of grass at the end of the street where the dog relieved itself.

"Rightio, queen. Will I mekk tea?"

"That would be most kind, Mrs O'Neill." Mrs O'Neill smiled approvingly at the closed door, then went down the narrow staircase to put the kettle on.

Tom Hartley stood up, careful not to slip off the shiny horsehair settee where Mrs O'Neill had put him, as the two young women entered the room. Mrs Brown really was the most glorious creature, even in her sombre black mourning dress. Like many women who were expecting a child her condition was not very obvious but she glowed, her skin like honey silk, her mouth a vivid poppy red. Her hair was like a living flame about her head, pulled up to a chignon but from which endearing tendrils escaped. Her blue-green eyes, such an unusual colour, gleamed as she smiled and as she had been taught by Holdy she held out her hand to him, indicating that he might sit. Her sister sidled beside her, shy with downcast eyes and when Mrs Brown sat so did she.

Mrs O'Neill, who had once been in service and knew the right way things should be done, brought in a tray covered with her best lace tray-cloth. There were three china cups and saucers with a teapot, milk jug and sugar basin to match, her most treasured possessions which normally never saw the light of day.

"Could yer eat a biscuit, Doctor?" she asked the caller and was rewarded with a smile like that of a boy. "Indeed I could, Mrs O'Neill. I wouldn't mind betting they're home-made."

She beamed and nodded and hurried away, returning in two minutes with three plates which matched the set, three linen napkins and a plate heaped high with her special coconut macaroons.

"Now get them down yer. You too, Mrs Brown. Yer'll need ter keep yer strength up. An' yer sister." Though Mrs O'Neill thought Mrs Brown's sister was a bit gormless and not a patch on Mrs Brown.

When she had left the room and the three of them had drunk a cup of tea and eaten the whole plate of Mrs O'Neill's biscuits Doctor Tom set his cup and saucer down on a small table whose surface was almost invisible beneath Mrs O'Neill's knick-knacks.

"I've come to tell you I think I might have found a suitable cottage for you, Mrs Brown," he announced. "You remember you asked."

Abby leaned forward eagerly. "Yes, oh, yes."

"My family is well known in Liverpool and we have many acquaintances in the city. The Hemingways, who are friends of my parents, own a great estate down by the river and there is a small – very small, I'm afraid – cottage almost on the seashore. It has been empty for some time since the old nanny they employed and who lived there when the children grew up, died in the winter. She was very old. The cottage is in a splendid position though some way from the city."

"It sounds ideal. Neither my sister or I are city people. It has a view of the river, you say."

"So I have been told and it is still furnished with the old lady's possessions. Mr Hemingway says you may have whatever you can use, although I did mention you might want to put in your own . . ."

Bramble, who had trotted down the stairs with them, leaned confidentially against Tom Hartley's legs, squirming in ecstasy as the doctor scratched his ears and even Cissie leaned forward and smiled with delight. To have their own place would be wonderful and out of the city, too, which she was not sure she cared for.

"Can we go an' see it, Doctor?" she asked excitedly, then hung her head shyly. Cissie Murphy was still a child and, apart from the hours she had spent in the schoolroom learning her lessons, had never been far from her mother's skirts. She loved and trusted her older sister but so far the great adventure was not quite what she had imagined. She had always said she longed to see the world but the bit she had seen had frightened rather than thrilled her. Abby had promised her last night that when they were settled they would buy some new dresses, at least for Cissie, since it would be a waste of time for herself, at least until the child was born.

"'Ow long will we be 'ere, our Abby?" Cissie had asked wistfully, staring round the stark cleanlines of Mrs O'Neill's bedroom.

"Are you homesick, Cissie? Do you miss Mam?" Abby had put her arms round her and held her close. "Would you like to go home? I can put you on a train to St Helens and send a telegram to Mrs Bennett to meet you and take you—"

Cissie pulled away in great agitation. "Oh, no, our Abby,

I couldn't go on me own. It's just so . . . so strange 'ere, but I suppose I'll get used to it." Leaving Abby to wonder if perhaps she might have done better to come alone.

"Of course, Miss Cissie," the doctor answered, smiling at the girl and standing up. "I've arranged for a cab to take us and I have a key. From what was said you can move in tomorrow if you care to. Mind, I'm not sure what state the place is in but I'm sure the structure will be sound. Mr Hemingway is most responsible about such things." He hesitated and Abby, who had stood up and sent Cissie flying upstairs to fetch their shawls, looked anxiously at him, for there was evidently some problem he wished to discuss.

"Yes, Doctor?"

"There is one thing I would ask of you. A condition, if you like."

"Doctor . . . ?"

"That boy, the one who came for me when you fainted in the market. Do you remember him?"

Abby looked perplexed. "No, I can't say that I do. I was not really . . ."

"Of course you weren't. Well, the lad lives on the streets earning a farthing here and a farthing there. God knows where he sleeps at night but he's a good boy and deserves a chance to better himself. Not too much but an improvement on his life now. I'm sorry, I have this tendency to go on but would it be too much to ask you to employ him?"

"Doctor Hartley . . ."

"Tom, please . . ."

"Doctor Tom, I'm not sure what my plans are to be. How long I am to stay in Liverpool after my child is born. Besides which, my funds won't really stretch to employing a servant. I'm sorry."

"He would expect nothing but a bed to sleep in and his meals. He would work at whatever you asked him and . . .

well, besides doing him a favour I would feel better if you had someone to run for me if needed. Your sister—"

"Doctor, let us—"

"His name is Archie." He smiled winningly and Abby began to laugh.

"Do you provide all your patients with a servant, Doctor Tom?"

"I wish I could, Mrs Brown. Many of them are in such dire straits someone to look after them would be a godsend."

Abby looked into his kind face and wondered at the fates which had sent this man into her life. Not only had he administered to her when she fainted, but he had found her a cottage which sounded most suitable, in fact, exactly right for country girls like herself and Cissie, and was now offering them a lad to help them. She had not thought to employ anybody. Cissie was strong and used to working and she herself, though she had lived a soft life for four years, was not averse to reverting to the domestic duties she had once known. In fact she would welcome them. She was well aware that this was a temporary passage in her life. That some day when the child was born she must return to . . . to . . . she supposed it would be to Noah, for he was her husband and the probable father of her child. He was the most likely one to have impregnated her, for he made love to her almost every night and sometimes in the mornings as well. The child would bear his name no matter which man had fathered him but she comforted herself with the thought that when the baby was born, with a mother's instinct, she would know. Roddy's or Noah's? Something would tell her. Some likeness. The colour of its eyes, surely, or its hair which would make her decision for her. In the meanwhile she would have this time of peace to prepare herself, not only for the birth of her child, but for what would come after.

"Well, Mrs Brown. Will you have Archie as well as the

cottage? I'm not saying you can't have one without the other but you would be doing me, and yourself a great favour, not to mention Archie."

"You are very persuasive, Doctor Tom," she twinkled, flinging the shawl that Cissie handed her about her shoulders with such grace Tom Hartley was fascinated. "Let's go and see the cottage first."

"And if you like it?"

"You can send for Archie!"

26

Biddy, Laura Bennett's young maid, opened the front door and fell back in great alarm into the narrow hallway when the man, who she was convinced was going to attack her, flung himself over the threshold. She squeaked and wrapped her hands defensively in her apron, backing away up the hall as he advanced on her, and it was not until the kitchen door at the end of the hallway was opened and Cook put her face out to see what all the commotion was about, that Biddy came to a stop. Even so the man still had his face in hers in the most fearsome way.

"Now then, what's ter do?" Cook said belligerently. "What d'yer think yer doin', me lad?" Cook was a large woman who had dealt with a drunken husband and six strapping sons in her time and given the provocation she'd wipe the floor with this chap.

At her words Roddy Baxter came to his senses, realising that he was frightening the young lass, though it was clear the older woman had no fear. He stepped back, then, remembering his mission, leaned wearily against the wall. The tall, cheerful, undeniably good-looking young man was gone. He had been humorous, boyish, engaging once, but now he looked older than his years, dragged down by life. His mind was in turmoil with thoughts darting like a flock of swallows in flight, picturing his Abby in some strange town or, worse, in the clutches of some monster and her with only that bit of a sister of hers to protect her. Why had she gone? Why had she left him without word? Why had she not written to *him*? She had said not a word to him the last time they had met and he just couldn't believe that this was happening. He couldn't believe she would go away without telling him. She knew how his life was nothing without her in it and besides, it was not like her to be so callous as to leave him with this appalling anxiety. It must be something to do with that bastard of a husband of hers. He must have done something so dreadful she could stand no more so she had fled, but then why hadn't she come to him? His head was aching with the clanging of these questions and none of them had any answer and if he didn't get some from Mrs Bennett he was going straight to Edge Bottom and demand to see Noah Goodwin.

Cook took a step forward, brushing past the trembling little maid. The young man was in a dreadful state, his back to the wall, his head hanging and though she had known a few knocks in her life, *and* dealt with them, she felt compassion for him move in her.

"What's up, lad?"

"I'd like to see Mrs Bennett. It's important."

"I can see that but she's got one of 'er meetings an' I don't like ter—"

Roddy raised his head. "Please, I must see her." His face was so haggard with strain Cook was tempted to put a hand on his arm and draw him into her kitchen which was calm and homely but she resisted.

"Does she know yer?" she said instead.

"I've met her a couple o' times. I've been to meetings. Please, ma'am, ask her ter come out an' see me. I'll only keep her a minute."

Cook hesitated then turned to Biddy. "Go ter't parlour an' tell Mrs Bennett there's a . . ." She cocked her head enquiringly in Roddy's direction.

"Roddy Baxter."

"A Roddy Baxter ter see 'er if she could spare a minute. Say it just like that, Biddy." For the little maid, in her effort to please, sometimes got messages a bit mixed up.

Roddy was put in the small room where John Bennett smoked his pipe and pored over his medical records. It was barely bigger than a pantry but there was a desk and a couple of chairs. Roddy sat in one but leaped to his feet when Laura Bennett entered the room.

"Roddy, I know we've been introduced at a couple of our meetings but what can I do to . . ." Her voice petered out, for she knew full well why he was here.

"Where's Abby, Mrs Bennett? Please, I must know where she is. Mrs Woodruff told me she wrote ter yer but . . . Dear sweet Christ, I can't stand this, not knowin' where she is or why she's gone. Mrs Woodruff said it was of her own free will but I can't believe . . . she'd not go willingly. I *must* find 'er. I must know she's safe. I can't stand it, not knowin'. Please, Mrs Bennett, help me, please."

He held out his hands to her and Laura took them in both of hers. She looked into the distraught face of the young man and was overwhelmed by the awful, unbelieving worry and grief she saw there. She had always known of the love that was shared by Roddy Baxter and Abby Goodwin. Years ago Abby had nursed him back to health against the express orders of her husband and there had been between them, obvious to anyone in their presence, or at least anyone with feelings in their own heart, some bond that was invisible and yet unmistakable. She had only been in their combined company a couple of times when Roddy, who was interested in the betterment of his fellow man, which included *women*, had attended meetings in Manchester where speakers such as John Stuart Mill, amongst others, had taken the platform. He was a self-educated young man, a *well*-educated man, interested in philosophy, astronomy, chemistry, besides the usual mathematics, reading, writing and literature. She supposed he had nothing else to do with his time, which he spent studying. He was rising fast in the Mulberry Glass Works and had a splendid future ahead of him but his love for Abby, his *hopeless* love for Abby would always hold him back. Abby was further put out of his reach by her pregnancy, which Roddy knew nothing about, for the child, which biologically could be his if he and Abby were lovers, would be claimed by Noah Goodwin. Noah had been gone for days searching for it, and his wife. It was a mystery to both men why Abby had vanished so suddenly, but whatever the reason they would neither be satisfied until she was found and brought back. God in heaven, what was to happen when she was? It didn't bear thinking about. She had wept in John's arms last night, for there seemed to be no way out of this chaos for her friend or for this young man who was clutching her hands in desperation, his narrowed cat's eyes boring into hers as though they would pry from her the secret of where Abby had gone.

"Roddy, I wish I could help but I'm as much in the dark as you as to her whereabouts. I had one letter which was posted in St Helens before she boarded the train."

"Which train? Where to?" His grip was so fierce she winced.

"I don't know. Noah set off at once—"

"Where to?"

"Roddy, can't you see I am not really at liberty to tell you—"

"Where to?"

Laura shook her head. "I shouldn't say because she was not found there but—"

"Where?" Roddy let go of her hands and moved towards the closed door as though in preparation for the quick getaway he intended. "I'll find her an' bring her back. Not to him but ter live wi' me."

"Roddy, has it occurred to you to wonder why Abby ran away?" Laura turned away from him and moved to the small window, staring out at the long bare strip of garden at the rear of the house. A cat sat in a patch of sunshine grooming itself and she watched it unseeingly.

"It must've been something he did to her." But Roddy looked somewhat confused as he stood with his hand on the door knob.

"Or you?"

He moved back towards her, looking at her in consternation. "I did nothing to 'er. I did nothing but love 'er so it can't—"

"She was like a beautiful strand of silken ribbon with you on one end and Noah on the other, pulled between you until she was ready to snap. I believe, I *know* she has gone away to . . . to find peace, to have a few weeks, or even months in which to think of what she must do. She is Noah's wife and has a duty to him in the eyes of—"

"But she doesn't love him!"

"Perhaps not but—"

"There's no perhaps about it. Me an' her have loved one another since we were bairns. We would've been wed but for that old bastard who took her. Anyroad, that's past history." He shook himself, like a dog coming from water. "That was then and this is now an' if you'll just give me the name of the place she's gone I'll go after her."

Laura sighed heavily. "Manchester."

"Thanks." He flung himself through the front door, banging it behind him.

The booking-clerk at St Helens Railway Station stared with open-mouthed amazement at the young man who almost had his head through the opening of the booking-office window which allowed the passengers to hand him the necessary fare and for him to pass them a ticket. But it was what he said that confounded him.

"Have you seen two women with a dog, pass through here in the last few days? A . . . a lovely woman with hair the colour of copper, long and . . . the other one, not more than a girl really with, I think, brown hair. They were said to take the train ter Manchester."

"Bloody 'ell, 'ow many more're goin' ter ask after this lass, tell me that?" The clerk shook his head in bewilderment then sighed deeply as though all he had done for the last week was answer questions about this elusive woman. First the toff who had caused great offence not only among the staff but the passengers who had been doing their best to buy tickets. Now this chap who, being of the same class as himself he felt he could speak to plainly. "'Oo is she that every second man 'oo comes ter me window wants ter know—"

"Never you mind who she is," the man snarled, thrusting his face even further into the opening. The clerk realised his mistake. This one was going to be just as belligerent as the other one who had been here more than once, getting on and off trains to here, there and everywhere in his search for this mysterious woman. "Tell me what yer know or I'll be in that office of yours an' tear yer bloody 'ead off. I'm askin' a simple question in a civil way and I expect a civil answer."

"Now look 'ere . . ."

"No, *you* look here. Which train did these women take an' what stations did it stop at between 'ere an' Manchester?" Roddy reverted to some of his old speech pattern is his angry fear.

"That's what t'other chap asked and there's the answer." He fiddled with some leaflets on the counter and handed one to Roddy. "He went off like a bullet from a gun ter ask at 'em but 'e still keeps comin' back 'ere and I'll tell yer summat, I'm gettin' manderous sick of it. I don't know where they fetched up, like I told t'other chap, I only know they bought a ticket ter Manchester. Now, if that's all, I'll ask yer ter gerraway from me winder an' let me gerron wi' me job."

"Give me a ticket ter Manchester."

"Rightio, an' the best o' luck. T'other chap don't seem to 'ave 'ad any."

The cottage was just as Abby hoped it would be, set in a half-acre of garden practically on the strip of beach that bordered the River Mersey. It was reached by a tree-lined rutted lane off Aigburth Road, its garden gate facing the river leading down a few rough steps and directly on to the sand. Lark Cottage, it was called and it stood on Jericho Beach. The meadows and farms to the right of the cottage as you faced it from the water all belonged to the Hemingways, so Doctor Tom told them, a great family who owned a shipping line and who lived at Silverdale which also led on to the beach.

The hansom-cab that brought them was forced to stop before they got to Lark Cottage, the driver complaining that he couldn't chance his horse's legs nor his cab's wheels on such a surface.

"Will you wait here then?" Doctor Tom asked him. "We'll be no more than ten minutes or so."

"Well, as long as it's no more. I'm losin' business hangin' about . . ."

"You'll be paid for the time you wait."

Doctor Tom had the key to the cottage and as soon as he pushed open the door and allowed Abby and Cissie to step inside Abby knew this was the place. She stepped over the threshold, noting absently that the step appeared to have been freshly scrubbed. The cottage was tiny. There was a narrow passage that led to a kitchen, the biggest room in the place, she found out later, and off the passage was a parlour. She glanced inside, noting its neat and cosy appearance but it was towards the kitchen she headed. She gazed round her, standing for a moment to draw into herself the peace, the slightly hazy atmosphere which spoke of warm fires in the winter and, as today, the slanting sunshine in which dust motes floated and the simplicity of the lives that had been led here. Countless loyal servants of the Hemingway family had spent their last days here, not turned out to fend for themselves when they grew old or to end up in the workhouse, but cared for in tranquillity.

From the kitchen there was a steep crooked staircase leading to a small, square landing and two low-ceilinged bedrooms. The windows were set almost at floor level and the ceilings sloped so that Doctor Tom had to bend his head to peer inside. The cottage was scrupulously clean and smelled of lavender with a faint whiff of baking bread. There was a bed draped in a beautiful hand-sewn quilt in each bedroom, evidence of the clever fingers of the last occupant in her winter years, with a pine dresser and wardrobe, and on each low, wide windowsill stood a pretty washbasin and jug. On the landing was a set of pine drawers which, when Cissie hesitantly opened them, disclosed piles of lavender-scented bedding, pillow cases and sheets edged with hand-sewn lace and embroidered with what was known as "whitework", a white stitch worked on white fabric, and dozens of spotless white towels.

Without speaking and trailed by Doctor Tom, they descended the crooked stairs and inspected the kitchen, a mellow room furnished with functional simplicity. There was the pine table in its centre and the dresser against the wall held a great deal of stoneware, dinner plates, cups, saucers, gravy boats and tureens all decorated with bluebirds sitting on a branch laden with blossom. There was a rocking-chair piled with cushions before the cast-iron grate, which was set in a recess providing warmth and the means for cooking, and a tuffet on which the old lady who had lived here had rested her feet. There were rag rugs on the flagged floor and, as upstairs, the windows were low with wide sills. There were gingham curtains at the window and along the wall on shelves a dozen pans of varying shapes and sizes.

The parlour was just as trim but much more stiff and formal as though it had been not much used. On the mantelshelf above the small fireplace were rows of old photographs, children, six of them, in artificial poses, two boys and four girls of various ages, presumably once in the charge of the old lady who had lived and died here.

"She must have been well thought of," Abby said musingly. "To have been cared for in such comfort at the end of her days."

"The Hemingways have always treated their servants well. They keep this place for their old retainers but at the moment it is not needed, which is why, when I dined with them at my parents' house, they suggested this. They have no wish to rent it out since it stands in their grounds but when I said you were two respectable ladies, sisters, they were willing. I spoke of rent but Mr Hemingway would not hear of it. What's five shillings a week to a man like him? He was only too glad that it would be cared for perhaps over the winter. He said he and his wife might walk down to see you. Anyway, what d'you think? It's a long way out of town but . . ."

"But we couldn't possibly live here rent free, Doctor Tom. Perhaps if I was to go and see Mr Hemingway . . ."

"He would be most offended, Mrs Brown."

"Abby." Abby's voice was distracted.

"Abby, then. And Cissie?"

Cissie smiled shyly from beneath her long lashes and nodded.

"Well, it's exactly what we were looking for and I shall find some way to repay the kindness of Mr Hemingway. I don't know how but I will and we'll accept his offer. When may we move in?"

Doctor Tom laughed. "Today, if you wish. If you can find someone to move your things, that is if you have any . . ."

"Perhaps, we'll see. This is perfect, isn't it, Cissie?" taking her sister's hand in hers.

Cissie nodded, still inclined to be anxious, for this was such a long way from home and the familiar muddle of the cottage in Sandy Lane. She looked out of the door towards the river, overwhelmed by the great stretch of water and the faint outline of the far shore, hazed by the heat, and at the ships that crowded it. Where were they all going and where had they been? But already her young mind, as curious about the world as her older sister, was becoming fascinated by this new experience. This was a lovely little cottage and though she had no idea what they were to do here she felt safe in the capable hands of Doctor Tom who seemed to have everything under control.

But Doctor Tom had something further to say. "Right, Abby, but before you take up residence so far away from town I want to have young Archie living here, though I'm not sure where he'll sleep. I know if something were to happen . . . some, well, Cissie could run up to the big house but . . ."

Cissie turned from the doorway, her young face clouding over, for Cissie Murphy had never spoken to any member of the gentry in her life and the very idea of running up to the *big* house and knocking on the door was too alarming for words. Even the servants would be far superior to her, she was sure, and again she wondered what on earth had persuaded her to accompany their Abby on such an adventure. She had been so excited at first, so overwhelmed at the thought of seeing something that was further than five miles from her own home but now she was not so sure. She felt very confused. Frightened and excited at the same time.

"What's that little building by the hedge at the back?" Abby was leaning down to peer from the kitchen window, doing her best to distract Cissie from what was evidently a moment of great unease. She herself longed to step out on to the strip of beach beyond the front door of the cottage. To walk along it, to stand and watch the great flurry of activity that was taking place on the grey rippled waters, but first things first and it seemed Doctor Tom would not rest until he was certain that young Archie, who had yet to be persuaded, was to be on hand in case of an emergency. Perhaps the lad would not care to live in such an isolated part of the great port of Liverpool. Perhaps he liked the bustle and noise in which he lived and earned a few pence, but Doctor Tom seemed to be convinced he would come.

"I don't know but we'll soon find out. Let's take a tour of your new property."

They waded through grass which had not been cut for several weeks and in it, as though it were a meadow, grew wild flowers, the pale pink of knotgrass, common sorrel which turned the garden into a vivid crimson mixed with the white and lilac of lady's smock, the yellow of buttercups and the pink of clover. There was also a great clump of stinging nettles which they skirted to reach the building. The building was only small and proved to be a washhouse with the privy attached but above it was a small space in the roof, snug and watertight which, so Tom said cheerfully, would make ideal sleeping quarters for Archie.

They stood for several minutes on the edge of the water. Ignoring the increasingly impatient gestures of the cab driver, they watched sea birds, gulls Tom called them, float on the slight wind above the moving ships. A large, dark bird stood swaying on a buoy moored in the estuary, its wings outstretched as though to dry, and Tom said it was a cormorant, some of which nested in these parts and were inhabitants of the estuary. As they stood watching, Tom noticed that Cissie clung to her sister's hand and wondered uneasily how helpful the girl would be when Abby's time came. He was longing to know the history of this lovely, pregnant woman who seemed so refined next to the pretty but obviously lower-class girl who was her sister but felt that this was not really the time to enquire.

They moved in the next day. Wally, who had guided them to Bolton Street, proved invaluable, for it was he who knew a chap who knew a chap who could loan them a small cart pulled by a sad donkey which would take them and their belongings to Lark Cottage.

"We'd no need to buy all this stuff from the market," Abby complained to Cissie as Mrs O'Neill helped Wally to load it on to the cart. "There's certainly better bed linen at Lark Cottage."

"Don't yer dare lift that there bundle, Mrs Brown," Mrs O'Neill admonished. "Me an' Wally an' that there lad'll see to it," meaning Archie who had agreed to come along for a trial period, he said. Mrs O'Neill eyed the man who was loaning the cart with some indignation, but as he said he had been asked to *loan* the cart not load it. Doctor Tom had meant to help but at the last minute a difficult confinement in one of the squalid courts had called him away. "I don't like the idea of you goin' all the way up there," Mrs O'Neill added, just as though they were off to Bootle or Southport, "not on yer own, anyroad." Mrs O'Neill eyed Cissie with a disapproving stare, for though the girl, give her a task, would do it well, she seemed not to have the gumption to think of it herself.

Mrs O'Neill stood indecisively as Mrs Brown was helped up on to the cart by a solicitous Wally, then as though making up her mind darted indoors, coming out with her shawl draped about her. She banged her front door, and telling Cissie to "shove up, lass", scrambled up on the seat next to her. The cart lender nearly fell off the other end, much to the amusement of several of Mrs O'Neill's neighbours, but at last they were under way, Archie perched like a sparrow on top of the load. Abby kept repeating that Mrs O'Neill was more than welcome to visit them at any time in their new home, she knew that, but they really could manage this move. Mrs O'Neill took no notice, watching the driver sternly, ready to advise him on any bumpy surface in the road, which did not please him. The poor donkey leaned into his harness and picked his way along Renshaw Street, making his way towards the edge of the city and out into the open countryside towards Aigburth Road. The hedges were weighed down with honeysuckle and wild roses. They passed farms and the big mansions of the wealthy families, most of them come by their riches from the sea, the ships and all that passed along the great highway of the River Mersey.

Abby sniffed the fragrant summer air and from her perch on the cart's seat looked over the hedgerows to where cows grazed and men walked behind ploughs pulled by massive horses. It was all so lovely out here, with as much peace as she could have wished for, but her heart dragged with pain and loneliness as she grieved for Roddy who must surely be out of his mind with worry. And strangely she thought of Noah who would, since someone would have told him, be looking for her if only to claim the child she carried for his own.

27

They said in St Helens and Edge Bottom that Noah Goodwin must be losing his mind and if he didn't pull himself together he'd lose his glass works as well. For the past six weeks he had spent his days in the search for his missing wife which in itself was a source of great mystery, totally ignoring his obligation to the business which previous Goodwins and then himself had built up into a thriving concern. His young engineer and foreman, a Scot by the name of Euan MacNair, was hard pressed to keep everything ticking over, making decisions, which his master couldn't seem to be bothered with, and somehow holding the wobbling construction from tipping slowly into chaos. A ship that has no captain at the helm and only a young, untried mate to put his hands on the wheel can soon run into squalls, but give the lad his due, he did his best. He was ambitious, clever, and though it was daunting to be in sole charge, in a way he welcomed this chance to show his employer his true capabilities. He had been apprenticed to a Glasgow engineering firm and was interested in improving the apparatus for grinding and smoothing plate glass, crown glass and sheet glass, which was why he had attracted the attention of Noah Goodwin. But he was not yet experienced in the actual *running* of the business. The maids at Edge Bottom House had become used to seeing his anxious young face at the front door with an urgent request to have a word with Mr Goodwin and more often than not being turned away with the information that the master was not at home. Somehow, so far, he had managed to keep things running in his employer's frequent absences. Now and again Noah Goodwin showed his face at the works, impatiently listening to Euan, obviously longing to be away on his search for his young wife, giving instructions for this and that and, as Euan's old grandmother would have said, with the help of perspiration, cork and glue, the business tottered along.

Noah was constantly amazed by Abby's ingenuity in covering her trail. He had patiently followed her from St Helens to Manchester, soon realising that she must have left the train at one of the stations in between. Newton in Makerfield where a lady fitting the description of his wife accompanied by a young girl had bought a ticket to Warrington. No, the station-master told him, for Noah insisted on speaking to the man at the top, no one had seen her actually getting on the train . . . well, they hadn't the time to take an interest in every passenger, had they, but there were several junctions on that line, one that led to Parkside Station which had a connection with the line to Wigan.

He criss-crossed Lancashire a dozen times, haunting large and small stations, Preston, Wigan, Bolton, Chorley, Ormskirk, Lancaster, Blackburn, the small fishing village of Lytham where he thought Abby might have settled, even travelling as far as Carlisle in his search for his wife and his child which she carried. Now and again he was rewarded by some porter or booking clerk who had vague recollections of a shawled woman in mourning black who was accompanied by a younger girl and a dog and he wondered if Abby had realised the inadvisability of carting the animal about with her, for more often than not it was the dog the station employees remembered. He was becoming desperate, for he knew the longer she remained hidden the colder became her trail.

His only consolation was Laura Bennett and not in the way he would have liked her to console him years ago. He often wondered how he could have been so crass as to imagine he could have seduced her. She and her husband were devoted to one another and whenever he was back from his searchings he spent time, sometimes taking a meal with them, in their rather shabby house in Claughton Street.

"How far along was she, John, do you know?" His face was thinner, and about his eyes was a stain which spoke of sleepless nights. He smoked one cigar after another as though he had to have something to do with his hands. Something to hold on to, not even asking Laura's permission to smoke, which was the mark of a gentleman. Laura studied him as he spoke, knowing he could not continue to carry on as he was doing for much longer, wondering at the change in him who once had thought of nothing but his business, his own pleasure, the women he was said to have, gambling and drinking, his trips abroad to further his concerns, his love of the good things in life. What had changed him? Surely it was not just the hope of a son that Abby might be carrying. He was obsessed with finding her, but was it just the child? Laura was beginning to wonder and perhaps have a faint inkling of what drove Noah Goodwin in his search for Abby.

"I couldn't tell you that, old man," John was saying. "I had no idea she was pregnant, none of us did, until she told Harriet and then vanished. Perhaps you may have . . . have more idea than . . ." He paused delicately.

"If you mean when did I make love to my wife then the answer is probably the night before she left and every night since we were married, which is no help at all. I wanted a child, you see."

Laura began to suspect at that moment that there was more to it than Noah's longing for a son. That it was not the only reason he made love to her.

The servants moved about the strangely empty house in a daze of unbelieving sadness. They knew by now, of course, that their young mistress was to have a child, for how could such a secret be kept hidden. Whispers from one to another, none of them quite understanding how it came about and who had first told another. It seemed Harriet Woodruff had the mistress's confidence but that was no help, was it? It didn't explain why she had left or where she had got to. They cleaned and polished and cooked meals which were scarcely touched when the master was at home, which wasn't often, and had it not been for Harriet would have become slack, skimping their work and lolling round the kitchen table drinking tea all day. It brought about a blazing row between her and Cook and had Laura Bennett not chosen that moment to call might have brought disaster.

This time Noah Goodwin had been missing from home for almost a week when it happened. They were sitting round the table sipping tea when Harriet entered the kitchen from the yard. Cook had made a few scones, to cheer them up, she said, and Nessie was spreading one hot from the oven with the best butter delivered only that morning from the dairy at Updale Farm. Harriet had taken Todd and Harry up to Miss Holden in the nursery and after a word with Clem who was grooming Lysander, for the horses still needed caring for, didn't they, had decided to pop into the kitchen to see if there was any news. She knew there wouldn't be, for if there was one of them would have been over to the cottages to tell her but still, you never knew.

"What the devil's this?" she asked, frowning at the sprawl-ing maidservants about the table. Cook even had her boots off! Nessie, May, Kitty, Ruby, tucking into Cook's scones while in the scullery sink the pans used for their breakfast were still waiting Nessie's attention. There was flour and bits of dough on the marble slab at the end of the table and a clutter of baking trays ready to be taken to the scullery. There was even flour on the floor and some suspect stains that might have been fat which the cat was getting her tongue round.

"What d'yer mean?" Cook asked, reaching for another scone and nodding to Nessie to pass her the butter.

"What do you think you're up to, lounging about the place as though you were at a tea party? You're not paid to indulge yourselves in behaviour that is not only lazy and inefficient but dishonest. You wouldn't behave like this if Mrs Goodwin was here and I'm surprised at you all."

Nessie stumbled to her feet, her face flushed with guilt, and the others had the grace to look shame-faced but Cook held up her hand and waved them back to their places.

"And who are you ter tell us what we may or may not do in *my* kitchen? This is my place, not yours and I'll thank you to keep your nose out of what don't concern you. If me an' my staff want to have a cup of tea an' a little break then that's our affair. At least mine since I'm in charge." She turned a look of triumph to those at the table but they were inclined to avoid her eye. It was not so long since Mrs Woodruff, once Harriet Pearson, had had sole charge of not only this kitchen and its running, but this house. She had married Clem Woodruff who was merely a groom and in a way had moved down in the servants' hierarchy. In fact she was really no longer a servant. Not since Mrs Goodwin had run off, for her position as companion and friend to their mistress no longer existed.

"You may be in charge, Cook, of the kitchen, but since the mistress went away it is I who have taken over the running of the house, or hadn't you noticed? Hadn't you noticed that I am the one who deals with the merchants, orders the food you eat, the changing of the beds, who attends to the master's laundry and settles the accounts? And until Mrs Goodwin comes home, which, make no mistake, she will, I say what you and your kitchen staff may do. And I say now that these *little breaks* will cease immediately. I have no objection to refreshment mid-morning and a half-hour for lunch as before but I will not have . . ."

Cook stood up and for some reason picked up the rolling pin with which she had rolled out the scones. The rest got to their feet in horror, for surely she didn't mean to brain Mrs Woodruff with it.

"Now listen 'ere, madam, just because you an' the mistress are marrers, though God knows why, it don't give yer the right to come in here flinging yer weight round. You clear out of my kitchen an' get back ter yer cottage where yer belong, as the wife of a groom. I'm sick of you tootin' where yer don't belong."

"Oh, Cook," wailed Kitty, horrified at the swiftness of this row, which had blown up over nothing really. They should not have been lounging about as they had been, but really Mrs Woodruff was going too far, as was Cook and she supposed it was the strain and the tension that had settled over this house since the mistress had disappeared. They never knew where they were these days with the master away most of the time and the mistress God knows where and her in the family way, which should have been such a happy time.

"Never you mind, 'Oh, Cook', Kitty Spencer. I'm havin' me say an' if this—"

It was at that precise moment that the front doorbell rang and everyone in the room jumped nervously but with great relief.

"Answer the door, Kitty," Harriet said imperiously, still glaring at Cook as though to say defy me at your peril. They stood almost nose to nose, watched by the others and when Laura Bennett entered the kitchen they barely noticed, still enveloped in the madness of the moment.

"What is going on here?" Mrs Bennett's well-bred voice demanded and at the tone of authority they jumped apart guiltily. The rest bobbed curtseys, their faces pale, ready to weep, for this had been such a happy house until the mistress vanished. Cook was a bit of a tyrant and sharp-tongued but she was fair and rarely ruffled. Mrs Woodruff, because of her friendship with the mistress, was held somewhat at arm's length, not because they didn't trust her but because she was not really one of them and never had been. Heavens above, she had once been the old man's *mistress*, but since the birth of her son and their great fondness for the lad, she had been more freely accepted.

"Nothing really, Mrs Bennett," she answered politely. "Just a difference of opinion which has been resolved, hasn't it, Cook?" Harriet turned to smile at Cook, who returned it.

"Kitty seemed upset when she answered the door, that is why I ask." Laura looked round the room, knowing that if Abby didn't return soon this house would fall apart, for Noah Goodwin cared little what his servants did in his absence. "But if you say there is nothing wrong then I will take your word for it. Now, I just came to tell you I have had a letter from your mistress . . ."

Before she could finish they had all crowded round her, chattering like magpies, one voice overlapping another so that none made sense, laughing, ready to cry or jig about, for surely this meant that Mrs Goodwin was coming home. Harriet took Laura by the arm, ready to shake her if she didn't hurry up and divulge the contents of the letter. Where was she? Was she well? When did she mean to return? But Laura stepped back before reaching into her reticule and producing a single sheet of paper on which lines of writing were neatly inscribed. They quietened and nodded to one another, waiting for Mrs Bennett to read it to them.

"The letter was posted in Hull and is dated the day before yesterday."

"'Ull?" Nessie murmured. "Where's 'Ull?"

"Nay, don't ask me, but be quiet will yer. Mrs Bennett'll tell us."

"It's on the east coast but I doubt that is where she is. She doesn't want us to know where she is living and somehow has contrived to have this posted in Hull."

All except Harriet wondered what she meant but they remained quiet, for surely they were going to hear good news.

"She says she is well and living in a pleasant cottage with her sister. She has a good doctor caring for her so we are not to worry." For by this time Laura was aware that the news of Abby's pregnancy was common knowledge. The only puzzle was why Roddy Baxter had not been on the warpath, for if the servants and the residents of Edge Bottom knew, so did he. He had not been seen for weeks and was, presumably, on the same quest as Noah. John had been over to the Mulberry Glass Works and was told by Jack Harrison that the grand position held by Roddy Baxter had been filled by a chap who was willing to come to work every day and not go searching for a will-o'-the-wisp as Baxter was doing. What turmoil had resulted from this dreadful tangle of possessive love. What damage had been caused to so many, and would it ever be resolved?

"Does she say she's coming home, Mrs Bennett?" Harriet asked hesitantly.

"No, I'm afraid not. I came to give the news to Mr Goodwin, though perhaps he has received a similar letter?" They didn't know. There was a pile of unopened letters on his desk but that was all they knew.

"Very well, then, I'll be off, but I think it would only be fair to Mrs Goodwin to keep her home exactly as it would be if she was here, don't you?" Letting them know that she was not foolish enough to believe their story of a difference of opinion.

"Will you let Clem drive you home, Mrs Bennett?" Harriet's voice was diffident, for they all knew Mrs Bennett's independent spirit. They were all surprised when she agreed.

Roddy opened his cottage door, bewildered to find it unlocked, and threw his old portmanteau on to the kitchen floor. He sighed and shook his head, convinced he was losing his reason, for he was sure he had locked it when he left a week ago. But was it any wonder his mind was in such a whirl, making it hard for him to concentrate or even remember the simplest things? Well, it didn't matter, for there was nothing in this home of his worth stealing. He had the barest essentials needed to live in it as he had been waiting, for years now, his sorrowing mind brooded, for the day when Abby would come and live with him and put her own special mark on it. To choose what she wanted in her own kitchen and bedroom. He had a bit of money put by for the day when it came, since he was earning good wages at Mulberry. At least he *had* been earning good wages but he was pretty certain that Mr Harrison would have long decided to replace him after his many absences. Six weeks he had been darting about the north of England, following sightings of two women with a dog, often facing astonishment at railway stations where porters and clerks told him there was another chap looking for what sounded like the same woman. It would, of course, be Noah Goodwin who, though he didn't love her would not readily let one of his possessions be lost to him. He anguished over the thought that her husband might find Abby before he did, but he was pretty certain he would never persuade her to live with him as his wife again. If she had liked being his wife she would never have left him, would she, though he did worry over the fact that she had not come to him when she left Edge Bottom House.

"There yer are, my son," a voice said to him from a corner

of the kitchen and when he whirled round he was bewildered to see his mother sitting in the one comfortable chair, sipping tea and nodding at him in her plain, sensible way. Dorcas Baxter would have liked to leap up and drag this son of hers, this beloved, ill-fated young man whom life had treated so shabbily, into her arms, but that was not her way. She'd lay down her life for him right gladly but instead she greeted him calmly and with a no-nonsense simplicity that he was accustomed to.

"Ma, yer give me a shock. I wondered why me door was unlocked. I knew I'd turned the key when I left but, I don't know, these days I seem not to know whether I'm on me head or me heels."

"I'm not surprised, lad, the way yer goin' on. But there, that's nowt ter do wi' me. Yer a grown man an' mun choose what yer do wi' yer life. If yer want ter waste it runnin' after another man's wife, that's your affair. No, I'm not 'ere ter argue. I just come ter see if yer was all right an' 'appen do a bit o' cleanin' fer yer. I found spare key under t' brick by't door. I knew yer'd 'ave one." She was referring, of course, to Abby Goodwin's visits which she was well aware of and the key Roddy left for her should he not be at home.

"Mam, have yer not enough cleaning ter do without coming ter do mine an' all, or is this just an excuse ter come an'—"

"When did I need an excuse ter visit me own son, Roddy Baxter?" she interrupted him. "Am I not welcome then?"

"'Course you are, Ma, yer know that." But he was dwelling on the time she had nearly caught him and Abby in bed together and since then had kept his door locked when Abby was there. Still, it could be awkward if . . . well, he knew his mother wouldn't tell a soul of his relationship with Abby, but it was an embarrassment to them both.

"Is there a cup in't pot?" he asked, doing his best to be cheerful.

"Aye, an' then you an' me 'ad best 'ave a little talk, my son."

"Now, Mam, we've 'ad this out a dozen times an' it does no good. I'll not give 'er up, not while there's breath in me body. I've loved her since she was a little lass, an' she loves me. She was tricked into marryin' that bastard but she doesn't love him an'—"

"Why does she stay wi' 'im, then? If there's nowt but business between them, which your sayin' it is with the glass works, why is she still with 'im after all these years? Why don't she leave an' go away wi' you an' start a new life where yer not known?"

Roddy Baxter had asked the same question, of himself and of Abby, a hundred times and had never, from himself, or from Abby, had a lucid answer. Abby spoke of vows in church, the law, her obligations to . . . to . . . well, he couldn't remember what those obligations were said to be. But it made no difference. He could as easily stop loving her as he could stop breathing. She was inside him, buried deep and secure and yet she was outside him, wrapped around him, keeping him safe and sure, her love for him fused with his for her. It was strong and fixed, like two pieces of metal that have been welded together and which nothing could drag apart. The very idea of being without her in his life was so ludicrous it was almost humorous and surely his mother must have realised that by now. Didn't she recall the way Abby had nursed him back to life when even she, with her mother's strong love, could not do so? Those days when Goodwin had thundered his way into her cottage and demanded his wife come home. Abby had refused, simply and with dignity, and he was determined, now that Abby had made the break, that when she was found it was to Roddy Baxter she would return.

His mother put her cup of tea on the top of the oven

beside the fire she had lit. She looked down at her old, work-worn hands, studying the broken nails, the dirt which was so ingrained that no matter how she scrubbed them would not go. All evidence of the love she bore her sons, the work she had done on their behalf, and would go on doing until the day she dropped dead in the traces. She didn't know how she was to tell her son what she had to, for it was obvious he didn't know or he would not be hanging about here.

"There's summat yer should know, my son," she said quietly. "The whole of Edge Bottom knows but wi' you bein' away yer'll not've 'eard."

"Oh yes." Roddy held himself stiffly, aware that a great terror was growing in him though he didn't know why. She'd come home and was at this moment with her husband, perhaps in his bed . . . she'd been found discovered dead on the moor . . . Noah Goodwin had found her sick unto death . . . she'd . . . she'd . . . Oh, sweet Jesus, give me the strength to bear it.

"She's . . . oh, lad, I'd give anything not ter 'ave ter say this."

"Fer God's sake, Mam, tell me."

"She's ter 'ave a child."

There was a long and terrible silence broken only by the crackle of the fire and a blackbird singing his heart out in the hawthorn hedge at the front of the cottage. It went on and on and Dorcas watched her son's face as it became ashen with shock, with horror, with hopelessness and then, as something trickled into his desolate heart and mind, it slowly began to come to life, ready to smile, to grin, his mouth stretching in what would surely be a shout of joy.

"Roddy?"

"Mam, oh, Mam, don't you see, it's mine! She's carryin' my child. We've bin . . . well, I hate ter use the word but we've bin lovers, yer knew that."

"Aye, I do, but what mekks yer think it's yours?"

"Of course it's mine. All these years he never managed it. She's been married fer five years and it never happened. She doesn't love him an' he doesn't love her so . . ."

"Are yer sayin' that in them five years he didn't tekk her ter bed?"

Roddy's young face aged before her eyes and became savage with pain and she was ready to defend herself in case he should, in his mindless fury, become aggressive.

"No," he hissed through clenched teeth. "She had ter."

"Then why could the child not be 'is?" Dorcas sprang to her feet, her face creased with compassion for this tragic man who was her dearest son. She loved Willy and Eddy and all the others who had died in her arms scarcely before they drew breath, but this was her first born, come when she had been young and hopeful and not overwhelmed by life itself. She didn't want to torture him like this but he must be made to see, to face it, to accept what had just as much chance as the one he claimed. That it was Noah Goodwin's child in Abby Goodwin's womb.

"Roddy," she implored, but her son sprang away from her and flung himself at the door.

"Son, where yer goin'?"

"Ter see that bastard an' 'ave it out with him."

The blackbird sang on but in Dorcas Baxter's heart was only desolation. She sank down into the chair and put her face in her hands.

28

Noah Goodwin stepped wearily down from the hansom-cab in the lane that ran beside Edge Bottom House. He paid the cab driver and, carrying the portmanteau which had gone everywhere with him during the past weeks, opened the wrought-iron gate that led into the garden and began to walk up the smoothly raked gravel path to the front door. His shoulders slumped and his usual upright, arrogant manner of walking was missing. His feet seemed to drag, disturbing Mr Renfrew's careful work with the rake, giving the impression that he was within inches of reaching the end of that tether we all know.

He was halfway along the path, moving beneath the shade of the enormous oak tree that stood before the house when a man stepped out from behind its wide trunk and took up a threatening stance directly in front of him. He seemed to be trembling with some great emotion, his face rigid, his mouth clamped tight, a tension about him that might have alarmed Noah had he not been so bloody tired. The front door had opened as though the sound of the cab had alerted those in the kitchen and Kitty appeared on the step, ready to smile and bob a curtsey in welcome, then her hand went to her mouth and without a word she turned and vanished and the man and Noah were face to face.

"Who the devil are you?" Noah asked irritably. He was not afraid even though the man had been hiding and was obviously up to no good. He really hadn't the energy to be frightened. He was so bloody drained. He had just come from Hull from where Laura had received her last letter from Abby and though he had known it was a wasted journey he had been obliged to go.

"I know she's not there, Laura. She's too astute to send a letter from the very town where she has settled. It's a red herring. She has apparently found someone who has posted it for her from there but I must go."

"Why don't you let those men you have employed to find her do their job, Noah? You are paying them and then doing the work for them. Surely they are more experienced in these matters than you are? And then the police are keeping a lookout for her in all the major cities. There is no need for you to—"

"There is every need, Laura," he interrupted savagely. "Do you think I can calmly go on with my day-to-day life with the knowledge that my wife and the child she carries are lost?"

"Not lost, Noah. She has written to say she is safe and well."

"Bugger that. I beg your pardon, Laura. I want her here where I can . . . can watch over her. You know how head-strong she is. She might be . . . be acting foolishly. She's so young and this is her first child. How do I know what sort of a girl her sister is? She might be some flibbertigibbet with no thought in her head but having a good time. Oh God, Laura, what am I to do? Why did she go? I've searched the whole of Lancashire. Station after station where she might have got off the train and where, for Christ's sake, she has been *seen* or at least women who answer their description and the dog have been seen, then they vanish again."

He had sat with his head in his hands and Laura Bennett was astounded, for was this the man who had married Bradley Goodwin's granddaughter solely to possess all that she would inherit when the old man had gone? Was it the child for whom he had longed or was it the woman herself who had turned him into this hagged, heavy-eyed, dog-weary man who could not rest until they were returned to him? His business was staggering on thanks to the young man who was his manager, but they were saying in St Helens that if Noah Goodwin didn't pull himself together and attend to his glass works it would go under.

He had just returned from Preston where a porter remembered heaving a trunk from a goods van some time ago and trundling it across the lines to await a train to Liverpool. The man had seen no woman, no women, no dog, but the trunk he remembered since it was heavy and had required two of them to lift it on to the train for Liverpool. Of course it might not have been the right trunk, for there were several a day. Had there been a label on it, perhaps with a name? He didn't remember only that it was addressed to Liverpool and was to be picked up there. Mind you, as he said, this was some time back and he did attend to a lot of luggage.

So, tomorrow Noah was to take a train to Liverpool and see if a trunk – God, there must be hundreds of trunks – had arrived and been picked up. To see if any of the men who worked at Lime Street Station remembered a woman with hair that glowed like the sunset in winter, with eyes a cool, blue-green and a mouth as red and ripe as a raspberry with a young girl and a dog. She had been in the black of mourning, that he had gleaned from his enquiries and had been dressed like a working woman. Dear God, how many women would fit that description?

He sighed wearily as the man stood silently on his path, wondering what the devil the matter was now. He really felt he couldn't stand any more. All he wanted was to have a hot bath and fall into the bed he had once shared with his lovely young wife and sleep the sleep of the dead in preparation for yet another probably fruitless trip in his search for Abby.

The man was flexing his hands and his white face bore an expression of such bitter hatred Noah was astonished and inclined to take a step back, for it seemed there might be some harm intended.

"Might I ask what you are doing standing on my path, barring my way? Indeed may I ask who the bloody hell you are?"

"You don't recognise me then," the man spat out.

"No, I can't say I do. Should I?" Noah answered, doing his best to be civil, though he longed to push past this intruder and enter the house.

"Roddy Baxter ring any bells?" the man sneered. "Abby Murphy an' me were ter be wed before you decided you fancied her fer yerself, helped by that old bastard whose glass works yer also fancied. She an' I were close . . . still are fer that matter an' I believe the child she carries is mine so . . ."

For the fraction of a second Noah froze in total disbelief and horror, unable to decipher what the man had said and send the message to his stunned brain. The words had no meaning, made no sense, were incomprehensible. In fact they were obscene, words uttered by a mad man intending to shock and horrify and they had done both, rendering him speechless. This wasn't happening. He vaguely remembered the man who stood before him, or at least his name, but the last time he had seen him he had been no more than an emaciated lad on his sickbed. Abby had been nursing him, refusing to get in the carriage and come home and on the same day, on the same errand as himself, the old man had collapsed and died. Abby and this man – dear God in heaven, it was four or more years ago – had been childhood sweethearts, innocent and vulnerable against the machinations of the old man. No more had been heard about him, at least *he* had heard no more about him and now the swine was standing on Noah Goodwin's property and claiming ... claiming that ...

A mist swam before his eyes and the blood pounded in his head and through his body, and with a roar that lifted the heads of the horses in the paddock he dropped his bag and launched himself at Roddy Baxter with the firm intention of killing him. Shutting his coarse mouth so that never again could it utter the words just spoken. *Lies, lies, all lies.* Not his Abby. *Not his wife, his woman, the woman who was carrying his child.*

Roddy Baxter was not the slightly undernourished young man he had been four years ago. He had grown into the big man his young manhood had promised, strong and fit. He had spent the years in between in the foot races so popular in St Helens, in training at the gymnasium at the Mechanics Institute, in the occasional prize fight whenever the police relaxed their vigilance. He had played football in the winter, cricket in the summer, pastimes which, as well as giving him something to do when he was not with Abby, had given him a body well able to defend itself. And he was on the attack. Though it was Noah Goodwin who had made the first maddened move, Roddy was ready for him, more than ready for this contest which he had longed for ever since he had come home and found his Abby belonged to another man.

But despite his weariness Noah Goodwin was no weakling. He was older than Roddy by ten or eleven years but he had been wild in his youth and had been just as athletic, a big, powerfully built man with broad shoulders and handy with his fists. He was shrewd, cunning, with an ability to survive and, if necessary, fight dirty. He was still tough and had the aggressive nature that had made him successful years ago in the prize fighting ring. They were well matched, despite the difference in their age, for Noah had learned to fight in the school playground. His nature was more ruthless than

Roddy Baxter's and in a moment they were on the ground, rolling across Mr Renfrew's flowerbeds and crushing the plants which were still blooming. Each was doing his best to swing a fist in the other's face, wanting to hurt, to blind, to maim, to kill, grunting as each landed a blow somewhere on the other's body.

Warned by Kitty and galvanised into action by the sounds coming from the front of the house, Olly and Clem rounded the corner, followed gamely by old Mr Renfrew brandishing a pitchfork, by Charlie Potter and by the two gardening boys, Jacko and Frankie, who were wild with excitement. It was not the first time this man had been up at the house this week. Insane, they had thought him to be when he came thundering on the front door, bellowing the master's name and terrifying the women so that none of them would answer the door. It had not discouraged him. Round the house he had come, hammering on the back door and, finding it unlocked, bursting into the kitchen to confront the four maidservants and Cook who cowered in the corner, too frightened even to scream.

"Where is 'e? Where's the bastard who stole my Abby? What's he done wi' 'er? What did he do to 'er ter make 'er run away? It must 'ave been summat awful or she'd not have gone. Where is he? Fetch him out, tell him Roddy Baxter's here and wants a word." But by this time Olly and Clem and Charlie had burst into the kitchen and had him by the arms, dragging him out of the house and into the yard where Charlie commenced to pummel him.

"Leave 'im, Charlie. Send one o't lads fer't constable." Clem and Olly were having a bit of a job hanging on to the intruder's arm and were ready to put him in Charlie's little workshop which had a good lock on the door, but at that precise moment Harriet, warned by the commotion, appeared from the back of the stables where her cottage lay and where she had been making an apple pie for Clem's tea. Her hands and arms were still coated with flour and her hair was falling about her face. She recognised Roddy at once and her voice rang out, surprising him and the others.

"Leave him, Clem, let him go."

Clem stared in consternation at his wife, but Harriet was remembering the trusting young lad she had sent to the woods and to a terrible fate as a soldier on the other side of the world. She had been obeying Bradley Goodwin's orders but she had never forgotten that moment, nor forgiven herself, and never would. Had she been more courageous none of this might be happening, but then who knew what might have occurred had the circumstances been different. But she couldn't allow him to be locked up. She knew why he was here and she knew she could not prevent what was to happen, Roddy's next words confirming it.

His voice was quiet. "She's mine. She's always been mine and I mean ter have her and the child she carries. I'm its father and—"

"Yer filthy sod," Clem bellowed and would have knocked Roddy to the ground had not Harriet hung on to him and screamed to Roddy to run. He didn't run, but he left nevertheless and here he was again, mad as a bloody hatter, attacking the master. They would never forget the last few days when they had crept about the house, hardly able to look one another in the face, for though it couldn't possibly be true that their lovely mistress had consorted with the wild-eyed ruffian there had been something about him, a dignity, the sound of *truth* in his words which had confused them.

It was difficult for the men to get a hold on the two combatants. They were like wild cats whose claws could just as soon injure those who tried to separate them as each other. They were both mouthing obscenities as each man tried to land a lethal blow on the other. The maidservants were at the front door, Harriet among them, all of them sobbing in fright and watching in horror the young man, who they had begun to recognise now as the anguished lad who had plagued them years ago over Mrs Goodwin. But he was a man now and if something wasn't done either he or the master would inflict some injury that might never be mended.

"Clem, for God's sake, stop it," Harriet screamed. "Olly, help him." And as though the sound of his wife's voice had unlocked some part of him that had been paralysed Clem sprang forward and grasped his master by the scruff of his neck while Olly did the same with the intruder. They were both strong men, for they had worked physically since their childhood, dealing with horses, many of which had been wild and mettlesome. It had taken some muscle to calm Lysander when the master first bought him, for he was a thoroughbred, born of thoroughbreds and would have no man as master. The two gardening lads, daft as lads are, leaped enthusiastically into the fray and Mr Renfrew poked his pitchfork into Roddy Baxter's bare neck, drawing blood. The struggle went on, the combatants screaming to be allowed to get at each other but gradually, soaked in sweat and blood which was coming from one of them, they were dragged apart, swaying and ready to fall.

"Fetch constable," Clem gasped at one of the lads but neither wanted to miss anything, and they ignored his order.

"I'll kill you for this," Noah hissed into Roddy's face, doing his best to shake off Clem's strong hands but too weakened by the last few weeks and the last few minutes to manage it.

"You'll have ter find me first. Her an' me an' our child."

"Fuck you, you bloody liar. You'd better get off my land before—"

"I'm going, yer ruttin' sod. An' when I find 'er—"

"You'll never find her."

"Watch me, an' watch me tekk 'er back where she belongs. Her an' our bairn . . ."

Noah strained to get away from the strong hands of Clem Woodruff, his face contorted with such a rage Harriet was convinced he might have an apoplectic fit. Spittle sprayed from his mouth and were those tears in his blank eyes which were as hard as agate. There was blood streaming from a gouge on his forehead, dripping fiercely to his shirt and as he surged forward, ready to start again, Roddy Baxter began to laugh. A young man's laugh that said he was done with competing with an old man.

"I'll find 'er, old man, an' yer'll never see any of us again." He turned on his heel and swaggered away, young, confident, his belief that the child Abby carried was his strong and vibrant within him since he had seen the wreck who was Abby's husband.

"Get your hands off me, Clem. I'll . . . I'll . . ."

None of them knew what he was going to say as he staggered to the door and entered the house. He brushed past the maidservants and they cowered away from him, for he looked as though a killing devil was in him.

"Fetch the doctor and Mrs Bennett, Clem," his wife hissed at him, then turned and herded the appalled servants back into the house.

He was drinking brandy when the hansom-cab clattered up the lane and stopped at the side gate. John was first out, handing down his wife, both still stunned and rendered speechless by the terrible tale Clem had related to them. Clem had been lucky to catch the doctor at this time of the day, or his wife who had been on her way to a meeting entitled 'The Campaign for Democratic Voting Rights' in a hired room at the town hall. John had his medical bag with him, for it seemed Noah might have sustained some injury from Clem's tale of blood and blows and other things!

He was seated in the drawing-room, a room he rarely visited except with his wife before dining, for he considered it to be essentially a feminine domain. A 'withdrawing-room' to which ladies could retreat from the dining-room, and also a place where a well-to-do lady met her social obligations. It was a pleasant room, furnished years ago by Bradley Goodwin's wife with five long narrow windows at one end swathed in cream silk which looked out over the garden at the front. At the other end was the wide doorway that led into the conservatory. The walls were cream and decorated with dados and garlands of flowers painted the same colour. There was plump furniture in pale, pretty colours, chairs of velvet over which Noah Goodwin still dripped blood, and seated opposite him, watching over him, Laura decided, was Harriet, still in her apron and her arms coated with flour. She stood up when the Bennetts entered the room and would have left but Laura waved her back to her seat, for of all the servants Harriet was the one who would tell the clearer tale.

"Now then, old man," John said, kneeling down at Noah's feet and opening his bag, "let's clean this up before we go any further. That looks to be a nasty cut and might need a stitch. Will you ring for hot water and towels, Laura. No, not you, Harriet. Why don't you pour Noah another glass of brandy and perhaps one for yourself. That's right, good lass." For it was evident that Harriet was on the fringes of shock and must be pulled together.

Noah sat through the whole procedure without a murmur, staring off somewhere into a nightmare only he could see, though those about him could imagine it. He had just been told that his wife had been unfaithful to him and that the child she carried might not be his and his mind, normally so calmly analytical, astute, clear, able to see through any crisis and solve it, was muffled, blinded and unable to function.

Kitty crept in and cleared away the detritus of the cleaning and sewing up of the wound, her eyes darting from her master who wore a jaunty bandage about his head to Harriet who still sat like stone.

"Perhaps we might have some coffee, Kitty?" Laura enquired graciously, smiling at the elderly housemaid. "And tell the others to . . . to make tea and rest for a while. Mrs Woodruff or myself will be through directly to speak to you."

"Yes, madam." Kitty bobbed a curtsey, then hurried back to tell the others that they were to sit on their backsides – which they were already doing anyway – and rest. Orders from Mrs Bennett, she said, and after taking through the coffee, hurried back and flung herself down beside Cook and allowed herself the indulgence of a good cry. It started them all off, for they just couldn't believe it, no, not if the mistress herself stood before them and told them it was true. What had happened to this once happy household? Was it the fault of that young man who – it was hard to believe – had been . . . well, they didn't like to use the word, some of them didn't even know what it was, but he and the mistress had been . . . and then there was the baby – *whose* baby: his or the master's? It just didn't bear thinking about. Clem, Olly and Charlie shared their tea and their dreadful despair, nobody saying anything, waiting, waiting for what was to happen next, while up in the nursery two children huddled up to their governess's knee, their eyes wide and frightened, as hers were, for the noise at the front of the house had been very upsetting.

In the drawing-room Noah sipped his drink and continued to gaze blindly at nothing while Harriet, Laura and John stared at him and then at each other. Where to start? What to say to this man who had retreated into himself as though what was happening could not be borne and so he must hide from it?

Which was not the true nature of Noah Goodwin. He was
a man who dealt easily with any challenge. He was a man
of unquestionable charm and arrogance, a masculine and
attractive animal who had ridden roughshod over anything
that might stand in his way. He was inclined to shout if his
shirts weren't ironed to the perfection he liked or complain
bitterly if he was served the same meal twice in a month.
His tastes were complicated, sophisticated and in his business
and in his home he demanded and received exactly what he
needed. It was as though his world had split open and he had
fallen into a space he did not recognise. He was confused.
His anger appeared to have gone, leaving him in turmoil. His
sharp, incisive mind had disintegrated for the moment and he
had a grip on nothing but his brandy glass. His friends and
business acquaintances would not have known him. He was
dishevelled, stained from the grass and gravel he had been
dragged across, and his face was bruised, his lip torn and the
eye beneath the cut in which John had put two stitches was
already turning a rich plum colour.

Suddenly he stirred, putting his glass carefully on the side
table. He spoke, his words vague and hardly more than a
murmur as though he were talking to himself. "She was a
virgin when I married her and yet she has turned out to be
a whore."

Laura stood up sharply. "No, Noah, oh no. Not that. I
won't have you calling her that. She was . . . *is* a good
woman."

"About to have a child, uncertain as to who is the father.
And I can't believe that I was the only one in ignorance. What
about you, Harriet Woodruff? You know about whores since
you played one for many years. Don't tell me that your
mistress didn't confide in you about her . . . her lover."

Harriet broke then and began to weep, bending her head,
the tears falling silently to the white apron she wore. She made

no sound and Noah studied her dispassionately. "Ah, I see she did but you did not see fit to tell me, her husband. No, I suppose not. You two were always as thick as thieves. Did you arrange her clandestine meetings with her lover or did she learn over—"

"Please, Noah, she was my friend and I could not betray her."

"Well, it is done now. There is nothing more to be said so you and your husband had best collect your things and leave my house. I cannot employ servants I do not trust. Go to her, for you must know—"

"I don't, I swear. I wouldn't allow her to be alone." Harriet lifted her head and the truth shone from her eyes. She looked steadily at Noah but she could see he was in the world he had wrapped around himself, probably in self-defence, and did not hear her. His words were distinct and dangerous, soft as they were. Nobody would be forgiven for this desolation that had struck at Noah Goodwin. His face, like his eyes, was quite blank and once again Laura spoke.

"You can't blame Harriet for this, Noah. She has served both you and your family well. You call her whore but she only did what she had to do, for we must all defend ourselves against life. She and Clem have done nothing to justify your dismissing them—"

"Is that so, Laura? And what of you? Did you know that my wife was lifting her skirts for that man? Bradley Goodwin had the right idea when he sent him to the other side of the world and I wish to God he had never come back. No, no, I had nothing to do with that but I wish I had. Anyway, I shall make sure the bastard never works in this area again. Well, I must ask you all to leave me now, for no matter what has happened I must continue my search for my wife. She has . . . she has my child in her belly and though she can go to hell for all I care, the child must be found."

"Dear God, Noah, it's not even born yet," Harriet broke out.

"When you leave this house I would advise you to—"

"Noah, don't do this to Harriet," Laura said desperately. "She is not to blame."

"Is she not? She seems to know how far along my . . . my wife is, for she has just told us the child is not yet born. When will it be, Harriet?"

"I believe it to be December," Harriet mumbled.

"Right, then I must get on. I want her here for the birth, not for her sake but for the child's."

He stood up and strode from the room, his face set in such lines of implacability Laura began to weep.

29

Mrs O'Neill followed Doctor Tom down the crooked stairs, on her face an expression that said she was not altogether sure she agreed with his treatment of his patient. He had just given Abby, as Mrs O'Neill had been told to call her, an extensive examination which, to Mrs O'Neill's mind, had seemed somewhat unnecessary. In her day, though she herself had never given birth to a child, women just got on with it and, when their time came, a handy woman who called herself a midwife was brought in to deliver the child. Doctor Tom seemed to be worried about something, though it appeared he was disinclined to discuss it. Just a murmur under his breath that they must keep an eye on her, which was exactly what Mrs O'Neill was doing and had been ever since Abby and her sister had moved out to Lark Cottage.

"Will yer tekk a cuppa tea, Doctor? It's cold out there. There's some left in't pot, in't there?" she asked the young woman who sat up to the fire side by side with Abby's sister who was as useless as the damn dog who was forever under your feet. Pots for rags, as they said in the part of the country she came from, and as unlike her sister as a fish from a bird. The other woman, older and as plain as a pikestaff, was Miss Jane Hemingway, who often wandered down to Lark Cottage from Silverdale where she lived with her grand family. A spinster with a heart of gold and willing to do anything for anyone in trouble, but Mrs O'Neill, who had taken Abby under her wing, resented what she saw as Miss Hemingway's interference. She was quite capable of watching over Abby Brown – if that was her real name – in these last months of her pregnancy. She had her boarders to see to, of course, for they were her livelihood, but when they had gone to wherever they spent the day she would put on her well-worn but serviceable coat and hat and walk the distance from Bolton Street to Lark Cottage in no time at all. There was absolutely no need for the grand Miss Hemingway to bother herself, but just the same the woman came a couple of times a week fetching flowers from Silverdale's glorious gardens, perhaps grapes from the hothouse, apples and pears from the orchard and the offer of help with the garden, for that lad, though he did his best, was a city lad born and bred. Bertha O'Neill would never admit under any circumstances that she was a bit jealous of Miss Hemingway and the manner in which she and Abby "got on" but she certainly let it be known to them all that she was the one in charge.

Bramble jumped up at Doctor Tom's knee, his tail wagging nineteen to the dozen and though the doctor did not rebuff him, indeed scratched his ears, she told the thing sharply to get down. Damn thing was always in the way, trekking sand and God knows what off the beach and had even brought a dead, decomposed fish into the cottage. Abby idolised the animal so it had to be put up with.

"Is she all right, Doctor?" Miss Hemingway asked anxiously, standing up to reach for the teapot, ready to fill a mug with the scalding, almost black tea which was how Mrs O'Neill liked it. Mrs O'Neill felt the irritation move in her, for what right had Miss Hemingway to pour tea, the tea that she herself had made, for the doctor. Just as though she were the hostess in her own home!

Miss Hemingway had knocked at their door a few days after they had taken up residence at Lark Cottage; after all it belonged to her family. She had been somewhat shy, diffident and eager not to be thought intrusive, which was the last thing they wanted, she was sure, but if there was anything she could do for them they only had to send the boy . . . yes, she had noticed him doing his best to turn over the garden at the back of the cottage and she would come at once. She had stepped inside and accepted a cup of tea and she and Abby had become friends. Not friends like Abby and Laura or Harriet were friends, for Jane was too self-effacing to be another Laura but she was good-hearted and friendly.

"Oh yes, quite well but she must be made to rest more. She is so . . ."

"Yes?"

Aware that the three women were hanging on his word Doctor Tom smiled and accepted the mug of tea and a chair at the table. "She's a healthy young woman and will give birth to a healthy child. No worry on that score."

Cissie looked from one face to the other, her own anxious, unaware that had Abby not been afraid she would give away her hiding place she would have been sent home to her mother weeks ago. Cissie Murphy, though willing and hardworking, had not the strength of character her sister had at the same age and was constantly alarmed by the smallest thing. She couldn't seem to settle to the quiet, peaceful life that Abby had chosen and was forever talking about her mam, wondering how she was, had she had her baby yet and was she managing without Cissie. For a clever girl academically who had done so well at school and could, with her sister's help, have made something of herself, she was out of her depth in the company of Jane Hemingway, Doctor Tom and even Mrs O'Neill. The beach frightened her, for it was alien to her country-bred nature and the water was so wide, and what if it should come up to the door of the cottage and drown them all. She had heard that the tides were high in the spring and autumn, and autumn was already here. She was reluctant to go into the city with Abby, even to look at the shops and visit the library or the art gallery which Abby loved, for the people there were always rushing about and noisy and besides, what would she do if she and Abby became separated?

"Now, Cissie," Doctor Tom said, making Cissie's heart leap uneasily. "If there is something you are not sure of over the next weeks—"

"Like what?"

"Well, anything at all that seems to be—"

"What? Eeh, Doctor Tom, I can't . . ."

"Didn't Abby tell me you are the eldest of the family, now that she no longer lives at home?"

"Aye, but—"

"Did you never help your mother when she was in labour?" Tom Hartley did his best to be patient with the child who was Abby's sister.

"Well, Agnes next door helped more'n me."

He sighed and exchanged a glance with Bertha O'Neill, then put his mug down on the plush-covered tabletop. At that moment Abby Goodwin lumbered down the stairs still fastening the broad silk sash around her thickening waist and at once the three of them, Mrs O'Neill, Doctor Tom and Jane Hemingway leaped to their feet to help her. She had put on a lot of weight during the last three months. Her face was somewhat puffy and her hands and ankles too, though only Doctor Tom and Mrs O'Neill had seen the latter.

"Good Lord, will you stop fussing me. I'm as fit as a fiddle. I get a bit out of breath when I walk on the beach but that's because I try to keep up with this scamp," bending to stroke the dog which was jumping up at her knee.

"Well, stop it, d'you hear. Walk on the beach by all means but don't run after Bramble."

"Doctor Tom, I don't run—"

"I've seen yer, Abby Brown," Mrs O'Neill interrupted.

"Pickin' up shells an' such an' fetchin' 'em 'ome an' what about t'other day then. Yer come 'ome wi' no shoes nor stockin's. Paddlin', yer said an' if yer don't watch out yer'll come down wi' pneumonia."

They continued to wrangle good-naturedly though Mrs O'Neill was half serious.

"Well, it's too cold for paddling now so I promise I won't do it but I'll not give up my walks."

From the first day Abby had fallen in love with the wonder of what lay just beyond her front door: the rough grasses starred with golden buttercups and dainty white daisies at the bottom of the stone steps, the grasses running the whole length of the beach; with the flat, rippled stretch of golden sand, wet and gleaming, the small pools formed when the tide was out filled with tiny darting creatures, with seaweed and small crabs. She loved the sparkling waters of the wide river itself. The beautiful winged birds that were the ships that flew across its surface.

She and Cissie had found a bookshop in Bold Street by the name of Henry Lacey. The shop sold sporting prints, albums and scrap books, writing paper, Bibles, writing cases, playing cards and the most extensive collection of books Abby had ever seen in one place, even the library in the town hall back home. Browsing through the shelves, she had come across a book in which every kind of sailing ship was named and described, and also some of the steamships which were more and more coming into service in the world of commercial shipping. Cissie had become absorbed with the first few pages of *Sense and Sensibility* by Jane Austen which, having been published so long ago, over fifty years, had been reduced in price. There was another that caught her fancy, *The Woman in White* by Wilkie Collins, published only seven years previously, so, parting with one of her precious guineas, and to help her to settle in to her new life, Abby had given in to her pleadings to purchase them. The book on ships, named *The Life of Shipping*, she bought for herself.

During those first weeks her book went everywhere along the shore with her, a reference book with which she identified the shipping of the River Mersey. She became so familiar with them all that she could recognise a topsail schooner or a square rigger at a glance without reference to her book. She sat on the shore and watched them skim the waters, Mersey flats from Cheshire, fruit schooners from the Mediterranean, brigantines, gig boats, which helped ships in and out of the estuary, coastal schooners loaded with coal and clay, paddle steamers, frigates for the Indian trade, ferries plying between the Pier Head and New Brighton and Birkenhead and, the loveliest of them all, the great clipper ships coming from across wide oceans halfway round the world carrying tea and silk, porcelain, paintings, fans, silver dishes, ornate ivory and lacquerware, all the beauty of the Far East brought to the crowded dockland of the greatest seaport in the land. The river had the wide outer estuary of Liverpool Bay, the narrow middle section where Liverpool itself stood, and the wider, shallower upper estuary that finished twenty miles beyond Warrington. Jericho Beach, where Abby and Cissie sat, Cissie reading, Bramble digging and Abby just gazing, was nearer the inner estuary. The tide swept through at the rate of seven or eight miles an hour, the difference between high and low tide thirty feet, so that sometimes the beach was wide and flat and rippling and at others no more than a strip barely big enough to walk on.

She thought of Roddy and Noah at such times, brooding sadly on the anguish Roddy at least must be feeling, but accepting that there was nothing she could do to help him. She had taken the only course she could in the circumstances, torn as she was between two men who would claim her child as their own. Roddy's life had revolved round hers, his every activity, apart from his job at the Mulberry Glass Works, fitted round the visits she made to his cottage. He would be searching for her, she knew that, remembering how *she* had felt and how she had searched for him when he disappeared. She knew exactly how he would be feeling, for had she herself not known the terror, the despair, the grief of his disappearance and he would be the same. But in a way it would be worse for him, since he would know by now from Laura that she had gone voluntarily. That she had left him of her own free will and it would hurt him as much as her disappearance.

Wally had given the letters she wrote to Laura to men who worked on the railway, guards in the luggage van and once to an engine driver to post somewhere along the route of their journey. Three now to Laura and one she had written to Noah but which she had torn up. She didn't know why. She knew Noah would also be looking for her, not because he loved her as Roddy did but because he would believe that the child she carried would be his. So what was she to say to him in a letter? He was not a man to understand her need for this peace in which to carry her child. She had slowed to the pace of a brood mare, existing in a dreaming stillness and calm that she would not have known in his house, for by now he and Roddy would have clashed, she knew that, over the paternity of the child.

It would need to be faced one day but here, in the little cottage by the river, she lived from day to day, walking the shoreline, often with Archie who was as fascinated as she was by the flotsam left by the tide. He always called her "Miss", running to her with sea urchins and sea anemones, excitedly holding them out for her to examine and put a name to from the second book she had purchased at Henry Lacey's bookshop. It was called *The Natural History of the Seashore* and she and Archie would turn the pages until they had found the picture and the name of the creature he had found.

Archie was a cheerful, gregarious child with all the characteristics of those born in Liverpool. The peoples of the world poured through Liverpool streets, a cosmopolitan population bringing their alien habits, cultures, thoughts, speech and religion into the life of the city. Some remained, not having the wherewithal to go further, settling down, breeding, independent and self-reliant, fighting for themselves. Archie was the result of one such culture, his beginnings unknown to him. His mam was never at home in the squalid tenement – of which there were thirty thousand plus twelve thousand cellars and twenty thousand lodging houses – in which he had been born and raised and if asked he would say she was at "work", though Mrs O'Neill was of the opinion that she spent her days down at the docks meeting the ships that came in. Archie was one of a dozen children born of her coupling. His father was unknown. His speech was typically adenoidal, in it mixed the Irish, the Welsh, the speech of his mother who came from Sweden and the accents of Lancashire. He was "made up" as he put it, with his new life, ready to lay down his life for Miss though he did his best to keep out of Mrs O'Neill's way.

"What yer doing, yer cheeky monkey?" she would ask suspiciously when she found him hanging about the garden at the back of the house.

"Nuttin'," he would reply jauntily, "me shears need sharpnin' ter cut me grass." It was always *his* grass now, or *his* path that needed sweeping, or *his* flowerbeds that needed weeding. Rigged out in the clothing and boots Jane Hemingway brought over, once belonging to her brothers and put away in an attic, he had taken to the life like a duck to water and in the three months he had lived at Lark Cottage he had grown five inches and put on a stone in weight. He had no idea how old he was and didn't care. He was fed three good meals a day and slept in a warm bed at night. What else could any man wish for? He never strayed far, for the doctor had impressed upon him his need for speed when Mrs Brown started her baby. Oh aye, he knew all about babies, for he had watched without interest since it occurred so often when his mam gave birth.

"Well, get on with it then," Mrs O'Neill would say sharply.

"I am doin'." And with a cheerful whistle or a mischievous grin he would apply himself to his task, keeping an eye out for Miss who would need his company and his support on their daily walk. Sometimes the other one would come with them but she was no trouble. In fact she seemed to need him more than Miss, for the slightest thing frightened her, even a mother duck with a row of ducklings in a string behind her. She would shriek that they might attack her, or the crab that lurched about a pool might climb out and pinch her. He and Miss would laugh behind her back and watch as she hurried to return to the cottage and the safety of Mrs O'Neill, whose company she found comforting. Aye, it was a grand life and he would be sorry when that baby came. For would it mean the end of his days on the seashore? If it did he'd go on one of the ships, since he must be over ten years old which was the usual age for boys to go to sea.

Bertha O'Neill was on her knees donkey-stoning her front step when the man spoke to her. She always did her step on a Saturday morning while she was waiting for the washing to dry before ironing it. Saturday was bed-changing day and she had been at the boiler, the dolly tub and the mangle since six o'clock. Many of her weekly boarders left on a Saturday and they, along with her regulars, were rooted out of their beds whether they were ready or not. A splendid breakfast of bacon, eggs, fried tomatoes, fried bread and mushrooms with toast to follow stifled their resentment at being made to get up so early on a Saturday, for Mrs O'Neill could not be surpassed when it came to good grub.

"Good morning," the man said to her pleasantly. "I hear you have rooms to rent."

Mrs O'Neill rose to her feet, ignoring the hand the man put out to help her. The day Bertha O'Neill needed help to stand on her own two feet would be the day they put her in her coffin.

"I might 'ave but I'm pretty full at moment." She wiped her hands down her rough sacking apron, the one she put on for dirty jobs, bending to pick up her bucket of water, dismissing the man, she didn't know why. She only knew she was uneasy.

"I'm not actually looking for lodgings." He smiled, a smile that lifted his rather gaunt face and put a glow in his eyes. She was startled by the transformation but still guarded.

"Oh aye," she said, waiting for him to continue.

"No, I'm searching for a . . . for a friend. A lady. Two ladies, actually, with a young dog. Have they perhaps sought shelter in your establishment?"

"What mekks yer think they come 'ere? I don't tekk in ladies, especially wi' a dog. Nasty dirty things trekkin' muck on ter my clean step."

"A porter at the station told me you might have seen them. He directed a couple of ladies to your lodging house several months ago. They answered the description, particularly the dog!"

That bloody Wally! She'd give him what for next time she saw him. This chap had probably given him a few bob and Wally had opened his gob and let it all pour out and now Abby, who obviously was in hiding – Bertha O'Neill had come to that conclusion weeks ago – was in danger of being found. He seemed nice enough, the man who looked for her, courteous, sober and not at all threatening but if he *was* something to do with Abby he must have treated her badly or she'd not be hiding from him. Bertha didn't know, of course. She didn't know anything about the lass, or at least her past, but what she did know was that she, Bertha O'Neill, had taken a real shine to her. Abby must be hiding for some reason and until Bertha found out she certainly was not going to tell this chap anything.

"Well, as I said, I don't tekk females. They mekk more trouble than they're worth so yer'd best look elsewhere." She sniffed and wiped the back of her hand on her nose, then turned on her heel and made for the door but the chap was not satisfied.

"Perhaps you know of other boarding-houses where the ladies might have gone. Does any other house in the street take in lodgers?"

"Nay, yer'd 'ave ter ask them. Now, if yer'll ger outer me way I'll gerron. You might 'ave time ter stand about mitherin' burr I 'aven't. I'll bid yer good-day an' don't put yer foot on me step. I just done it."

She shut the door in his face.

Bertha sent next door's lad to call her a cab, for the walk down to Lark Cottage was a long one and took at least three-quarters of an hour and she hadn't time to loiter. She must get down to Abby's and tell her there was a chap looking for her. She was not sure what the urgency was but she·felt there was one and the sooner Abby knew the better. She didn't know what the lass would do, since she was in no state to be dashing about. It was nearly the end of October and the baby was due in six weeks' time and Bertha could tell Doctor Tom was flummoxed about something and so was she, for the mother-to-be was so big and clumsy she could barely get about. Her ankles and feet were swollen and she had confessed to Bertha that she had a bit of a problem passing water. No, she hadn't told the doctor and Bertha was to keep her mouth shut, but if she knew of anything she could take she'd be grateful.

"Can yer 'elp yersel' ter them apples in Miss 'Emingway's orchard?"

"Oh, yes, she often—"

"Then mekk up some apple juice an' drink plenty o' water. It's good fer kidneys."

And Abby had taken her advice and reported that she felt much better. But she was still not fit to go gadding off looking for somewhere else to hide from the chap who had spoken to Bertha on her doorstep.

She banged the door to behind her and climbed into the cab the little lad next door had fetched for her.

Noah strolled along Bold Street, stopping for a moment to watch the antics of a monkey perched on the shoulder of an organ-grinder. There was quite a crowd, for it was a Sunday, a cool but sunny day and the world and his wife – and family – were out for a stroll. All the lovely shops that catered to the rich were closed, but throwing a few coins into the organ-grinder's cup he moved on, stopping now and again to look into a window. There was a jeweller's, Thomas Dismore, who proclaimed that he was Silversmith and Jeweller to the Queen, and Noah studied the window display, noticing a bracelet of aquamarines and diamonds linked by a fine gold chain. The blue-green stones were the exact colour of her eyes and he vowed that tomorrow he would come down here and take a closer look at them. If the diamonds were as fine as they looked from this side of the window, he would buy them.

He turned into Berry Street and then into Duke Street until he came to a subterranean passage which intrigued him. Strolling through it, he came out into daylight, turning right again and coming to the mount of St James Walk. The walk was a gravelled terrace four hundred yards long with fine views over the river where, it being a clear day, the beautifully indented smooth chain of the mountains of Flintshire and Denbighshire could be made out. To his right was the lighthouse and signal poles which guided the ships that came in from the sea. He turned, leaning his back against the railings, looking towards the grove and shrubbery behind the terrace, entered through a wicket gate and was just in time to see the familiar figure of a man disappearing through it. The man was shabby, hatless, his hair needing a barber's attention. He wore no overcoat though the day was cool and he was in need of a shave. In fact he had a small beard and moustache. It was Roddy Baxter!

At once, almost knocking down a lady and gentleman who, arm-in-arm, were admiring the view, Noah raced towards the gate, moving so rapidly it was still swinging to, and on to a path that led through the shrubbery. The man he had seen was not running but was walking rapidly towards Upper Duke Street and with an oath Noah chased after him, catching him as he crossed Berry Street. Neither looked to the right nor the left and several vehicles were forced to get out of their way or collide with one another. The horses that pulled them reared frighteningly and women screamed.

"Yer bloody fools," the driver of a hansom-cab swore.

"Look where yer goin' or d'yer wanna kill yersels," cried another.

"Yer want lockin' up, yer daft buggers," bellowed a third, but the two men were oblivious to it all and to the dismayed shouts of the passers-by. Noah grabbed Roddy by the lapels of his jacket and pulled him up close so that they were face to face, but Roddy was not to be intimidated. With an oath he put his elbow under Noah's chin and forced his face away, knocking him off balance so that they both fell heavily to the ground.

"What the hell d'you think you're doing, following me about, you bloody bastard," Noah spat out, doing his best to give Roddy what those in the area called a "Liverpool kiss," which was a head-butt to his nose.

"Following you about! I've just as much right ter look fer 'er as you. More like you're followin' me."

"You swine, who the devil d'you think you are?" Several ladies, who had never in their lives heard such language and from what seemed to be the lips of a gentleman, were ready to faint, it seemed, but suddenly in their midst were two police constables, big, burly men who each grabbed one of the pugilists and hauled him to his feet. One of them, though shabby and of the lower classes, was neatly dressed but the other was obviously a gentleman. They were still trying to swing at each other but the constables, well used to fisticuffs in this city of sailors, drunks, and the short tempers of men who were accustomed to beating up their wives every Saturday night, had them handcuffed and in to the horse-drawn wagon that had been summoned, still both using obscene language and doing their best to get at each other.

It was thought prudent to put them in separate cells, but Roddy Baxter and Noah Goodwin spent the night in the Borough Gaol, coming up before the magistrate the next morning. They were bound over for three months to keep the peace.

30

Abby felt herself sway and had it not been for Mrs O'Neill's quick arm about her thought she might have fallen. She sat down heavily in the rocking-chair then wished she had chosen something steadier, for the chair rocked wildly. She thought she might be sick but Mrs O'Neill's brisk voice brought her round.

"I told 'im I didn't tekk lady boarders burr 'e weren't best pleased. Said a porter'd sent two ladies an' a dog ter my place a few months back. That'd be that bugger Wally."

"What did he look like?" Abby could feel the quiver in her voice and wondered why she was so surprised, for after all had she really believed that Noah would calmly get on with his life when the woman who was carrying the child he longed for was wandering about unchaperoned, unprotected and without him to see she was behaving herself?

"Tall, dark, 'andsome in a way . . ."

"That could describe either of them," Abby said musingly, unaware of the look of astonishment that crossed Mrs O'Neill's face.

"Yer what?" Mrs O'Neill sat down heavily, placing herself at the kitchen table where Cissie was sorting shells. Cissie had found a new hobby which Jane had shown her and that was sticking shells on to a box, making necklaces, or frames for pictures which she cut out of the periodicals Jane brought from Silverdale. With the weather turning colder and Abby becoming increasingly bulky they did not get out as much as they had, which didn't bother Cissie, and the pastime absorbed her. Jane had also lent her books from the library at Silverdale and she was quite happy glueing her shells or reading Jane Austen, Sir Walter Scott and Charles Dickens.

"I must think," Abby said, putting her hand to her forehead. "He's bound to find me. He'll ask every cab driver at the railway station until he finds the one that brought us here and—"

"It were Doctor Tom 'oo hired the cab what brought us 'ere," Mrs O'Neill began, still bewildered and doing her best to get to grips with what Abby was saying. *It could be either of them!* What the devil did that mean? That there were two men looking for Abby Brown – if that really was her name – so was one of them the father of the child or . . . or, dear sweet God in heaven, had she got the wrong end of the stick altogether? Was it a member of her family or . . . or . . .

She sat up and thrust her chin out and her eyes were sharp with suspicion. She had grown extremely fond of this lass and would do anything to help her, but before she went any further she would have the truth and if that wasn't forthcoming she'd put on her bloody hat and hightail it back to Bolton Street.

"Right, lady, 'appen yer'd best tell me what's goin' on 'ere. 'Oo was it that spoke ter me this mornin'? Someone's lookin' for yer an' if you an' me's ter stay friends I want the truth. 'Oo is it looking for yer?"

"I think it's my husband but then again it could be someone else. If you could be more explicit in your description I might recognise—"

"*Yer 'usband!* I were led ter believe yer was a widderwoman." Bertha O'Neill was mortally offended. She had befriended this young woman and her timid sister, been genuinely sorry for her and had done her best to make her life easier while she awaited the birth of her child. She'd even neglected the comfort of her lodgers, who were her livelihood, to walk over here nearly every day to check up on her, for it was her belief that neither Cissie nor that Jane Hemingway were sensible females who could be trusted with a pregnant woman. She'd had no children herself but she had helped during the confinement and the birth of many of her neighbours, for that was what they did in her class. They helped one another, coming to the aid of anyone in trouble and that's what she had done with this one. But unless she was told the truth, which she had a feeling was going to upset her, she'd come no more. Let the lass manage with her daft sister and that spinster from Silverdale.

"I'll 'ave the truth, lass," she said quietly, and so Abby Goodwin opened her heart to Bertha O'Neill, leaving nothing out from the day she and Roddy, no more than children, had pledged to marry one another. From the rocking-chair she gazed out of the low window, her eyes on the waters which were grey today and on the ships that crowded them, for the Mersey was a busy highway leading from Liverpool to the four corners of the world. There were seagulls swirling on a raw wind, screaming, coming inland, which was a sign of bad weather, or so Archie told her, and at Archie himself who was throwing sticks on the beach for Bramble.

Her illegitimacy, her father's death and her grandfather's wickedness. The horror of what Roddy had suffered and the strength of their love for one another which had survived through it all. Her forced marriage to Noah and the life she had led. Roddy's involvement in it, glancing at Bertha to make sure she understood what she meant by that remark and her flight to Liverpool when she discovered she was to have a child.

"I don't know who the father is, you see, Mrs O'Neill. I felt I would be torn limb from limb between Roddy and Noah, each claiming me and the baby, and to bear a child I felt peace and calm was needed. I know many women don't have that but I had a little money so I . . . I ran away. I thought I had covered our tracks but my husband, and Roddy, are determined men and so I would like to know which one it was who came to your door."

"'E were well dressed. A gent, I'd say. 'E looked right put out when I told 'im ter clear off."

"You told him to clear off."

"Well, as good as."

"It sounds like Noah and he'll find me, Mrs O'Neill, with or without your help."

"Is Noah yer 'usband?" Mrs O'Neill asked, perplexed.

"Yes, and Roddy won't be far behind. I bet if you asked Wally . . ."

"I'll do fer that bugger."

". . . he'd tell you that there was more than one man asking about me. Oh, God, what am I to do? I can just imagine the pair of them turning up here, bristling up to one another like a couple of dogs and I can't stand the thought. I must get away. Please, Mrs O'Neill, help me to find a place where I can hide until the baby is born."

She struggled to get to her feet and instinctively Mrs O'Neill stood up to help her. She had never heard such a tale in her life and she hadn't yet made up her mind what her next move was to be. She was badly shocked by the revelation that Abby, the ladylike, loveable, good-natured, steadfast, *honest* young woman she had known for all these months, had not only a husband but a *lover* and could not say which of the two was the father of her unborn child. Talk about being taken in! It was not something Bertha O'Neill was used to and she was amazed at the ease with which it had happened.

"Well, I dunno, chuck." And with the last endearment Bertha knew that the decision had been made. There was no way she could cast off this young woman who had no one, unless you considered Doctor Tom, to look after her until the babe was born. After that Bertha had a feeling she would be quite capable of dealing with husbands and lovers and anyone else who tried to interfere with her life.

"Perhaps you know of someone who would take me in for a few weeks, just until after the child comes. It would be—"

With a sudden lurch she put her hand to the base of her belly and winced. Her face drained of colour and sweat broke out on her forehead.

"Oh dear," she said comically, "I shouldn't have eaten those plums Jane brought."

"You've bin eatin' plums! Of all the daft things ter do when yer . . ."

She put out her hands and took Abby's then they both looked down in bewilderment as something splashed on their boots. They could not have looked more astonished if the dog had cocked his leg and urinated on them, and it was Cissie, who had taken little interest in the previous conversation, though the bit about Roddy Baxter was an eye-opener, who said carelessly, "Looks like yer waters broke, our Abby."

It might have been amusing had it not been so horrifying. From what Doctor Tom had told her and from her own calculations, Abby was certain the child was not due for another five or six weeks. It was almost the end of October, November next week and here she was in the middle of one of the worst crises in her life and from the signs, which she should know having seen it happen to her own mam, she was just about to go into labour.

"Sit yer down, lass," Bertha said quietly. "Let's face us ull stand cloggin'." Which was her way of saying she and Abby must be determined to see the situation through regardless of what happened. "Now think on, Doctor Tom'll be over at once. See, Cissie, fetch Archie in. Don't sit there gawpin', do as yer told an' shout fer Archie. Shape yersel', lass," she added sharply as Cissie continued to sort her shells.

Archie, when summoned, removed his new boots, which were taking a bit of getting used to, placed them carefully just inside the door and, barefoot, started off up the lane in the direction of Aigburth Road like a hare chased by a dog, doing what he had been waiting to do ever since he had been employed by Miss. Miss had started with her baby and it was up to him to get the doctor here in the shortest possible time.

He passed a hansom-cab on his way from which the occupant was just alighting.

Doctor Tom never left her side and neither did Mrs O'Neill, but the pain, which never stopped its tiger-prowling somewhere in the small of her back, became worse and worse, striking her again and again, faster and faster until there seemed to be no interval between each thrust of its claws.

"It's not time yet," she panted to Doctor Tom when she had breath to speak.

"No, but there's nothing to worry about, Abby. An eight-month baby is quite as capable of surviving as one that goes full term."

"But I must leave here, Doctor Tom. Ask Mrs O'Neill, she'll explain. I must hurry up and have the baby and then I'd be glad if you'd call me a carriage." She clung to his hands in a grip so fierce he winced. It had been twelve hours since he had arrived and though he did not know why, despite his suspicions, the child was reluctant to leave the warm haven of its mother's womb. She struggled against the pain, her pains even closer together and very sharp, so close that she could scarcely draw breath.

Another twelve hours later she was so exhausted she was barely conscious, her lovely face lovely no longer as it sank into dark hollows, black rings about her eyes and the man who hovered at the door of her bedroom looked no better.

"It's not going well, is it?" he snapped as though he blamed Doctor Tom for it.

Abby was far away in the clutches of some gigantic monster which was doing its best to eat her alive when the arms went about her, holding her so comfortingly she felt the monster recede a little as though something stronger was threatening it.

"I'm frightened," she whimpered from between lips that were bitten and bleeding.

"Nothing will frighten you while I'm here."

"I don't want to die."

"You'll not die." The arms cradled her more firmly, tender, compassionate and yet strong and the calm settled about her even though the beast, the dragon, was still circling looking for a foothold. The arms held her, rocked her, stroked her hair and there were kisses that were warm and soft on her cheek and her brow.

"I'm going to give her some laudanum now, sir, if you'll step away," another voice said.

"And about time too and no, I won't step away. It seems to comfort her to . . ."

She awoke to peace and quiet and warmth, the only sound the cracking of the fire in the grate and the shrieking of the seagulls who were riding the rain squalls that sliced across her window. It was daylight but there were candles lit, bright pools of glowing light which flickered and made dancing shadows on the ceiling. She turned her head. Mrs O'Neill sat by the fire in a chair Abby had never seen before, a low button-back of deep red velvet with arms. Later she was to learn it was a present from Jane Hemingway, for she would need somewhere to sit and nurse her babies, wouldn't she? Mrs O'Neill was placidly stitching on something, her face tranquil and yet tired and Abby smiled, for wherever Bertha O'Neill landed she always

found something to do. She'd probably been scrubbing out
the scullery, her knees on a bit of sacking, her bum swaying
from side to side as she moved the brush. A devil for work
was Mrs O'Neill and Abby brooded for a minute on how she
would have managed the last few months without her.

She stretched and yawned and immediately something
inside her wrenched in pain and she gasped. At once Mrs
O'Neill was out of her chair and across the room.

"Now none o' that," she admonished as though Abby
had been about to leap from her bed and begin a day's
"bottoming". "Just lie still, chuck, an' that sister o' yours
can gerroff her backside an' fetch yer a nice cup o' tea.
Milk, doctor ses, bur I reckon a cuppa would go down a
treat first off."

She leaned over Abby and stroked her hair back off her
forehead lovingly and for a moment Abby thought she was
going to kiss her, which would have convinced her there
was something seriously wrong. That she was on her deathbed even!

"What . . ." she began to croak, wondering why her throat
was so dry, but Mrs O'Neill shushed her then went to the
door and called out softly.

"Put kettle on, Cissie, an' yer'd better wake Doctor Tom.
She's come round an' 'e might want ter look at 'er. All them
stitches . . . eeh. Now look sharp, lass."

She turned and came back to the bed and took Abby's
hand in hers, continuing to stroke her hair gently, smiling
down into her face. "Lass, lass, yer give us a rare old fright
an' no mistake, an' a surprise an' all, though I 'ave a feelin'
Doctor Tom 'ad an idea."

Abby tried to sit up, all of a sudden alarmed about something, though in her confusion she was not sure what it
was. She felt light-headed as though she were under the
influence of some drug but Mrs O'Neill pushed her back

gently. "Nay, don't fret, lass, they're doin' fine, even at eight month."

"They?"

"Twins, chuck. Two lovely girls. No wonder yer were so big an' 'ad such a 'ard time. But all three of yer are as right as rain but 'ere's doctor ter tell yer."

"Twins," she said dazedly.

"That's right, my dear Abby, and two healthy specimens though they were so early. Small, of course but . . ."

"'Ere, 'oo are you callin' them specimens. Right pretty little girls they are."

"I know, Mrs O'Neill, and I'm sorry but now I must examine my patient before I get off home. And there's a very anxious young man downstairs who insists on seeing Miss."

"Well, 'e can wait, little monkey," Mrs O'Neill said sharply, for at the moment Abby Brown . . . no, Abby Goodwin as she was called, was hers and she would guard her and the babies with her life. She wanted no noisy lad coming up here disturbing her lass and even that daft sister of hers, who had done nothing but wring her hands and cry for her mam all night, could stay where she was.

"Where?" Abby ventured, looking about the room. She supposed she should show some interest in these shocking babies to whom she had given birth but it terrified the life out of her to look at them for fear of who they might resemble. *Two babies!* Dear God, the thought of facing one was bad enough but two of them, two babies whose paternity was unknown. Well, not quite but there were two bloody candidates and which one did she want to be the father? There had been someone here, she remembered, a man who had put his arms about her and held her comfortingly against his chest. He had rocked her and murmured over her, even stroked her back where the tiger prowled and she had been comforted, she remembered that too. When Doctor Tom had finished his rather painful examination, when he had sounded her heart and felt her pulse and studied her eyes and even her tongue, she would ask about it but first she must get through the . . . the ordeal of seeing her daughters . . . *daughters, ye gods.*

"She'll do, Mrs O'Neill, but she's not to stir from that bed until I say so. Now then, perhaps you would bring in the two . . . the two Miss Goodwins and I'll have a look at them. They are tucked up in the other bedroom, Abby, where Mrs O'Neill is to sleep for a few nights. Just until I'm satisfied you can manage with just your sister. Miss Hemingway has had a truckle bed brought over for Cissie. She did offer to take her back to Silverdale but Cissie wouldn't go. Now I want you to put your daughters to the breast as soon as you feel able and when I return later I'll bring a couple of feeding bottles and teats and some milk suitable for newborns. D'you understand?"

"Yes," she murmured.

They put the babies in her reluctant arms, two tiny parcels of blankets and lace and in them two faces lay sleeping peacefully. Long dark lashes fanned their rounded cheeks and two rosebud mouths sucked as though already they were at the nipple. Delicate arched eyebrows, dark and fine, and on each head was a cap of dark hair, somewhat skimpy but with a ripple in it that said it might curl. One of them squirmed for a moment and Abby looked up anxiously at Mrs O'Neill, ready to hand her back, then the smallest hand she had ever seen appeared over the edge of the blanket, the fingers delicately curled in perfect innocence and her heart slowed and warmed with love for these two amazing little creatures who were hers and . . . and . . .

"What about clothing?" she said worriedly. "We weren't expecting two and have only enough for one so . . ."

"Abby, that can wait until you're up and about. Already

Mrs O'Neill and Miss Hemingway are stitching and embroidering."

"And we'll need another cradle."

"One has already been delivered." There was an uncomfortable silence.

"Who by?"

"He said he was your husband."

"My . . ."

"Noah Goodwin. He spent some time with you last night and I must say you seemed to rally when he came to you."

"Noah . . . it was Noah?"

"Yes."

"Is . . . is he still here?"

"No. He had to leave."

"Of course, he would have more important things to attend to. His glass works and his other businesses. Now he has laid claim to my children . . ."

"He said he would be back later today. I got the impression he is still in Liverpool. He is staying at the Adelphi where he said he might be reached should . . ."

She suddenly felt exhausted and without a word handed the babies back to Mrs O'Neill who gloated over them as though they were her own. After that first and surprising rush of love she felt curiously detached again as though the children belonged to someone other than herself. Perhaps it was the knowledge that Noah had been here and was to come again. Perhaps it was just the consequence of the long labour, or the shock of giving birth to two children.

For ten minutes, which was all Mrs O'Neill would allow, she was dragged back from the edge of the strange melancholy into which she had fallen by the cheeky, smiling face of Archie, who had hacked a great branch off a beech tree, which at this time of the year positively glowed with colour, a brilliant mosaic of russet, orange and gold. He had gone to a great deal of trouble cutting it into smaller branches which he had tied up with a bit of ribbon. It was quite beautiful and she was reduced to surprising tears, for she was not normally what her mam had called a "crier". Jane brought chrysanthemums from the gardens of Silverdale, again the colours quite glorious, and even Cissie had a present, a frame of cardboard with delicate shells glued round its edge.

She slept then for over four hours so that it was dark when she awakened. She was alone and from some part of the cottage a baby was wailing. A thin sound, weak and hopeless, and she knew she couldn't just lie here while one of her children was in trouble. Mrs O'Neill would be with them, and probably Cissie, but these were her babies and as their mother she was needed. She had not nursed them yet and she pondered how one went about feeding two babies but she supposed if Doctor Tom brought feeding bottles and the babies took it in turns things might work out. Dear Lord, she was tired and sore and wanted nothing more than to snuggle down beneath the blankets and sleep and sleep. Let someone else do the worrying, but then she was their mother and that's what mothers did. Worry! She thought she might tell Mrs O'Neill to bring the cradles in here to be with her at all times so that when they needed her – and this moment seemed to be one of those times, by the way the baby was crying – she would have them by her side. In fact she was obsessed with the sudden idea that it might be a good idea to have them in her bed where she could watch over their vulnerability.

She began to cry helplessly, she didn't even know why. She didn't remember her mam crying after the birth of one of her children but then she supposed Mam never had the luxury of lying in a warm bed with time to feel anxious. Up the next day, Mam had been, and back at her cleaning the day after. So why did she feel so weepy? She felt too weak even to shout out for someone to come and tell her what was happening.

She turned on her side away from the door weeping desolately and was bewildered when those same arms that had held her during her labour came to hold her again. To shush her and murmur in her hair that everything would be all right and she was not to worry, nor weep. She was to be strong, as she had always been strong and she would get through this agony and despair, for that was what she felt. Not physical agony, though her body was still wounded, but an agony of mind. The arms were familiar. So many times she had lain in them at night but never once had they given her comfort, or soothed her to peace. Strong arms they were, and gentle with her but they were not the arms of the man she wept for.

31

She was out of bed in a week, against the wishes of both Doctor Tom and Mrs O'Neill, and though she was sore and had to walk carefully she said she had never felt so well in her life. Motherhood appeared to agree with her. Her babies were beginning to thrive, for it seemed she had enough milk for both and to spare and though during the first few days she and Mrs O'Neill had to resort to the feeding bottles, they were soon, to Mrs O'Neill's secret regret, put aside.

The strangest was Cissie's behaviour. She had sat throughout the long hours of Abby's labour alternately pacing the kitchen, reading her books with her hands over her ears, glueing her everlasting shells and had even ventured out on to the strip of grass in front of the cottage. But from the moment she had crept up the stairs, persuaded to peep at her new nieces, she seemed to fall under some sort of spell. Wonderingly she had picked up number one as she had been temporarily called since she was born first, holding her carefully and gazing down into the tiny, yawning face. She placed her finger in the shell of the baby's hand, fascinated by the way the fingers curled round hers. Watching her, Abby was amazed, for after Cissie's birth Betty had borne five more children and Cissie had been indifferent to them.

"What yer goin' ter call them, our Abby?" she had asked.

"I hadn't given it any thought, Cissie." For how could she name these children whose paternity she was not sure of? But why would that make any difference, she asked herself, for they must be called *something* no matter who their father was?

Cissie, who had just read *Pride and Prejudice*, put the baby back in her cradle and picked up number two. "I like Elizabeth," she murmured. "We could call her Beth."

"Elizabeth. Beth. That's nice."

"Beth Goodwin." Cissie gazed down into the baby's face then replaced her in her cradle. "You know if Mrs O'Neill wanted ter go 'ome I wouldn't mind 'avin' one of them in wi' me. If she needed feedin' I'd fetch her in to yer."

And so, to the relief of Mrs O'Neill's lodgers, who had been muddling along under the somewhat heavy-handed care of one of the neighbours who was glad of the extra money, their landlady returned home, coming up each day to Lark Cottage to supervise "that there daft lass" as she privately called Cissie, in the care of the babies.

"Elizabeth," she sniffed when told of the suggestion for number one and who had thought of it. "Beth, well, I suppose that's nice enough but wharrabout t'other poor little mite? Is she not ter 'ave a name?"

"Perhaps you have a suggestion?" Abby said diplomatically, for she was not unaware of the tension between Mrs O'Neill and Cissie.

"Well," Mrs O'Neill ventured hesitantly. "Me mam were called Emily. She were a good woman. She an' me pa were right fond o' one another an' 'e called 'er Milly."

"I like that, Mrs O'Neill. Elizabeth and Emily. Beth and Milly." And so it was decided and when Noah Goodwin knocked on the door a few days later Beth and Milly lay side by side in the makeshift double cradle where they spent their days. It was a large wooden crate, the top of which had been sawn off by the odd-job man up at Silverdale, and which Jane had padded and covered with the prettiest muslin in pale peach. There were satin bows at each corner and lace around the edge and they themselves were dressed in white dresses of broderie anglaise threaded with pale pink ribbon over lace-edged petticoats. They were for "best", Jane said, but they were so pretty she just hadn't been able to resist them. She had bought them in town only the day before from Anne Hillyard's baby linen warehouse in Bold Street and promised to bring more for everyday wear, white petticoats and plain frocks which she would embroider. She was already hard at work on christening robes over which she was careful to consult Abby. There were christening robes and to spare at Silverdale, for she was one of six children and most of them now had children of their own but she had thought it would be more appropriate for these two to have brand-new. Long, of course, the skirt at least thirty-six inches but ruched in the bodice and with pink bows about the hem.

Beth was sleeping peacefully, her arms firmly tucked into the lacy shawl wrapped about her but Milly, whose nature was already different from that of her sister, had freed her miniature fists and was waving them about in what looked like rage at being so confined.

Noah stood quietly on the doorstep, waiting to be asked in or told to clear off, whichever Mrs O'Neill decided was appropriate. She knew who he was, of course, since he had got in everybody's way on the night of the twins' birth. He had gone away calmly enough and now, two weeks later, here he was.

Abby looked over Mrs O'Neill's shoulder and her heart began to pound, for was this the start of it. She had been surprised he had not been here before this. Doctor Tom was apparently keeping in touch with him on the progress of the babies at his request but it was not like Noah to be patient. He would want to have everything out in the open, dictate his terms and ride rough-shod over hers, whatever they might be. She did not even know if he accepted Beth and Milly as his daughters, or at least would pretend to for the sake of his pride and standing in the community. Perhaps because of their gender he would not be overly concerned since a son is what all men want, but here he was, standing patiently – again unlike him – on the step.

"May I see my wife?" he asked the dragon who guarded her.

"Nay, it's up to 'er," Mrs O'Neill bristled.

"Come in, Noah," Abby said at her back and reluctantly Mrs O'Neill stepped aside and allowed him over the doorstep. He looked tired, older, pale, as though he had not been outdoors for a long time, which indeed he hadn't, for ever since he had found Abby and assured himself of her health and safety he had spent every moment, apart from an hour's sleep here and there, mending his neglect of his businesses. Euan MacNair had done marvellously well considering his inexperience, but there were many fences needed mending among the men who purchased Noah's glass and bricks who had been highly indignant regarding his negligence, which had affected their businesses. The strain of it all showed clear in his face, staining his eyelids, engraving lines she'd never seen before from mouth to chin.

"Will you sit down?" she murmured politely, never thinking to ask if he would care to examine the babies who might or might not be his.

"Thank you, but if I could . . ." He indicated with a tentative hand the pretty box where the babies lay.

"Of course." She was amazed when he crossed the room and squatted on his haunches, looking down into the cradle with narrowed eyes. She knew he was looking for any sign of family likeness, the Goodwin copper hair, his own dark brown, almost black eyes, but they still had the slightly squashed look of the newly born: small pug noses, rosy lips and scarcely any hair. Beth slept and her long silken eyelashes curved on her cheek but Milly had her eyes open and though it was said that babies of that age cannot see clearly, she seemed to fix Noah with a stare and even, as he did, narrow her eyes speculatively. He smiled and reached for her hand with his finger and she gripped it fiercely. He stayed where he was for perhaps two minutes, the child and he considering one another, then he gently loosened her grip and stood up.

"Hmm," was all he said and for a moment Abby thought he was about to turn on his heel and leave. He had done whatever he had come here to do and was off back to the real world of power and profit and progress, but instead he sighed and then looked at her, studying her as though for the first time.

"Has Roddy Baxter been here?" he asked her, his voice soft and low.

"No, he . . ."

"So he's not claiming these as his own?"

"Noah, I'm not sure we should be—"

"What? Discussing their parentage? Perhaps if this lady" – turning to look at Mrs O'Neill – "would leave us alone . . ."

"She knows all about me and . . ."

"Roddy Baxter?"

"Yes."

"Then perhaps we might talk about your future, and the future of these children. But not today. It's too soon. I need time, as I'm sure you do to make such life-shattering decisions. If I may I'll call again and perhaps things will be clearer in both our minds. I have no wish to force you to come home and indeed do not intend to do so, even if I could, and if I wanted to! So, I'll leave you. I have a hansom waiting at the top of the lane. Good morning to you, ma'am." He nodded politely in Mrs O'Neill's direction, opened the door and left.

Abby moved to the window and watched him as he stood for a moment looking across the river. He bent and picked something up, studying it carefully, then walked to the lane, turned into it and out of sight.

"Well, what d'yer mekk o' that then?" Mrs O'Neill said, watching Abby carefully, for it was not really up to her to make comment on this woman's life. She herself knew exactly what would be best for her as far as security went. And her husband seemed a nice enough sort of chap, but then she really didn't know him or the other one who had not yet been seen. Abby had run away from them both in her fear and confusion, but it was clear she couldn't stay here though it would break Bertha O'Neill's heart to lose her, and the babies.

"What d'yer think?" she asked tentatively, then wondered if it mattered what Abby thought, for it seemed the husband wasn't at all sure he *wanted* her and her children.

"I don't know, Mrs O'Neill. As Noah said, I think it's too soon to make any decision. He's gone through so much in the last few months and I've been the one to cause it. What man would . . . well, it seems he's undecided and I think he's probably right, for it will give both of us time to consider what must be done. What is best for the children and . . ." Her voice trailed away and without a word she threw on her shawl and stepped out of the cottage and on to the beach. Bramble had been lying patiently by the door waiting to be let in and as she set off up the beach he fell in beside her, not frisking about as usual but keeping close to her leg as though in sympathy.

She allowed it to escape then. The great, tamped-down emotion that was her grieving love for Roddy and which had lain safe and secret in the depth of her heart and soul. During the last months she had sealed her mind from him, for the pain was too great to bear. Being pregnant had seemed to cocoon her in some protective refuge which perhaps all gravid women are blessed with. Now that she was herself again, a woman in control of her own body, and even though she was not with him, she felt the intense harmony they had known together ever since they were children which, as she walked, swayed her body so that she thought she might fall. She knew a warm tide of feeling carrying her towards him though he was not there. No one else existed anywhere. She was alone with him on the empty beach, body and spirit blending together as rivers blend at their joining place, a complete and final moment of love. And yet they were many miles apart and it was tearing her to shreds. Where was he? Was he searching for her as Noah had done? She was aware that he did not have the resources that were at Noah's disposal, the money, the time, the arrogance that enabled Noah to demand the attention of men at the top – as at the railway stations – and to pry from them every scrap of information they had. Noah could shout or bribe, and had done, and had followed every railway line from one end of Lancashire to the other and he had found her.

But he was not pressing her and she was grateful for that. He seemed inclined to let her have her precious recovery time and, indeed, seemed to need it himself. She must regain her full strength, bask in the glow of peace and tranquillity which would heal her and close off from her mind what the future might hold. She was safe. She had friends and she would get through it. But Roddy . . . she needed to see Roddy. Dear Lord, let him be safe, let him not be broken as he had been broken before. Roddy, Roddy . . .

They settled into a routine that was not unpleasant and had it not been for her worry over and longing for Roddy she would have known great peace and even content as her babies grew and became recognisable as little people. She had letters now, from Laura and from Harriet, and she marvelled at Noah's generosity who must have given them her address. Laura promised to catch a train and visit her, but there was an outbreak of fever in the poorer quarter of the town that kept John busy and she did not like to leave him at the moment, but as soon as it was under control she would come. Harriet said much the same, mentioning the fever as though it were nothing much to be alarmed about but she was looking forward to seeing Abby and her twins. Both letters were somewhat stilted, non-committal, but she put that down to awkwardness, for Laura was Noah's friend and Harriet his employee.

They had a small christening service at St Michael's Church, which was a short walk across the lane and the field from Lark Cottage. Jane and Mrs O'Neill were god-mothers and Doctor Tom godfather. Archie was there in a second-hand suit from Jane, the trousers cut down, his thin legs like knots on cotton as Mrs O'Neill said privately to Abby. He was the only other guest and, disregarding the vicar's astonished air at the smallness of the party, it was enough in the circumstances. He had been twice since that first time but Noah did not attend though he had been informed of the date. It seemed he was still in that cold and depthless place into which her desertion and adultery had cast him and she wondered why he came at all. When he did he studied the two children, though he made no attempt to touch them again. Even when Milly made a wobbly attempt at a smile he did not respond but merely nodded at Abby, Mrs O'Neill and an open-mouthed Cissie and went on his way. He had asked her if she needed money and if she did she had only to write and he would see to it. He had not mentioned the future nor what he wanted from it, or her, and she had been strangely saddened by it.

Afterwards they trooped back across the cold February field with Elizabeth and Emily Goodwin to a small tea party Abby and Mrs O'Neill had arranged and tucked in to small pork pies, lemon cheesecake and home-made scones with strawberry jam, also home-made, and whipped cream. They drank a toast to Beth and Milly from the bottle of good wine

Doctor Tom had brought, and were just about to make their farewells when a knock on the door, so quiet and hesitant they might not have heard it had Bramble not barked, brought forth an irritable "tcch-tcch" from Mrs O'Neill.

"'Oo the dickens is that at this time o' night?" for the winter day was already drawing in. "Open door, there's a good lass, Cissie," and when Cissie did so they all squinted into the fading light at the tall figure of the man who stood there. None of them knew him except one and she moved, thankfully, it seemed, light and graceful as a fawn, straight into his waiting arms. They all gawped and exchanged startled glances, but perhaps the stillness and length of the embrace warned them, for one by one they faded away.

"I couldn't find yer. I knew yer were in Liverpool because he was. I saw him a while back. I nearly killed him. We were put in gaol, did he not tell yer? Aye, I knew he'd have found yer by now but without money ter bribe folk I had ter follow every snippet of information meself and it took a lot longer. I tried ter follow him once but he got in a cab oh, love, my love, I thought never ter see yer again. And the babies, two of them. When can I see 'em? Are they like me? Or Willy and Eddy, 'appen? Oh, Abby, my Abby." He groaned and then was so overcome with the terrible depth of his sorrow he bent his head in despair.

They were sitting at the table in the kitchen while upstairs Beth and Milly Goodwin could be heard wailing their disapproval of the bottles with which Mrs O'Neill and Cissie were trying to feed them. Abby stood up and put her arms about his shoulders and held his beloved body to her. This was her love, the man she had loved for as long as she could remember and he was suffering. He was sick and shaken and trembling and she pressed his head against her breasts which were straining with the milk her babies were crying for, resting her cheek on the top of his tousled hair. He looked shabby, down at heel and, though it was February with a cold, raw wind blowing off the river, he had no overcoat. She suspected he had sold it for money to buy food and shelter. Where had he been during his search in Liverpool, where had he stayed? In one of the hundreds of cellars probably, where a small space lined with straw might be had for a penny? His arms were round her and she knew he was weeping as though already he knew what was to happen. She didn't! Noah was just as unsure as herself but this man in her arms who knew her as well, if not better than any person living, knew what the future held. Was it with him?

"I love you, Abby," he whispered sadly against her breast. "That's how it is an' always will be." Some sound worked its way from his throat, a sound so deep and harrowing it seemed to come from the years of painfully remembered sorrows. "It doesn't matter ter me whether the babies are his or mine, I promise I'll treat them as mine. I've no job, only a small cottage to call me own but I can work."

"I know, my darling." Something inside her broke and like him she silently bowed her head. She kissed his tears and he kissed hers, clinging together, not with the passion they had joyfully known in the past, but as though they were one entity slowly being ripped apart.

He stayed for three days, sleeping with Archie in the little room above the outhouse. He ran on the beach with Bramble who seemed to remember him, shovelled great platefuls of Mrs O'Neill's food inside him, accepted the greatcoat which Jane brought across and sat for hours of an evening with a sleeping Beth and Milly on his knee. They all loved him, even Mrs O'Neill, the slanting silver gleam of his eyes, his endearing grin, his effort to be cheerful when all he felt was sadness and it was perhaps then that she truly began to realise what had forced Abby to act as she had done. Why she loved this man as she did. A woman who is married and yet takes a lover was an outcast in Bertha O'Neill's decent world, but having seen those two men and heard Abby's story she began in a small measure to understand.

When he left, promising to write and come again as soon as he could, they clung together, still the two youngsters who had loved in innocence and trust years ago. He was going to see Doctor Bennett, he told her earnestly, looking down into her face, and ask his help in getting his job back at Mulberry Glass Works. If he could start work again he could provide a home for her and the babies and though it might be hard going at first their love was as strong and endurable as ever. She must promise to write to him. No, she was not to cry, though he felt like it himself, he said, sniffing and doing his best to smile, and then he was gone, tearing himself from her arms and running up the lane, the overcoat Jane had given him flapping behind him like wings.

It was that night that she first began to notice how unalike Beth and Milly were. They were three months old now, lovely children with dimpled hands and rounded cheeks touched with peach. Their skin was the colour of honey. They had ready smiles which revealed little tongues quivering over pink shining gums and when they were perched on her knee, or Cissie's or Mrs O'Neill's, who fought over them hourly, they sat straight with only the occasional wobble, beaming round in great good humour, a burbling, gummy grin. They had both developed a short cap of copper-coloured hair which promised to be exactly like their mother's but it was their bright eyes that caught her attention for the first time and she wondered why she had not noticed them before. Her mind went back to the days when she and Roddy roamed the fields about Edge Bottom village. He had smiled down at her and she had likened his eyes to those of Mrs Hodges' pampered striped tabby; a slanting pale grey fringed with dark lashes, a silvery grey almost. And from Beth's baby face they looked at her again.

Her heart lurched madly and began to beat at a terrifying speed. These were Roddy's children then and now she could see it in the way Beth lifted her head and turned to look up at her. Her small jaw was a baby jaw but it had a slight cleft in the chin, barely noticeable but exactly like Roddy's.

She shifted her gaze to Milly, who was struggling to escape the firm confines of Cissie's arms, though what she would do at three months should she manage it was a puzzle. She was more active than Beth. She slept less and was more demanding, doing her best to lift her head from the cradle and not miss anything that was going on around her. She grabbed at Bramble if she was lying on the rug before the fire, hanging on for grim death and shrieking her displeasure should he escape, but sweet-natured when she received the attention she seemed to need.

She was like Beth except for her eyes. They were enormous, a deep, velvet brown, long-lashed like her twin but with a certain shape to them when she smiled that was so familiar Abby's heart raced even faster. They were sisters, for God's sake, and sisters often had different coloured eyes yet it was not just their colour that marked them but the shape of their heads, the curve of their rounded chins, their personalities, for where Beth had a placid, patient nature, willing to wait her turn at nursing or bathing, smiling with great good nature at them all, Milly shouted her displeasure if she was not immediately attended to. When it came to bedtime and Abby was trying to settle them Milly made it clear that the last thing on her mind was being settled!

So what was she to make of that? she wondered hesitantly. She could not doubt for a moment that Beth was Roddy's child, for not only had she the velvety grey eyes that had smiled at Abby ever since she could remember, she had seen them in the face of Dorcas Baxter. Exactly the same shade and shape and Dorcas Baxter's only claim to beauty. She had given them to her son who, in his turn, had given them to his daughter.

And Milly, lively, demanding, a certain arrogance in the way she lifted her head and at three months the centre of all their lives. They loved Beth and shared their devotion with her but it was Milly who set them running to please her as once they had all done at Edge Bottom House in the service of Noah Goodwin.

32

After a harsh winter when storms lashed the waters of the river to fury and several ships came to grief with loss of life, spring did not begin until late April and when it did it was as warm as summer. Outside the cottage in the fringe of grasses that lined the beach appeared shy cowslips to stand beside the miracle of wild daffodils which, in March, had exploded in trumpets of gold. There was lady's smock, all silver white, with violets of blue, and Abby wondered where they had come from since surely no one would plant such things on a deserted strip of beach.

"It's the birds," Jane told her knowledgeably, who had it from the gardener at Silverdale. "They eat seeds and then . . . well, you know," dipping her head in embarrassment, for Jane Hemingway had been brought up to believe that bodily functions, even those of birds, were not spoken of. It was so warm a rug was spread just outside the front door and the babies lay on it in the sunshine, but they had to be watched every minute. Milly, who was more forward than Beth, would roll over from her back to her stomach and inch her determined way to the edge of the rug and beyond, where there were pebbles, strands of seaweed from the high spring tides, interesting bits of mouldering fish, flotsam and pieces of debris that she thought intriguing. Anything she could reach she stuffed into her mouth, watched with great admiration by her sister who could do no more than shuffle on her stomach, her arms and legs going like a swimmer breasting the waves.

Abby was restless. She felt a sense of unease that was hard to understand. She took long, lonely walks, but for Bramble, along the beach towards Liverpool, going as far as Brunswick Dock where she could go no further, or along the inner estuary beyond the Garston Salt Works, standing to watch the vessels that were beating their way to Warrington and the canal there. She went further afield, worrying Mrs O'Neill, for what was the matter with the girl that she felt the need to leave the cottage as soon as she herself arrived and stay out for most of the day? The babies were six months old now and were being weaned from the breast, so she and Cissie were quite capable of dealing with the bottles, the changing and washing, but still their mam was strangely vague, saying she had been cooped up so long and with the weather taking a turn for the better as spring advanced she needed to take long walks which she couldn't do with Beth and Milly. Mrs O'Neill suspected that the girl, which she was to Bertha O'Neill despite being the mother of two daughters, was getting away by herself in an effort to untangle the twisted skein of her own life. To be alone. To be still and silent inside her own head. To clear her mind of all thoughts but the ones that dealt with her future and that of her babies.

She took the horse-drawn omnibus, she told Bertha, from outside the George Hotel in Dale Street to the Zoological Gardens where she had stood and watched the so-called *wild* animals in their cages, pitying and feeling sympathy for their restless, confined wandering. She strolled aimlessly along neat paths where the spring show of primroses, daffodils, narcissi and blue-eyed Mary thrived side by side with tulip and the cheerful yellow-centred daisies. Men dug the rich soil in preparation for the coming of summer and others mowed the smooth lawns. There were budding crab-apple trees in the spinney and wall butterflies, which she had seen in the gardens at Edge Bottom House, danced crazily, drunk on the smells and taste of the coming summer. Swallows dipped over the trees towards the sheds at the back of the gardens where they had built their nests and a pair of chiff-chaffs headed towards the undergrowth carrying scraps of something in their beaks with which to make more secure their own small home. There was an extensive lake with wrought-iron seats where you could sit and watch the stately progress of swans and the dip and dive of ducks. She caught the admiring eye of many a gentleman, for she had regained her figure which maturity and motherhood had carved into magnificence but she did not notice as her thoughts were far from this park, this great seaport in which it was set. Her hair beneath her demure hat, nothing more that a flat saucer covered with wild flowers picked in the lane beside the cottage, caught the sun's rays and glowed with fire and her blue-green eyes were cloudy with her thoughts which darted and buzzed with a fervour that surprised her. She was approaching some point in her life where a crossroads would be reached and a choice made, and though she knew it alarmed and upset Mrs O'Neill that she could not share it with her there was nothing else she could do.

She went one day with Jane down to Woodside ferry and would return by the Seacombe ferry, for, as Jane said, as long as she was in Liverpool she might as well take in some of the sights. It was as though Jane, in her quiet way, knew of the conflict that was slowly coming to its climax in Abby Goodwin. She said little, merely leading her down the floating walkway to the waiting ferry boat that would carry them across the water. Jane pointed out Bidston Hill, the lighthouse from where a good view of Liverpool might be seen, the Welsh mountains, the charms and interests of the landscape, the undulating country studded with herd and fold, doing her best to be the perfect guide, but though Abby was polite, nodding and smiling as Jane spoke, it was very evident that her mind was else-where.

It was from one of these outings that she returned to find a letter from Harriet. In it she spoke of the fever that was spread-ing in Greenbank where the Irish community seemed to have taken root and where poverty and disease ran side by side, for though it was 1868 and the ocean tide of Irish immigrants had reduced to a trickle by comparison with twenty years ago they still came. They brought the famine fever, dysentery and smallpox and it was in one of these "Little Irelands" as they were called that the fever was growing, spreading so that the town was becoming frightened and those who lived outside went there only if absolutely necessary. Cook wouldn't allow even the tradesmen to come to the back door with their goods but made them leave the provisions at the back gate where Clem or Olly would collect them. Thank God the air was fresh and clean up here at Edge Bottom so at least the two boys were safe and could play without risk in the gardens, the orchard and paddock. They were getting so big now, Abby would hardly know them, Todd, who had just had his third birthday, the ringleader in every escapade. It was evident from the tone of the letter that Todd Woodruff could do no wrong and was his mother's pride and joy. She was longing to meet Beth and Milly, Harriet wrote, wondering somewhat plaintively when that would be.

The next day by the early morning post there was a letter from Laura which, after Harriet's rather perfunctory description of the spread of the fever – since it did not come to Edge Bottom nor threaten young Todd Woodruff – began to alarm Abby.

> . . . *John is rarely at home now, spending most of his days at the infirmary and though he forbids it I go there too, helping where I can though I am no nurse. They are so pitiful, particularly*

*the children who go so quickly. John is forever – and has been
for years – fighting with the mayor to give them a decent water
supply but so far to no avail. One of those afflicted is Dorcas
Baxter who . . .*

"Oh, great God," Abby blurted out so loudly both the
babies turned to stare at her in astonishment and Beth's lip
began to quiver. They were being fed Mellin's Food Biscuits
recommended by Doctor Tom which were mashed up with
milk and given on a spoon which the twins did not care for.
Most went up their noses, down their bibs or was pushed away
so violently it went on the floor where Bramble lapped it up
eagerly, but it was the first step towards solid food. They each
sat in high wooden chairs with restraining bands to prevent
them falling out or slipping through to the floor.

"What's up?" Mrs O'Neill enquired, doing her best to get
Milly to open her mouth.

"It's a friend . . . she's seriously ill." Abby stood up and
began to pace the room.

"Not that doctor's wife?"

"No, it's . . . it's Roddy's mother. You know who I mean?"

"Aye, I remember Roddy but surely if Mrs What's-'er-
name 'as got 'er eye on 'er . . ."

"She has two young sons and only Roddy to care for her
and . . ."

Bertha O'Neill became very still, her eyes on Abby so that
when Milly grasped the bowl of food in her hand and threw
it with great glee to the floor she didn't show any interest, to
Milly's surprise and disappointment. She had thought herself
to be very clever but it seemed no one cared.

"Yer not thinkin' what I think yer thinkin'?" Mrs O'Neill's
face was aghast.

"She was very kind to me when . . . How can Roddy
manage? And the boys? In his last letter he had high hopes

of returning to Mulberry where John Bennett had spoken for him and if he's started there and is forced to look after his mother . . . I must go, don't you see?"

"And what about these babbies? Yer'll not tekk them inter a house o'sickness. Over my dead body." Mrs O'Neill stood up, her face the colour of a ripe plum in her outrage, the spoon still in her hand and Milly watched with wondering interest.

"Of course not. I hoped you and Cissie . . ."

"I see, while yer run off to a place where fever's—"

"If you won't or can't have them then I must take them with me and leave them at . . . at Edge Bottom House. There are plenty of women there who would be glad to—"

"Not my lambs! Yer not tekkin' these."

"Then let me go alone. You and Cissie can manage."

"An' what about me lodgers, tell me that? 'Oo's ter see ter them, eh? They'll soon find somewhere else ter—"

"Then let them, Mrs O'Neill. Give it up. Come and work for me. Noah is more than generous with the money he sends and I need someone I can . . ."

She had been about to say "trust", for though Cissie was devoted to Beth and Milly and looked after them assiduously she was young and easily panicked. At once Mrs O'Neill knew what she meant and within her began to glow a lovely flicker, not quite a flame, for it needed a bit of thinking about, but it burned there just the same, the meaning of Abby's words, which said that Bertha O'Neill was to live out her life in the service of this woman who was as dear to her as the daughter she had never had, and these babies whom she adored. She was in her sixties now and though she would never admit it to a living soul, often wondered what was to become of her when she was *really* past it. She hadn't a living relative. She had been an only child, as had her William, and they had had no children. What a joy it would be to see these babbies grow up, to . . . well, she couldn't think beyond that and already Abby was turning away, ready to dash off, she supposed, to that place she came from.

"Eeh, lass, I couldn't . . ." she said hesitantly.

"Yes, you could, Mrs O'Neill, but we'll talk about it when I get back. In the meanwhile I'm counting on you to look after my babies."

She had sent a telegram to Laura and was not surprised to see her waiting anxiously on the station platform at St Helens. She looked thinner, pale, exhausted, and for a moment hung back from Abby, for what might she carry on her clothes, but Abby dragged her wordlessly into her arms and held her for several moments then she stood away from her, still holding her by the hands.

"Tell me," she said. "Dorcas . . ."

"She's hanging on, Abby. Willy, he must be the eldest, has just started at Edge Bottom Glass Works, fetching and carrying, sweeping up, that kind of thing and Eddy still goes to school at Roddy's insistence."

"Is Roddy back at Mulberry?" They were walking towards the arched exit of the station where a line of hansom-cabs waited. It was nearly a year since she and Cissie had caught a train here going she was not really sure where, escaping, fleeing the havoc in her life and here she was back again and there was still havoc but now she knew she could manage it. She had matured, attained a tranquillity that allowed her to be the woman she was meant to be. She had been scarred and hesitant in her past life but now she was free and whole, strong, self-sufficient, aware of her own strength, knowing where her destiny lay.

"Yes, but now he refuses to leave his mother, and Jack Harrison, though he is sympathetic, can be patient no longer, he told John. He's a decent man, Abby, but he has a business to run and . . ."

"I know. Now I must go to Dorcas."

Laura looked aghast. "Will you not go to Edge Bottom House first?"

"No, not yet."

They separated affectionately. "I'll send John over as soon as I can and come myself and if there is anything you need send one of the boys. Oh, my dear, good luck and . . . and take care."

There was the usual consternation when the cab drew up outside Dorcas Baxter's house, the neighbours crowding in their doorways to see who the caller was. They fell back in amazement when they saw the elegant figure of Mrs Noah Goodwin, wife to the man who employed most of their husbands, descend from the cab and knock on Dorcas's door. Jinny Hardacre answered it, the woman who lived next door and who once had given a hand when Roddy himself was ill. Abby didn't remember her.

Abby smiled at her and without being asked stepped over the threshold and looked straight into the gleaming catlike grey eyes of Beth Goodwin's father. The likeness to him was uncanny and yet vague and unformed, for how could a baby of six months look so like a man of twenty-two? He had been bending over the truckle bed that had been placed in the corner of the small kitchen, evidently sponging his mother's face and neck, for there was still a cloth in his hand. Jinny watched with great interest, storing it all up in her mind to recount to the neighbours. Jinny was not a bad woman, indeed she was the only one to offer her help to the beleaguered family, but she was only a human woman after all and they all liked a bit of gossip in Edge Bottom Row.

"Abby?" His voice had a question mark in it as though he didn't quite believe that it was really her. "Abby?"

"Yes, I heard your mother was ill and so I came to help you."

"Jesus, Abby . . ." And before the astonished eyes of Jinny Hardacre he held out his arms and Abby Goodwin moved into them. Dear Lord above, what a tale she would have to tell Martha Jolly and the rest of the neighbours. They stood there, the pair of them, wrapped about in some strange thing Jinny could not understand. It was not of the flesh, like the lusty performance her Jed put up every Saturday night but . . . well, she could think of no word to describe it. They seemed unaware of her presence and if at that moment the woman on the bed had not begun to mumble and mutter, to twist and turn as she had done for two days now, she thought they might have carried on for God knows how long.

Abby Goodwin turned at last to Jinny and smiled, a lovely smile which had in it her thanks and grateful acknowledgement for what Jinny had done.

"Thank you, Mrs . . ."

"Hardacre, ma'am," ready to bob a curtsey before she remembered this lass came from some sod cottage out Sandy Lane way.

"Thank you, Mrs Hardacre, you have been kind and brave and I'm sure Dorcas, when she is recovered, will thank you personally. But I'm sure you have your own family to tend to and now that I am here I'll take over. Roddy must go to his work." Turning, her hand still in his, to look at him, ready to argue if he did, then back to Jinny. "If there is anything my family can do for yours at any time I shall personally see to it that it shall be done."

"Thank you, ma'am," Jinny blurted then did drop a curtsey, for she knew she was addressing a lady. She left quietly and went at once to her own house, turning away the women who wanted to hear all about it, for Abby Goodwin had been kind and Jinny, at the moment, did not feel like gossiping about her.

It took a while to persuade Roddy to leave his mother and go to work, though if he was honest it was not his mother he could not bear to leave, but Abby. He wanted her in his arms, in his *bed* if it had been possible, but she allowed him only a few minutes to tell her what had happened in his life since his last letter.

He was indeed back at Mulberry Glass Works and though Mr Harrison had been inclined to mutter about reliability and such, he had reluctantly given in to John Bennett's importuning. He had been back a fortnight when his mother had complained of feeling a bit under the weather, which was so unlike her he had immediately been concerned. His mother never complained, never admitted even to being tired but when it came out that several of the men, Irishmen, who drank at the public house where she was barmaid had gone down with the fever that was prevalent in St Helens, he had begun to fear the worst. Two days he had been here and in that time his mother had become delirious. She had violent attacks of vomiting and diarrhoea so that she was in a constant state of soiling. He was at his wits' end in his effort to keep her clean; they had run out of bedding and had it not been for Jinny who loaned them some of her threadbare stuff, would have had to leave her in her own filth.

"Go to work, Roddy. For God's sake, you must keep your job, for it's clear it will be a while before your mother can return to full employment. You must not worry. I know that's an easy thing to say and not an easy thing to do but I promise she will be safe in my care. I shall send to Edge Bottom House for clean linen and—"

"I'll have none of that bastard's charity in my house," he exploded, leaping from the chair in which he had collapsed in relief.

"Not even to save the life of your own mother?" she asked quietly.

"Abby, how can I?"

"Because you love your mother. Now go and show your face at Mr Harrison's and leave her with me. You know I will care for her as though she was my own mother."

And so he went. She found a lad loitering in the street and gave him a note, containing a list of her requirements, and sixpence to deliver it at once to Mrs Woodruff at Edge Bottom House. Harriet was not to come herself, which Harriet needed no telling, but was to send Olly or Clem in the trap and leave what she needed on the doorstep. She would not open the door until the trap had gone!

It came within the hour, an anxious Olly driving it. He had strict instructions from his Ruby, who was expecting their second child any day, that he was to leave the stuff at the end of the street. No, she didn't care if it was Mrs Goodwin, or the queen herself, she would not have him breathing in the same air as the mistress. He could knock on the door and then run like hell, for what if he should bring it back to their Harry? Fever! Dear Lord, the very word struck terror into the hearts of all mothers. Her own little brother had died of it, burning up and with his skin turning the most peculiar colour, dark as though there were blood under it. And it was quick, so quick that a man whistling on his way to work in the morning could be wrapped in his winding sheet by teatime.

The boys, Willy and Eddy, crept home of an evening, Willy from the glass works and Eddy from school, and it seemed not to occur to anyone to keep them at home. Willy had a job of work to do bringing in a few bob a week and surely it was better for Eddy to keep up his normal routine? Abby boiled every drop of water they drank from the water butt at the back of the cottage and it was perhaps this supply of clean water, falling straight from the clouds, that kept them free of the disease.

It was cholera, Laura told them. Not just fever but cholera and she was afraid for John who worked every hour God sent to save the lives of the dozens and then the hundreds who were going down with it. It lived on dirt and bred in rotting garbage and there was enough of that in Greenbank, God knows, and John had ordered chloride of lime so that the houses in the stricken area could be limewashed. She came as often as she could be spared from her work at the infirmary, which was filled to overflowing. The grave-diggers were increasingly unable to cope. Abby felt she was unable to cope herself as she set about boiling fouled bed linen and sat for hours bathing the withering body of Dorcas Baxter, who was shrinking away before her eyes, the foul odour of her sickness sickening *her*. She slept a little on a mattress on the far side of the room from the bed on which Dorcas tossed and mumbled while Roddy, overcoming his shame that he should see his own mother naked, bathed her body in the cool water that was thankfully always available in the water butt, unlike the poor souls who used the water in the puddles that collected in the rutted lanes of Greenbank.

Dorcas Baxter died that night, her hands held by her son and the woman he loved and who loved him. She seemed to rally a little at the end, smiling weakly at the woman she believed would look after her family when she herself was gone and Abby's heart broke and inside her something wept and would not be comforted. They washed her wasted body together, feeling no awkwardness, and dressed her in her Sunday frock though it was far too big for her now. A note was sent to Laura and a few hours later a coffin arrived, ordered from a sorely pressed undertaker, and with her hair brushed and her face serene, with her sons beside her, the coffin was placed on the kitchen table so that those who wished might come to say their last farewell.

Nobody came. None of the neighbours wanted to take the

risk of entering a house where sickness had been. They did not know as yet that it was cholera that was decimating the Irish population in Greenbank, that was striking at the heart of the town, for they lived and worked almost in the country where the air was fresh and untainted but still, best be safe rather than sorry. Fever. There was always fever of one sort or another to carry off their children and though Dorcas had been well liked, they stayed away.

They talked then, Roddy and Abby, on the day of the funeral, for there must be no delay in quickly putting under the ground those who had died. She told him about the babies and spoke of their progress but she was constrained by the need to keep from him the difference between the two girls, by her belief that one was his daughter and the other Noah's. She meant to talk to John about it, to find out if such a thing was possible, but until she knew she would keep it to herself. She didn't even know why for it would make no difference to the outcome, to the way her life led her.

Laura and John attended the small funeral service and on the edge of the churchyard Harriet stood with Clem. It was soon over, for the minister was in a rush to carry out the next committal. She and Roddy walked side by side towards the gate and as she reached the spot where Harriet stood, her arm through Clem's, Abby was ready to smile, even to put her arms about her dear friend whom she had not seen for so long, but Harriet backed away.

"No, Abby, don't come any nearer."

"Harriet, there is no danger now. With Dorcas . . . well . . ."

"It's not that, Abby." Harriet's face was drawn and Clem held her protectively against him as though she might fall. There were daffodils about their feet and the trees were budding in spring glory as though to make mock of the death all around them, but suddenly the world tipped a little and Abby felt her heart begin to pound.

"What? Who?"

"It's Noah. Olly's gone for Doctor Bennett but now he's here . . ."

"Have you come in the carriage?"

"Aye."

"Take me home, then." And with no more than a touch on his arm Abby Goodwin said goodbye to Roddy Baxter, who leaned against a tree trunk as though his strength had been drained away from him.

33

It was a long time before the door opened, as though the servants were reluctant to admit what might be further disaster to Edge Bottom House but when, as she and John were about to go round the house to the back door, it opened a fraction, Kitty's face was a picture! Her expression changed from one of apprehension to delight, amazement and the shriek she uttered could be heard at the back of the house where Olly was grooming the horses.

"Madam . . . oh, madam, I can't believe it's you. Lord bless yer an' us in such a sad state wi' the master. An' Doctor Bennett, thank God. Come in, come in. I'll go an' tell the others. Oh, ma'am, we haven't half missed yer. Dear God, will yer listen ter me babblin' on an' you standin' on doorstep—"

"How is he, Kitty?" Abby interrupted, brushing past the maid and heading for the stairs with John Bennett close on her heels.

"Eeh, she won't let any one of us up there, Mrs Goodwin. Ringin' bell every five minutes fer us ter fetch things but we're right glad doctor's here . . . an' you. Eeh, missis." Kitty was so beside herself she lapsed into the Lancashire way of addressing a married woman.

Joanna was bending over the figure of her brother who lay in the bed he had shared for so many years with Abby. She was wiping his face with a damp cloth and murmuring to him that he was not to fret, for she was here and would make him well again. There now, she was saying, didn't that feel better. Aye, sleep a while, for it was well known that sleep was a healer. She seemed not to be aware that he was not asleep but semi-conscious and even as Abby and John entered the room he began to toss about, muttering irritably that she was to leave him alone and stop her damn fussing.

She turned sharply as the door opened, ready to give what for to whichever servant had dared to disobey her, her face aflame with indignation, for Joanna Goodwin felt that at last she was about to come into her own and she wanted no interference. For nearly five years she had been thwarted in her efforts to guide the girl her brother had so rashly married in the way she, Joanna, thought was the best way to go about things as the wife of a prominent and successful businessman, which her brother undoubtedly was. When the little madam had disappeared she had been triumphant, ready to move into Edge Bottom House and be its mistress but Noah had been curiously – in her opinion – reluctant to allow her to do so. They had argued fiercely, for she was as stubborn as he but he would not give in. But now, with the onset of this illness, she saw her chance to get her own way and when he was better Noah would have become used to, and be grateful for, her presence.

She was speechless with consternation for a moment then, "What are you doing here?" she hissed. "You're not wanted nor needed. We've heard the tales of your wantonness and those illegitimate children you gave birth to and my brother and I have no need—"

"Stand aside, Miss Goodwin," John Bennett ordered curtly. "Your brother is probably a very sick man and what he has is—"

"How dare you come in here with that trollop and order me to—"

"Let me have a look at him."

"Get away from that bed. Doctor Andrews has been sum-moned and will be here directly. So you see your services are not required. Doctor Andrews has been my doctor for many years and I have every faith in him. Dear God . . ." She began to shriek as Abby darted past her and kneeled beside the bed. She watched with horror as Abby put her hand on her brother's forehead and smoothed his hair back, then cupped his face with gentle hands, gazing down at him in a way she had never done before. Then she wrinkled her nose and with an imperious look ordered her sister-in-law to ring the bell.

"Get away from him," Joanna was thundering, ready to tear Abby to her feet and hurl her from the room, but John rang the bell himself then took her arm and led her towards the door.

"He needs changing at once," Abby said. "Can't you see he is soiled and lying in his . . . Good God, woman, have you lost your sense of smell?"

With Joanna hovering at the door ready to drag them both away and have them thrown into the garden, John leaned over the bed and with kind, gentle hands began to examine Noah Goodwin while Abby watched anxiously. She was still soothing Noah's face with her own gentle hands and he seemed to quieten.

"Is it . . . ?"

"Oh, yes. It usually takes the very old and the very young, at least to begin with, but as it grows it begins to take everyone in its way. Noah comes into contact with a lot of people in his day's business. Some of the Irish work at the glass works and he has been low in spirits recently; it will involve massive vomiting, his bowels will open – they already have begun – and the body can retain nothing."

"What shall I do?"

"You will do nothing, madam," the voice from the door

shrieked. "You will leave this house and go back to your lover and your bastard children. Noah is my brother and I will nurse him."

She might have been the fireplace in which a good fire burned, or the tallboy in which Noah kept his beautifully ironed shirts for all the notice they took of her and when Kitty knocked hesitantly on the door she flung it open and glared into the maidservant's face. "And you can get downstairs again where you belong. When you are needed I will send for you."

Abby stood up and moved across the room to where Kitty hovered uncertainly. "Kitty, I will tell you the truth because I know you can be trusted not to panic the others. Mr Goodwin has cholera . . . yes, yes, I know it frightens you but he is strong and will pull through. But I shall need your help. Mrs Woodruff and Ruby must not come up here. They have children and will be frightened, but if you could help me with the linen which will be constantly fouled and anything else I shall need I should be grateful. You must not come into the room but if I know you are there to bring anything I need and . . . and take away the dirty linen to be boiled I would be easy in my mind. There is nothing else to be done except keep the master clean."

"I will not allow this. I simply will not allow this woman to come anywhere near my brother," Joanna was howling and Abby sighed before she spoke.

"Joanna, you may help to nurse Noah if you wish but I will not have this tirade which may upset him."

"*Upset him!* What do you think your behaviour has done to him over the past year, tell me that? I will not be shut out of his room—"

"*My* room, Joanna, and if you don't leave it at once I shall call Clem and Olly to remove you and give orders that the doors are to be barred against you. I have enough to do without your—"

"How dare you. How dare you speak to me like that. As for being silent I will not . . ."

Clem and Olly were to remark frequently and with great satisfaction in the days that followed that they had never enjoyed anything so much as lifting the shrill figure of the master's sister and frog-marching her down the stairs and out of the front door where Kitty politely handed her her coat and bonnet.

And so it began, the fight with death which Noah Goodwin battled alongside his wife. John, against his will, for he had a great regard for Abby Goodwin, was forced to get back to the infirmary where folk were still pouring in, vomiting and shivering and dying. Before he went he helped her to strip her husband naked, wash his soiled body and lift him into the clean bed for which Kitty had left the linen at the bedroom door. Unwilling to risk the bed linen which would most certainly be contaminated with the fever, the family laundry room to the side of the kitchen was not used, so a large metal tub had been erected in the yard with a fire beneath it and every soiled sheet was boiled in it, a job Nessie and May begged to do, for they had no other way of helping the mistress who had come back to them. They had heard so many weird and terrible tales about her. Lovers and children that could be his. There was that lad who had haunted the place years ago and the young man who had fought with the master last back end who, it seemed, were one and the same person. So many rumours, whispers, not among themselves but if they were they *kept* them to themselves. The master was forever chasing off somewhere and folks were wondering why and really could you believe any of it? They tried hard not to, for they had become very fond of her and wished nothing more than to see her, and her children, twins would you believe, reinstated at Edge Bottom House.

Despite Kitty's dire warnings they brought cans of hot water, towels, soap to the bedroom door, scuttling back to the kitchen where a state of nervous tension existed. Neither Mrs Woodruff nor Ruby came to the house, keeping to their own cottages with their precious children at Mrs Goodwin's request. They took trays of delicious food up, though it was reported by Kitty that Mrs Goodwin had said she didn't want it but she must keep her strength up. She ate it.

Abby crouched in a chair beside the bed watching, watching, waiting for what was to come, for had she not seen it with Dorcas. He was quiet at the moment, inclined to mumble, and once she heard her own name but he did not respond when she leaned towards him and took his hand. She was devastated by the fierce heat of it.

"Noah," she whispered, lifting the hand and putting the back of it to her cheek, but he continued to toss and mumble, unable, it seemed, to hear her.

On the second day he began to be devoured in a stinking gush of sweat, then in a burning dry flame that threatened to consume him. His skin turned to a sulphurous yellow as he boiled in his own sweat and the smooth brown layers of his firm skin seemed stripped away. The bones of his pelvis, his ribs, his collar bone stood out. Abby bathed him again and again in cool, boiled water, changed his bed a dozen times a day, struggling with him, for though the weight of him was falling away he was still heavy. He moaned in pain when she moved him, doing his weakened best to fight her, not knowing her, and when John Bennett came, which he often did in the middle of the night, he was appalled by the frailness of her, her strength which would not give in to the frailty.

"I'll sit with him for an hour while you sleep," he told her and when she refused he became angry. "What will he do if you go down, tell me that, Abby Goodwin? If you're sick there will be no one to tend him but his sister and I don't think you want that."

She had acquiesced, falling at once into a state almost of unconsciousness and while she slept John ventured outside the sickroom door and rang the bell that had been placed there. Immediately Kitty was there, for it seemed that none of the servants was getting much sleep either.

"Send Olly or Clem for my wife, will you, Kitty. Your mistress can't manage this on her own."

"Let me come in, Doctor," Kitty begged but a voice from behind John, the voice of her mistress, spoke coolly.

"You'll do no such thing, Kitty, and neither will Olly. I have slept and I'm rested. I can manage. If I need anything I will ring the bell."

Kitty went downstairs defeated and reported to those who lolled at the table, their heads on their arms, that the mistress would accept no help. The doctor left, shown out by May who could not stop crying, she said, at the thought of their little mistress – despite the fact Mrs Goodwin was taller than any of them – all by herself up there.

Noah was mumbling, muttering, shouting at times, flinging himself from side to side so that she was afraid he would throw himself out of the wide bed. The room was hot, for the fire was kept in, fed by the coals that were left in buckets outside the bedroom door.

"Hush, Noah, hush." She tried to soothe him but he would not be soothed, so that finally she took off the dress which she had put on aeons ago and lay down beside him, his head clasped firmly to her breast, her arms tight about his shoulders until they were both soaked with the outpourings of his sweat and his foetid breath rose around her but it seemed it did not matter.

She must have dozed off, for she woke to the sound of her name.

"Abby . . . ?" Amazed. The voice was weak, hoarse and it was accompanied by convulsive swallowing as though its owner's throat was excessively dry, making it hard to form the word.

"Yes, I'm here."

"Have you come home, my love?" he asked drowsily.

"Yes." It was her turn to be amazed, for it was true. She *had* come home and it was not until this moment that she realised it.

"Why?"

"Because I was needed, I think. Who else is there to look after you?" And to her own astonishment she realised she spoke the truth. "Joanna was here but she . . . well, she wasn't able to . . ."

"But you – were . . ."

"Yes." His head rose and fell on her breast as she breathed and she thought she heard him sigh, whether from weariness or content.

"I'm glad."

She sighed herself, for it seemed the worst was over, but it was not as she was to discover over the next few days. The disease followed its course as John said it would, recovery for an hour or two when Noah would watch her, his eyes clear but somewhat wary, then relapse as his body slowly succumbed again to the fever that had invaded it. She slept in snatches, waking to find John bending over her, his hand to her forehead, and once it was Laura. Abby's voice rose in anger, telling her to get out but Laura only smiled and turned to bend over Noah who was dreadfully quiet. She struggled to rise, her own body enfeebled by days of weary, watchful nursing of this man who was her husband and yet was a stranger, but somehow she could not find the strength to argue any more.

It was on the fourth day when she lay on the bed holding him to her, knowing he was dying, that her own spirit seemed to die little by little, as his was doing. She really did not think she could stand the thought of it, let alone the reality. Noah, vital, vigorous, stubborn, arrogant, witty, strong as a lion and yet he lay against her like a limp doll. He had gone in the crucible of his illness, burned away in the fire of disease, this man she had hated, this man who had made her laugh, made her cry, infuriated her, this man who had hardly seen the daughter she had borne him, for there was no doubt that Milly was his just as Beth was Roddy's.

Roddy! Where was Roddy, the man, and the boy; she had loved for the past ten years, while she was a child, a young girl and as a woman? As though some telepathic wave had passed from her to Noah he spoke to her. His voice was weak, strained, but it was alert and knew exactly what it was saying.

"Do . . . you want . . . me to send . . . for . . . Roddy Baxter?" it asked and it was with these words that she knew he loved her and with that knowledge a small flutter began in her chest then moved down to her stomach where it stayed. She suddenly felt panicky, as though she had strayed too close to the edge of something. He was weak, not himself at all. Not the Noah Goodwin who, if he recovered, would fight her and fight Roddy every step of the way, but he was lucid and was inviting her to make her choice. He was offering to step aside and allow her to leave him and go to Roddy. If that was what would make her happy he was willing to give her to another man. Her head was spinning and not just through weakness and plain exhaustion but with the knowledge that she did not know this man at all. She had thought him selfish, self-willed, greedy even, and he was all these things but he was ready to put her feelings before his own, so was this a sign that he loved her? It was amazing, magnificent, bewildering, a wondrous joy she could not understand, just as she had not understood the Noah Goodwin who had married her to get his hands on her grandfather's glass works.

"I don't . . . know why . . . I'm saying this . . . Abby." And there was a small measure of his normal irritability in his voice as though he was himself bewildered. "I . . . I don't understand myself . . . and I certainly don't understand . . . understand you and why you are here . . ." Though his voice was no more than a straining whisper it was becoming stronger and she could tell the effort he was making to let her see what was within him, perhaps before the next relapse came which might be his last.

"We have never understood each other, you and I, Noah. We were forced . . . at least I was forced into marriage with you when I was too young and inexperienced to realise what was happening to me."

"So . . . will you stay?"

"Noah, rest easy, this is not the time for decisions, or declarations. You are not yourself."

He made a sound that might have been laughter. "Perhaps . . . this is . . . the time to . . . believe me while I am . . . weakened. Stay with me." His voice was blurred now and he stirred restlessly against her but she held him close to her, his cheek on her breast. He tried to keep his eyes open but they were heavy and though neither he nor Abby was aware of it he fell into the peaceful, relaxed sleep of a child, a *healing* sleep, and so did she. Their bodies settled against one another as though it was the most natural thing in the world.

When Abby woke, pleasantly refreshed, she turned at once to the man in her arms, feeling his cheek, his brow, the skin of his chest, finding them damp but cool. She was considerably startled when a voice from the chair by the fire spoke up.

"So yer awake then, mistress, and yer'll be wanting a cup

of tea, I'll be bound. I'll just ring fer May ter fetch you a tray, you an' the master."

Abby eased herself away from Noah, who still slept peacefully, and crept from the bed in order to give Kitty the rounds of the kitchen and to send her downstairs and out of danger. She longed for nothing more than to plunge herself into a bath, to strip off the stinking garments she had worn for so long, she couldn't even remember exactly how long, but she knew she was barely recognisable as the elegantly clad woman who had fled from Dorcas Baxter's funeral.

"Nay, don't fret, lass." Kitty grinned. "Doctor were here in the night and said master were past worst an' it were safe fer us ter help yer. Hot water's ready and Nessie'll bring up tub so yer can both . . . well, not together, like" – blushing furiously – "then I can change bed an' 'appen a bit o' breakfast . . . porridge, Cook thought, a coddled egg an' hot buttered toast an' then—"

"Tell this woman to go away, Abby. She is wearying me," a voice from the bed muttered and both women whirled round to confront the apparition which was doing its best to sit up. Abby smiled at Kitty, for they both knew that Noah Goodwin was fast becoming, at least in his mind, himself again, then rushed towards him, marvelling and yet saddened at how easy it was to force him down among the rumpled bed covers. It would probably be days, even weeks before he was fully recovered but the iron, bull-headed conceit of him was already beginning to rear its head. And yet there was an expression in his eyes, a brooding expression of . . . of *hope* as he looked up into hers that told her he had not forgotten what he had said and was waiting for her reply. This once powerful, handsome man had not wanted her as a girl but now, as a woman, he did. The glass works were no longer a monument that stood between them. She felt quite giddy and her hands were inclined to linger on his shoulders.

He smiled in triumph, himself again, though he was, like her, barely recognisable as the man she remembered.

"I make a lot of money, Abby," he whispered, as Kitty gave instructions to an excited May at the bedroom door, "but I've been a poor man for the past year. I've missed you. I'm tired . . . now but . . . later, will you let . . . me . . . allow me to tell you . . . and . . . one more thing . . ."

"Yes?" She smiled down at him and her hand went of its own volition to smooth his lank hair from his brow.

"Send for the children. I have a need to see my . . . my daughters."

The excitement was intense and upstairs the man in the bed fought with his wife to get out of it.

"Bloody hell, Abby, can't you see how much better I am. That damn doctor's an old woman and I've a good mind to send him packing the next time he pokes his head round that door. I'm perfectly capable of getting dressed and going downstairs to join in the fun. *Fun!* Good God, woman, two babies, an old woman, a young girl, a street lad and a dog to be added to the household and I'm describing it as fun, but I suppose after all they did for you and the babies I can't turn them away, can I? Now come here and sit on the bed and let me hold your hand. Godammit, every time I get you alone some bloody woman comes poking her nose in the door, simpering and smirking as though she expects to see us . . . come here, please. Dear God, let me get my damned legs back and I won't give you a minute's peace."

She let him rant and rave, smiling at him from the window where she was watching for the small cavalcade which was expected any minute. Both Clem and Olly had gone, Clem driving the carriage and Olly the gig, for two babies and their gear, two women, a boy and a dog took a bit of shifting.

"Bertha will bring them up the minute they arrive, that's

if the women let them get past the kitchen. They've waited for this day for a long time, Noah."

"And so have I, my love."

My love! That's what he called her and it caused a surge of excitement to move in her. She felt like a girl again, for it was very obvious that her husband valued her, not as a means to the business he had craved, but as a woman, a wife, a mother, the mother of *his* children. She was having the hardest job not to allow him to pull her into his bed at night, sleeping on a truckle bed which he threatened to set fire to, but he was still weak, still emaciated, his face gaunt with the remains of his illness.

There was suddenly a great commotion in the lane, cries of welcome and even weeping from downstairs. She could hear Bramble barking and Clem shouting for Harriet.

"I won't be long," Abby told her husband, then, unable to wait for Bertha O'Neill, ran on flying feet to fetch Noah Goodwin's daughters up to him.

34

Though she was filled with wonder and a kind of joyous anticipation, walking through her new life with languorous smiles, wanting to stretch herself in the scented, sunshine air she shared with Noah, Roddy Baxter walked daily in her thoughts. She was sadly aware that he would never cease to live within her in a secret corner that she would teach herself not to visit too often, but in the meanwhile she concentrated on settling her *Liverpool* family into their new home.

To say the Edge Bottom servants were astounded at the appearance of Bertha O'Neill, Cissie Murphy and Archie, whose surname even he didn't know, was an understatement of the highest order, but as Mrs Goodwin explained to them, two babies needed a great deal of attention and she was preoccupied with restoring her husband to his former health. She knew they would understand and welcome the newcomers with the warmth they had shown her and she also told them that Mrs O'Neill was not one for sitting around on her . . . she nearly said *bum* as she once might have done, but when the babies did not need her attention would certainly give a hand in the kitchen, if it was needed.

"Mrs O'Neill is to be Beth and Milly's nurse, or nanny as they call her in higher circles, while my sister Cissie will be nursemaid. The rooms on the top floor are to be completely refurbished, a night nursery, a day nursery, a schoolroom where, naturally, Todd and Harry" – nodding at Harriet and Ruby – "will continue their lessons with Miss Holden. Later

Beth and Milly will join them. There will be three bedrooms, a bathroom and a small kitchen where Mrs O'Neill can warm milk or make up baby food and bottles for Beth and Milly."

The lad would be harder to place but if Mr Renfrew could find some work for him he could share the room above the stable with Frankie and Jacko.

Beth and Milly! The joy that the two babies had brought even in such a short time into the lives of the maidservants was indescribable. They were the loveliest little things, they told one another with their quite glorious cap of golden copper curls, which came from the mistress, of course, and their wide smiles for anyone who happened to glance their way as though they had been waiting specially for a friendly face to greet them. They were alike in some ways and Milly was the image of the master with those enormous dark brown eyes. But where had Beth got those cat's eyes of silvery grey? Anyway, did it matter? They fought with one another whenever the nursery bell was rung on who was to answer it and when the tradesmen moved in to make the renovations to the top floor Mrs O'Neill complained jealously that she never knew where to find her precious charges. Holdy had moved down into the master's study for the time being to continue the boys' lessons, for he was unlikely to need the room for a while and Mrs O'Neill, her full title being insisted upon, and Cissie had to park themselves wherever there was a space.

There was one unusual event that took them all by surprise. Young Archie, thin as a stick and shy as a fawn, was found to be interested in what Todd and Harry were up to in the study and Holdy, seeing his interest, allowed him to sit in on the lessons. Todd and Harry were overjoyed for, as younger boys do of an older, they looked up to Archie who enchanted them with tales of ships and lands across the sea, of sailors and cargoes, most of which they had never heard of.

Cissie walked over to see her mam and pa, proud of her

smart appearance and wonderful new job and was the talk of Sandy Lane and her mam's pride and joy.

"An' when's t'other little madam ter come an' see 'er old mam? Tell me that, Cissie Murphy?" she said sourly, for Betty Murphy could not quite forgive their Abby for stealing their Cissie away and without a word to a soul. She could have told her mam, couldn't she? And then all those terrible tales that had been whispered from cottage to cottage. It had turned out to be untrue, thank the Holy Mother, otherwise Mr Goodwin would never have taken her back, but still, it had been hard for Betty to hold up her head, and to feed her children, another of which was stirring in her womb.

"Mam, Mr Goodwin's been that ill, an' still is, she can't leave 'im but she sent these," these being a couple of large baskets filled to overflowing with food and a guinea wrapped in a scrap of paper. "I could have 'ad the carriage if I'd wanted," Cissie boasted, "but I fancied a walk across fields. You can't manage that load, our Abby said, take the carriage but I said no an' here I am." Cissie Murphy's speech had improved enormously under the influence of her sister and Jane Hemingway.

Abby and Noah spent a great deal of time together, first in their bedroom where it seemed he could not bear her out of his sight, and then in a secluded corner of the garden as the weather turned warmer and the summer flowers began to burgeon. Mr Renfrew reported they sat close together and never stopped talking and though no one knew what was said, they were all satisfied that their world was once more on an even kilter. Theirs and their employers'.

"I've missed you. You don't know how much I've missed you, my love. I know I could say anything to get you back and you'd not know the difference but I mean it, Abby. I miss what we might have done, what we might have been to one another and what we could have together now. God, I've missed you, Abby."

"Yes . . . ?"

"What d'you want me to say now?"

"I'm sure you'll think of something."

"How about this then. Will you marry me, Abby? Really marry me, in church, if it's allowed and if not then a blessing on what we have now? I think I know what you need of me now, my love, and I think I can provide it."

"Noah, I think you can."

"Then you'll do it?" He reached forward and took her hands eagerly in his, then kissed her tenderly on the inside of her wrist.

"There is something to be done first."

"Yes?"

"I must see Roddy."

"The devil take you," he roared, throwing off her hands, then the tension around his mouth relaxed and he managed a small smile. "I don't like it."

"I know but it must be done. He has loved me for so long and waited. I cannot just . . ."

"Of course. I remember when I was delirious I asked you if you wanted me to fetch him for you. I didn't mean it, of course, and you never answered me. Do you? Want me to fetch him for you?"

"No . . . no. But I must go and say goodbye to him. Complete the circle. Let him go to find the life he deserves."

On several mornings she walked with Bramble on the rough pathway that led up to Old Fellows Edge. There was a mist on the top, shifting and thinning, a mist that promised heat, swallowing Bramble as he ran, his nose to the ground, in search of all the many scents that a dog finds so intriguing. She leaned against the pile of rocks where she and Roddy had sheltered so many times, waiting for him, since she had no doubt that he would come. It was almost June now and though there was a pall of dirty yellow smoke over St Helens, up here as the mist wisped away in the increasing warmth of the sun the air was so clear beyond the rocks at her back she could see the blue of heather mingling with the prickly yellow of gorse and under the shade of the heather the stunted shape of bilberry. On three separate days she waited, in a dream-like state, which was not to say she felt composed, far from it, and on the fourth day, a Sunday, not a working day, which should have occurred to her, he was there. His face was set and closed and his eyes, the lovely silvery grey that she saw every day in the face of her daughter, were wary, vulnerable. About him, the way he stood, the lift of his head, his hands which were stuffed in his pockets, probably to hide their trembling, spoke of an unutterable sadness. Bramble, stiff-legged with excitement since he recognised him, ran towards him and jumped up at his leg.

"Hello, lad," Roddy said gently, bending to put a hand on the dog's head, giving both Abby and himself a moment to compose themselves.

He looked up at her and she wanted to weep, for no matter what her feelings towards Noah had become, this man had been the light of her life, her love, *her first love*, and it was no easy thing she was about to do.

"I've been waiting each Sunday since you left me."

"I know. I couldn't come. Noah was ill and then the children keep me busy."

"Of course." His voice was scrupulously polite. He wore a somewhat frayed blue coat and corduroy breeches. His shirt neck was open and around his neck was a flaunting red scarf which did not hide the frantically beating pulse beneath his jaw. He looked better, somehow, more controlled, steady as if some decision had been come to, some choice made, and though it might be an agony to him he at least had made it. She felt a warm tide of feelings carry her towards him but they stood a few feet apart as though afraid if they came closer it might spell disaster.

"The time has come, hasn't it?" he said. "That's what you've come to tell me." His voice was gentle, low, sweet with his love for her. "I suppose I always knew it would."

"Yes."

"Your . . . husband is recovered." He might have been an acquaintance asking after someone he barely knew.

"Yes."

They walked for a while, leaving the shelter of the rocks, moving along the pathway and away from the edge above St Helens and when his hand clasped hers, as it had done a thousand times in the past, she did not pull away.

"I've loved you for so long," he said musingly, "ever since we were both bairns, I can't imagine not having you in my life. It has been . . . a great pain to me for the past three or four years, the only joy in it when you were with me and it's not a way for a man and woman to live, even if you were willing which I have come to realise you are not. And neither am I, Abby. You are blocking my way to other things, another woman, perhaps a family of my own." She felt a twinge, which might have been jealousy, for this man had been hers, had loved her for so long the thought of him with another woman did not sit easily.

They walked in silence for a while. The mist had burned off completely and the low moorland stretched, serene and lovely, before them. A feeding curlew performed its beautiful liquid song as it flew above its territory, reminding Abby of the gulls that hovered over the seashore on the Mersey. They stopped for a moment to watch it, their hands still clasped, then turned to look into one another's eyes. She put her hand on his cheek and her mouth carefully, carefully on his, as one would kiss a sleeping child, lingering to retain the odour and texture of him in her mind, to carry him with her for the rest of her days, for she knew she would never see him again. She had loved this man to the extent where she had been prepared to go as often as she could to his bed. She had lived a life perpetually ill at ease, undressing and dressing hurriedly, rushing home breathlessly, fearful, covering her tracks with tales of visiting her mother. No love could surely survive such furtiveness but theirs had. Had they been happy? The answer, of course, had been no. They had been prepared to lie and cheat – or at least she had, for Roddy was free to do as he pleased – to continue the one true loving relationship they shared, but as Roddy had just said, it must come to an end and the end was now.

He smiled. "Do you remember the skates?"

She smiled too. "Yes. The dam was frozen and we both played truant. I fell on me bum" – reverting to the vernacular of their childhood – "and went home with bruises all over me. It was the day of the accident."

"Aye." The day that Richard Goodwin died. The day that distorted both their lives beyond recognition.

Again they were silent as they continued on the stony track which broke off suddenly before a great outcropping of rock with sloping, identical stretches of moorland on either side. Disturbed by the dog a snipe rose swiftly from its nest, which was well hidden in a tussock of grass. They stopped and leaned against the rock, his arm companionably about her shoulders and though she sensed the need, the desire in him, he merely stood, his hip against hers and looked out on the world that was so familiar to them both.

"I'm going away." His voice was abrupt, almost angry. She held herself very still, doing her best to quell the sudden sense of loneliness she felt, for Roddy had been beside her, even when they were apart, for as long as she could remember.

"Where?" she managed to say through a throat that was thick with tears.

"Belgium. There are many glass works there. With my experience I have been promised a job. Mr Harrison knows—"

"*Belgium!*" She buried her face in his shoulder and shuddered, for though she had come up here to say goodbye to him she realised that she had believed he would still be in St Helens. Belgium was across the Channel, hundreds of miles away and not somewhere . . . Oh, dear God, she really was never to see him again.

"I must, my love. I can't live here with you so close. You have a husband and children, a home, people who rely on you and I must let you go as you must let me go."

"The boys?"

"Willy and Eddy will come with me, of course. I have been offered a good job and Willy will be apprenticed to the same firm."

"I'm not sure . . ." She realised that tears were pouring across her cheeks and dripping on to the fine cotton of her simple day dress, the one she had put on this morning, sadly, she knew that, but with the belief that now she and Noah were to be *properly* married, that he truly loved her, she could say goodbye to Roddy with dignity. How wrong could she be? She had not meant to shed tears. Their parting would be hard but with so much to look forward to with Noah she had believed she would manage it calmly. Now she was ready to wail like Milly did when she could not get her own way. The shock of parting was rippling over her in waves but Roddy hushed her, the more composed of them both.

"Don't cry, lass. You know it's the only way. I'll always love you and you must . . . Do you love him? You are to stay with him but do you love him?" His voice had the remnants in it of the savagery he had once shown against Noah Goodwin. "Do you?"

"He loves me, I know that," she gulped, doing her best to get a firm grip on her scattering emotions. "I am to live with him as his wife so . . . please, Roddy, don't ask me."

"You can't, or daren't tell me, is that it? I think you do and though it tears me apart, I'm glad, for you must have someone to love. One last thing and I need the truth, though it makes no difference to my decision. The children? Are they mine or his?"

She knew quite positively that Beth was his daughter just as she knew that Milly was Noah's. They were twins, or so everyone believed and she had confided in no one her belief that they were not, except John Bennett. He had been quite astonished, but on reflection he had decided that it would be possible for two babies to be conceived by different fathers providing the conception took place on the same day. His face had been stiff with embarrassment, for though he knew of Roddy Baxter and her relationship with him it was an awkward subject to discuss.

"I cannot tell you. But this I know. *They are mine!*"

"Yes, of course."

They stood for perhaps ten minutes, gazing about them, their bodies close but their minds slowly drifting apart. His arm left her shoulders and he stood away from her, on his face an expression which told her that though they had been scarred by what had happened, first to him and then to her, they would heal one day and she was to accept it. He was the stronger of the two though he had more to lose.

"I'll go now, Abby."

"Yes."

"I must know before I leave how your life will be. Will you be happy?"

"I shall be well . . . and happy as you have taught me with your love how to be happy."

"Go then and . . ." She did not know what he had been

about to say, for he turned abruptly and began to hurry along the track. She watched him for a moment then turned to face the rocks so that she would not see him disappear.

When she turned in at the gate from the lane and started along the garden path between the borders of lavender, Noah was sitting in the corner where the sun hit it. He had a baby in his arms, the other at his feet on the rug. The baby in his arms was Roddy Baxter's daughter.

They all three turned to look at her as she approached. Milly smiled and showed off her latest trick which was an attempt to stand up, pulling at her father's trouser leg. Beth sat up and though she recognised her mother she snuggled herself against Noah's chest, smiling too but happy to stay where she was.

"We missed you," Noah said and held out his hand to her.